Jhanes nodded. "Inari admire courage. If anyone wants to kill you, it will be in the open Circle in a one-on-one fight. Who is your interpreter?"

"That problem we haven't solved. We hope to find someone before we leave the castle. There are traders in the city who speak Inari."

His heart sank. *What can I say? Why did it have to be now?*

"Well? What is it, man?" Zoysana frowned. "I can see you're not happy. Don't just sit there; tell us."

All three of them stared at him.

He shook his head slowly. "It won't work. Those traders only speak Chinotuk. The Inari won't talk serious politics in Chinotuk. It's a trading language, and they look down on traders. The Inari diplomatic language is full of conventions and traps, highly dependent on a sense of irony. Word-for-word translation may mean something completely different from the intent. You need one of your own people who speaks Inarituk."

Zoysana took a moment to think, then turned her face full to Jhanes. "And that person is you? You speak this Inarituk language?"

He shot a glance at his new wife. "I'm sorry, Sarha."

She was mute, unmoving, and he knew what was going through her mind. *Only three days respite from the last danger, and now...?*

Zoysana touched the other woman's hand. "I know it's a difficult sacrifice, Sarha, but if he can help in any way, he could save hundreds of lives. Thousands, perhaps. If the tribes attack en masse, they could overrun the whole realm."

There was no argument from Sarha, only a lowering of her head to stare at her calloused hands on the table in front of her.

Jhanes felt walls closing around him.

THE INNKEEPER'S HUSBAND

PETRELLAN SAGA BOOK 5

Gordon A. Long

AIRBORN PRESS
Delta, B. C.

The Innkeeper's Husband
Petrellan Saga Book 5

Gordon A. Long

Published by
Airborn Press
4958 10A Ave, Delta, B. C.
V4M 1X8
Canada

ISBN: 978-0-9952687-8-4

Printed by CreateSpace

Cover Design by Mihaela Voicu

More from Gordon A. Long

Available at Smashwords, Amazon and other outlets

"Zoysana's Choice" The Petrellan Saga Begins
Coming in early 2018
"Mercenary's Dream" Final book in the first trilogy of the
Petrellan Saga
"Out of Mischief" World of Change Book 1
"Into Trouble" World of Change Book 2
"Mountains of Mischief" World of Change Book 3
"The Trouble with Tents" World of Change Book 4
Coming This Fall
"Queen of Mischief" World of Change Book 5
"A Sword Called...Kitten?" Romantic Comedy with an Edge
"The Cat with Many Claws" Sword Called Kitten Book 2
"Why Are People So Stupid?" Social Humour with a Point

Look for Gordon's books, selected reviews, poetry and short
stories at <airbornpress.ca>
Gordon's opinions on humanity are at the
"Are People Really That Stupid?" blog
http://airbornpress.ca/arepeoplestupid/
Find his weekly reviews and his ideas on writing at
"Renaissance Writer"
http://airbornpress.ca/newdir/

Thanks to Cas Peace for her help and support

CONTENTS

PROLOGUE — CHILD OF WAR

The boy hated uniforms.

He avoided them whenever possible, but he could not ignore them completely, as they were often the only source of food in the ravaged countryside. He stole from them when he dared, and hid, snarling, when he had to. But he hated them with all the pent-up emotion of his undernourished soul.

Frey had been an early casualty of the war. Certain scenes were walled safely away in his small mind: scenes of fire and blood and flashing steel, and a screaming that seemed to go on and on and never stop until he woke in the cold night with the sound on his own lips.

He had a hazy memory of sheltering with others at the beginning, but then the uniforms had come again and the harsh scenes were repeated. Thrown on his own resources, he had learnt to rely on himself alone, shunning the poor wretches who huddled together in the meager protection of their former homes. He scorned and avoided them, stealing from them when his hunger drove him.

But for the uniforms he reserved his own, special, hatred.

He had seen them run, once. He still cherished that scene, drawing it out before his mind's eye in his moments of peace, reliving it again and again like a recurring dream he could experience at will.

The soldiers were marching as usual, with their cruel weapons, their horses, their full supply wagons. He crammed himself into the hollow under an uprooted tree to watch in longing and hatred as they passed.

But then they stopped. Had they seen him? No, they were confused, making unhappy noises, moving restlessly in place. He liked that. They almost looked afraid. He felt a grim satisfaction, but it was nothing compared to what came next.

A disturbance moved gradually through the line of soldiers, beginning at the head of the column and advancing towards him. The turmoil approached; something was moving along the road through the army. Before the moving *thing*, uncertainty prowled. Men shuffled and strained to see; others pushed ahead, some pushed back. After the *thing* passed, pandemonium reigned. The horses of the mounted men reared and plunged, unseating riders and running free. Soldiers fled in terror or froze; some fell to their knees in prayer.

Intrigued and pleased, the boy squirmed higher, pressing his face behind the screen of a projecting root stub, his matted hair against the dirty bark. He had never seen soldiers act like this. Whatever made soldiers afraid, he wanted to know about it.

Then, from the trees opposite him, came a scream that rose and wavered and died, then rose again, repeated and echoed throughout the forest. The terrible sound startled him, and at first he was afraid, but then he saw the soldiers. They panicked and ran in many directions, one almost stumbling into the boy's hiding place in his haste. The urchin scuttled down under the broken wood but kept one eye to a crack.

Soon, the sounds died away, and he was alone again.

Except for the figure on the road. The cause of the disturbance. No, there were two figures, and the one behind was a dog. Or sort of a dog. It terrified him. It was larger than any dog he had ever seen, with a wide head, huge teeth and great furry feet with strong black claws. It was almost as tall as its master, revealed now by the fleeing soldiers.

Its master. She must be the animal's master, the small dark woman in the swirling robe. The dog followed her with its head and tail low. Frey knew what that meant. It meant that She was the dominant one, and the vicious beast was trying, like a scolded puppy, to win Her good will. He watched Her. Was She the one who had frightened the soldiers away? How could She be? She must be. There was something different about Her walk, as if She was in a trance, for Her head stayed absolutely still, Her eyes focused far ahead, and Her body swayed in a dance-like motion, hidden in the flowing cloth. Then as he watched, She sat on a roadside boulder, the huge dog fawning at her feet. After a while, She rose, shook herself awake, comforted the dog and continued, walking normally now, around a corner and out of his sight.

For a long while he lay there, savouring the pleasure of the experience. The soldiers had run! They had been afraid of her, as he was afraid of them! Who was this Woman, with so much power? She must be magic. The word came from somewhere in the storehouse of his mind: a concept from another time, another life. But magic was the right word. She must be magic.

Then he saw something more important. A supply wagon lay on its side, horses gone, a wheel broken. Spilling out of it was more food than he had seen in months. Meat! Loaves of hard, dark, bread! Dried fruits!

Abandoning his cover, he slunk over to the wagon. He picked up a loaf and held it for a moment, unable to believe his luck. It smelled marvellous. He took a bite, tearing the tough crust with anxious teeth. It was real. It tasted heavenly. His saliva flowed, and he gulped the bread down. He grabbed a handful of nuts from a torn sack. They were real; they went the way of the bread. He was in his own fearful version of paradise. His eyes darting from his feast to the road and the surrounding woods, he gorged himself.

He heard footsteps returning through the forest. Men's voices. Finding a rag, he scrabbled as much food as possible into its folds, slipped back into the woods and started towards his hideout.

Then he stopped. The Woman. But She was gone. He thought of Her with longing. How could he see Her again? How could he go to the One who made the soldiers afraid? Would She kill him with her magic? The soldiers must have thought She would kill them; they ran away so fast. Where had She gone? How could he follow Her? His food was too heavy, and he must not leave such riches.

He stood, torn by his two desires. Opening the makeshift pack, he ate more bread, but he was too full. He closed it again and gazed around. There! A good hiding place, under a rock surrounded by thick thorns. Easing his treasure in and under as far as he could, he backed out and observed it from several angles. Yes, it was well hidden. He started away.

After a few steps he stopped and looked back. The food was safe. He turned and went on. Then he stopped again. He looked over his shoulder. He could not see the food! He rushed back. Yes, it was still there. So hastily that the thorns scored his back, he dragged his prize out and opened it. Yes, it was all there. He grabbed a handful of fruit and stuffed it in his mouth. His stomach hurt, it was so full.

He stood for a long time, his arms held tight around the bag of food, staring longingly in the direction the Magic Woman had departed. He could not leave the food. He must take it back to his den. By then She would be gone. If She went into the town, he dared not follow Her. They would chase him in the town, throw rocks. But he must not leave the food. Winter was coming.

Maybe She would come back to save him. Yes, that was it. He would stay with his food and wait. Then She would come back. When She came back, he would go to Her. He would put his head down, like Her big dog did, and She would know She was his master. He must practice. Placing the bag on the ground, he crouched and cringed. Did he have it right? He tried to look at himself. On hands and knees, he arched his back, tucking in his buttocks and holding his head near the ground, neck exposed. Yes, that was it. That would work. He would practice, so when She returned, he would ask Her to be his master. He would wait. He would eat the food, and his master would return. He would wait for rescue.

And the war-ravaged realm waited with him.

1. BARGAIN

"I wouldn't touch that if I were you." The big man's eyelids were almost closed, but he was wide awake.

The hand shrank away from the shiny dagger hilt.

"Don't think of running. Inn's locked up tight. Nowhere to go."

The hand froze.

"Come out and let's have a look at you, now. Come on, I won't bite. Not if you're good. And you better not bite, either. Lady be praised, and aren't you a little thing, after all of that? No, don't run away. I didn't mean to hurt your feelings. You've been avoiding me all evening. Are you bolder now?" A soft chuckle escaped the man's lips. "So you want to see my dagger?"

The tangled hair nodded. The gleam of a calculating eye peered up at him; the lip forgot to snarl.

"Go ahead. Pull it out. But you be careful with that. It's sharp enough to lop a finger clean off. You happy now?"

The little boy, if boy it was, gripped the knife with care, enjoying the play of reddish firelight along the slick blade. As he held it, the snarl returned, and he sank into a fighting crouch.

"You've seen your fill; put it back, now. Right now! Go ahead. That's a good lad. Now, you run off to bed. I see you down here again, I'll tie you to a bench for the rest of the night." A fierce scowl sent the young would-be thief scampering up the shadowy stairs, although there was not a whisper of sound.

Rolling over onto his back, Jhanes winced as his splinted arm caught in the cloak that covered him. The firelight flickered on the low, dark ceiling, and soon he slept again, the light, semi-aware sleep of a man in pain and uneasy with his surroundings.

So he roused the moment a creaking door upstairs accompanied the first grey glimmer of dawn seeping in through cracked shutters. He continued to doze while his ears followed the landlady's morning preparations. Soon, the smell of bread roused him further, and he sat up, stretching.

"Oh, you're awake, then, sir." A lined face peered over the counter that separated the kitchen from the common room.

He grinned. "I sleep light, Mistress. Especially when I have small visitors."

"Ach! Frey wasn't down botherin' you, was he? I can't keep him to stay in bed for the full night. Always up and about, creepin' and pryin'. It was his upbringin', poor lad."

The man yawned. "And what kind of upbringing was that?"

"We don't really know. Found him in the forest, we did, nested up in a fox's den. Must have lost his family in the Troubles and was livin' off the land. And him a child so young."

"Might explain why he was wary of me at first. Probably didn't get on too well with soldiers." The big man shook his head. "It's too common a tale, Mistress. So why is he here?"

"Where else would he go?" The landlady shrugged as she placed a mug of light ale and a round of warm bread in front of her guest. "I can use the company."

The big man shot her a glance, respect forming. "It's good of you, Mistress. Business can't be good, what with the Troubles and the bad weather."

She shrugged again. "Someone had to take him in." Humour crinkled the corners of her eyes, and he lowered his estimation of her age by five years. "It was that or have him steal everything we had left."

"So he's a thief, is he?"

"And what would you expect, with nothin' to eat in the countryside and winter comin'?"

"True, true. A few times I've been tempted myself, when things got difficult. Soldiering is an up-and-down business."

"Well, it's a credit to your mother's teachin's that you resisted." She shot him a sideways glance. "If you did resist."

He laughed, holding out empty hands. "For the most part I did, Mistress. You see before you a man, no less honest than any other, but no less poor than most, mainly because of that same character flaw."

She sniffed. "I'd not be calling honesty a character flaw, sir."

"And that's why your inn is small and your shutters cracked. Shall I open them and see what kind of a day it is?"

Caution flashed in her eyes. "Just you take a look before you go openin' anything. You never know what might be out there, even at this time of the mornin'."

He raised his eyebrows but did her bidding, opening the shutters a slit and peering through first before flinging them wide, then closing the pane behind to keep out the cold. "Nothing but winter sunshine, Mistress. And not a bad day for the first month of winter."

The rutted road that ran past the inn was frozen, with puddles cracked open by passing feet. A few skiffs of snow drifted against the outbuildings, but for the most part the ground was bare. Tufts of dead grass, grey and brown, littered the common between the houses of the village, and barren trees crowded the fallow fields on every side.

"Not a pretty time of year, but better for travelling than sleet or rain."

"And you'll be travellin' today, then, sir?"

Jhanes turned and looked around the inn's cramped common room, dark now with his shadow across the window. *It isn't much. But then, what choice do I have?* He sighed, but only in his head, and glanced at her. "That will depend on you, Mistress."

She laughed. "It's been many a year since a man gave me the power to bid him go or stay, sir. I had thought I was long past that stage o' my life."

His cheeks burned. "I didn't mean…"

"The Lady save us, of course you didn't. I was just havin' some fun with you. Please don't grieve yourself."

He grinned. "Sorry, Mistress. These days, it's a long stretch between times when a man is free to joke."

"Take it as a compliment. It has been a pleasure to have you stayin' here, if you don't mind my sayin' it. We haven't slept half bad, with you down here."

"Glad someone had the benefit of a good night's sleep."

"Ach, I'm that sorry, the child botherin' you."

"Well, when his hand was closing on my dagger hilt, I did worry. But there seems no harm in him."

"Nay, and there isn't, sir, I'm sure of it. In fact, there's somethin'...I can't tell what. He's like to be waitin' for somethin' or someone. He'll be in the middle of some mischief, and of a sudden, all of his own, he'll stop, as if listenin', then go on about his business proper-like, as if someone had told him to be good."

The man considered the strangeness of the waif and the heart of this woman. *No matter what she says, she must put up with a deal of turmoil in aiding the lad. He's lucky. A child needs a family. Not that I'd know much about that.*

He glanced around the room again. *Why worry about the innkeeper's personality? The place is warm and dry. I've mostly had worse since the day I was born, and I can't afford better.* A deep ache settled in his bones. *I'm getting old for this soldiering business. But what else am I good for?* The woman was waiting, and he shook the cobwebs loose.

"I'm looking for a place to stay for a while."

Her face brightened, the lines disappearing. "And how long a while would that be?"

He indicated the bandaged arm. "Until I'm ready to hire out again, I suppose."

"A clean break? No wound?"

He grimaced. "Yes. A strange injury for a soldier, you would say."

4

"I wouldn't think to judge on what happens in battle."

"Battle? Hah! Mistress, you see before you a veteran of The War That Never Was. You are in the presence of the very first casualty in the Battle That Never Happened."

"You speak in riddles, sir."

He sat down on a nearby bench, which creaked beneath his weight, and swept a hand towards the matching seat. "Have you ease, Mistress, to hear a story, and so early in the morning?"

A smile that verged on coquetry took another few years off her face. "Since you are my only customer, I should find time to humour you, sir."

"Then listen well, and learn from the Past, as the Future will look to you."

If she found the Bard's Preface strange coming from the mouth of a rough soldier, she did not show it. Seating herself opposite him, she leaned her elbows on the table and gave him her full attention. If truth be known, a part of her was also assessing the man before her as any lone woman must, but it was part and parcel of the story he told and the way he told it.

"What you now call the Troubles might have been a war, except there was no opposing army. King Barent's soldiers took over Rawden's territories with ease, with the cooperation of most of Rawden's people. Hardly even a battle. The famine and social rupture that followed could not be called a war. The mighty enemy, poised with invading army, never materialized."

"But everyone knows about the Battle of the Lady's Wood. Surely that was a true battle?"

His shout of laughter startled the boy, who had crept near their feet to listen. The child burrowed behind the woman's skirt, but his sharp eyes peered out at the man with uncommon interest.

"The Battle That Never Was. Do you know what vanquished Barent's army?"

"None has ever told. A powerful force, either of arms or magic, to perform such a rout."

He laughed again with pleasure. "Five scouts with bows and one small woman."

"What? Never!"

"Just what I say. The total opposing force in the Battle of the Lady's Wood was a troop of bowmen and a short, dark woman dressed in the style of a Kyabran. That was all."

She stared across the table, but his face held no smile. "You're sure of yourself."

He waved his injured arm. "I told you. There it is. The first injury in the Battle That Never Was."

"You were there?"

"Oh, yes I was. And I hope to never see the like again."

"Tell, tell!" Her eyes brightened and she hitched forward, unaware of the gap in her blouse that afforded him more than the accepted view of her bosom. He was too intent on his story to take notice.

"It was the most amazing thing you could dream of." His hand swept the scene out before her. "Picture us, tramping down an empty road. No resistance, no trouble. Could have been a training march. Five score light horse, fifteen armoured Warlanders on heavy destriers, four hundred foot. And no raw recruits, believe me. All seasoned veterans. Say what you like about Barent, he knew how to build an army."

Her enthusiastic nod propelled his narrative.

"There we are, marching along, enjoying the day as much as a man can when he might be headed for his death, when there's a disturbance in the cavalry up front. They're slowing down. Now, as I say, we're all capable men, and anything out of the ordinary sets us on edge. We check our flanks, but there's nothing. I'm taller than the rest, but there's too many horses in the way to see. So we keep marching. Blind. We've been told naught else. But soon we can hardly move.

"A disruption of some sort is moving back through the cavalry. A horse bolts to the side, his rider trying to control him. Another rears and his mates scatter. It's like there's a

6

boulder rolling down the middle of the road through the army. Slowly.

"Then it reaches the tail end of the lancers, and I can tell because all the horsemen are looking back towards us. I'm in the centre column, and I can sort of see what's happening because the spears are wavering and the ranks are breaking. But we're soldiers, so we try to keep marching. I'm watching this thing come down the lines toward us, like a gust of wind across a field of wheat, and I know there's something strange going on. So I shuck my pack and out with my sword. Nothing takes me unawares.

"As it gets closer, the ranks in front of me break apart, and there she is."

"She?"

"A woman, I have no doubt. And you know who I mean."

His glance dropped and the landlady, aware of her posture, drew back, her hand on the pendant inside her dress.

"Yes, it's a woman in the robes of the Lady, followed by the hugest damned armigerent you've ever seen, and him twice as big as usual with his hackles all standing on end and his teeth bared. But nobody's even looking at him. It's her.

"I tell you, at first I feel a fool, standing there all alone with my sword up and this little woman coming at me. Then I see her eyes. It's like I'm not even there. She's staring somewhere away past me, yet through me, and down into a place in my soul where I don't want to look.

"And I don't feel foolish any more. I'm scared as I was in my first full battle, when I was a lad with a rusty old sword and boiled leather for armour. But I stick it out. I don't give in for that. Fear is part of the job, and if you can't deal with it, you had better give up the mercenary's trade. So I square up my weapon, but she just keeps walking. Straight at me. And I know she won't stop. She'll walk right through me and down into my soul and tear up whatever gets in her way.

"I tell you; now I'm scareder than I've ever been in my life. But you can't let that kind of thing get in the way of your duty. So I bring up my sword, ready to strike.

"Now, I know what you're thinking. What does it look like? A man my size with a big sword up in the air, ready to hit an itty bit of a woman who only comes up to my armpit, and her without any weapon. But it wasn't like that. When I drew my arm back, I looked in her eyes and I knew beyond any doubt in the world I was never going to hit her. But I had to try.

"I start my attack, and you have to believe there's not many men in Petrella or the Inner Duchies or anywhere else who will stand in my way when I get a clear swing. And do you know what happens? All this time I've been staring into her eyes. And this look comes over her, like a child just broke a goblet and she's got to give it a spanking, though she doesn't really want to.

"And right in the middle of my cut she reaches out, casual-like, with one hand and brushes me aside like I'm a branch sticking out over the path. Catches my forearm, here," he touched the injury, "with the side of her hand. Felt like a sledge hit me. Broke the small bone clean as anything, tossed me over like a forkful of hay. And all the while she has this apologetic look, like she's sorry I got in her way, but I should have known better."

The big man shook his head, rubbing the bandaged arm. "I've never seen anything like it and I hope I never do again. I tell you, she was going somewhere. She was headed for her destiny, and we were on her path. That was it. We didn't matter any more than a trail of ants across a road."

"But what about the casualties? Wasn't there an attack?"

"That." He snorted a laugh. "A few of the braver lads went back the next day, picked up what was left of the supply wagons, read the ground. There must have been a troop of scouts trailing us, partisans or bandits or what-have-you. Keeping well back from the road and checking our progress.

They found sign of five of them. And some smaller tracks, come to think of it."

He looked with renewed interest at the small figure hidden in the woman's dress.

"Did you find him north of here?"

"Yes. How did you know?"

"Explains the other tracks. I imagine he saw the whole thing. What do you say, lad? Did you see the lady with the big dog?"

The skirt twitched and the child disappeared.

The big man laughed. "Strange kid. Anyway, when the scouts saw us in such a commotion, they decided to take a hand. Started keening and shooting. Killed a few and spooked the others completely. When everyone had run away, they took what they could carry from the baggage train and faded.

"I don't remember much of what happened. I skedaddled with the rest. There was nothing supernatural about those arrows. We trickled on to the village and regrouped. Then nothing happened. They move us here; they move us there...next thing we know the war's over and we're all paid off. And here I am."

"I see."

"Right. And that's where you come in."

"I do?"

"Aye. Can't hire out like this. I have to den up somewhere until the arm heals. Nowhere too expensive, since we didn't make much. Somehow you never do when your side loses." He knitted his eyebrows. "Of course, we won the war, I suppose."

The woman leaned forward again, all business this time. "So you're lookin' for a room for a month or so."

"Maybe two or three. No sense moving in the winter. Nothing happening anyway."

She held her gaze on him longer than necessary. "Tell you what, soldier. I'll make you a deal."

"A deal?"

"Yes. If you stay the rest of the winter, you stay free."

9

"Free?"

"Free." She took in his heavy shoulders and the bulge over his broad belt and smiled. "But you pay for your food."

He returned her smile. "So I'm hired, am I?"

"You could call it that. I won't say as it ain't a comfort to have someone like you around, what with the Troubles and all."

"At the moment, I'm not much use in a fight."

"I don't expect it to come to a fight. If it did, I'd do what I done before, and I'd expect you to do the same."

"And what's that?"

"Run."

He nodded. "I know the worth of that tactic. Not to my liking, though."

"That's your choice. There's little in this place worth stealin', and with the stone walls, they can't do much damage if we ain't here. I've lived in this place almost forty years, even had the roof burned off once. I won't say it's fun, but we can start over if we still have our health. No, runnin's the smartest move," she fixed him with a stronger stare than he expected, "and I figure you're smart. Do we have a deal?"

He rose, stretched his left hand across the table. "We have a deal, Mistress. I think I'm going to like staying here."

Her bony fingers disappeared in his huge fist. She held them there a moment, looking up into his face. "You won't get bored? Little village like Lanil's Rock ain't got much entertainment. 'Less some minstrel plays here, and they don't make much, so they don't come much."

"I need little entertainment. I don't sleep too well because of the pain, so I lie around a lot. It isn't fun, but I've been through it before."

"All right, then, get your pack and let's go upstairs."

"Upstairs?"

"You weren't thinkin' of sleepin' down here, were you?"

"No, but I thought maybe the stables, or...?"

"What good are you out in the stables if I need you inside? No, you sleep in one of the upstairs rooms. Why not? They don't exactly get used on a daily basis. In case you ain't noticed, travel is off this year."

"I suppose."

She grinned. "Besides that, there's only two beds in the house big enough to fit your feet in." Then she reddened, spun away from him and hurried up the stairs.

He hoisted his pack and ducked his head through the narrow opening to the staircase. *And I'm guessing I know where the other one is…*

His room was up under the roof. It wasn't large, and the sloping ceiling meant he could only stand up in the half farthest from the outside wall, but it had a long enough bed that didn't sag too much under his weight and a window that could be opened for an emergency escape.

After he had settled his few belongings to his satisfaction, the soldier returned to the common room. The landlady was sweeping, so he carried a bench outside and leaned back against the warm, dark, old wood of the doorframe. He was vaguely aware of several curious villagers who passed him, but they mattered little compared to the sense of accomplishment easing its way through his mind. A fine place, this. *The landlady…what's her name, Sallya? Sarha?… is much more interesting than I first thought. Have to keep a close eye on my gear, with that wild boy around…*

"Dog story."

He opened his eyes a slit. The voice had come from somewhere near his feet. Sure enough, the ragged waif was sitting as close as possible to his left leg without quite touching it. "What?"

"Tell dog story."

"What dog story?"

"Dog with big teeth. Lady and soldiers. Tell story."

The landlady leaned out the window, shaking the dust from a rag. "That's the most words I've heard him string together since he came here. He must like your storytelling."

The soldier shrugged. "All right, Sonny. I've got lots of stories. You pick yourself up out of the mud and I'll tell you a story."

The tousled head shook. "Dog story. Lady story."

"Just that one?"

"Dog story."

The soldier looked around. The sun was almost warm, and he had nothing better to do. "You want to come and sit up here?"

Again the shaking head. With a curious, dog-like movement, the boy curled up, his back just touching the soldier's foot. Careful not to disturb the tenuous connection, Jhanes made himself comfortable and started his tale again.

* * *

In the months that followed, the three settled into a pleasant routine, creating a sheltered island for themselves in the seething morass of a land healing from war. As his arm improved Jhanes took on more of the rough jobs around the inn. One night a bully with too much to drink took an unexpected flight with a hard, damp landing, persuading the locals that the injured arm was no hindrance to the soldier's ability to keep peace. This incident of violence resulted in more business. There was a security to the place that brought the men, and even their wives, out to socialize, although few had more than a penny for a single mug of light ale, which they nursed all evening.

The heft of the soldier's purse faded with the departing winter, but he felt a strange reluctance to move on. A vague disquiet sometimes urged him, telling him that the levies would be forming for the early fighting, if not here in Petrella, then over in the Inner Duchies. But still he stayed on, basking in a sense of comfort that pierced deep into places he rarely visited. He rested in a limbo of ennui like a man just roused from sleep but reluctant to rise and face the day. And so he waited for a sign or an event that would give him direction, spur him into action.

The wild boy, it turned out, had no interest in stories other than the "Dog and Lady," but always appeared when that tale, a favourite with the villagers, was told. At the end of the telling he would exhibit his strange dog-like behaviour, whining and wriggling in an ecstasy of some sort. After consulting with the landlady, who considered this the least of the poor child's symptoms, the soldier decided to let it ride. There was nothing he could do to stop it, and little Frey was so enchanted with the story it would be cruel to disappoint him.

As the weather warmed and the ground thawed, the lad's voice returned. Soon he was talking in sentences, although trying to find out anything about his past brought a relapse into silence.

Likewise, time did its job on the soldier's arm, and one day he went to breakfast without the splints. "I think it needs strengthening." He twisted his wrist back and forth, rubbing the muscles with his other hand. "Feels stiff."

"Let me see." Sarha probed with work-hardened fingers. He winced a few times, but the pain was minimal. "The bones feel straight. Lucky you got it set right."

He grinned. "The surgeon hadn't much to do after that battle."

"Hmm. Well, don't overdo it. Light duty at the beginning."

His smile widened. "Aye, Mother. Whatever you say."

She scowled. "I'm nowhere near takin' your mother's place. Who'd want you?"

His big hand trapped her arm on the table, holding her facing him. "I'd like to thank you. It has been a great benefit to me, staying here."

"Then you'll be leaving soon?"

He checked for disappointment in her face. "Only if you want me to."

"No, no, not half. Our deal still holds. I just didn't expect you'd be hangin' around, what with your arm healed and the summer campaigns startin'."

"Well, I didn't expect my money to last so long, what with staying here. So if you don't mind, I'll wait for something to come up. Tell the truth, the idea of going back to a regiment doesn't appeal any more. There's plenty of other jobs a man can do that don't get him in the middle of a battle quite so regular. I've seen my share of the world, proved I can stand against any man. Maybe there's other things to look for, now."

She shot him a sly grin. "Why, Jhanes, it sounds like you're growin' up."

"After thirty-five years, you'd think it would happen."

"Go on with you. You're never born so long ago."

"That's what my mother told me, and she was there at the time."

"I suppose she was. And not likely to forget it."

"I doubt she would. I was a big baby then, and I didn't stop growing for a long time."

"Well, I'm that glad you're stayin', soldier. We done better this winter than I had any right to expect. More people come to a safe house, you know. You tarry as long as you like.

"But if that arm of yours needs exercise, there's a mighty big garden out back that needs turnin' over before plantin' the early vegetables."

"And if I grow my own food, do I still have to pay for it?"

"Only till your money runs out. Then we'll see."

"And I'm supposed to be the mercenary around here." He lumbered to his feet, stretching till his shoulders cracked. "I suppose if we had a mule, we could plow."

"We could, that. If we had a plow."

"I'll get the shovel."

14

2. OUT OF THE STORM

Spring brought warmth and light and good spirits to the village. It also brought travellers on the road: some less welcome than others. The soldier found more and more need for his presence at the inn.

"Do you often have this type of trouble?" He was panting, having just persuaded two ruffians that they didn't want to argue so forcefully within the crowded common room.

"Throw their bags out after them." The landlady suited action to her words and slammed the door. "We don't need their sort in here, anyways. And no, it seems there's a lot of people of a type we don't usually get travelling south this spring."

"Vultures. Happens every time."

"Vultures?"

"When a war's over, there's those who come to scrounge the leavings. Some are more or less decent merchants looking for new markets. Others are crooks and thieves of all stripes. You watch. Look for new faces in the freehold farms and shops. There'll be more theft, beating and robbery on the roads this summer."

"The king should do somethin' about it!" The speaker was the local blacksmith, the closest thing the small village had to a civic leader.

"Oh, he will, sooner or later. Gerth's a good sort, I hear, so it might be sooner. But until he sends his patrols our way, we're on our own. So, tomorrow I'm going to repair the lock on the pigsty, and I will also be less gentle with that type." He gestured in the direction of the newly departed customers. "We have a good reputation and it won't hurt to add to it."

"Are you expectin' trouble?" The town carpenter looked up at the soldier with worried eyes.

"Not on any large scale. Since Barent's death the word has gone out that the kingdom is settling. Nobody like Lupent is likely to try grabbing a little niche for himself." He chuckled. "Especially with the threat of the Lady and her big dog hanging over us all."

"Are you a Believer, then?"

"Probably not in the sense that some of you are. But believe you me, that day on the road I ran across something, and if I have any second thoughts about it, I have only to feel my arm to tell me otherwise." He was distracted by a call from another table for more ale and spoke no more philosophy that night.

But the thought niggled at him, and he started looking at the village from a defensive point of view. *Anything could happen. It often has. Best be prepared.*

The inn itself was perfect: built in a hollow square with thick walls and small windows, the shutters all repaired now and fitting closely. Of course, a few weeks of dry weather and a torch to the roof would finish it all.

The town was less easily defended, especially against footsoldiers. The outside walls of the buildings crowded together to form a decent line of defence, but the road was open through the middle, and an enemy, once inside, could control the central common and pick off individual houses at will. Unless, of course, there were bowmen in the windows and a barricade at each end of the street, in which case the enemy would discover how it felt to be fish in a shallow pond.

He wasn't likely to find a squad of archers anywhere near, but surely a few of the locals were at least proficient. *I'll ask around.*

He sighed. *I come here to give up soldiering, and here I am at it again. Why can't it just leave me alone?*

His thoughts were interrupted by the rumble of thunder. A spring storm was approaching from the west, darkening the twilight. Most of the customers took this as a signal to leave, since they would be up with the sun tomorrow. He was closing the last shutter when the rain came down, washing the village

16

from sight. The soldier turned inside, tossed another log into the fireplace, sat in the warmth and grinned at his hostess.

"A fine night to have a tight roof and plenty of firewood, Mistress Sarha."

"Aye, it is that. Is all secure outside?"

"As good as we'll get without a squad of archers on the rooftops."

"You're still thinkin' about that, are you?"

"An old soldier can't keep his mind from turning."

"Old soldier! Hah! Not forty yet, and soundin' like a greybeard."

She had mentioned his age several times recently, and he wondered where it was leading. He waited with a soldier's patience, sure that when the time was right she would let him know.

"Just trying to get used to the idea of not going out on the road again."

"Thinkin' of stayin', are you? There's not many places like this one. Dry roof, thick walls, good customers, a soft bed upstairs." She paused a moment, took a deep breath. "There might even be a softer one, if you had the notion."

"Why, Mistress, I believe that sounds like a proposition, and not completely a business one."

She did not respond to his smile. Instead, she sat down opposite him, pulling his hands across the table and squeezing them to hold his attention. "And why not? Look, I'm near forty. But I'm still strong and healthy, got most of my teeth and I got this inn. You're a bit younger, but if you want to leave soldierin', you need a place like this, somewhere to make a start. We work well together. We live well together. I know I'm no beauty, but we're both long past the time when love was so important."

"Hold on, there. Just hold on a moment. I wouldn't like to think I was ever past the stage where love was important. If you're talking more than a business proposition, then you're talking about the rest of our lives. At least, that's the way I've

17

always considered it. And beauty's got nothing to do with it either. I've seen beauty, and it doesn't make a whole lot of difference in the long run. Don't sell yourself low. I'm no bargain, either. Handsome? Not likely. Sure I'm big, but that just means I eat more. Worse, I'm not sure I'm ready to become an innkeeper, just like that. Be a big change, all of a sudden."

"You wouldn't need to be tied here. I can handle the place myself. I done it for years. You could still travel, maybe do some buyin' and sellin'..." She paused, looked him up and down, then slipped her hands away. "Ach, what am I thinkin' about? This is no life for the likes of you, a wee village like this. You, who've been out in the world, and educated and all. Oh, yes, I can tell by the way you talk. We get enough travellers through here that I can tell, accent or no. I'm sorry I brought..."

He reached across the table, cutting her words short with a squeeze of her upper arms that stopped her breath. "Never be sorry. Never sell yourself low. I know you're a fine woman, and what education I scrounged doesn't make me any better a man."

He released his pressure and slid his grip down, taking her hands in his, looking at her earnestly. "I'm pleased you see me this way. Don't think I haven't considered it myself. Should have mentioned it, but I didn't. Just slow, I guess. But now you've brought it up, and it's something to talk about. I don't know if it would work, but I'm not saying it won't."

She smiled in relief. "There's no hurry, that's for sure. I've been meanin' to speak to you, but I worried I'd be drivin' you away."

He laughed. "Not much chance of that. Haven't had a woman propose marriage to me for years. Tell the truth, haven't had a woman seriously propose, ever. Does a man's heart good to know he's wanted."

"Well, I'm glad of that, soldier. You are most definitely wanted."

His fingertips slid gently up her arm where the skin was soft. "And so are you, Mistress. So are you."

She looked down a long moment, then up at him. Her hands were shaking, ever so slightly. "So, do you want to go upstairs, try out that other bed?"

He smiled, gently this time. "So we can discuss that part of the deal?"

"It's one place to start."

He considered for a moment. "Maybe we ought..."

But she didn't get to hear what he was about to say. There was a banging at the door and a muffled voice calling out.

He stood. "Damn! I never heard anyone coming. The storm must have covered them."

She grinned. "There were other things on our minds, soldier."

He patted her shoulder. "That there were, Mistress. Now, you slip back into the kitchen and I'll find out who this is." He approached the door, listening. More banging, but it was a gloved hand, not a sword hilt. He slid open the peephole, but could see nothing in the outer darkness.

"Who is it?"

"Travellers, Innkeeper." The voice came from below. "Looking for shelter from this Lady-sent storm."

The Kyabran expression clicked with the accent, and Jhanes had the man placed. He swung the door open. "Welcome, travellers from the north. Come on in out of the rain."

A short figure swathed in a sopping cloak stepped in, and the soldier knew a reconnaissance when he saw one. Quick eye-sweep of the room, another glance at himself, registering his size and the short staff leaning within reach of the door. A moment for decision, then a quick nod. "Thank you, Innkeeper."

The stranger merely glanced backwards, but a signal was passed and the second person entered the room, indistinguishable in a similar cloak.

"Come in, friends, and keep the storm out." Jhanes hurried to shut the door.

"There are animals..."

"I'll see to them myself as soon as you are settled. We have a dry barn and some of last year's hay. Not much body left in it, but..."

The travellers were slipping out of their cloaks, shaking water out of their dark hair. The second was a woman, of similar height to her companion but lighter of skin. She smiled and was about to speak when a sudden commotion attracted everyone's attention.

It was Frey, and he was acting in the strangest way. Whining and cringing, he raced across the common room towards the visitors, almost reaching them before dropping on the floor, his head turned away, body wriggling in a strange fit. The mistress followed quickly, but she was too late. "I'm so sorry, my Lady, I can't think what's got into the poor thing. He's never acted like this before." She reached out and was about to pick up the child when the woman gestured.

"Wait. Look at him." Her voice was low, unaccented, and she seemed not at all put out. "See his actions? Like a dog. A junior member, greeting the prime of the pack. See how he rolls over, exposing his throat, his eyes turned down?" She knelt, laying a hand on the tousled head. "What a strange child. Is he yours?"

"I'm truly sorry, my Lady. He's mine now, but we don't know where he come from. Lost his family in the Troubles, I guess. Lived by himself in the woods."

The woman nodded. "Yes, but there's more to it than that. If he's never acted like this before, why now? Why me?" She rose gracefully, and the boy crouched at her side, pressing against her leg. She left a comforting hand on his head and turned to her companion. "The horse, Tadeo?"

The Kyabran man stepped forward. "Of course, Lady Zoysana. We have three animals, Innkeeper. One of the horses is lame. Slipped on a patch of clay and pulled something, perhaps." He gestured at his mud-splattered boots. "Not an easy night for walking, as I soon found out."

"I'll take special care of him, sir. Please seat yourselves."

"I'll come with you."

"Nonsense, sir. You've been out in the rain enough tonight. I can tend three horses, even if one is lame."

"Only two of them are horses."

Jhanes waited for more information, then shrugged. Grabbing his cloak from its peg, he slung it around his shoulders and stepped into the storm. The man followed, and they led the two horses around the main building and into the stable. There was no sign of a third animal, and the soldier was too concerned with his charges to worry about it. The injured steed, a fine, sturdy pony with an air of speed about him, was content to stand and be checked over. The two men inspected the leg but there was no reaction from its owner, no matter how hard they prodded.

"I'm no horseman, but it doesn't look serious to me."

The Kyabran nodded as he left the stall. "A day of rest wouldn't hurt him." He looked around the stable. "Is that stall in the corner available?"

The soldier nodded. "Kept ready, in case. Clean straw, hay in the manger, nothing fancy."

"That will be fine. Could you stand aside a moment?"

Puzzled but not worried, Jhanes stepped back. The small man walked to the door and whistled a strange, sliding tone. There was a splashing in the innyard and a huge armigerent stalked through the door. The Kyabran gestured towards the empty stall, but the creature was in no hurry. First, he gazed around, noting the positions of the two horses. The huge, craggy head turned towards the soldier. Two sniffs, deep enough that Jhanes could feel hot breath, told the animal all he needed in that direction. Politely walking to the far end of the stable, the armigerent shook himself thoroughly. Then, like a king entering his throne room, he strolled into the stall, circled twice and flopped into the straw. His chin dropped onto his paws and he gave a great, gusty sigh.

"He's settled for the night. Let's go inside."

The soldier snapped from his reverie. "Will he need feeding, sir?"

"No, he ate well this morning. Thank you for thinking of it. I'm sure he appreciates it, don't you, Patu?"

The eyes opened, and the thick tail thumped twice against the planks.

The Kyabran laughed. "He's very polite, but you have to look for it."

The soldier smiled, though his mind was elsewhere. Opening the door that led through to the house, he indicated for his guest to precede him through the kitchen.

Back in the common room, the lady was seated before the fireplace, her steaming boots upside down on the irons, damp stockings smoking on her outstretched feet. "Come over here, Tadeo. You have to admit, a hot fire after a storm is one of the true luxuries of life."

"Once again, the Sponsor imparts wisdom to her pupil."

She chuckled, a deep, pleasant sound. It was a long while since the soldier had heard a laugh so confident. Her face held long shadows as she turned from the flames, and he moved to get a better look. He tried to stop staring, but it was too late. With incredible grace she rose, standing before him, peering up.

"What is it, Innkeeper? Is something wrong?" Then a faraway look came over her face and she stepped back. "Have we met before?"

"I believe so, Lady." He slowly raised his hand as he had held the sword that day on the road.

"Ah." Her right arm moved, a brushing motion that ended with the side of the hand against his arm. Shaking off her dream, the woman took the injured area in both hands, feeling the lumps on the bone with probing fingers.

"It broke, didn't it?"

"Yes, Lady. A clean break, quickly healed."

She looked up at him, her face normal now, perhaps even friendly. "Well, I won't apologize. You did have a sword."

"I did, Lady, but it wasn't much use."

"That was a brave stand, soldier."

"More stupid, Lady. Like stepping in front of a runaway wagon."

Her hands dropped from his arm, and she returned to her place by the fire. "I always wondered about you. Whether it was brave or stupid. Having met you, I think brave is the word." She smiled at him again. "I would like to think brave, anyway."

"Oh, so would I, Lady, but do the arithmetic. Three hundred experienced men in front of me turn away, but I have to be the one to stand firm. Stupidity."

"Bravery. I'm sure of it now." She relaxed back, and the question was closed forever. "So how do you now become an innkeeper?"

"Oh, I'm not the innkeeper. Sarha is mistress of this house. I'm just a...well, I suppose you could call me a long-term guest."

It was disconcerting how that quick glance, flicking to each of them in turn, seemed to bare their whole previous conversation. "Very long-term, I suspect?"

"My Lady is pleased to meddle."

The soldier glanced to the Kyabran, surprised that the man would correct his mistress so sharply, but she only laughed. "Oh, Tadeo, you're spoiling my fun again. No offence taken, I hope, Mistress?"

The landlady, puzzled by this byplay, could only shake her head. "I have no complaint, my Lady. But I do have stew for supper, if anyone is hungry."

"Hah! The lady has an unanswerable response to my wit. Food, and hot at that? Truly, Tadeo, we have come to heaven." Her hand rested on the head of the boy, still crouching by her chair. "And don't let's have this 'Lady' business. I have no rank in Petrella. I am merely Zoysana, and this is my sometime Guard-of-Life but more often friend, Tadeo Priya."

23

The Kyabran bowed. "Lady Zoysana chooses to be informal, but those of us with manners help her keep proper etiquette in mind." He smiled, but the soldier knew a hint when he heard one.

He too, bowed, even deeper. "We are honoured, Lady Zoysana. I am Jhanes, mercenary soldier. At least, I was. It is a pleasure to meet you, Guard-of-Life Priya. Your training and abilities are not unknown to students of war in this realm."

Priya's face warmed. "I had you pegged for a soldier. You are also a student of warfare?"

"Only in a small way, when the occasion permits. Surely any soldier who wishes to stay alive will take some of his time to study his trade."

The Kyabran laughed. "How correct, and how often untrue. Tell me, where were you trained?"

The conversation continued through the meal of stew and bread the landlady served. The soldier was at first uncomfortable about eating with the guests, but the Lady soon persuaded him otherwise, an ironic twinkle in her eye.

"Since you are only a guest here yourself, why would you not eat with us?"

With such an invitation, he gave in gracefully. *I like people who say what they mean instead of doing things for all sorts of reasons of politics and manners.*

It was only after the food was cleared away and they sat with mugs of the landlady's best strong ale in front of them that the conversation got serious.

"What are the conditions here, soldier?"

He considered. "Not bad, for the moment."

"Explain."

The word came pleasantly enough, but the tone told Jhanes he was now reporting to a commanding officer, and a sharp one at that.

"Well, Lady Zoysana, it wasn't a terrible winter, but it wasn't a good one. Not too cold or too long, but there are stories of those who starved; no surprise considering what was destroyed or stolen during the previous summer. But most resisted the temptation to eat their seed grain. It will be rough until the first food crops come in, but the forest is starting to green up and the people here know how to use the forest."

"But soon...?"

"The vultures are gathering, my Lady. You might have noticed the traffic on the road. Some rich ones, some poor ones, but all with the same glint in the eye."

She nodded and shot a glance at her companion. "As we suspected." She turned back to the soldier. "That's why we're here. Oh, Gerth is sending out his patrols," she smiled at him, "but you know how long it takes soldiers to get anywhere. And we don't want them sent to the wrong places. Tadeo and I move fast," here she grimaced, "at least we used to, and we wanted to make a swing through the worst of it so we could disperse the troops to their best advantage."

"Reconnaissance by one with the authority to ensure the information is acted on."

She laughed. "A shrewd guess, soldier."

"I know a superior officer when I'm questioned by one."

"And I know a superior soldier when I hear his answers. Are you set on staying here?"

Jhanes looked over at Sarha, perched nearby but not joining in the conversation. "I hadn't thought of hiring on with a troop, Lady."

"But if you could stay in the area and do some odd duties for me?"

Inwardly, he winced. *A few 'odd duties.' At least to start with. Then...?* He knew all the recruiting tricks, had played them himself. *On the other hand, if I want to be part of this village, I will have to do my share.* He dropped his head in a slow bow. "It would be an honour, Lady."

The warmth of her smile was hardly military. "Good. We'll talk more tomorrow." Another of those quick eye exchanges with her companion that seemed to convey so much information. "We won't want to move on for a while. Tadeo's pony needs a rest and the road will be terrible. If the weather holds us up, it will stop everyone else as well."

She yawned and stood, stretching full out like a cat. *More like a deep-woods panther.* "We have had a long but not entirely wasted day. We will go upstairs now."

As he expected, his guests asked for separate rooms, and soon they were settled in for the night. With difficulty, and finally a direct order from the lady, Frey was persuaded to go to his own bed, leaving the soldier and his landlady alone together. She looked up at him and sighed.

"You see? Even before we start, opportunity searches you out."

"This changes nothing. You heard what she said. I can stay here and still help her."

"Maybe at the moment. But I see possibilities for you, and I would never want to be the one to hold you back."

She pushed him towards the stairs. "Looks like you're better off in your own bed for a while longer."

3. A Better Deal

The next morning was grey and damp, with more water rising from the ground than falling from the sky. Jhanes was up early as usual, only preceded by Sarha. Their distinguished guests had left orders that they were not to be awakened, but the dim glow of dawn had barely reached the strength of day when they wandered down, yawning and regarding their surroundings in the brighter light.

In fact, Zoysana had something on her mind. She was definitely prowling. She stepped outside to view the inn from several angles, then returned, checking doors and windows.

The soldier observed this until his curiosity got the better of his manners. "Is there something you are looking for, Lady Zoysana?"

She measured the side of the inn with her eye. "There is another room somewhere."

"Yes, beside the kitchen." The common room stretched the full length of the building along the road, while the kitchen behind it was only two-thirds that size. Across the hallway to the stable was another room, which at the moment held spare lumber, broken furniture, and any number of insects and smaller rodents. In more prosperous days it might have been a private room for banquets and parties. One main advantage was its access to the stables.

"Could I see it?"

Jhanes glanced at Sarha for permission, then led the way. "Be prepared for a bit of dust."

Again his soldier's eye noted her precise inspection. A few quick glances calculated the lines of fire through the window, escape routes and other advantages of access. *She must have a use for the room. Could she be sending an agent? Do we want a stranger living here?* The money would come in handy. *Wake up, fool. You live in an inn, now. There will always be strangers living here.*

Soon she nodded, and without further comment returned to the common room and breakfast.

When she had eaten, she leaned back on her bench and stretched again. "A good meal, Mistress. I could eat like that more often on the road."

The landlady blushed. "I'm that sorry, Lady, but there's not much around for variety."

Zoysana chuckled. "I don't complain about lack of variety until after the tenth meal of the same bread. Right now, I'm quite comfortable." Her eyes slyly took in her Guard-of-Life, relaxing likewise. "But not comfortable enough to rest all day."

He didn't look concerned. "Were you thinking of some training, Lady Zoe? Perhaps a candle-length of quarterstaves in the mud?"

"I take your point. Perhaps more domestic duties are called for. Mistress, can you provide us with some soap and hot water? Our clothes have suffered from the weather and the road."

"Oh, no, Lady. You don't do that sort of thing. You leave them with me. I'll have them clean in no time."

"I don't want to put you to a lot of trouble. You have an inn to run."

The soldier smiled at his friend's sharp response. "Right. And two and a half guests to take care of. If I couldn't handle a bit of laundry on top of that, what kind of innkeeper would I be?"

Zoysana's feet hit the floor with a thump. "A very comfortable one, I'm sure. Tadeo, we must take our cue from this hard-working woman. We will leave her with our laundry and set out to do some work appropriate to our assignment."

She was at the bottom of the stairs before her companion's feet were on the floor. He grinned. "So much for a lazy day," but there was no reluctance in his movements as he took the stairs in doubles.

The bag of laundry was small, and the landlady whipped it away with a disdainful frown. "I do more than this every day of my life. You go have a walk, and it'll be dryin' by the kitchen fire before you've circled the village."

"The town is that small, is it?" Zoysana turned to the soldier. "Could you show us around? That is, if you have no other pressing duties."

"Only to see to the stock, Lady. Would the armigerent like something, now?"

"I imagine he'd like something most any time of day. He got fat and lazy over the winter, and I'm trying to slim him down to fighting weight."

"He looks pretty trim to me."

"We've been on the road a while, now. It's starting to tell. Still, he wouldn't turn down a few bones and scraps. He eats almost anything."

Armed with a platter heaped with all the scraps he could find in the kitchen and the meat safe, the soldier led the way to the stable. Tadeo insisted on watering the horses while Zoysana officially introduced Patu to the soldier. When she saw them together, she burst into laughter.

"Now, Patu. There's someone your size for a change. You won't be knocking him off his feet, nosing in for a treat. You'll have to behave yourself."

Sure enough, the huge animal pushed close against him as it left the stall. Taking the hint, he stood firm. The beast turned and looked up at him so reproachfully he had to give in. Ruffling the bristled mane, he placed the platter on the floor. "There you go, boy. I hope it'll keep you on your feet until dinner time."

"It will. I'll leave him inside today. I want to walk around without causing too much of a commotion."

"I can see that. He's not exactly an ordinary house dog."

She shook her head ruefully. "It's not just him. The two of us together...well, we create a bit of a picture. It's useful at times, but this isn't one of them. Not that I'm hiding or anything. In fact, I wouldn't mind being introduced to a few of the village leaders."

"Easy as anything. No one is going anywhere with roads like this."

After deciding that the pony was not feeling any ill effects from yesterday's slip, four of them strolled around the village, the child refusing to be left behind.

When speaking with the villagers, Zoysana's accent changed, and some of her expressions would never have been heard in a manor house. She was especially at home in the forge, asking the smith to continue his work while she watched and twice reaching over to hand him the next tool he needed. She did not pry into anyone's affairs, but left all the villagers with the impression that someone in Arlyn Castle cared about them.

"Any comments or problems, drop a word over at the inn. Sarha will see it gets to me."

The smith nodded as if it was normal that the local innkeeper should be promoted to the lady's assistant.

"I hope that's all right?" As they left the smithy, Zoysana stopped and looked up at the soldier. "I didn't ask her if she would do that."

"Why not? In the first place, it's you asking, and she'd never refuse. In the second place, it's common practice. The inn is the logical clearing house for messages in a small town."

She continued walking, lost in thought. When they reached the edge of the village, she turned and surveyed the area.

He watched her note the same tactical information he had gathered. "Perhaps a sliding barrier, hidden behind this shed?"

She grinned at him. "I was thinking along those lines. What about the other end?"

"There's those big trees on either side. A few long logs shoved between them and the houses and no one could get through. Not if they were being harried by a few well-aimed arrows."

"Are there any archers here?"

"Only four, including myself. One of the old men is very accurate, but he uses a small hunting bow, not having the strength to pull a big one. The other two are passable."

"And yourself?"

"Well, I always found it easy to pull, you know."

"No false modesty, soldier. I need information."

"I was considered good in most outfits. I take my time, but my bow's got more heft than most." He looked around. "I could probably do a man injury as far away as the other end of the town, there. If it wasn't too windy."

She peered down the narrow street, across the common. "That's a long shot."

"As I said, my bow has more pull than average."

She glanced at his thick arm. "I suppose it might."

"Would you like me to try for you?"

"No, I'll take your word for the moment. I don't want to create any kind of stir. Not until I need to. Let's go back to the inn."

When they returned, the mistress said nothing, pointing into the kitchen, where shirts and leggings hung on lines in front of the fire.

Zoysana smiled and nodded. "Anyone interested in tea?"

"I'm sorry, Lady, I don't have…"

"Ah, but I do." She bounded up the stairs, coming down with a small bag that she deposited in the landlady's hand. Sarha opened it, looked in, then stuck her nose to the opening and sniffed deeply.

"I don't know if I can do this justice, Lady."

"I'll take the fact that you recognize it as a good sign."

The mistress bustled off into the kitchen, returning with two cups the soldier had never seen. They were smaller and of finer material than the everyday kitchenware, and though they were dark in colour, they gave off a deep shine. She placed them on the table with a flair bordering on ceremony.

"Do you have four cups, Mistress?"

"I do."

"Please bring the rest. We have business to discuss."

Sarha's glance shot to the soldier, but he could give her no hint. She turned and made her way back to the kitchen for the extra cups, a trace of spring in her step.

Accustomed to the usual innkeeper's technique of thumping the drinks in front of customers as quickly as possible, the soldier noted how his hostess served the tea. Her movements were slow and measured. Each cup had its place; each step was performed with ritual grace. He hesitated, even when his cup was full, until it seemed the right time to drink. The tea was like nothing he had ever tasted: tangy sharp, but with a touch of earth. He drank again, then noticed that everyone else had stopped.

"Thank you, Hostess. It is a pleasure to see my blend treated with respect."

"Oh, Lady, I never thought to serve such a drink at my own table." Sarha rose and retrieved the bag, placing it near Zoysana's hand.

The dark woman pushed it back. "Perhaps not yet, Sarha. I have a proposition for you. For both of you." She took another sip of tea and they drank as well, watching her intently.

"I need a centre of operations. A place from which to come and go, a place I can be reached without fail."

Sarha frowned. "Surely there's a town more appropriate to your station than here, my Lady. Why, down the road a few candles in Alderly there's a fine inn with a carriage to rent and all."

"That's not what I need. If you had seen the place where I grew up, you would understand that I have no desire for elegant lodgings, and I would like to cause as little stir as possible. Your extra room would be ideal: a private place to keep our records, work on our maps. We could come and go from the stable easily, and up to our rooms without disturbing your other customers."

"You could also come and go with your horses without anyone noticin'."

"We could?"

32

"True enough. T'other end of the stable there's a door leads to the paddock. From there, you go out the back gate and down to the stream below. Nobody's windows look that direction. You can circle around to the road and be on your way with nobody the wiser."

Zoysana glanced at Tadeo with a satisfied smile.

The Kyabran grinned. "She likes to have a bolt-hole. Another part of her training."

"As I should. I'm not hiding my presence in this area and I might have to make unpopular decisions: unpopular in some quarters, at least. It would be premature to consider the war completely over." She turned earnestly to the landlady. "The risk is small, but there could be a problem. You can refuse if you want. I'll understand."

Sarha's back straightened. "If you're here to keep the peace after the Troubles, my Lady, I'll be proud to help. No matter what happens."

"Good. We'll try to make it worth your while. Now, as to the cost of the room..."

"We'll not be discussin' that, my Lady."

"No?"

"No. When you're here, you'll pay for your rooms upstairs, food, stabling, and what you drink, like any other customer. Going rate. But that room I wasn't using, and you'll not pay for that."

"I'm sure you could use the extra money."

"I'm sure you can use the extra money to help put this countryside back together."

Zoysana gazed into the other woman's eyes and read the determination. Then she nodded to herself as if she had made a good bargain. "I accept, Mistress. When we are away, we will leave all our extra belongings in the downstairs room. If the inn is full when we return, we can camp there. Otherwise, we will use the bedrooms upstairs, as we are now. At the going rate." Both women nodded, and the deal was struck. Then Zoysana grinned. "So keep the tea and put it away for when we want it.

"And if you won't let us pay for the room, you must let us help clean it out." She clapped her hands, startling Frey who was dozing at her side. "Hot water, my Hostess, and soap!"

Carried along by her enthusiasm, they attacked the mess, and soon it was a whirling mass of dust and suds, cobwebs and brooms. The inn's cat was torn between catching the mice they drove out and avoiding the soapy water they sloshed around, but even she had a successful morning.

It was long past time for the noon meal when they stood back to survey their task. The room was square, with one multi-paned window facing north. The wooden floor shone with new wax, the walls looked acceptably white and a merry fire crackled in the draw of the freshly swept chimney. A large table stood askew at one end awaiting a leg repair, but it gave the right effect.

"I'll have to work on the upholstery of those chairs. Straw's leakin' out all over."

"Will it cost? I could..."

The landlady fixed her guest with a firm eye. "My Lady, you and I both know what your presence is goin' to do to my business. I won't be needin' any extra money from you. Keep it for them as needs it."

Zoysana chuckled again. "It's your house, Mistress. I bow to your authority."

The soldier was surprised to see Sarha wink at Tadeo. "As long as it suits her, she does."

He was even more surprised to see Tadeo wink back.

4. FOXES

"Soldier." The lad trotted into the inn yard, glancing over his shoulder.

Jhanes turned and looked down. "What is it, Frey? Found another fox?"

The small head nodded. "Big foxes. Sly foxes."

The soldier raised his eyebrows. *Who knows what goes on under that mop of hair?* "Big foxes, hey?"

A serious nod. "Shouldn't be there."

He went on sawing the plank to repair the gate. "Shouldn't be where?"

The grubby hand swept a half circle. "Went 'round t' village."

Something about the conversation bothered Jhanes. *The kid's serious about this.* He set the saw down and sat on the plank. "What's this about foxes? Our henhouse is fine. Not a hole to be found. I wouldn't worry about foxes if I were you."

The boy stared at him. "Come." He started away.

"What? Just a moment. I don't have time for any games today. I've gotta fix this gate. Maybe another day."

Frey kept walking. "Bad foxes. Come see."

Jhanes frowned. *Never seen him this positive. Can't hurt to take a look.* He put the saw down, and something about the boy's wary posture made him reach through the front door and pick up his staff as he went by.

Frey led him up the road out of town to the north, through fields that were just sprouting with early crops. The greenery of the forest was at its full spring growth, now, and Jhanes almost missed the faint game trail the boy turned onto.

"See."

He looked where the boy pointed, peered closer. Then he glanced at the lad. "What do you read, Frey?"

35

"Three of 'em. One big, two reg'l'r. Big One limps. Ridin' Boot's short. Got a staff. Moccasin, he's good."

"Aye, Moccasin is careful where he steps. At the first, I thought there was only two." He peered through the screen of bushes and indicated the Frey-sized tracks beside and sometimes over those of the adults. "Where'd they go?"

The boy swung his hand around.

"They circled the village? You follow them all the way?"

Frey nodded once. "Back on t'road after."

"Did they stop or turn aside? Meet anyone?"

"Ate. Chicken, bread, cheese." The boy smiled. "Old bread." He held his nose and grinned. Then he became serious. "Big One 'n' Ridin' Boot sat. Moccasin, he don't sit, he don't move. He c'n be still, that one."

Jhanes nodded. "See that moccasin?"

The boy stared at the print, then up at him.

"It's not Inari. Must be a foreigner from somewhere in the North. Inari moccasins have a line of stitching across the back of the heel, there. Got it?"

"No stitch. Not Inari. Got it." The boy looked up. "Why?"

"Inari this far north means trouble. Maybe big trouble. You see Inari tracks, you tell me quick."

"Got it."

"Anything else?"

The boy shrugged.

"Fine. Back to town."

They returned to the road and strolled side by side back to the inn. "So we've got three men who don't want to be seen. They've got bad food. Probably stolen from a farm up the road. Two of them aren't regular travellers: wrong footgear, limp. The third is a woodsman. This is not good, Frey. Anything else?"

Frey wrinkled up his nose. "Big One's got th' flux."

"Stopped a lot?"

36

"Aye." He held up his hand, thought, then showed four fingers.

"That'll be the bad food." Jhanes stopped and looked at the boy. "Ever seen the like before?"

"Aye."

"Recently?"

"First this year."

Jhanes resumed walking, a hand on the boy's shoulder. "Good eyes, Frey. You're out in the forest more than most. You keep looking and let me know."

The lad nodded and did not pull away.

Jhanes squeezed the thin shoulder. The boy looked at him. "And you be careful, you hear me?"

Frey shrugged. "I c'n be careful."

Jhanes dropped his hand, and they walked back home in silence.

The next afternoon, when Zoysana and Tadeo returned from a trip out to Alderly, he reported Frey's discovery.

The Kyabran woman ruffled the boy's hair. "Good work, lad. We need to know that sort of thing." She looked up at the soldier. "Not unusual, I suppose. We've noted the types that are moving on the road. There must be a few that are even farther over the line."

"Three aren't much of a problem. Nobody around here carries anything worth stealing, unless it's their lunch."

Zoysana's dark eyebrows went up. "And a farm girl coming into town on her own?"

He grimaced. "I suppose we'd better spread the word."

"You do that. Any chance of picking this lot up?"

Jhanes turned to Frey. "How long ago?"

The boy shrugged. "Coupla days. I wuz out there 'fore that."

The soldier nodded. "Not today, because it sprinkled rain last night, and you could tell. No, unless they hang around to pick up food, they're down the road a ways by now."

"And as long as they don't team up with more of their like."

He shrugged. "Not much more we can do. Once everyone starts watching, if there are any big foxes around, we'll soon hear about it."

After that, Jhanes paid more attention to Frey. Several times he inquired about foxes, but the boy only shook his head. As the sun warmed towards summer, the lad spent more time in the forest and often reported the animals and food plants he saw. Jhanes suspected he had a hideout somewhere close by, because there was a sudden shower one day but the boy came home afterwards completely dry.

He's ready for more training. I'll have to find some time...

5.   THE FUTURE

Like a small, dark tornado, Zoysana whirled the inn and its occupants around her as her plans matured. In spite of his reservations, the new innkeeper found himself drawn deeper and deeper into the Kyabran woman's confidence. So a few quarters later, there he was, saddling the large, if aged, riding horse she had purchased "for the king's business" and slinging his pack up behind the cantle.

"These lords out at the back of beyond ought to be the easy ones, Jhanes. They are the ones who pay the most for everything because of the fees and tariffs the others charge for passage through their lands. Here is the king's letter."

Shaking his head, but only after he was out of her sight, the former soldier rode off on a mission of...diplomacy? *Strange to think of that. I'm used to solving problems with my sword.* Still, he passed the messages he was given, answered the questions that he could, and did his best to reassure people with what they wanted desperately to believe; the king was firmly in power, the kingdom was settling, and prosperity was just around the corner.

As the spring turned toward summer, he spent more of his time on the king's business, passing along information and sometimes orders. His knowledge of Zoysana's plans increased, and he found himself taking a more active part in cajoling the reluctant lords to follow the king's new plans. He managed to accomplish some of his own business along the way, searching for new sources of supply for the inn, and getting word out that the quality of service was improving at Lanil's Rock.

One beautiful early summer's day Jhanes swung his sturdy mount, shaggy now with falling winter hair, down the road towards his village. *Funny to think of it as my village. I haven't had a place to call my own since I was fourteen, and I wouldn't call that small corner of my owner's tent a home. My village.* It was a pleasant feeling.

Well, he'd had enough of romance and adventure. It would be nice to have a place of his own, a hearth to sit by. *'Nice.' Not a word I've had occasion to use, at least not up to this point in my life.* A middle-of-the-road word, 'nice.' Not a word with a lot of interest to it. *I wonder if I'll be satisfied with a 'nice' life. Not that this life is exactly middle-of-the-road, even so...*

He sat straighter on his horse and it picked up speed in response. He had done well, this trip. Not that anyone could tell whether the mountain lords would come through, but most of them could see where the wind was blowing.

He slapped the slack bag slung across the horns of his saddle, and it gave a weak slosh. *Not much of that hill-apple cider left. Too bad.* He was saving the rest so that those back at the inn could have a taste. A couple of barrels would be delivered to the inn a few days hence.

Not long now. He began to recognize landmarks from his short forays over the winter. Soon he could see the Rock, leaning over the trees on the hillside above the village. His eye was drawn to a slight fold of the land ahead. *If I remember right, that small draw comes out at the rear gate of the inn.* It would be a good joke to slip in the back way, stable his horse and wander into the common room as if he'd only been gone a moment.

The idea appealed. He was not lacking in a rough sense of humour in keeping with his soldier's life, but a subtle trick like this was new for him. He grinned at how Sarha would react. How would she greet him, after a half-month away? With a bit of show, he hoped. After all, they had been discussing marriage. Not that she had let him open the subject since Lady Zoysana arrived. Still, the words were there, even if not recently spoken.

He reined his horse off the road, ducking the slash of a freshly greened twig. The narrow trail was a cool respite from the strengthening summer sun, and he felt even more pleased with his decision.

It was easy to approach the inn from this side, and he was sure no one had seen him enter. There was no sound from the inn and no movement save for Patu, absorbing the sun in the courtyard. The armigerent heaved himself upright and strolled over to greet horse and master before returning to his nap. Jhanes slapped him on the ribs, feeling the tightness of the muscles under the curling wire of the outer coat. The animal was getting into shape; Zoysana and Tadeo had not been resting while he was away.

In the stable, the soldier savoured his little joke as he rubbed the horse down and fed him. Still no one around. He strolled down the corridor to the inn, not making much noise but not hiding his presence either. The fire was banked, a pot simmering, but the kitchen was empty. The sunlight lay across the floor in a band, dust dancing in the movement of his passage. He leaned on the counter to look into the common room. Another bar of bright light dimmed the corners, but he could make out a small figure, motionless in the gloom.

It was Zoysana. She sat, her elbows resting on the scarred table top, her arms folded, her eyes straight ahead, seeing nothing. He was about to speak when something about her posture stopped him. She must be aware of his presence, but he knew, somehow, that he should not break her reverie.

A soft step and a light hand on his shoulder turned him. Sarha peered past, then motioned him to follow her. She left her hand there, warm on his arm, as she led him.

The kitchen door was shut behind them, but they were down the passage and almost into the stable when she spoke. "She's like that sometimes."

"What's wrong?"

She leaned against the passage door to close it, then remained there, looking up at him in the dimness.

"Can't make it out. She gets that way. Sits staring into nothin', and nothin' gets through to her. Usually doesn't let anyone see." She shook her head. "There's somethin' sad, there.

41

I know it. She is a powerful person, more powerful than even you could ever hope to be, but I think she paid a price."

He nodded. "You don't get to where she is easily. When will she come out of it?"

"Oh, any time. She's not one to mope around, that's for sure. Come supper, she'll be as chipper as ever."

"And what about you, my Hostess? Are you as chipper as ever?"

The landlady smiled up at him. "More than chipper, now that you're here."

"Oho! Kind words. Did you miss me?"

She stepped back and tilted her head, as close to being coy as a woman like her could ever come. "I won't say I was lonely and I can't say I was bored, but I missed you." She nodded as if satisfied with the truth of the words as she spoke them.

It had been a whole lifetime since he had felt the soft, awkward glow that tied his tongue and heated his face. All he could manage was to hold out his arms.

She chuckled as she reached up to his shoulders, pulling him down towards her. It was an unfamiliar embrace, warm and strangely satisfying, yet not passionate. She was slim and strong and she smelled of the potent lye soap she used to scrub the floors. She would never achieve the plumpness of a rich woman, but he was satisfied with that. Her strength had been earned and it suited her. He held her against him for a long time.

Finally, she chuckled again and leaned back, letting him support her weight, just looking up at him.

He smiled in return. "Is this what it feels like?"

"What?"

"Being married."

Her brow wrinkled. "I suppose so. It feels like it to me."

"Um. Not a bad feeling. Strange, though."

She pulled back. "Well, thank you very much!"

He tightened his grip. "I'm not joking. I always thought the passion came first, and you only felt this way many years after. When you were old and comfortable with each other." He broke off to look closer at her face. "Now I've really insulted you."

Instead of answering, she reached up again and held him, tighter than before.

All this bending over was beginning to hurt his neck. He swung an arm down behind her legs and picked her up. "This is more comfortable."

After the first startled gasp she relaxed against him, her head on his chest. "It is a good feeling, isn't it?"

He could think of no response, so simply enjoyed the feel of her weight in his arms. Then he felt the dampness against his shirt. Looking down, his glance met tear-brimmed eyes. "What's wrong?"

She made no move to wipe the tears away. "Nothin's wrong. Happiness comes too seldom in my life. I guess I don't handle it very well."

"We'll just have to give you some practice."

She shook her head, motioned for him to put her down. "Let me back on my feet so we can discuss this rationally."

He set her down but did not release her. "I think, my dear, that there is a time not to be rational."

She pulled away but did not drop her hold on his arms, looking up into his face firmly. "A romantic notion from a man your age, but I thank you for the thought all the same. This is no time for sentimentality. Both you and I have lived through too many disappointments to be so naïve."

Now she wiped her eyes, tossing her hair back. "All right. So you missed me too. Fair enough. That doesn't mean you're goin' to be happy stuck here as an innkeeper the rest of your life. Don't make any promises."

"Why not? Is there something wrong with being an innkeeper? Wasn't your father an innkeeper?"

She shrugged. "I suppose there's nothin' wrong with it. I just don't see you in the role, somehow."

"If you mean the type of innkeeper who sits behind the bar, drinking half the ale he pours and never stepping outside his inn, you're right. But what about the kind of innkeeper who moves about, buying a bit here, selling a bit there, keeping his inn supplied better than most? What about a man who spends his time taking an active part in the realm?"

She considered this. "I never knew anyone like that."

He tucked an arm around her waist and urged her towards the sunlight. "I've met plenty of innkeepers in my life, and there's all kinds. I can be the kind I choose. So what do you think?"

She pulled away, studying him earnestly. "I only want to make the right choice. Right for both of us. I don't want to spoil anythin'."

"We're in no rush. Just let things roll along as they will." He grinned and swung her around, planting a serious kiss on her lips, feeling a rush of warmth through his body as he held her. "I think we can be quite satisfied with the latest developments."

She chuckled again and leaned against him as they strolled out of the stable. "I suppose you could say that."

They stood that way a while in silence, letting the warmth of the sunlight seep into them. They were finally broken from their reverie by a deep "whuff" from the armigerent behind them. Turning, they found Zoysana leaning in the stable doorway, regarding them with a distinctly forlorn gaze. They broke apart, then stopped, aware they were doing nothing wrong.

The smaller woman smiled, sadly, but at least a smile. "I see we're all glad to have you back. How was the trip?"

"Fine. Just fine. The weather was great, and all the innkeepers are being really friendly these days. The roads are drying out quickly..." He realized this sounded like babbling, and got control of himself. "Would you like a full report?"

She waved a negligent hand, then brought it to rest on the neck of the armigerent, who had pushed close to her. "Not right away. I'm sure you have things to attend to."

"I'm already unpacked, my Lady. Whenever you are ready."

"Oh. Well, if you're sure..." She looked back and forth between the two of them. It was the first time he had ever seen Zoysana look unsure.

The landlady laughed. "Don't worry, my Lady. I'm finished with him. At least for the moment, anyways." She looked up at him, pushed him, not too gently. "Go on with you. I know you're dyin' to talk about it. I got washin' you barged in on."

Zoysana smiled, now. "A welcome interruption, I gather."

Sarha lifted her nose. "I won't deny it. It's that nice to have him back." She looked steadily up at Jhanes. "But I won't let it get in the way of what has to be done."

In spite of her sharp words she reached out, just for a moment, and rested her hand on his chest before stepping smartly around the armigerent and into the inn.

Zoysana's chuckle made the soldier realize he was staring at an empty doorway. "Has anything changed enough to affect our arrangement?"

He tilted his head toward the departing Sarha. "I think you can figure the lay of the land. If an innkeeper is any use to you..."

She took his arm and led him around the front of the inn to the bench in the sunlight. Patu regarded her, then, reassured that she was staying, stretched his bulk at her feet.

"Explain, if you wish. I don't want to pry into your personal life, but if this is going to affect our work...if you don't want to travel, for example..."

He held up his hands defensively. "Certainly not, my Lady. There is no problem there at all. The opposite, in fact. These developments aren't all that new. If things should turn out well for me here, then I need to establish myself in this area, and your work does that. Also, I think I can do better than just make this inn run. As I was telling Sarha a moment ago, I have

45

spent a lot of time in a lot of inns, and some innkeepers are more successful than others. The ones who are more…more…outward looking, I suppose.

"If I was content to sit in this place and wait for whoever comes, then I could make an easy but not prosperous living. If I go out looking for customers, if I bring in food and drink that will attract them, then I can do much better than that. I can also use my travels to do some minor buying and selling. I haven't been talking to all these lords about the advantages of trading without spending some thought on it myself, those long days on the road. I can do very well here, and still get to move around enough to keep me happy."

"And doing these small tasks for me fits in with those plans."

"Yes."

"But…"

"But?"

"But there is something else. I can hear it in every sentence. There is something you aren't saying, something that balances all this fine planning, this perfect fit."

He sighed. "There is." He turned to face her. "I was a soldier. I still am. You don't just stop. But I decided, over the winter, to stop being only a soldier, to try being an innkeeper."

He sat back. "And so far I think it was a good decision. Not a perfect one, but a good one. And that's my problem. Just as I'm getting settled down at innkeeping, along you come with all these other plans and ideas. As long as I can combine them with innkeeping, I'm fine. But I know you, Lady Zoysana. At the moment you're a diplomat and an ambassador. But you're also an officer, and a fighter and I'm pretty sure a spy of some sort…" he glanced over, saw he had caused no offence and continued.

"I don't want to go back to being a soldier. Especially not until I've given this innkeeping a good try. It would be too easy to slip back into the old habits and let this chance slip. And I don't want to do that. I like innkeeping. I like the freedom."

He shifted on the bench. "I haven't ever really been this free before. Being a soldier is a pretty restricted life, and I had even worse before. So I like this and I want to make a good try for it."

"This is freedom?" Her hand indicated the inn and all it contained.

"Aye. Strange, isn't it? I think it's the freedom to choose that I like. I know I have to do a lot of things, but I'm free to choose when and how I do them. It may sound strange to you, but if you came from where I did…"

She didn't take the opportunity to pry further, just nodded.

"Sarha told me I'm finally growing up. I'm making progress, staying here. If I go soldiering again, I'll be going backwards."

Zoysana sat for a moment, and he wondered if she had been listening when she finally spoke. "Yes. You can sometimes move ahead much better by sitting still." She glanced at him. "Wisdom from Sarasha the Lame."

There was no more forthcoming, and as he waited, patient in the comfort of the rough wood bench and the sturdy wall against his back, he began to understand what she meant. "So I would like to stay here and continue to travel whenever you need me to, as long as I can get in some of my own business as well, if it doesn't interfere. If there is an attack, of course I will fight, do my share for the village. But I don't want our agreement to be anything to do with soldiering."

Zoysana's head snapped around. "More than perfect. Innkeeper you are. It is much better that you have your own business to occupy you. Not that we are trying to hide your role as my voice in the area, but it just seems less obvious, somehow."

She looked up at him, smiled and shrugged. "I know it sounds devious, but I can't break away from my training."

"That's fine, my Lady. I always try not to be obvious, though it is often difficult for a man my size. Anything that smacks of subtlety appeals to me. Perhaps I can learn some finesse from you."

"Oh, you'll learn finesse, soldier, if you ride with me for any time at all. The Sivan used to say I was downright sneaky at times."

"You knew the Sivan, then...of course you did, living at the castle."

"I did. More than I wanted, sometimes. How did you know about him?"

"I don't know. I thought everyone knew about him."

She raised an eyebrow. "Everyone? He wouldn't be pleased. What did you know?"

He took a moment. "Now you pin me down, not that much. I know, at least I heard, that he was Barent's spymaster, and that no one could ever unravel the plots he wove. That he was an old man, no one knew how old, with scars all over his face and hands, maybe all over his body for all anyone could tell, and thick grey hair, peppered with black. They made a big thing about the hair, as I recall, said it turned overnight for some reason. I don't know. Most of it sounds like legends."

She laughed. "That's about right. He couldn't hide his presence, but he could shroud it in rumour and myth until no one knew if any of it was true."

He nodded. "There was not one fact about him I would say I knew for sure was fact, and many things I'd heard different, or even directly contradicting other things I heard." He shook his head. "If he did that on purpose, that's pretty clever."

She laughed louder. "If the Sivan heard you call his techniques 'pretty clever,' he'd be incensed at the insult. But you see what I mean, soldier. You're already getting lessons in subtlety."

He laughed and leaned back against the inn again.

"So, would you like to tell me all about your trip?"

He nodded. "Would you like to go somewhere more private?"

She looked around. "Second lesson in subtlety. The best place for this conversation is right out in the open where no one can sneak up on us. If I was really worried, we'd go right out in the middle of the common as if we were taking a stroll, and you could tell me there. That way, unless someone could read lips, we'd be perfectly secure."

"Read lips?"

"Yes. You can train yourself to understand most of what a person is saying by how they move their lips as they talk."

"And people can really do that?"

She nodded. "I can do it some. It's not very reliable, though. Unless you know what they're talking about, it's almost impossible. At least for someone with my level of ability. Some deaf people are much better."

She sat up and shook herself. "This spring sunshine is definitely not letting my mind get moving today. End of Spy Lesson Number Three. Start your report, Innkeeper."

Shaking himself mentally as she had physically, he began his report.

* * *

They celebrated at supper that night, just the four of them. Five, if you counted the small figure of Frey, glued to his usual spot at Zoysana's side. The hill cider was well received, although Jhanes got his share of ribbing about the size of the original waterskin and the small amount left for the others.

"It was a long trip and the sun gets warm, these days," was his feeble defence.

Zoysana's face sobered. "Yes, and the roads are drying. Time for us to move on."

He nodded. Their conversation this afternoon had been leading in that direction. "Where are you headed next? If you want to tell us."

"Oh, yes. I want you to know as much as you can about my plans, so you can find me if necessary." Zoysana picked up her mug. "Let's go into the map room. If our hostess can find some of her own good cider...?"

The innkeeper scooped up his own drink. "I'll bring a jug of the first pressing."

As they trooped in and settled themselves at the newly repaired table, the soldier looked around the room. Yes, Zoysana had been busy. Maps of the area, each with a different set of arcane symbols peppering its surface, hung in various places. A goodly number of the pristine sheets of paper she had brought were now covered with writing or drawing and stacked in piles on whatever surface was available.

"You seem to use a lot of paper, Lady Zoysana. Do you need a storage place, perhaps something with a lot of shelves?"

She looked ruefully at the piles. "I suppose I do. Paper always seems to multiply, once you start using it."

Her face became thoughtful. "Do either of you write?"

The soldier shrugged. "I read fine. Write well enough, but not that neat."

The landlady shook her head. "Simple things, my Lady. Enough to keep my records straight for the taxes, and this inn has always done a very small business."

"Good enough. If you need paper or ink, there's always some here. If we need more, feel free to order it in the king's name." She waved a hand towards one pile. "If you have time, go through those over there. The results of my meetings with the local landholders. It might be useful if you knew what was in them. The rest won't mean a whole lot to you, but look if you please. Anything I don't want you to see will be kept out of sight."

Jhanes met Sarha's eye, pleased at this show of confidence. "I hope we can live up to your needs, my Lady."

Zoysana grinned. "I think you can, and I'm either a shrewd judge of character or a fool. I've been called both, one time or the other."

No more was said on the matter, but the soldier knew he and his hostess had passed whatever tests the dark woman had set for them. He was determined not to be the cause of anyone calling Zoysana a fool.

The lady hauled out her largest map, which covered the table. "Here's this whole region of Petrella and a good slice of Velikii as well. You, soldier...I'm sorry, innkeeper...will be responsible for this section, from the border to the Perston River and as far west as Alderly. Be on your best behaviour near Cdeile. That's Lord Feister's demesne. He's a good man, and we don't want to step on his toes.

"Only two day's ride in any direction." She grinned up at him. "I know you'd like to think I chose this town based on your sterling qualities, but you can see that it also has a certain central nature."

"I still don't see why you didn't go on to Renalk. It's not quite as central, but that's where the keep is. The road there is much more travelled."

"For one, I prefer not to be in any lord's demesne."

"But that's not the only reason?"

Zoysana just looked at him. She wasn't going to answer, so he turned again to the map. He stared at the winding lines representing the roads and paths, blending his soldier's training with his knowledge of the plans she had told him.

"I see. The Renalk road runs through to the centre of the Inner Duchies. That's how most of the trade goes."

"Went. Up until now."

"But now, with more trade coming in from farther north and east..." He turned towards Sarha to see if she got the implications.

Her brow furrowed, and she traced a line on the map. "If this is the road from the northeast border, then we're goin' to get way more traffic through here. Foreign traffic."

"That's right."

Her eyes slid around the room, and the three of them laughed, all knowing where her thoughts were moving.

"You won't have time to rebuild the inn, Hostess. I'm sure my compatriots have stayed in many worse places. Ask Tadeo. He has travelled more than I have."

Tadeo grinned. "At least in conventional fashion."

Jhanes wondered what that meant.

"Anyway, don't worry. If the traffic warrants it, you'll just have to build an addition over against the hayloft and use that extra space above the stable and the tack room."

The soldier grinned at the width of this woman's interests and the quickness of her mind. He glanced upwards, thinking with pleasure of how the expanded inn would look, and how he would deal with the extra stock in the stable. *We might have to extend the kitchen as well...*

Zoysana's voice brought him back to the present. "But that's not what we're here to talk about. Once Tadeo and I are back on the road, you will have less to do, and you can use the time to make your preparations." Her attention returned again to the map.

"We will be setting up another post like this farther east, in this area over here." She pointed. "Probably in Jaspen, as it's the biggest town and the traffic patterns will not change so much there.

"We'll be in Jaspen for the next few quarter months, then we'll swing back over to the south. But I have to get to the castle before the end of the month. There's something stirring in the South, but we don't know what."

"The Inari." A pang went through him. "What kind of stirring?"

She glanced at him. "That's right. The Inari. It's time for the raiding to start."

"Is it a late spring in the South?"

"I think the winter was rough up there. What does that have to do with it?"

"Just wondering. Any special information?"

"Maybe, maybe not. We sent out the Guides as usual, but there have been losses. Other than that, we don't know. I'll be reporting to Gerth..." she smiled at Tadeo, "I mean his Majesty, and by this time Loreline will have more to go on. Then we can make our plans."

Inari. I don't like the sound of that. They should have started raiding already, unless the winter was hard. And if it was a hard winter… not my problem. I'm an innkeeper now. He pulled his attention back to Zoysana.

"Loreline is your contact at the castle, if you need to send any messages. She has her hand on what's going on day to day and will decide who needs to know whatever information you send. I've already written to her about our plans, here. You might drop her a line once in a while, so when I get to the castle she can bring me up to date. Once a quarter should be often enough."

"What about messengers? Do you want to use any special service?"

"I've been thinking about that, Jhanes. I don't want to depend on the king's messengers too much. It wouldn't hurt to have our own man, you know. He can't really be a farmer; he'd be away from his fields, with summer coming on. Do you know anyone around here who could be trusted?"

Jhanes turned his eyes to Sarha. "You know the people around here."

For some reason, she blushed. "What kind of person are you looking for, my Lady?"

Zoysana steepled her fingers. "His occupation doesn't matter a whole lot. He needs to be able to travel, preferably mounted. He needs to be free of other responsibility, as I said. An independent thinker who can keep his eyes open and see what's going on around him. Also, someone who can handle himself in any situation. I'd as soon not have too many of my messages go astray."

"I…I do have someone in mind, my Lady, though I don't think he'd fit in too well at the castle."

"He doesn't have to fit in at the castle. He'll be reporting to Loreline, who started out as a kitchen maid. Second best, we just need someone we can rely on to take messages."

"Oh, he can keep his eyes open, my Lady. And handle himself in most situations, I suppose. If he chooses."

"Who is this person, and what is the mystery?"

The landlady looked around the table, her face reddening again. "My brother, my Lady."

Jhanes leaned forward in interest. She had mentioned her brother once or twice, but had not volunteered more information. Given her reluctance, he had assumed there was some problem, and had felt it best to ask no more.

Glancing around the table to meet their stares, Sarha continued. "He's a trapper, my Lady. Works in the mountains out to the west. He'll be comin' through any time now with his winter furs. Goin' to the city because that's where he gets the top prices. He finds the best bearskins for the Warlanders' capes, so the furriers always buy from him."

Zoysana nodded, then smiled. "Sounds fine. Now what's the problem?"

"Problem? Ach, not really a problem. It's just when you said 'independent thinker.' He is all of that. A bit too independent for many. That's why he's a trapper, I suppose, instead of doin' more usual things. He goes his own path, does my brother, and very little changes him from it."

Zoysana tilted her head slowly back and forth in a sideways motion. "I don't know. Sometimes people can't be objective when it comes to their relatives. I would ask Jhanes, here to check him out, but he's maybe too close to the situation as well." She threw up her hands. "Try him out. Make him see the importance of what we are doing and maybe he'll come in with us. You're his sister; if anyone can figure out what to do, you can."

The landlady returned the smile ruefully. "I suppose it's me can persuade him, if anyone can."

"Sounds like a man after my own heart. I'm sorry to have missed him."

"Perhaps, my Lady."

Zoysana's glance showed that she was not completely happy with her decision, but then she turned to other subjects.

6. FAMILY TIES

A quarter-month later, the new innkeeper stood in the middle of the bare inn yard wondering if he had made the right choice. He looked around at the rain-splattered mud, the blank walls, and the tattered eaves of the thatch.

Dull. That's the only word for it. Zoysana and Tadeo had been gone for several days, the inn was empty and he felt utterly bored. Certainly, there were chores to be done, but that's what they felt like: chores.

With a sigh, he turned towards the stable to finish cleaning the stalls: one of his least favourite jobs. He mused about a time when there would be so much trade he could hire someone for this kind of thing, but his practical side told him to enjoy that luxury when it happened.

It was easy, talking about changed trade routes and new business and profits to be made, with Zoysana full of enthusiasm and Tadeo nodding in his quiet, knowledgeable way. Now, it didn't look the same. The weather had been cool, muddy and ugly, there was little money coming in, and to top it off, it was starting to rain. Again.

At least the stable was dry. He consoled himself with the thought as he forked the manure-soaked straw out the trap door to the dung heap. The job completed, he racked the dung fork and slouched back into the inn. In an uncharacteristic move, he ran himself a mug of ale and slumped down at a table, staring out at the pouring rain.

"See what I mean?"

He started at her voice, so close to his ear. "Don't sneak up on a man!"

"I didn't sneak up on you. You were so lost in your own misery, a horse coulda kicked you, and you wouldn'ta knowed 'til you hit the ground. In fact, it'd likely be better if a horse did kick you."

The sarcasm got through to him: that and the tone of her voice. "What's the matter? Can't a man have a bit of quiet time to himself without someone jumping him?"

She simply looked at him, and he saw the slouch of her shoulders, the sadness in her eyes.

He came instantly to his feet. "What's the matter?"

She dropped her gaze to her work-reddened hands, folded at her waist.

"What's wrong? You look as if your best friend died."

She sighed, refusing to meet his eye. "Maybe he did."

He took her shoulders, forcing her to face him. "What do you mean? Who died?"

She shook her head, but the look did not leave her face. "Nobody died, soldier, exceptin' maybe a silly dream or two."

The bitter edge to her voice brought him up short. "What is it? What's wrong?"

He could see her mouth working, but no words came. He reached out to take her in his arms, but she evaded him. Dry-eyed, she sat on the bench, staring out at the rain just as he had done. Then it came to him.

"It's me, isn't it?"

No answer. But he knew the answer.

"It's me. I've been moping around here like a child that missed the puppet show, haven't I?"

She shrugged.

"Well, what do you expect? It was wonderful having them here, wasn't it? Didn't it make you feel you were important, that you were part of vital events in Petrella?"

She turned to look up at him. "That's right. It did. And now they're gone, I have to go back to my usual life. I can do that. It ain't easy, but I can do it. Can you?"

He stared at her, then dropped his gaze. "I see."

"See what I've been saying all along? This is my life. This is the way it goes for an innkeeper. Days and days when nobody comes, when you don't know if you can pay the bills, when nothin' happens to break the monotony." She stood, facing him squarely.

"Days when there's nothin' to do and nothin' you can do about it. You can't take a sword and beat somebody's head in, 'cause there's nobody there to beat. You just sit and wait and hope things get better. Can you handle that? Because if you can't, then you're in the wrong trade and you'd better start lookin' for another one."

"I see."

"Yes. Now you see." She turned to lean one hand on the table, the curve of her back more eloquent than her words.

For a moment he stood, thinking. Then he walked around to the other side of the table to face her. "So that's what's bothering you? You think I won't stick to it?"

She did not look up. "Don't even try. If you force yourself to stay here, it will only be worse later. You'll feel more and more tied down, and then you'll blame me, and then you'll hate me, and I don't want that."

Then he knew how much he didn't want that to happen either. He moved around the table to stand behind her. "Sarha, don't be like this. I understand what's going on, now that you've shown me. I've made enough decisions in my life to know it doesn't matter whether I stay or go, I'll still have days when I wish I'd done the opposite. That's the way of life. You make a choice and you live with it. Regrets are part of the business. The test of a man is how he deals with it.

"All right. I've been pouting. Acting like a spoiled brat. I promise to stop. I promise to be cheerful. From now on, I will smile more than twice an hour and I will dance a jig of joy at least once every day."

Still she refused to smile, but she turned to him, holding him earnestly by the shoulders. "Don't do it. Don't force yourself. I couldn't bear it."

"I'm not forcing myself. Honestly, I am not forcing myself. Lady take it, isn't a man allowed to have a bit of a down day without it turning into an epic tragedy?" He enfolded her shoulders in his hands, shook her gently in time with his words. "I am not, I repeat, not, going to run out on you. I am not, and I repeat again, not, going to blame you for my own decision, freely made. Your problem is that you are so afraid something will go wrong that you are afraid to take a risk so that something might go right."

"An easy thing for you. Soldiers are used to taking risks."

"That's right. But don't make it sound like an insult. When a soldier takes a risk and it goes wrong, he loses his life. We don't take any risk lightly, and we appreciate it doubly if it goes right. So cheer up."

She sighed. "I don't know, Jhanes. I just don't know."

"That's fine. Neither do I. Nobody does. All we can do is guess. My best guess is that you and I get along very well and we will continue to do so for many years to come, probably the rest of our lives. I don't promise we won't disagree, because I know we will. Anybody as strong-headed as you is not going to put up with anybody as willful as me without a bit of friction. But that won't matter. Not in the long run. What matters is that we respect each other, and treat each other like, well...like..." the soldier threw up his hands.

"I don't know, Sarha. I don't have the words to say it, but I think we'll be just fine."

She chuckled, her mouth twisted in a smile. "Isn't that about the way it goes? All my life, I've waited for a gallant Warlander to come ridin' in and sweep me off my feet and carry me away to his castle where servants will look after my every need.

"Instead, I get a broken-down soldier who hasn't two words to put together, nor two coins neither, who has persuaded himself he wants to live in my castle so I can look after him. I don't know why I put up with it."

"Can I take that as a 'Yes'?"

"A 'Yes' to what question?"

"To a question I'm not going to ask, because it has been there for a long time and now is not the proper time to ask it. Now, if you'll excuse me, I have chores to do."

58

Placing the unfinished mug of ale on the counter, he rolled up his sleeves. "Now, how difficult will it be to raise the roof over the stable high enough to put some rooms up there? Or do we just take it off completely and start fresh?"

"Jhanes, we got no money for that sort of thing!"

He laughed. "You're right. <u>We</u> don't have the money right now, but sooner or later, <u>we</u> will have. Lady Zoysana says so, and if Lady Zoysana says it, then <u>we</u> had better be prepared. Because it will happen."

He started towards the back, then turned around and strode over to Sarha, kissed her squarely on the lips, then turned again and marched out, leaving her shaking her head behind him.

Later in the afternoon, Jhanes was feeling better. He had inspected the roof structure and had a chat with the local carpenter, and he was confident that the new work could be done with little disturbance to the working of the inn, weather permitting, although at a price much higher than he had hoped. Which was as things usually went.

He was sitting in Zoysana's map room, allowing himself the luxury of a piece of drawing paper, when a clamour of barking rose from the front of the inn. They were not the familiar voices of the local dogs, but deeper. Nor were they warning barks, but sounded more like animals in a joyful mood. Intrigued, he made his way through the common room and opened the door.

There stood Sarha, her back pressed against the inn wall by two large grey-and-black hounds. The animals, as tall as her waist, were barking furiously at each other and competing to press as close as possible to her, while she alternately cuffed them and rubbed their ears. Standing in the middle of the road was a roughly-dressed man of medium height, laughing and slapping his leg.

The stranger paused for breath. "Now, Sarha, you say I let them go too much. Show them a little discipline, why don't you?"

The landlady was laughing, too. "Some chance, and them so glad to see me, the only one who ever loves them properly."

"Overfeeds them, you mean. Oh, hello!"

Jhanes stepped forward. "Hello. You must be Sarha's brother, or I've missed something."

"I am," he stepped forward holding out his hand, "and you'd be the soldier I've heard about."

As Jhanes grasped the work-hardened arm he shot a glance at Sarha, who shrugged eloquently. Word got around whether you sent it or not. "That I am. Jhanes is my name, and I'm pleased to meet you."

"If you're treatin' my sister well, I'm pleased myself." He looked around. "At least the inn seems in good shape. As good a sign as any. Never had time to do that type of work."

His sister was at his side, an arm around his waist. "Never had the gumption, you mean. I've never known an idler man. Month after month, nothin' to do but lie around and do nothin'."

He returned her gesture, and the two stood comfortably side by side, akin in their spare frames and strong, even features. "You know well, my sister, that I work hard enough through the winter to earn my time off during the rest of the year."

"A rest, certainly. But six months?"

He shrugged. "The pelts are no good in the summer, even a town lady like yourself knows that."

"And that's your excuse, is it?"

The trapper turned his eyes to Jhanes. "I don't know why I should feel like apologizing for my sister's argumentative side. You've had plenty of opportunity to discover it for yourself. Can you give me a hand with the horses?"

Jhanes grinned. "As much as I do for any customer. Bring them around." He regarded the heavily laden animals. "I don't know that much about the trapping this side of the Barrier Range. Is this a good haul?"

The trapper shrugged. "Middling. It was an easy winter out west, so there were lots of animals, but the fur's not as thick as in a harder year. I'll do all right if the buyers haven't cooked up more than their usual tricks, and if the cold they had up in the South hasn't given the Inari hunters an edge on me."

"The Inari?"

"Aye. Word is they had a cold winter up there. Makes for tough trapping but good, thick pelts."

The men led the horses into the inn yard, the dogs playing around Sarha's legs, butting against her for attention.

"Will the Troubles have upset your markets any?"

"I won't find out till I hit the city. Probably less than last year. We don't hear political news up in the mountains, but rumour has it that everything is settling out real quick. Much quicker than expected, in fact. Trade is supposed to be moving too. Think it's so?"

Jhanes nodded. "King Gerth has made a great effort and has managed to get most of the landowners behind him. Having The Lady on his side makes a difference."

That brought a shout of laughter. "I heard that one, too. Apparently, she appeared beside him at his Presentation, and now she's wandering the land, seeing that things are done right. And they call us backwoods hicks gullible."

Sarha's eyes glinted with humour. "I don't know, Ferlen. What would you say if you met a little, dark woman in a robe with colours that seemed to swirl constantly, with an armigerent," she paused to pat a rugged head, "twice the size of Rositea, here?"

"I'd say I drank too much cranberry wine. Wait a minute. Are you saying you've seen this apparition?"

The only answer was a shrug.

"Come on, now. You're joking with me." He turned to Jhanes. "Tell me she's joking. She doesn't really believe all that about The Lady."

It was Jhanes' turn to shrug. "The woman Sarha is talking about stayed here last month."

61

The trapper looked from one to the other for a moment. "You're havin' fun with me."

"That we are, and loving it, but she did stay here."

"The Kyabran woman and her armigerent."

"That's right, Brother. Her name's Lady Zoysana, and she's half Kyabran and half Petrellan. Her armigerent is named Patu. He's just as big as everyone says, and he's a real sweetheart. Lets Frey snuggle up to him and eats from your hand as dainty as you please."

The trapper dropped his hands. "Well, doesn't that show you can't trust rumours. Just when you think they're the worst, you find out they're true. So, what's she doing in this neck of the woods?"

"Exactly what everyone says. Travellin' around as the king's agent, makin' sure the rebuild of the realm is goin' well and that people are bein' treated fairly. She moves faster than a squad of soldiers and has more effect. Jhanes has made several trips on her behalf." She took his arm proudly. "He's her agent in this area."

"It's more like the two of us. I do the travelling and Sarha keeps track of things from here. Zoysana is using the old lumber room to keep her maps and such, and that's where she works when she comes by this way."

The trapper absorbed this, shaking his head. "And to think I came down here worried to see whether you'd made it all right through the winter, and whether this soldier you took up with was taking advantage of you."

Still shaking his head, he turned to the horse he was unpacking, and they worked for a while in silence. Once they had stabled the animals, they entered the inn.

"Well, this calls for a mug of ale, Sister, and a toast to the future. Sure sounds like there's going to be one."

"There's always going to be a future, Brother, whether we like it or not." She headed over to the tap, pushing the two men towards the window where the sun shone warm through the open shutters. They each swung a leg over a stool and sat, elbows on the table, sizing each other up.

"So you must be serious about Sarha."

"That I am."

"This new occupation suits you, does it?"

Jhanes rocked a hand back and forth. "Like any trade, it's got good days and bad days. Difference is, in this job a bad day might end up with me losing my temper at a horse."

The trapper chuckled. "Your old job, a bad day might end up with you losing a whole lot more than that."

"Exactly. So I think I'll be happy here. She's the problem, not me."

"Of course she would be. She wouldn't be Sarha if she wasn't. She afraid you won't stick?"

Jhanes sat back, unsure how to deal with this frankness.

"Of course she is. That's my Sarha: always looking for the worst in things, afraid to love something in case it goes away."

"Easy for you to talk. You who's got nobody, and never did." It sounded like an easy jest, but Jhanes could hear tension in her voice.

"I've got my dogs: sweetest companions a man could have, and never answer me back. Besides, I've just not met the right woman. Find me the right one and I'd be married like that," he snapped his fingers under her nose.

She batted his hand away and sniffed disdainfully. "And what kind of woman would want to marry a trapper, not see him half the year and then have him under her feet for the other half?"

"Well, there you are. If I thought I was going to be a trapper forever, I'd just have to give up hope."

Her head swung towards him. "What do you mean?"

He laughed, raising his mug. "Here we are, not half an hour after I meet your new man, and we're talking deep philosophy and solving all of life's problems. Probably borin' him half out of the room. Here's to the future. May we all be here for years to enjoy it."

Jhanes lifted his mug. "I can drink to that with a will."

"And I."

Their mugs clashed together top and bottom, and they drank.

"Good ale."

"We'll have better soon."

"Yes? How so?"

"Things are changin', Brother, if you haven't noticed up in the mountains. New ideas, new trade, new routes..."

"And one of them's comin' from the coast of the Inland Sea, right by our door."

"You always was quick to catch on. Right by our door. Jhanes was just out this afternoon, measurin' the inn for new rooms."

"Well, if that doesn't set your head to spinning. And how does a ordinary man get in on all this wealth?"

Jhanes had a thought. "You don't own part of this inn, do you?"

The brother regarded him a moment. "And what difference if I did?" An edge had crept into his voice.

The soldier made his laugh easy. "No difference at all. I just like to know where things stand. In fact, and I'm only thinking of this now so I haven't discussed it with Sarha, but will you have a whole lot of ready cash when you sell your furs?"

Sarha snorted. "Ready to be someone else's, and quick."

"Now, Sister, you do me wrong. Have I ever come to you for help?"

"Not to me."

"So there you are." Ferlen's voice took on a cultured accent. "I may expend a certain amount of my yearly funds on a well-deserved spate of relaxation, but I have never been improvident enough to dissipate it all, tempting as that may be."

64

The soldier interjected. "But you will have some cash. Adding to the inn will cost money, which we don't have as yet. But we will have. The custom is coming. We know it. You could buy in and have a regular share in the profits. A good safeguard against the ups and downs of the fur market."

"And what if the custom doesn't come? What if this great change in trade never happens?"

Sarha laughed. "Then you have part-ownership in an inn with plenty of free room for you when you visit." She became serious. "But it will happen. Lady Zoysana says so, and I believe her."

He matched her mood change, leaning forward intently. "You put a lot of faith in this Zoysana. That's not like you, Sister. Will she come through for you?"

"You have to meet her, Brother. You'll see."

"And do I get a chance to meet this paragon?"

Sarha shot a glance at Jhanes, and he nodded. "You could get more than a chance to meet her. You could work for her."

"Me? Work for the king's agent, who may or may not be a reincarnation of a goddess I'm not sure exists?" The trapper chortled. "Now that's a tale for around the campfire when the nights grow long."

"I'm serious, Brother."

"Never thought you weren't. I've rarely seen you so serious, Sister. This soldier of yours is either very good or very bad for you. I suppose we'll find out sooner or later. Now what's this about working for the king's agent? How can you be offering me such a job," he swung to face the soldier, "or are you more than you seem?"

Jhanes shrugged and held up his hands with exaggerated innocence. "I had nothing to do with this one. Zoysana was asking who could take messages to the castle for us, and Sarha suggested that, at least this once, you could do it as easy as not."

"Take messages to the castle. That's all? Just deliver mail. To who?"

65

"There's a woman there named Loreline. I don't know what she does..." Sarha wavered a hand, "but she's the one we make our contacts with. Seems she used to work in the kitchens, but Zoysana trusts her. All you do is take her the messages and bring back whatever she gives you. There's no real danger involved."

"I'm not worried about danger, Sarha. I just want to know what I'm getting into. And it's just the once?"

"That'll be up to you. Zoysana likes people who have jobs that let them move about freely without causin' suspicion. You could take messages back and forth from here to the castle and elsewhere, if you liked. You can move quick and know how to handle yourself, needs be. An independent thinker, she said, and I knew you were right for it."

The trapper sat back, looking from one to the other, light dawning on his face. "This is a spy system."

Jhanes held out a hand, palm down, rocking it back and forth. "Not really. More of an information system, if you get the difference."

"I'm not sure I do. Explain."

"We aren't spies. We are official agents of the king, here in the Free Counties. Everyone knows that. We want everyone to know that. We want people to bring us information, so the king finds out what's going on.

"On the other hand, we don't want to advertise when we are sending that information on to the castle. It would be better if no one knew who our messengers were, not every time. It's hard to explain it the way Zoysana does, but it just works better."

"She's right, I'll give her that. If someone knew what was important to the king, they might use that knowledge to make trouble or to feed faulty information. I can see that. So you want me to take a package for you, slip it up to the castle as quietly as I can, then bring back the answers. And you want me to do this on a regular basis?"

"More likely an irregular basis."

Their new ally nodded. "That's good planning, too. I really would like to meet this Zoysana of yours, now. She sounds like a good mind."

Jhanes regarded the man in front of him. *Speaking of good minds, his country accent is almost gone and his vocabulary gets bigger as he gets more interested.* "So you'll take the job?"

The man shook his head. "Me, a messenger for the king. Now that's a good laugh. Too bad I won't be able to tell anyone. Don't worry; I'm not stupid. Things aren't that settled. I could tell from the people I met on the road down here. Your Zoysana hirin' a soldier, even an old beat-up, worn-down one like yourself, for an agent, instead of a regular innkeeper. Yes, it will be some time before the duty stops being dangerous, and I'm one who knows how to walk a quiet trail when there's a bear around. Certain, I'll take your work, Sarha, and with pleasure."

He stopped, took a long pull of his mug and grinned. "Gods take it, it must have been a slow winter, me doin' a thing like this at the end of it when I should be thinkin' about my well-deserved rest."

He was about to raise his mug when he hesitated. "You know, you've really spoiled my fun. Now I won't be able to go on a tear when I hit the city. Too much responsibility."

The soldier raised his mug as well. "Well, now, I don't think it would be good to draw attention to yourself by changing your habits. Maybe just a little tear would be necessary."

"A man after my own heart. And I'll be back with whatever I have left to invest in our little business here." They all lifted their mugs again and downed them to the bottom.

"It's a changing world, Sarha, and our best move is to change with it."

While they held their discussions, little Frey wasted no time in getting acquainted with Ferlen's dogs. The moment he saw them he plunged between them, making small animal sounds but none of the passive wriggling he had shown with Zoysana. To him, they were simply other pack members to be dominated

67

so he could retain his status. At first they tolerated him, but soon he was ordering them around, wrestling and playing with them at will.

Sarha was worried the first time his skinny arm disappeared between the keen fangs, but her brother calmed her. "He's doing just fine. They treated him like a puppy at first, and he took advantage of that, then made the switch to human leader before they knew what was going on. Very impressive for his age."

"He spends a lot of time with dogs. Watches them, plays with them, bosses them. Maybe he thought he was a dog for a while. He gets along better with them than with people. He disappears when we get customers."

Jhanes nodded. "He even had Patu following him around."

"Do you think he has that Trainer talent for armigerents Zoysana was tellin' us about?"

"She says he might have, but it's hard to tell at this age. His strange upbringing makes it even more difficult."

The brother was intrigued. "You'd only had him a few days when I was through in the fall. Find out anything new, since?"

Sarha shook her head. "Jhanes says he might have been at the battle on the road, where Zoysana put Barent's regiments to flight."

Jhanes responded to the brother's raised eyebrows. "They found child-sized tracks in the woods and a stash of food stolen from the supply wagons. He was picked up near there a few months later. So he probably saw the whole thing. He sure knew Zoysana. You should have seen the to-do he put on when he first met her. Just like a dog, all whining and wiggling and eager to please."

"Strange little guy. Seems friendly enough, though."

"He's easier with the strangers, now. But he's got a long way to go."

"He's young, yet."

The brother stayed a few days, resting his horses, sorting and repacking his loads and chatting with his sister. They were close, despite how little they saw of each other. Jhanes soon got used to Ferlen's direct and challenging style of conversation. He was glad he got along so well with the man. Theirs might be a long relationship.

Soon Ferlen was eager to travel again, and one dry morning he packed his string of mountain ponies with their loads of furs and headed south, a small, tightly wrapped packet of papers tucked inside his coat.

Life settled down again, but either the soldier had thrown his funk aside, or there was too much to do to worry about it. He began his plans for extending the inn, but one warm evening Sarha led him out behind the inn. "You see that patch of field, there?"

"I do. Even an old soldier knows a field when he sees one. For all it's a scraggly, weedy one like that. "

She shrugged a shoulder. "I got a line on some late-harvest oat seed, and the ground's still soft, what with the wet spring."

"And if we have more customers, we could provide oats for their horses at a better price if we grow it ourselves."

"And in case you didn't notice, we now have a horse."

He grinned at her. "You mean, if we had a plow, we could plow?"

"It's a small field, but the choice is plow or shovel. Which would you prefer?"

He looked thoughtful. "Given the choice, I suppose I would prefer the horse to do the larger part of the work. Do you know how to drive a plow?"

"No, but you can learn."

"If we had a plow."

"We can find a plow."

He regarded her. "You've had a plow hidden behind your back the whole time, haven't you?"

She tried to look innocent. "Well, you know plows don't get used a whole lot. Most of the time they just sit around waitin' for the right season. And it happens that Mattos, the third farm up the hill south of town, is long finished with his plowin'. So his plow is sittin' around for the next few months, twiddlin' its fingers, so to speak."

"It doesn't take much of a soldier to know when he's been outmaneuvered. When do I start?"

"Mattos is bringin' the plow down tomorrow afternoon if he comes into the village. If not, some time the next day."

"How convenient." A sudden thought struck him. "This Mattos, now, he's not a usual customer of ours."

"No, he lives too far out to come regular."

"So what are we doing for him? Or is there some history that a polite person like myself wouldn't be asking into too closely?"

She grinned. "As it happens, Mattos and I were friends once when we were about five years old. Then he grew up into a boy and wasn't interested in my dolls anymore, and next thing I knew he was married to someone, and there you have it. As far as the plow is concerned, he's happy to lend it. He's that kind of man. He won't keep track, but some day, we'll make sure we help him out."

"And that's what makes the wheels go around in a little town like this."

"And in a lot of the rest of the world, I suspect."

"It's that way in the mercenaries, too. Creates a great company spirit, good morale. You know, I never thought of it, but a village is a lot like a company of soldiers."

"It is?"

"Yes. A small group of people united in a common cause: in this case, wresting a living out of the land. People dependent on each other, rubbing shoulders a little too close at times, not always happy with each other but pulling together when needed. Any good officer knows how to foster that spirit, keep it going, even when things get tough. It's the same in a village, I'll wager."

Again she nodded. "I suppose you're right," she smiled up at him, "and now that you're going to be a village leader, you can practise some of that officer stuff you wouldn't go for when you were a mercenary."

"Me, a village leader? How could I be? I've just got here. They won't accept any leadership I give them. I'm almost a stranger. Why would they?"

"True, they will! You are a smart man with experience in the world. Experience they're gonna need when the world starts movin' through their little town. Because you're the king's agent, and they will soon figure that your word carries weight beyond the village. Because you're someday goin' to be one of the richest men in town, and that carries a whole lot more weight, as you are well aware. And also because you are a leader. You can't help it, and they can't help but notice it. Just you wait."

He shrugged in his usual manner. "I never thought of myself as a leader. If you're right, I guess we'll find out sooner or later. For the moment, let's deal with the moment's problems. Who is going to teach me how to plow?"

She laughed. "We'll figure it out. I seen plowing done lots. I can give you some pointers."

"Oh, that'll be a great picture, that will. Half the village ought to turn out to see its future leader being towed around on his nose by a horse while his woman shouts orders at him."

She laughed, too, but soon sobered. "Is that what you think I am? Your woman?"

"I'm sure everyone else does. No one could believe the two of us have shared a roof all these months without sharing a lot more."

"I wasn't askin' about everyone else."

"No need to ask about me. You know how I feel. You're the one that's the problem."

"I am, ain't I? And I know it's foolish. In fact, havin' my brother here made me realize how foolish it is. You know, I'm always after him to get himself married, and he tells me the right woman ain't come along, and I tell him he's just scared. Now I look at myself, and I'm doin' the same thing, except the right man has come along and I'm too scared to reach out and take him."

He nodded. "That's pretty foolish, all right."

The colour rose to her cheeks. "I'm allowed to say that, you ain't."

"Why not? I've got a stake in this, too."

"Well, it's not great politics. You don't woo a woman by insultin' her."

"I never said I was any good at politics. I just think we're right together. I'm not saying I'm madly in love or anything like that. I'm not going around writing poems in the moonlight. I'm telling you the truth. Sorry, that's just me."

She shook her head, slowly. "I never wanted all that nonsense. I just want someone to be with, someone I respect, and who respects me. Someone so we can plan our life together, have some simple hopes and dreams to try for."

"I do."

"What?"

He grinned, now. "If anything sounded like wedding vows, that was it. I agree perfectly. If you agree, it's all settled."

"Just like that?"

"Why not?"

"With no ceremony, no witnesses, nothin'...?"

"Oh, we ought to have a ceremony and a big party, just for fun and for everybody else. But for you and me? We don't need it. We both know, and that's all it takes."

She looked into his eyes, then her gaze travelled over his face. Then she nodded and rose abruptly. "Fine. Let's go."

"Let's go?"

She took his hand, pulled gently. "Upstairs, of course."

"Right now?"

"Why not? You just said we didn't need any of that other stuff. So we've made up our minds, why wait?"

A big, silly grin stretched his mouth. "Why wait? A woman after my own heart."

As she led him up the stairs, he reached out and put his hand on her waist, just at the curve of her hip. She stopped and looked back, her eyes level with his.

"I've been wanting to do that for a long time."

She smiled. "You are a romantic, aren't you?" She laid a palm against his cheek, stroked it slowly downwards. "I've been wantin' to do that for a long time, too. So there!" Then she broke away and ran up the stairs, pulling him along. "Let's see what else we been wantin' to do!"

7. NIGHT AND RAIN

The soldier sat upright in bed, listening. If someone had asked, he couldn't have said why, but he listened. *There. Hoofbeats: slow, tired hooves, slogging through the mud.* He lay back, but quietly so as not to miss anything. He had a lot of sympathy for a rider out in that downpour at this time of night.

He pulled the warm, rough wool up under his chin. Sarha, feeling a draft, murmured something and moved closer to him. Sympathy he had, but he could still hope they would ride right on by.

No such luck. At the muffled pounding from below, he swung his feet to the floor and dressed. Not hurrying, he admitted to himself.

When he reached the common room, Sarha was already there, laying more wood on the fire and lighting another lamp. She smiled and reached up to smooth his tousled hair. "Times like this, it's good to have a man in the house."

He nodded and yawned. "Certain. Someone to go out there in the rain and put the horses away while you stay here in the warmth."

"That's not what I meant."

"I know."

Another tattoo shook the door. "I better open that."

"The doorjamb will thank you."

He lifted the latch, standing sideways, one hand near the staff propped close by. There was no sudden movement, so he swung the door open. A short man in bedraggled livery stood there, water streaming from his hair and running down his face.

"Come in, sir, please come in."

"Thank you, my good man." The traveller entered, wiping his face and shaking the drops from his hand, setting a large brass carriage lamp on the floor.

"Not a good night to be out without a hat."

Two bright eyes glared up at him, their pupils black in the dim room. "The subject of my hat is not one I would prefer to bring up. Especially," and here the man made a brief bow to Sarha, "in the presence of one of the fairer sex."

"Can I take care of your horse, sir?"

"No, the unfortunate animal has more work to do tonight, as does her master. I must return to my party as soon as I have obtained assistance."

"Oh. What kind of help do you need?"

The man shrugged. "Whatever it takes to pull a carriage out of a river and repair what is broken, I suppose."

"River?" Jhanes looked to Sarha for confirmation. "There's no river near here."

The visitor waved a dismissive hand. "Oh, I imagine it wasn't so much like a river this morning before the rain started. Believe me, when the wheel crashed through that pitiful excuse for a bridge and I was looking straight down into the water, it looked a whole lot like a river to me."

Sarha stepped forward, handing him a towel. "North about a mile? A small bridge, a bit of a drop to the stream?"

"You may call it a 'bit of a drop,' my Hostess, but I assure you it seemed much more when I was hanging over it. I must admit to a certain apprehension around that time. It was important to get my weight to the high side, you see, and I was in too much of a hurry, I suppose. Hence my hatless state." He sighed as if he carried the burdens of kingdoms on his ample shoulders, and dabbed at the water running down his nose.

"So you have a broken carriage down at the bridge. Would you like to bring your party up here for the night, and we can straighten things out in the morning?"

The man considered a moment, then buried his face in the towel. When he surfaced he smiled, rolling his eyes towards the ceiling in bliss. "Ah, that does feel better. Thank you so much for your thoughtfulness, my Hostess, but I don't believe I can accept your hospitality. Not that we would eschew the comforts of your inn, please believe me. No, no, it is just that I could not ask my patron to come out in the rain. The carriage, while not exactly level, is well-constructed and continues warm and dry."

He patted his ear with the towel, careful not to disturb his hair. "No, if we cannot free the carriage, I think my Lady will wish to stay there."

Jhanes shook his head. "It must be a very important trip, to make you take such a risk."

"Risk? What risk do you mean? Are there bandits? We are well-protected, I assure you."

"No bandits at this time on a rainy night. It's just that there are three more bridges and two steep hills between here and the next town. I don't know how you managed to get this far in the darkness."

"Oh, we are well-equipped for darkness, I assure you." He gestured toward the expensive-looking item on the floor. "Our lamps are quite sufficient." Then he frowned. "At least they seemed so, until the wheel broke through and everything went topsy-turvy."

Jhanes frowned. "I was over that bridge two days ago. I didn't notice any weakness."

The man grimaced. "Well, there is a weakness now, believe me, and the offside rear wheel of our carriage is stuck in it."

"I suppose I had better have a look." He reached for his cloak. "Did you say it was also broken?"

The man shrugged. "The driver says the axle might be cracked. I do not concern myself with mechanical details." He paused, thoughtful. "A situation I may have cause to regret."

"We don't have a wheelwright in the village. Shall I bring the smith? I doubt if he will be able to mend anything decently at this time of night."

76

The man looked up at Jhanes. "You are a person of a decisive nature, I can tell. Perhaps you would be so good as to come yourself and give me your view of the situation."

Jhanes nodded, then shot a meaningful glance at Sarha. There was no possible way for these travellers to move on tonight, and she would prepare for them while he was gone.

On a thought, he threw pulling harness instead of a saddle on his horse. *It's less than a half-candle's journey, and his back will be warm.* Without comment, the little man swung up on his own animal, opened the carriage lamp and led the way back through the gloom. When they left the cleared area near the town and entered the forest, Jhanes shook his head that anyone should be travelling at this time of night. Outside the glare of the lamp, the horse and man ahead were a mere blob of darker murk and the road was only a lighter smear on the obscurity of the ground.

As they neared the stream, a bright source of light appeared up ahead. Approaching, Jhanes spotted several lights close together, and it became even more difficult to see his surroundings because of their glare. He felt uncomfortable moving forward in near-blindness, but there was no reason for suspicion, so he let his horse step ahead and kept his ears open.

"Who goes?" A man's voice: young, firm. *No fear in that one.*

"I have returned with assistance, my Lady."

"Oh, well done, Gavess. I knew I could count on you." The new voice was low, but female.

Young. Used to being obeyed. They rode forward into the glare of the lights, and Jhanes stopped his horse in amazement. There in the middle of the bridge, canted crazily to one side, its lanterns pointing skyward, was the biggest carriage he had seen in years. Two carriage horses, finely matched but not large, slumped in the traces, heads low. *No wonder.*

He turned to his companion. "How far have you come today?"

"Only from Cdeile. The roads are so terrible, we couldn't make any time at all."

77

He nodded. The roads around here weren't wonderful, nor had they been kept up recently, and he pitied the two horses, hauling this gaudy wagon in such weather.

By this time they were approaching the carriage, although he still couldn't see much past the lamps.

"What help have you brought us, Gavess?"

"I have brought the local innkeeper, my Lady."

"The innkeeper? One man?"

"He has agreed to assess our situation in view of his knowledge of local facilities, my Lady."

"I see. Well, carry on, then."

"Thank you, my Lady. All right, lads, out of there and let's see what we can do."

Three shapes huddled under the tilted side of the carriage. They resolved into two slim young men and one older, all dressed in the same livery, all in a similar damp state.

Jhanes addressed the older man. "What's the problem? Besides the obvious."

"Axle's broke."

"Would pulling her out damage it further?"

The driver shrugged. "Horses'r too tired."

"My horse is fresh and he's a puller. Should we try?"

"Whatever you say."

Jhanes scanned the sodden group and received no denial or encouragement. *Someone better take charge.* "May I use the light?"

Gavess handed him the gleaming brass driving lamp.

He hefted it, noting the solid weight. *Expensive.* He walked around to the higher side of the carriage, knelt and peered under.

It was difficult to see, but it did look as if the axle had cracked when the wheel dropped through the bridge deck, the whole weight of the carriage having come down directly on it. However, the iron rods on either side seemed to be intact and would probably hold it together. The problem was how deeply the wheel was imbedded in the decking.

He stood. "Do you have an axe?"

The driver reached into the boot at the back and produced a large hatchet.

Testing its weight, Jhanes moved to the edge of the forest, holding the lamp high. Selecting a smaller tree, he dropped and limbed it and carried it back to the bridge.

"We'll use this to pry the carriage up. Then, with my horse helping, we might get it to move."

Again, no one offered any comment. It took some manipulation and fiddling, during which Jhanes discovered that the driver was the only man in the group who was any use. Finally, they were satisfied. "All right, now. We're ready to try it. You three swing on the pry bar," he indicated his original guide and the two footmen, "and we'll drive the horses."

He paused a moment. "But we should lighten the carriage, first."

"Out of the question."

"Pardon me?"

The butler straightened his back, trying to look taller. "You really cannot expect my Lady to allow her luggage out in this rain."

The soldier shrugged. "You're the ones lifting it. Go ahead."

The three swung all their weight on the log, but nothing moved.

"Wait, don't stop." Jhanes laid a hand on the end of the pole, testing. "Not a chance."

"You didn't even try."

"I can tell by the feel. There is no way that carriage will move with all the weight in it, even if I pull as well. We have to lighten the load."

"Gavess," the curtain of the carriage parted slightly.

"Yes, my Lady?"

"The man speaks logic, Gavess. Take out the luggage. The trunks will keep it dry."

The servants obeyed, and soon a huge pile of trunks and bags stood at the end of the bridge.

"Are you finished, Gavess?"

"Yes, my Lady."

"Are we ready to proceed?"

"All ready, my Lady."

There was movement inside the carriage, and the door swung open. "Come on, Lateda. You first." A hesitant figure appeared in the doorway, staring up at the rain. "Go on, dear. A bit of rain won't hurt you." The figure, that of a young woman, stepped down, the butler rushing to assist her.

A larger person appeared, to the concern of the butler. "Wait! You can't come out here!"

"You can't come out here, my Lady," the woman's voice carried a touch of asperity.

"I'm sorry, my Lady."

"Apology accepted, Gavess. And of course I'm coming out there. You heard the man. Lighten the carriage. I think I can handle a bit of rain, and I certainly qualify as weight." The heavily cloaked figure stepped down to the bridge deck, slipping and leaning against the poor butler, who had some difficulty getting her back on balance.

"Thank you, Gavess. The planks are very slippery, aren't they?"

"Yes, my Lady. Take care, please."

"I will take care, Gavess. Now the carriage is as light as we can make it. Please proceed."

This time all five men heaved on the lever, which bent considerably. There was a loud creaking, and the carriage rose. The horses strained mightily, but nothing moved farther.

Jhanes kept up the effort for a moment, then gave the command to halt. The horses slacked their traces and the servants let off the pressure.

He knelt down and peered under the carriage again. It had not lifted quite far enough.

"We need a higher fulcrum."

He did not turn to see who leaned over him. "I know. But if we use a higher fulcrum, we can't get the lever under."

"So raise it up and stick something under to keep it up."

"That's what I was thinking..." Then he realized the identity of the figure at his side and rose quickly. "I'm sorry, my Lady. I didn't realize it was you. I...was busy thinking...didn't expect you to know what a fulcrum was..."

A deep chuckle came from inside the hood of the heavy cloak, now glistening with rain. "Well, I was surprised that you understood a geometrical term, so we're even. You're the innkeeper, are you?"

"Yes, my Lady."

"You seem to be very resourceful, for an innkeeper."

"We come in all types, my Lady."

She might have nodded, but in the hood it was hard to tell. "So let's not stand around talking all night. Lift it again, and we'll block it up."

"The problem, my Lady, is that it requires all our weight to hold it up, even the coachman. There's no one left to put the block under."

She considered. "I will help hold the lever down, and you can put the block in."

"My Lady!"

She spun on the butler. "Gavess! I am not some dainty fairy princess. In fact, I have been out in the rain for several minutes, now, and I don't feel like I'm dissolving at all." She turned to Jhanes. "So, innkeeper. I'm no lightweight. Will it work?"

"We can try, my Lady. You stand right here. When we get the carriage up, you take my place on the very end of the pole, like this. If anything goes wrong, just step back...not to the side, but straight back...and nothing can hurt you. Understand?"

"Certainly. Let's get moving, gentlemen. You too, Arderton."

Under the watchful eye of their mistress, the servants heaved with a will, and the carriage rose, staying up even when she and the soldier changed places. He jammed a log under the axle and returned to his position on the lever to guide the weight down. After that, it was a simple matter to slide a larger log under the lever and lift the carriage again. This time the three horses, with a great deal of straining and slipping in the mud, were able to haul the conveyance onto level ground.

"Bravo, men, bravo. Now let's get loaded up again and move on."

"You do still have a broken axle."

"Oh. Will it stand up?"

"Probably as far as the village. You'd be better to load the luggage in the front and keep the weight on the other side as much as possible."

"But where will the ladies ride?"

"Gavess, you worry too much. Lateda can double with the innkeeper. I'm sure his horse will hold two for that short distance. I will ride up front with Arderton. Now load that luggage and let's get moving. This little adventure is beginning to pall."

There was a snap to her voice that sent the men scrambling, and soon the small procession was inching its way along the road, the soldier and his passenger riding behind with a lamp to keep an eye on the axle. It was difficult to tell in her heavy cloak, but the maid, though slight, had little of the round softness he would have expected of a young lady. In fact, her arms tightened uncomfortably around him once when the horse slipped.

By the time they reached the village word had spread, and there was enough novelty in the situation to bring several of the locals out in the rain. Jhanes took advantage of their curiosity to get the carriage unloaded, and soon the pile of trunks was sending rivulets along the floor of the common room.

Once the horses were stabled, rubbed down and fed, the soldier returned to the inn to find the lady ensconced in front of the fire, fussed over by the butler and the silent Lateda. Sarha, a bemused look on her face, stood to one side as if not sure where she fit in.

The lady looked up as he entered. She was much younger than her deep voice and decisive ways had led him to believe. "My, but you are as big as I expected, even without your cloak!" A brief glance at the disapproving butler. "I'm sorry if I speak in a familiar manner, but I consider myself an expert in being large, and thus take a certain latitude in these matters."

She smiled. While she would never be beautiful, there was a pleasant, open quality to her face that would last far longer than beauty.

"Well, Innkeeper, it is agreeable to be so cosy. We had no idea there would be such a snug spot along this road. Have you space to put us up for a night or so?" Her glance at the butler was a definite warning this time. "Yes, Gavess, we are staying here." She looked around the room. "I know it's rather plain, but I'm sure it will be fine."

The butler did a very good job of seeming unconvinced while being too polite to say so.

With an exasperated sigh, the lady tossed him the towel she had been using to dry her hair. "Smell that, Gavess."

Startled, he caught the towel and stood holding it uncertainly. Under the power of her gaze, he lifted it gingerly to his nose.

"Well? Is it not clean? In fact, does it not have a certain delicate scent, more than just clean?" She turned to Sarha. "What do you use to get that fragrance, Hostess? It is very pleasant."

Sarha bobbed a curtsey. "A herb, my Lady, which I pick in the forest. A touch of it in the soap gives the cloth a pleasant scent, don't it?"

"Exactly. You see, Gavess? A lady who takes care of such little details will have a clean room. Did you notice the cat?" She indicated the large grey cat lounging by the fire.

Again, he looked puzzled.

"A cat eats mice, Gavess. So, no vermin. The roof is dry; the fire is warm. Is this not much better than sleeping in a slanted carriage in the rain?" She turned back to Sarha. "So, Hostess. Have you room?"

Sarha and Jhanes exchanged glances. "A moment, please, my Lady." He walked over to speak more privately. "We could give the lower room to her and her maid; the butler and the other three can use two more, if someone doesn't mind sleeping on the floor."

"Do you think Lady Zoysana will mind?"

"No, she told us to rent that room if we had to." He turned to the lady. "We do have a room that might suit you. It is large, but has no bed at the moment."

"Oh, I have all the bedding I need, right there." She waved a negligent hand at the trunks.

"My Lady, you cannot sleep on the floor!"

The lady shot a long-suffering look at her butler. "Gavess, what do you suggest we do? Turn the landlady out of her bed, which probably wouldn't fit me anyway? I have, thanks to your careful packing, all I need for such an emergency as this, and I will be quite comfortable, I'm sure." She turned to Jhanes. "May we see the room?"

Hiding a smile, the soldier indicated the door.

"Oh! This is very nicely done up."

"Yes, an agent of the king uses it when she is in this area, so we fixed it up for her."

The lady looked at the innkeeper thoughtfully. "An agent of the king? Her?"

He ignored her interest. "Yes, my Lady. A matter of convenience. She keeps some of her things here, and I take care of them and whatever business comes up while she is away."

"Aha! So you are an agent of the king as well. I thought you were more than an ordinary innkeeper."

"Actually, my Lady, I'm very new to the innkeeping job. Sarha, your hostess, is the owner."

A small smile played across the lady's lips, but she made no comment.

"Sarha, we'll have to move Lady Zoysana's maps to the storage room."

He was turning away when the lady's hand on his arm stopped him.

"Lady Zoysana? Zoe? She's your agent?"

"Yes, my Lady. Do you know her?"

"Not personally. But she's my cousin's friend. He talks about her in all his letters. Not that he writes me a lot of letters, but I have heard stories about her." She grinned. "Quite exaggerated, I suspect."

He shook his head. "I don't know, my Lady. She's quite a person when you meet her. She doesn't talk much about herself, but from what I've heard and from what she doesn't say, you know, sometimes you can tell."

"Is there any chance I will see her here?"

He shook his head. "It's hard to know. She is on her way back; I expect her in the next two quarters. That's as precise as I can give you. It depends on how long you intend to stay here. If you are heading for Tsalk you might meet her on the road, because she's coming in from Arlyn Castle."

The lady sent her butler one of those looks Jhanes was beginning to recognize. "I think we may be here for a while. Perhaps we can set the men to arranging things while we talk about that."

It took a while to put everything in motion, but finally Jhanes and the lady were seated at the table closest to the fire: he with a mug of ale, she with a drink of wine in the daintiest glass Sarha could find, a glass that fitted rather well into the lady's large hand.

"Now, Innkeeper, it's down to business."

"Yes, my Lady."

"First off, introductions. I dislike referring to people by titles. It's demeaning somehow. I am Talia of Lesser Trenet. I am travelling to Petrella to visit my cousin, Varlinden, who is squire to King Gerth. Perhaps you have heard of him?"

"I have, my Lady. He played a role in the end of the Troubles last year, and Lady Zoe has spoken of him several times. He is a great favourite of hers and quite a character, I gather."

She smiled. "I am not surprised to hear that opinion, although it is pleasant to find he may be as good a friend to her as his letters indicated."

"I'm quite sure of that, my Lady." He nodded, thinking. "As I recall, once she spoke of something that needed to be done, deciding that he was the one most likely to succeed. In fact, she led me to believe that the tasks she sets out for him are some of the most interesting and perhaps even devious ones."

Lady Talia laughed out loud. "It sounds like our Varlinden hasn't changed much. Perhaps he has found an outlet for his talents.

"But to continue our discussion. As I said, I would prefer not to refer to you as 'Innkeeper'."

"Of course, my Lady. I am Jhanes, most recently of King Barent's Fifth Irregulars."

"A soldier! That explains it. An officer, no doubt?"

"No, my Lady, merely a soldier. A mercenary."

"I find that hard to believe, Jhanes. Not a man of your obvious talents."

He shrugged. "I never stayed with any unit long enough, and didn't like to play the politics. There's room for a good man in the ranks, you know."

"True enough. But you're not a soldier any more, are you?"

"Not at the moment. I had a small injury and settled here to let it heal. And here I am."

Again that small smile. "I see that. Well, it's my gain, I'm sure. I don't know where I would be right now if you hadn't come along and pulled me out of there. Probably dozing in my carriage. At a slant. And Gavess worries about me sleeping on a nice, level floor."

"You know, my Lady, there is a bed in my room that you could have. It would fit you as easily as it fits me." He risked a reference to her size, since she had commented on it several times herself.

"That's good of you, but don't bother for tonight. Perhaps we can do some rearranging tomorrow. And speaking of tomorrow; what do you suggest we do about my transportation problems?"

"Well, my Lady..." he paused, wondering how to say it.

"Be frank, Jhanes. Speak to me as you would to an officer you trusted."

He returned her smile. "Right, my Lady. Military precision. Objective: to get Lady Talia to Arlyn Castle. Obstacles? A carriage that is too big. With a broken axle. Horses that are too small. And too tired. Roads that are in poor shape. Weather that will make them worse."

She nodded. "That sums it up, soldier. What about security?"

"Another thought. Are your men armed? Are they experienced?"

"Yes, more than you might think. My two footmen are excellent swordsmen, and the coachman is an archer."

"And the rest? Including yourself, my Lady?"

"I am an indifferent swordswoman. Frankly, I'm too clumsy. But I'm strong and I can whale away if necessary. Lateda is...let's just say she hasn't always been a lady's maid. Gavess, well, his strength is organizing things. He's the one who equipped us."

"If you don't mind my saying so, he did not account for conditions out here in the South. If you were going into some areas of this kingdom, the roads are so narrow you'd find yourselves cutting down trees on either side just to get the wide hubs of your carriage through."

"But between here and the castle?"

"Width of road is not a problem. But you will discover, especially with the rain, that the hills are much too difficult for your two horses to pull that huge boat you have out there."

"The solution?"

"A new carriage or a larger team."

"Is either available here?"

"Not at the moment. We can get horses and perhaps a carriage from Tsalk in a day or two. Fixing the axle may be more difficult: a day or two, perhaps more."

"So we are stuck here, if you don't mind my saying it, for at least two days, perhaps more."

"I think so, my Lady. We'll do our best to make you comfortable."

"I'm sure you will. Don't worry about me. I took on this journey because I wanted adventure. If I can't stand a small amount of discomfort, what am I doing out here anyway?"

"A good attitude, my Lady." He grinned. "If you'd like a little more adventure, we could arrange to have you sleep in the carriage."

She shuddered. "No thank you, Jhanes. I'll take your nice warm floor quite happily. In fact," she drained the rest of her wine, "I think I will take advantage of that bed. It has been a tiring day. Gavess."

He was instantly at her elbow.

"Are we ready to retire?"

"All is prepared, my Lady, although..."

Her raised hand cut him off. "I know, Gavess. It's not quite up to the standard we enjoy at home. However, we are not in the Inner Duchies any more, and I'm sure you have done admirably, as you always do."

She smiled at him, and the man swelled visibly at the praise.

"I will retire, Gavess. Please arrange with Jhanes for the rest of the party."

"Already taken care of, my Lady."

She winked at her host. "You see? The man is invaluable. If only we can get him used to life on the frontier."

"Ah, my Lady, I hesitate to be forward, but might I make a suggestion?"

She sighed. "Politics ill becomes you, Jhanes. Speak frankly, please."

"We out here 'on the frontier' don't consider ourselves to be quite so benighted as you indicate. Such jests are sometimes not taken as entirely funny by those who are more sensitive to their place in the world. So when you reach the castle…"

Her eyes rested on him a moment, thinking. "You know, Innkeeper…or is it Soldier…I think you are going to be a very useful agent to King Gerth, and I am going to tell him so myself."

It was a completely unexpected comment, and for once he was speechless.

She laughed, that deep chuckle that was so infectious. "There. I've finally managed to get through that super-competent facade of yours. Now I really feel I've accomplished something and I can go to bed happy."

With an unconscious motion, she held out her hand, and Gavess was immediately there to help her rise. Not that she needed it. She had just graciously established her command of the entire situation.

Jhanes bowed, then returned her grin as she swept, somehow regally, towards her room.

Soon they had all disappeared. Only Sarha remained, bustling about in the kitchen, wiping down an already-clean table with a fresh washrag. He leaned over the counter to watch her.

"It's clean enough, Sarha. Her ladyship was very impressed. I'm sure she never expected to find a place this neat in a village so small."

She flashed a smile at him, then returned to her polishing.

"What's wrong, Sarha?"

"Nothin'." She paused a moment, then looked up at his silence. "No, really. It's nothin'."

"But...?" He came around behind the bar and put his hands on her shoulders.

She started to lean back against him, then stopped. "But..." she turned to face him and dropped her voice. "Can't you see? Can't you tell that I'm out of my depth here? No, I suppose you can't. You deal so easy with these people. It shows me how much you are one of them, in spite of what you say. You talk with the right grammar. You got no trouble givin' your opinions. Me, I'm tongue-tied the moment that lady looks at me. She's a princess, Jhanes. Don't you realize that? Or next thing to it. I'm just an innkeeper's daughter. I never spoke to anyone like that before."

He chuckled. "And you did fine. Do you think she cares if you say 'ain't' once in a while? Does she look like the kind of person to make fun of you? You're more likely to have trouble with the footmen or the butler."

"Hah!" Her back straightened. "Those footmen are just boys. And polite ones, at that. The butler?" She glanced around to be sure no one was listening. "He's a bit up on himself, I suppose, but he's a good man. You shoulda seen how he got those people organized. Certain, he's fussy, but they like workin' for him all the same."

The soldier nodded. "That's something to be said in his favour, no doubt. So you're not really having any problems."

She considered, then smiled slowly. "I suppose I'm not." Then she sobered, moved even closer to him. "The maid has a knife on her leg."

"The maid?"

"Yes, the girl who doesn't talk. She has a knife strapped just below her knee. Handle down. I saw it when she was hangin' the curtains and she stepped down off the chair."

"Handle down, you say. A quick-draw then. All Lady Talia would say about her was that she wasn't always a lady's maid." He mused a moment. "You know, our Lady Talia might be better protected than might first be expected."

"Good for her."

"Anyway, I don't think you need to worry about getting along with these people. You're doing just fine and you'll get used to it. The only problem is that we'll have a lot of work for the next little while. You're going to want Elise in, for a start. Do you want me to go over in the morning and tell her?"

Elise, the smith's daughter, helped out on the odd occasion when there were enough customers that the inn was crowded.

"No need. Everyone in the village knows by now. She'll be here at daybreak, ready to work."

"Right. And I think we'd better be ready at daybreak ourselves. Off to bed with you."

She leaned against him. "Is this what it will be like?"

"Maybe. A bit scary at first, but you'll get used to it. Wait till word gets around that Lady Talia of Lesser Trenet stayed here. We'll be putting those extra rooms on sooner than I thought."

"And you really still want to stay?"

"Sarha, don't you see how this helps? How can I get bored with these things happening?" He put his arms around her, and she held against him for a long, comfortable time.

Finally, she gave him a push. "Go do your rounds. I'll bank the fires in here."

He ruffled her hair. "Yes, Mistress. Whatever you say."

8. REPAIRS

Jhanes was up with the first glimmer of dawn, determined to give their guests the best service possible. It was no longer raining but the ground was soaked, and he didn't look forward to crawling under the carriage. Daylight showed it to be every bit as large and ornate as he remembered: even more so, as it squatted aslant in the grey light, its gilt trim and shining black lacquer obscured by muddy hand-prints and splatters.

The horses were no more encouraging. The effects of the day's work should have been countered by a night's good rest, but both animals still stood with their heads down, uninterested in the awakening stable. One took an indifferent bite at the hay in the manger; that was all.

He returned to the inn to help Sarha and Elise with the fires and to bring whatever supplies needed carrying from the roothouse. It was funny to hear Sarha coaching the girl on how to behave and calming her fears in words similar to his own last night. Elise was a strong-minded youngster, used to the hard work and hard language around her father's forge, and he doubted she would stay in awe for long. *Which means I'd better emphasize Sarha's instructions.*

"Just don't let those handsome young footmen use their smiles to get around you, lass. They'll be here for a few days and they'll be bored. After that they'll be gone, without another thought for what they leave here. Do you get the picture?"

Her face was blank with incomprehension, and he turned to Sarha. "Talk to her. You can speak more plainly."

Then the girl's face lit up and she giggled. "Oh, that! I know what you mean, now. I just didn't expect it to come from someone like you, Master Jhanes. Thank you for being concerned. Don't worry; I can look after myself when the boys are around."

"I hope so."

Sarha turned the girl by the shoulder and pushed her towards the common room. "There's plenty of girls who thought that and ended up in trouble, and don't you forget it. Now, let's get those tables spread. Best linen on the one by the window. The men can eat at the bigger table next the door. They'll expect cloth too, I suppose, and they'll know how to use a fork."

When Elise was off on an errand, Sarha returned to Jhanes. "That was kind of you, to think of her."

He shrugged. "I've been in this situation enough times to know what happens when young blades get bored. Is everything ready for breakfast?"

"Ready as I can be until I find out what she wants."

He sniffed appreciatively. "I imagine she'll be happy enough with the fresh bread and whatever you have to go with it."

"She might at that. I sent Elise over to the Widow for some of last year's bilberry jam. If they don't like that, they don't know what eatin' is."

"Yes, Dame Yeager's jam is good, all right. Do you think we could get some more of it?"

"Not much left, this time of year. If it's a good season for berries we might do a deal with her: help her out with the picking in return for some of the jam. There's no chance of getting the recipe, so don't even ask."

"Fair enough. Let her keep her secret as long as we can serve the jam. It's that kind of little thing that makes people remember your inn."

"I suppose it is."

"Oh, yes." He gazed at the shabby common room. "Let's have no illusions. This is just one of twenty little inns where somebody might choose to stay, and they all blend together in your memory, except the ones that are special in some way, either good or bad. And it doesn't take much to tip the scales either way, believe me. Then a place starts getting a reputation as word gets around. If it's a good one, it makes a lot of difference."

"If the Widow's jam doesn't do it, your carriage-mending skills might."

"Don't speak too early. I haven't fixed it yet. It's a heavy beast."

"My father used to have a block and tackle. In the loft over the stable."

"I found it, but the rope was all chewed by rats. That cat's not doing her job. She's too fat, and it's not from eating rats." The cat strolled over and pushed against his leg to show she held no hard feelings. He rubbed her ears as he went on. "The blocks are good, though. We might be able to use them with some smaller rope."

Having settled the technical details as well as they could, the couple lounged in the cosiness of the kitchen, drinking tea and eating warm bread. Elise returned with the jam, and they found it necessary to test a bite to see if it had stayed good over the winter. Then Frey stumbled in, his hair sticking up all over, wandered over to Sarha, climbed up and fell asleep again in her lap. The boy was too large for the woman to hold, and Jhanes signalled that he would take him, but she smiled and shook her head.

Soon, the sound of activity drifted down from upstairs, and the butler appeared, looking as tidy as if he had just stepped out of a manor house. "Good morning, friends. Is that bread I smell?"

Sarha smiled. "It is, sir. Would you like a loaf and some good bilberry jam to go with it? There's back bacon and strong cheese as well, if you wish."

The butler surveyed the tray she placed in front of him, shaking his head. "Much though I am tempted, my Hostess, I will refrain from your sweets. A piece of cheese must garnish my bread this morning." He nibbled the loaf, then carved himself a generous slice of cheese. "Alas, I cannot allow my palate to overcome good sense."

She smiled in sympathy and placed a steaming mug of tea beside his plate. "A good, hot cup of tea never bothered anyone's waistline, Sir."

"Ah, that it didn't. Good bread, my Hostess, and good cheese. Is it local?"

"Oh, yes, from the farm just up on the hill outside the village. There'd be fresh curds, too, if anyone in your party wishes. You only have to say the word."

He leaned back. "I can only speak for myself, my Hostess, but I think this will be sufficient," he leaned toward her and dropped his voice, "although you will not be surprised to find that Lady Talia will take a very decent breakfast, if you catch my drift."

She smiled her thanks. "We have plenty, Sir, and will do what we can to make your lady as comfortable as she deserves. What a night! The poor dear must be exhausted."

"The more so because she insisted on getting out and walking up every hill." This could have been a complaint, but a glow of pride showed his true feelings.

"Good for her! It is a common act of kindness to the horses in areas where the hills are so steep as they are here."

Soon the footmen wandered in, followed by the driver, all taking their places at the table. They managed to demolish a large portion of the food, although Sarha did not offer them any of the special jam. When they had finished, they relaxed with mugs of tea as well, chatting about their misadventures of the past few days.

All was relaxed and pleasant until the side door opened, and a different air swept the room. No one moved but everyone was alert. The moment Lady Talia entered they were all on their feet: not rushing, but as if they had just decided at that moment to rise. Jhanes got the impression that, rather than feeling as if their workday was starting, they were truly glad to see her.

She, too, looked as if she had spent hours preparing herself. She was dressed plainly, at least for a noble lady, in dark colours and few frills: a good choice for one of her stature. Her hair was netted at the nape of her neck, and the only jewelry showing was a signet ring on her left hand, ruby earrings, and a fine gold chain. Her skirt did not reach the floor, and as she strode forward, the toe of a laced walking boot peeked out with each step.

With a general smile and a personal greeting to each, she accepted the butler's arm and was seated at her table. Lateda served her mistress, standing nearby until she had finished.

When all was cleared away except for a fresh cup of tea, Lady Talia looked around the room. "Well, everyone who is anyone is here. Shall we discuss business?"

They all faced her, and she nodded. "First, our transport. Arderton, what is your opinion?"

The coachman did not hesitate. "The horses need a rest, my Lady. As we discovered, the coach is too heavy for them when the road is this difficult."

Her hand hit the table with a smack that made her people jump. "I was advised to take larger horses. But Father's head coachman was adamant. 'Those horses have been pulling your father's coach for years,' he said. 'His heir will not be seen without the traditional matching blacks,' he said. And so I disregarded the prudent advice of someone I should have trusted." She shook her head. "And for what? Vanity." She turned to Arderton. "The axle?"

"I will check the condition of the axle immediately, my Lady, but I am sure it will need repairs, perhaps extensive ones."

She nodded. "As I thought. Jhanes?"

"I agree, my Lady. We'll have to take it apart, first. From there on, it is a matter of how much repair is needed. We might send for a piece of wood or a new axle, or do a temporary fix hoping it would last until you got somewhere a more permanent repair could be made."

She nodded again. "And we are moving forward into terrain where a weak axle would be a serious liability."

"True, my Lady."

"Arderton?"

"I agree, my Lady."

"And even with a repaired coach, the horses we have will not pull it?"

"They are still tired this morning, my Lady."

"They will get their rest. Jhanes, can we get other horses? Do we have enough harness to work a team of four?"

"If you just want horses, good pullers but not fast, you could get a pair here. If you want real carriage horses, we have to bring them from Tsalk." He didn't wait for her question. "Two days."

"Well, that makes the choice easy. Everything points to us staying at least two days. At that time, we will have the information to make a better decision. Any other comments?"

There were none. *We certainly know who's in charge, don't we*? "Do you need anything, my Lady?"

"Thank you, Jhanes, but we are," she shot a smile at the butler, "exceptionally well-equipped. Lateda and I will wait until the afternoon before we venture out."

Again, she merely gestured with her hand and Gavess was there, aiding her to rise and escorting her to the door of her room. The men gathered together and went about their business, whatever that was. The Arderton and Jhanes headed for the carriage.

"I have some old sacking we can lie on. Let's take a look at this thing."

They did not have to crawl far under the coach to see the problem. "It looks split lengthwise but not broken across." Jhanes stuck his dagger into the wood. "That's hard stuff: hickory or ash."

Arderton looked gloomy. "It has to come out of there."

"How are you fixed for tools?"

"Oh, we have everything we need to take it apart." The coachman dropped a panel at the side of the coach, showing a pocket filled with bundles wrapped in greased cloth. "It's just going to be a bugger lifting her up to get at it."

"I have a block and tackle. We could use that on the big tree limb, and my horse should be able to lift it. Then we block it up and drop the whole wheel-and-axle assembly out from under. What do you think?"

The coachman's face brightened. "You make it sound easy, Innkeeper. Let's get at it."

After an hour's worth of assembling and testing equipment, Jhanes's gelding was able to raise the carriage, and Arderton rushed to place the chunks of wood they had left ready. Then Jhanes backed the horse and lowered the coach to its new resting level. The wheels were left sitting loose under the rear of the coach, and they rolled them out by hand.

"By gar, Innkeeper, I never dreamed it would be so easy!"

"I always figure; if you're in a hurry and you have the muscle, you can do the job fast. If you don't have the muscle, you have to use your brain. Takes longer, but it still does the job and it's more fun."

The coachman shook his head. "I never figured on this sort of work as fun. It always seems to happen when you're in a rush, in the rain, and most likely in the dark, like it was last night."

"Let's look at that axle before we congratulate ourselves too much."

They gathered the tools again and began tearing the metal parts off the axle. As they worked, Laingot, the local carpenter joined them, digging a thumbnail into the wood. "It's pretty tough stuff, that there axle. Ash, I'd say."

"So, how do we fix it?"

"We could put a few pins in it, glue it back together, but the wood's wet. Once it dries, the pegs'r' gonna fall out and we're back where we started."

"Make a new one?"

"Ain't a piece of ash that big in the village."

"So we ship the axle to Tsalk and get a new one built."

"I'd just put the pins in it. Get you to Tsalk, anyways. You want to be real sure, you bind it with wet rawhide and let it dry. That stuff holds like iron."

"But then we can't travel if it's wet."

The man grinned wryly. "But then the wood will swell and the pins will stay in."

The coachman grinned at this logic. "Let's get the pins put in, then."

Jhanes was looking at the axle and thinking. "Yes, you put the pins in. I've got an idea."

This abrupt departure left the coachman staring after him. Then Jhanes heard the carpenter say something about "a man who always has an idea." *I'm already developing a reputation among the village folk.*

By supper time, the coachman was pleased to make a good report. "We'll have the axle done by tomorrow, my Lady. The carpenter's making a good job of putting pins in, and Jhanes and the smith are rigging up a clamp to hold it all together."

The lady turned to the soldier with a smile, but he held up a cautioning hand. "It's a rather expensive repair for a temporary one, using that much iron. You'll need a new axle sooner or later, and then our repair will just be an expensive piece of scrap metal."

Her smile only grew wider. "If it gets us to the castle, I'm sure they can take care of it there. Now, what about horses?"

Jhanes waited but all eyes remained on him, so he spoke. "I think you should send someone to Tsalk."

She nodded. "That'll be Arderton, and he'll have to carry money. Ranill, you'd better go too. Are the horses up to the trip?"

The coachman wavered a hand from side to side. "That's the reason we haven't gone yet, my Lady. If we wait till tomorrow, they'll be that much more rested."

"That sounds reasonable, Coachman. Gavess, can you arrange all that?"

"Certainly, my Lady."

"Good. So we're here for another two days at least." This thought did not seem to dismay her.

"My Lady, if you don't mind a comment..."

"Certainly, Jhanes. Your advice has served us well so far."

"Well, it's about the weight of the carriage. With a weak axle, the difficult road and four horses to pull you through, there's even more chance of a breakdown. So I suggest you lighten your load. You can leave things here and I can send them on the next empty freight wagon that comes by."

"A sensible thought. Gavess, we have our work cut out for us tomorrow. We must make some difficult decisions."

Gavess looked glum at this, but he nodded. "I must bow to the inevitable, my Lady. Perhaps the innkeeper would be so good as to look over our equipment and use his experience to tell us what would be least essential."

"Certain, Gavess. I'd be glad to help."

"Jhanes, you have been glad to help from the beginning. I hope you plan to overcharge us abominably for all this." Lady Talia cast a mischievous glance at Gavess.

* * *

"Ruffians. That's all they are, ruffians, and I cannot see how you can put up with them, my Lady."

"Oh, Gavess, don't be like that. We've been through this all before, and they are exactly what we need. And keep your voice down. What if they heard you?"

"What if they did hear me?"

"Gavess, they may not be polished courtiers, but they are people with feelings that can be hurt. Especially Lateda."

Jhanes moved back from the common room doorway. At first, he thought they were talking about himself and Sarha. He hadn't been sure whether to make them aware of his presence or not. Now it was easier. He took a few loud steps, then opened the door with a bang. "Good morning, my Lady, Master Gavess. Sorry not to be here to greet you, but I had arrangements to make. How was breakfast?"

The lady grinned at Gavess before answering. "Quite sufficient, Jhanes. In fact, Gavess has been pleasantly surprised at the quality, if not the variety of the fare. You eat heartily out here in the country."

"We do well enough, my Lady. I know there's more variety in the towns, but with the early greens coming up, we do fine."

"Yes, I was just discussing with Gavess the advantages of a rustic upbringing."

"Oh?" The soldier didn't know where this was leading, so he allowed only polite interest to show on his face. Gavess did not respond. He was standing, his hands working at his hat, which one of the village lads had brought in that morning.

"Yes. Please sit down. I would like your advice."

He took the indicated spot on the bench opposite her. "My advice, my Lady?"

"Yes, Jhanes. On a military matter."

"Of course, my Lady. What sort of military problem do you have?"

"Our safety. When we left Trenet, we felt that we were well prepared and had taken the best advice we could find in all respects: equipment, escort, routes. Now that we have travelled so far from home, we discover that our choice of conveyance was sadly mistaken, and I am wondering if we have made other mistakes as well. How safe is this road? Do you think I have a strong enough force to continue?"

"Well, yes and no, my Lady."

"Explain."

"You understand that 'enough force' is relative, my Lady. If you have something valuable to transport, you can take a large escort and risk all the attention. Or you can pick a smaller escort, hoping to slip through and not be noticed by anyone big

101

enough to overpower you, hoping to be strong enough to scare off anyone who does notice you."

She leaned forward, and he could see intense interest in her face. "Are there any other options?"

"Well, if you think like Lady Zoysana, you would slip through with a smaller escort that would attract very little attention, but was much more..." he paused and the light dawned, " much more powerful than it seemed."

She straightened, shooting a triumphant glance at the butler. "See how quickly a military mind catches on?"

Jhanes nodded. "How valuable is your cargo, my Lady?"

"Oh, not very valuable, Jhanes. The usual clothes, jewels, you know."

"And your escort of four men should be enough to discourage the petty thieves who might want to steal those. But..."

"Please go on."

"But your escort is more than it seems. Your two footmen are not exactly tender young servants from the castle, are they? Likewise your driver. Oh, he handles the team well enough, but not with the level of skill a driver of his age should command. I suspect he has spent his life at other tasks. Even your maid, as you hinted yourself. This leads me to suspect that you are carrying something more valuable. If you don't mind my asking, my Lady, who exactly are you?"

She roared with laughter, slapping the table and throwing her head back. "Innkeeper, or soldier, or whatever you are, I might ask you the same question." She sobered, regarding him. "That was a good analysis, and I hope not many around will be able to make the same connections."

"No one has the same information I had."

"Good. Because your analysis was precise. I am higher placed than my escort would indicate. In fact, I chose to travel this way precisely because I didn't want to attract attention. We found good advice from someone we trusted, and I managed to persuade Father that it would be smarter to travel incognito than to brazen it through with the number of troops he wanted me to bring. I said King Gerth might not want an outsider wandering his realm with that many men so soon after a war. So I put together as strong a unit as I could. The footmen are both mercenaries, young but experienced. The coachman, too.

"Lateda was an orphan with an unbelievably terrible childhood. My mother rescued her from a certain future of crime and prostitution, but not before the girl had learned to fight, steal and live off the land in almost any situation. Because of this, she is fanatically loyal to my mother and would protect me with her life."

"Hence the knife."

The lady grinned. "Which one?"

He nodded. "Point taken. So you want my advice on whether you should proceed?"

"Exactly. The balance between attention and strength that worked in the Inner Duchies may not work here. What do you suggest?"

"It's simple, my Lady. Get rid of the carriage."

"That's all?"

"Everything you have done strikes the right note except for that carriage, which, if you'll pardon my saying, shouts to everyone for miles that here is someone too rich and stupid to know what she is doing. It's an open invitation to any of the outlaw bands around."

"And there are outlaw bands?"

"They certainly exist, attracted here by the war and looking for victims. These are the ones Gerth's patrols are after. They are one of Lady Zoysana's main targets. There has been no information of any dangerous groups in this area, but I suspect that, with the pressure put on them by the patrols, they will be on the move."

"So what do you suggest I do?"

"Higher strength and lower status. No one would think twice about a merchant's wife in a small carriage with a couple of mounted escorts as well as her footmen. If you want to continue with the big carriage from here you might, but at Tsalk leave it for a smaller one, and get Lord Foreston to loan you a couple of good horsemen. These bandits are mostly on foot, giving riders an advantage.

"In any case, I'd be happy to escort you to Tsalk any time you decide you want to leave."

"Thank you, Jhanes. I would appreciate that. It is dawning on me how unprepared I was for the conditions out here. Only good luck got me this far, didn't it?"

"I wouldn't say that, but a small amount of bad luck could put you in a much worse position."

She let loose another peal of unladylike laughter. "You have such a delicate way of putting things. I'll remember that one!"

Then she became serious. "When do you think we should leave?"

He considered. "We can plan that as it comes: when the carriage is ready, the road seems dry enough and the weather isn't threatening. Let's see how the next two days play out."

"Good enough for me, Jhanes. Thank you."

He bowed. "It's only what any innkeeper would be pleased to do, my Lady."

She bowed her head formally in return, but there was a glint in her eye. "Of course, my Host. I had expected nothing less."

9. Attack

Jhanes sauntered his horse along the road, not really enjoying the sunshine because it caused too many shadows below the heavily leafed trees to either side, and his chainmail shirt was getting hot. At least he had plenty of time. The coachman was taking it easy on the horses, working the two teams together, knowing there were stiff climbs and a long day to endure before they reached Tsalk.

Jhanes had time, now, to wonder what he was doing. *I decide to quit soldiering, and yet here I am, three months later, back in armour on guard duty. How did this happen?* He had to be honest. *It happened because I wanted it to. I'm good at this. These people need me.*

But Sarha and Frey need me, too. Alive. But if I'm too cautious, I won't be much use in a fight, will I? He sighed. *I just don't see how this can work.*

He shook himself awake. *But here I am. Nobody twisted my arm. I'd better make the best of it. Do my duty.* He turned his attention to scouting.

Jhanes had ridden farther ahead at this point because the woods closed in for an ideal ambush point. He scanned the forest without seeming to, only turning his head for natural reasons, such as a bird's song or a squirrel's chatter. *In fact, that squirrel seems too upset.* Keeping his movements casual, the soldier concentrated on his senses. The birds were very quiet. He reined in, muttering a foul word to himself. He couldn't see them, but every instinct told him they were there.

With an exaggerated sigh he turned to look at the carriage, far back down the road. *This is going to take some acting.* Throwing up his arms, he shouted a curse.

"Come on! What's keeping you?"

He was too far to be heard, but they would register his movements. Waving his arms in large, meaningless gestures, he shouted again.

"Get a move on, dammit. We've got a long day...Oh, what the hell...!"

Playing up his exasperation, he slapped his horse into a canter back down the road, wanting to smile to himself but half expecting an arrow in his back. Sure enough, Arderton had stopped the carriage, not knowing what his signals meant. Those in ambush would not know what to do: wait or attack. If his acting had been good enough, they would wait for him to hurry their quarry along into their arms.

He kept his horse in check until he got right up to the carriage. Then he spoke in low voice.

"Ambush. Where can you turn around?"

"This four-horse rig will tangle easily." The driver nodded to a spot just ahead. "I could almost make a circle up there. What does the ground look like?"

"Pretty solid. I'll ride ahead again. If it's dry, I'll keep on going. If I stop, it means you can't use that spot. How long would it take to turn around in the road?"

"I'd have to back up at least twice, and these new horses aren't used to me or each other."

"Let's hope you don't have to do that." He turned his horse forward again, shouting and waving his arms as if he were angry. Then he moved ahead, again scanning the ground and the nearby woods. The turf on either side of the road looked dry, so he continued past the level spot, glancing back at the carriage now and again.

When the carriage reached the appointed spot, the driver seemed to have trouble with the horses. Jhanes stopped with an exaggerated gesture of rage. *This little play won't fool anyone much longer, but I'll buy as much time as I can.* He sat his horse in the middle of the road, looking back in disgust, hoping he was still out of bowshot of the waiting outlaws. One of the horses was rearing, and the coach and team jackknifed. Then it backed completely off the road and canted at an angle in a cloud of dust. He winced for the shock to the damaged axle.

Then the horses straightened out, and the coach surged forward in a smooth curve, hitting the road again headed north. Jhanes glanced over his shoulder to see horsemen charging out of the brush behind him. An arrow drifted past him to drop, spent, in the ditch at his side. Clapping his heels to his horse, he dashed after the careening carriage.

He glanced back. Only five riders. *Good. The rest of the band must be on foot.* Kicking his horse again, he took the reins in one hand and pulled his bow out of its case behind his right knee. Stringing a bow on a galloping horse was a trick he hadn't practised for a few years, but he could manage.

By the time he caught up with the carriage and its straining team, he had an arrow nocked. The coachman was on the roof, his own bow ready. One of the footmen was driving, and the other knelt beside the coachman. Lady Talia leaned out the window towards him.

"How many of them?"

"Only five horses. I don't think they'll dare close with us. Unless they have something waiting back along the road and we've driven into a trap, we should get back to the village."

"If the axle holds."

"If a horse doesn't go lame."

"If the Lady wills it."

There was no time to respond to this reference. He nodded and rode on, his eyes moving: forward, sideways, behind. The horsemen were now catching up as the carriage horses tired. He shouted to the men on the roof.

"Let them get as close as you dare. Stay down behind the luggage till the last moment. Tell me before you start shooting, and I'll hit them at the same time."

Jhanes wished he had a pile of luggage to hide behind. Another arrow zipped past, with more force but less accuracy than the first. He pulled ahead, scanning the road for boulders and potholes, and the surrounding forest for new signs of attack. Rising in the stirrups and looking back, he still counted five riders, only two with bows. For once, the size of the coach was an advantage, protecting the carriage horses from the arrows. He leaned back and pulled his helmet from its ties, careful not to drop it from the bounding horse. There was no time for the chinstrap, and blessing his forethought in fitting it tightly to his head for times like this, he prepared his bow again.

At a shout from the coachman, he reined his horse around. The coach thundered past and a flight of arrows sped back towards the approaching riders. Only when his horse was at a dead stop did the soldier shoot, aiming at a bowman charging directly at him. The bandit loosed at the same time, but his horse was moving at a full gallop and there was no contest. The man went backward out of his saddle, an arrow in his chest.

Then the four other horsemen were upon him. It was too late to turn, exposing his flank. Bow and reins in his left hand, he drew his sword and charged. He swung to the right so he only had one bandit to deal with. He drove his horse's shoulder at the smaller pony, smashing it to the ground, and beheaded its rider with a single sweep of his heavy blade. Then he spun his horse around and came up behind the other riders just as they began to turn. He thrust between two of them and slashed right and left as he burst through. They tried to turn again, but too late. He was gone down the road after the fleeing carriage before they could untangle themselves.

He glanced back. Only two horses after him, and no arrows. No, the third rider was coming now, but slowly. Too bad. *I really have to practice my mounted work. This big clumsy sword is no weapon to use on horseback, anyway.*

He kicked his mount again as it seemed to be slowing, favouring the near front leg. *Probably bruised when it hit the other horse. I hope that's all.* The riders behind had slowed more, waiting for their companions on foot. He pushed ahead, but those in the carriage had seen this as well and eased up. The chase was over for the moment, anyway.

There were smiles on every face as he rode up. Lady Talia leaned out of her window again. "I saw that, soldier. You took on five of them!"

"I had the element of surprise, my Lady." He slowed to a trot, glancing back to see that the bandits had stopped.

"You certainly surprised me. Why did you go back?"

"I had to get the bowmen, my Lady. Five swordsmen would find this carriage difficult, but one bowman could pick you all off if he hit our archer first." He looked up at the driver. "How did you do?"

Arderton smiled sheepishly. "I thought I did fine until you started in. I got one in the arm in the first barrage, and I think I hit a horse in the shoulder. Then you stopped them and they were out of range, what with you in there too."

"Thanks for thinking of me. I hope the one you hit wasn't the one I killed."

"If you got the one on our right, I don't think so."

"Well, we've done enough damage to hold them off. But we don't know what they'll do now."

"What might they do?" Lady Talia's eyes were wide.

"Depends how many there are. I think I'd better go find out."

"You're not going back there!"

"Just as far as the bend in the road. If they're doing what comes naturally, the ones on foot will have run out and caught up with the horsemen. They'll all be milling around in the road in plain sight and I can make a count. They might not even spot me."

"Don't do anything silly."

"Don't worry."

"After what I just saw you do, I worry."

"I only do things like that when I have to, my Lady." He saluted and cantered back up the road. Rounding the corner, he was dismayed at the size of crowd forming up to follow four mounted men, grimly pacing towards him. *Well, at least Arderton's guess about hitting a horse was accurate.*

He took a quick count, then wheeled his horse. There was a shout, but none of the horsemen spurred after him, so he trotted away. He knew what he needed to know. This was a big group, strong enough to be a threat to the village, and they were formed up openly on the road, following him.

He slapped the reins on the horse's neck, lifting him to a gallop. On reaching the carriage, he slowed. "They're coming after us, about thirty of them. I have to warn the village. Keep up a good pace and you'll be fine. I'll come back out after you as soon as I can. Are you all right alone, my Lady?"

She grinned, but her lips were white. "I'm not exactly alone, soldier. Go tell your people."

He galloped off, not pushing his mount too hard. It was still some distance back to the village, and he had to get there. The poor horse wasn't coping too well with the soldier's substantial weight on his bruised shoulder.

When he turned the last corner, there was action ahead of him. Men were piling logs across the road, and the central common was full of animals. All the houses were shuttered, and the alleys that led to the fields were blocked by upended carts and other debris.

As he galloped up, Sarha ran out, shouting. "Who is it? What's the danger? Where is Lady Talia?"

"Bandits. About thirty of them. Coming soon. The carriage is right behind me. How did you know?"

"Frey. You know he's got a lookout up on the Rock. Came running in a few minutes ago yelling, roused everybody. He could hardly speak, he was panting so much. Kept saying 'Bad men. Soldier come. Bad men!' Some of the villagers didn't believe him, but I figured if he saw you coming back and there were bad men, it wouldn't hurt to be ready."

"I'm going back out to check on Lady Talia. You have everything in hand here. Tell them what's going on. Could be a serious attack."

He brushed his way through the villagers and mounted again. "Talk to Sarha. I'm going to bring in the carriage. We'll use it to block the south entrance. Work on the logs at the north end of town while I'm gone."

He trotted his tired horse back up the road, but didn't get far before the carriage came rolling down, the horses lathered and at the end of their strength. As he swung alongside, the coachman shouted.

"They're coming again. Not so fast, but chasing us."

He nodded. "You're just about there, Arderton. Stop the coach right at the town entrance. We'll turn it around to block the road and take the horses to the inn."

The coachman nodded back, grim-faced. Four riders appeared in the dust behind, but he resisted the impulse to face them down. They would be wary of him, and if another bowman had taken up a horse, it wasn't worth the risk. He followed the coach.

Then they were out in the fields and thundering down to the village. The crowd manhandled the carriage into position and unharnessed the horses. Two locals with bows positioned themselves behind it, and the soldier took up his post in the slot between the carriage and the wall of the nearest house. Sarha hustled Lady Talia and the other non-combatants to the inn.

The bandits pulled up out of bowshot to watch, their skinny horses blowing and staggering with fatigue. They looked like they spent a poor winter, which meant these men would be desperate. If they were hungry enough to attack a defended village, they were a threat indeed.

After a few minutes, a straggle of them appeared down the road, slouching along in no hurry. They were a nondescript lot, dirty and tattered, with little armour and few good weapons, but all were armed and all stared hungrily at the little town.

He got a good count: thirty-one foot and four on horseback. There was no sign of the injured horse, which meant that either it was dead or there were non-combatants in the group who were tending it. Hungry as these men must be, a dead horse would be useful to them.

When the ragged bunch had assembled, they straggled out in an uneven line, and one of the horsemen rode forward. "You in the village!"

The soldier didn't move. "What." He didn't make it a question.

"We have no quarrel with you."

Voices muttered in derision behind him. "I'm sure."

The man raised his hands, palms up. "No quarrel at all. We just want the rich folks in the carriage. Send them out to us and we'll go away."

"They would, you know." He turned to see Sarha standing behind him.

"Of course. We're the ones with the strength here."

She shook her head. "Are they stupid enough to think we'd actually turn them over?"

"Some people might. If they were weak enough and afraid enough. And had little enough cause to love the rich."

"I suppose. Are you going to answer him?"

Jhanes turned to Arderton, standing by with an arrow on his string.

"Could you hit him from here?"

The man shook his head. "Not worth trying. Just make him mad if I try and miss."

The soldier grinned. "I don't think he's any too pleased with us already. Keep an eye open." He was beginning to trust this coachman/mercenary, after seeing him shoot from the top of a swaying carriage. He turned and stepped a few paces out from the barricade.

"I am an agent of his Majesty, King Gerth. There will be no deals. The travellers and the people of this village are under my protection and the king's. Your only hope is to get to the border as fast as you can, because the king's men will be on your trail the moment they arrive."

The man sat his lathered horse, staring at the soldier. "Well, Mister King's Agent, I don't see any of the king's soldiers around at the moment. But thank you for the information. I will have to act more quickly than I had intended. We will come in and take what we want, and it won't be pretty.

"Now, why don't you look the other way and let the village people do what's necessary to protect themselves? Then you can pretend we caught that carriage out on the road, and everyone will be a lot better off."

"Nice try. King Gerth doesn't work like that." Jhanes raised his bow, brought the feathers to his ear. "Last chance. Leave now."

The man cursed and lurched his weary horse around. "Bad move, Mister King's Agent. I'll attend to you personally if you survive my men."

There was no ceremony, no strategy. He rode back to his men, screamed an order and turned to charge. The other horsemen followed him, the footsoldiers yelling and running behind. The soldier slipped back to the safety the carriage.

"Hold your fire!"

He watched the charge, with the horses stumbling as they ran. It was too early, but his inexperienced fighters could wait no longer, so he gave the order.

"Shoot when you can hit something."

He aimed at the leader and loosed his shaft, the next arrow springing to his fingertips in a well-rehearsed motion. His second one was in the air before the first struck, and he loosed in a steady stream, enjoying the feeling of competence and power it gave him. Another volley of arrows flew from the coachman at the other end of the carriage, and a few slower shots came from the villagers.

Two horsemen went down and the others sped past him, circling to find a weakness elsewhere in the village wall. Then the footsoldiers came into range and he was able to pick off a few before they got too close.

At the last moment he placed his bow safely behind the wagon wheel, drew his sword and stepped forward. It might have seemed a foolhardy move, but with the wall behind him and a safe nook to slip into, he knew he could do more damage, both physically and mentally, if he took the initiative. If this rag-tag bunch had a swordsman who might endanger him, he would be ready to take refuge. This would be a stupid time to die a hero.

The first two enemy to meet him slowed their run and advanced cautiously, their last mistake. The moment they were within reach Jhanes attacked, his sword striking flesh at every stroke. His opponents melted away before him and he was not green enough to follow. The battle would spread away from this strongpoint, so he dispatched two more of them, then slipped back inside the village.

"Can you hold?"

The coachman grinned, his own longsword out. "After what you just did? They won't be back here for a while."

"Watch out for horsemen." He sprinted to the centre of the common, listening and watching. Sure enough, there was an uproar on the west side, where a wide alley past the smithy opened to the fields. He ran.

He arrived to find the smith pinned under a wagon, lashing out with his huge hammer at the legs of several enemy who could not pass him. Just as a spearman was coming to prod him out, the soldier was among them, driving them back, lopping the head off the spear and pushing the enemy into the fields again. They ran without looking back, and he took advantage of the gap to step out and reconnoiter. Stumbling bandits scattered from the village in all directions. As he watched, an arrow sprouted between one man's shoulders and he fell soundlessly. A quick count showed five bodies within sight and he figured on at least five more of his own doing, back at the carriage. If Lady Talia's two "footmen" were worth their salt at the north end of town, they would account for a few more. He turned back in, clapping the smith on the shoulder as he wriggled out from under the cart.

"Thank you, sir. I thought they had me."

"Were you by yourself, here?"

"Only for a moment. I sent Odred for help when I saw how many were coming my way."

"A brave move, but it almost cost you your life."

The smith wiped a bloody arm, examining the cut to see how deep it was. "I suppose so."

Jhanes slapped his shoulder again. "But it didn't, so now you're a hero."

"I am?"

"Oh, yes, as long as I don't tell them about the crawling-under-the-wagon part. You better stay here at your post. They might attack again."

He laughed and strode back to the carriage. The bandits had re-grouped and their leader was haranguing them from the back of his horse. The soldier noted that the bodies that lay nearby were not moving and stepped outside the village.

When the bandits noticed him, he stood, hands on hips. Then he spoke, loudly but not shouting. "I'll be coming for you."

He stepped forward. "For you. I will not allow anyone to harm my people. You came here with over thirty men. Now, through your stupidity, you have less than twenty. You will run, but I will be behind you. Now that I know how weak you are, I will not wait for the king's men. I will come myself. I will hunt you down like the vermin that infest my fields. I will find you, day or night, and take you, one by one, two by two, and more. You will never be safe as long as you lurk near my borders. Your only chance to escape is now, while I tend to my people and prepare them to defend themselves while I am gone. This is my last warning. Go."

He turned his back on them and strode into the village. He could see by the smiling faces in front of him that his words had made the intended impact. By the time he reached the barricade and turned, the ragged bunch was straggling northward, giving the town a wide berth. A small troop of women with heavy packs on their backs trundled in the rear, a few men with bloodied bandages limping in their midst, one leading a shambling horse.

As the last of this pitiful company passed out of sight, the townsfolk let out a rousing yell. People began to slap Jhanes on the back and soon he was surrounded by a cheering mob. It took him a moment to silence them. "It's not over yet. I need a couple of good woodsmen to follow that lot for a ways, make sure they don't turn back. Who?"

Two hands went up.

"No heroics, now. Stay off the road, don't let them know you're there. Did anyone think to send a warning ahead?"

"Sarha did. She sent Trethor and Kletch. They're good runners and too young to fight."

He nodded. "A bunch of you go bring in the bodies. Pile them by the garbage dump. Be careful; they won't all be dead, and they'll be desperate. Bring the wounded ones in but tie them up first, even if it hurts them. Don't be cruel, but don't be easy, either. Do we have any wounded?"

"At the inn, sir."

He grinned. "Don't call me 'sir.' The war's over. Let's go see who's hurt."

There were a few minor injuries, but all had been tend by the time the soldier reached the inn. When he entered, everyone was gathered around a moaning, bloody figure on the table. It was Mendar, one of the local farmers, and his forearm looked bad. He had slipped at the wrong moment, held up his arm to protect himself, and taken a sword cut directly across the forearm.

The soldier opened the soggy bandage carefully. The blood had clotted into a mess, but the wound was deep. Taking the hand and elbow, he gently rotated. The man screamed in agony as the hand twisted freely. A new seepage of blood began to show. The soldier replaced the bandage and applied a splint along one side, padding the arm, then strapping it to the board.

"One bone sheared through. It may or may not heal right, depending on if it gets set properly or if it gets infected."

"If it gets infected, he'll die." Sarha shook her head.

The soldier shrugged. "He needs better medical attention than we can give him here."

"How are we going to get that?"

"Take him to Tsalk. The sooner the better."

Sarha looked at the injury and the sweat beaded on the victim's forehead. "It would be a terrible trip for him."

"Not in my carriage."

They both looked up at Lady Talia.

"Do you mean that?"

"Of course. Why wouldn't I? It may be big and ugly, but it rides beautifully, even on these roads. We could make him up a bed, strap him in to keep him from rolling around. There's plenty of room if I don't take all my luggage."

The soldier looked grim. "We haven't had too much luck getting your carriage through to Tsalk."

"Are there likely to be more bandits around?"

"I suppose. There can't be too many bands that size, though."

"So having defeated one bunch doesn't make any difference to our chances with any others."

"That's about it. But you want to get through, and now we have another reason to try. The problem is, I can't go with you."

"I suppose you have to stay and protect the village."

"The village is able to protect itself. These bandits would have left them alone if it hadn't been for the prize they were sheltering."

"So this is all my fault." She looked very young, standing there, disconsolate.

"You probably had some effect. Nobody is laying blame. Look at it positively; we've broken the power of that bunch and they won't be able to do as much damage to others."

She nodded, unconvinced.

"Anyway, I'm not staying to protect the village. I'm going after those bandits."

"By yourself?"

He looked around the room, at the astonished faces. "Yes, by myself. If Lady Talia was staying here, I would take one or two of her men. No one else has the experience to do what I'm going to do."

Sarha's eyes met his, and he could see the pain. "What are you going to do?"

"What I said I would. Harry them, day and night. Pick them off, one by one, until they don't dare stop to sleep or eat for fear of me. I'm going to chase them all the way to the border and make sure they don't touch a hair of anyone on the way."

"But you, alone, against all of them?"

He grinned in honest pleasure. "They don't stand a chance."

She looked at him, her head slanted to the side a bit. "You know, I believe you."

"You should. Now, let's get things organized. I'll be off as soon as I have my equipment ready. You, Lady Talia, should leave as early as you can in the morning. Take Janus, here. He can ride my horse, if it's had a rest. I won't need it. My only worry is Mendar. He'll spend a pretty rough night, and then all day in a moving carriage."

"I can solve that problem. Lateda, get the medicine box." The lady turned back to look at the injured man, her face white. "I came well-equipped for any emergency. I brought strong sleeping powders. They will keep him from pain until we reach Tsalk."

Satisfied that everything was under control, the soldier went to pack. Spreading out his equipment, he made his choices. For armour he only took his helmet liner, a hardened leather vest and his bronze vambraces. Both liner and vest were reinforced with steel strips, a satisfactory compromise, since the full metal helmet and chainmail were too heavy and shiny to use for the type of warfare he planned.

Once he had strapped his various weapons about him and slung a small pack of dried food on his back, he returned to the common room.

"I could use a few extra arrows."

118

Quivers were thrust forward, and he selected the longest and straightest shafts. Then he stood, looking around the room. "Well, I guess I'd better be off."

They all nodded soberly. He grinned. "Don't look so sad. I've done this kind of thing before. I won't take any risks."

Heads nodded again as if they believed him. Taking Sarha's hand, he made for the door, and they parted before him.

"Stroll with me a ways."

She nodded mutely.

They walked through the village in silence. When they reached the forest at the end of the fields, he stopped. "It starts to get interesting from this point. You'd better go back."

"You have to do this."

"No, I don't have to do anything. I can sit tight and safe here until the soldiers arrive. But I'm the king's agent. If I'm to fill that office properly, I have to do the whole of its duties. These are the king's subjects who are being threatened. Not only here, but everywhere between here and the border. The king would want me to protect them, because I'm the one who can. Believe me, Sarha, I can do this. I won't be in much danger. I'm more interested in scaring them than killing them. I'll stay out of sight. No confrontations, no battles, I promise."

She shook her head. "Don't make any promises like that. You do what you have to do when it's necessary. Just promise to do your best to come back. What more can I ask?"

He took her awkwardly in his arms, trying to find her a place that wasn't jagged with weapons. "I have never felt it so important to come back before. I will be even more careful than usual."

She smiled up at him. "I won't ask any more. Good luck, Soldier."

He nodded, kissed her and strode away, determined not to look back in case there were tears.

10. CHASE

As he swung into marching pace his sadness at leaving her faded, and a feeling of pleasure suffused his body. It was good to be moving again. The weapons nestled against him in their familiar places, and again he knew that feeling of total confidence, supreme competence. He settled into the chase: eyes attentive, ears alert, his whole body receptive and wary. It was unlikely that the bandits would have left a rear guard, but he had good reason to take no chances.

His gaze dropped to the dirt of the road. The scuffed surface told him little he didn't know already, but he was looking for tracks that led to the side.

Soon, he found them. The first stragglers had wandered to a convenient fallen tree and sat awhile. Drops of blood completed the story; one of the wounded needed a rest or a fixed bandage. No prints led into the forest, so they must have moved on.

He slipped aside when he heard his scouts coming back and enjoyed himself by giving them a scare once they had missed him.

"You've got to keep your eyes open better than that, lads. I was sitting in plain sight, and you walked right by." It was an exaggeration, but they needed the lesson.

Abashed, they gave their report. The mob was moving slowly but should be well past the broken bridge by now. He sent the scouts back to town, buoyed with his thanks for a job well done but cautioned again about keeping their eyes sharp.

Striding ahead, he slowed only when the tracks showed him where his scouts had turned back. Now he moved more cautiously, taking the time to scan the roadsides and the surrounding forest for any other information. The rest stops were becoming more frequent. These people were tired and hungry and had fought a battle. They would be stopping soon, and with any luck there was no isolated farm nearby.

Around the next corner, a plume of smoke rising above the trees quashed that hope. With a muttered curse he left the road, circling to come in from the east side. He was getting back into the old ways now, the routines of the forest slipping about him like a concealing robe, and he moved without a sound.

Soon, shouts and curses ahead slowed him further. Approaching through a thick patch of young spruce, he crawled to the edge of the clearing. He was heartened to see that the farmhouse still stood, stoutly barricaded. The charred rubble of an outbuilding was sending up the greasy smoke. The bandits had started a fire just out of bowshot of the house and were roasting a goat. Several stood regarding the building as if trying to find a weakness. One stepped forward, and an arrow arced out of a window to fall, spent, at the bandit's feet. More shouts and jeers. Stringing his bow, the soldier crept closer.

The bandits were content to prepare their supper, so he settled in to wait, counting heads and chewing on a strip of dried meat to pass the time. Twenty-four looked like fighters and the rest were women and wounded. Four horses; the one with the drooping head would have the arrow wound.

As dusk fell, the mouth-watering smell of roasted meat overcame the rabble, and they dragged the carcass off the fire, snarling and arguing about who should have how much. The leader did not have the power or the interest to keep his mob under any form of control. When he had eaten the first and largest share, he strolled over to gaze at the farmhouse again, leaving his followers to quarrel over the remains.

When it was just dark enough to protect him but still light enough for easy shooting, the soldier made his move. He began to pick off bandits, always selecting a target far enough away from the others that the death wasn't noticed. Two victims fell silently, but the third moved as the arrow flew; it lodged in his shoulder, bringing a scream of pain.

Every bandit sprang to the alert, but the wounded man was too busy suffering to tell them the source of the arrow. Assuming it had come from the farmhouse, the bandits edged farther away, which only brought them closer to the soldier's hiding place.

Waiting even longer between shots now, he downed two more. Then he backed away and moved around closer to the farmhouse and waited.

One of his victims was discovered, then a second. The bandits huddled around their fire, weapons drawn, staring fearfully back up the road. Unable to resist such an easy target, the soldier put three quick arrows into the group, drawing screams of pain and rage.

Then, as the bandits caught on and scattered, he slipped off, running easily and quietly over the damp forest floor. When he was a good distance away he found a stream and drank, then ate some more and rested. He felt good. His injured arm had stood up to the day's work, and the walking hadn't tired him as much as it might have. Better still, his old stalking skills were coming back, though rusty from years of disuse in the clamorous marching feet and jangling metal of the modern mercenary army. It was hard to move silently in these heavy boots, but he had given up carrying moccasins long ago when his last pair wore out.

He waited until moonrise, then returned to the beleaguered farm. The fire was still burning, and the bandits sat around it in unmoving lumps of darkness. There was still no sign of life from the farmhouse, although a wisp of smoke trickled from the chimney, up against the stars. The dangerous part would come in the morning when the bandits, rested but hungry, decided to attack. He doubted if the farmer had the manpower to fend off a serious assault from a band this size.

He would just have to even the odds. He checked the camp's periphery. Sentries were posted at the obvious positions. Calculating that they wouldn't be too scared yet, he moved in closer. A hunched figure leaned against a tree, silhouetted in the firelight. It took him half a candle to get close enough. Then

122

he reached around the tree and crushed the man's skull with the pommel of his sword. As his victim slumped to the ground he was away again, moving to the next man, who was smart enough to stand in the open. That one was rewarded for his intelligence by an arrow in the chest.

Slipping nearer the fire, the soldier dispatched two more sentries. He took the time to leave no wounds, and rearranged their bodies so that they looked to be sleeping before he retreated to the edge of the woods. He considered stealing the horses, but it was too dangerous. The leader kept them close to the centre of the camp. Not wanting to kill the animals out of hand, the soldier decided to wait for a better chance. He was breathing heavily now, and judged it time to rest.

Sure enough, his victims were soon discovered, and a new clamour arose in the camp. The leader shouted, punched, and beat his followers into silence: a silence that was broken by the whirr of an arrow downing another unlucky bandit.

Time to move on. They saw where that arrow came from. The soldier slid back into the forest and circled behind the farmhouse. No bandits would dare rush him in this direction for fear of attack from the farmers. On the other hand, he might be shot at himself, so he stayed well clear.

He was beginning to feel the strain of the day, so he withdrew to his place by the stream. Rolling into his blanket, he lay and looked up at the stars, reviewing his progress. *Reasonable. They have no one that endangers me. I just have to be careful. I have family to think of.* That stopped him. *Should I have come at all? I didn't have to. In fact, I could go home now.* He knew it wasn't good enough. He had to see it through. The king would require nothing less. *And neither would I.* He rolled on his side and dropped into a light slumber.

It was a thin blanket and a clear, early summer night, and he awoke near dawn when the cold drove him, shivering, into motion. He drank from the stream when he could dimly see the foam flecking its sides. Hurrying to the clearing, he approached from a new direction and studied the situation in the growing light. It was too dangerous to approach the sentries, so he satisfied himself with leaving one pinned to the tree where he had been leaning, an arrow through his heart. Then he lobbed several arrows into the huddled figures around the dead campfire, evoking screams and scrambling, although he had no illusions about his accuracy at this distance.

The bandits settled down again, but there would be no more sleep for them. They hobbled around, stretching, yawning, complaining, building up the fire and getting whatever meagre breakfast they could, shooting fearful glances at the surrounding forest. When the leader started eyeing the farmhouse again, it was time for a change of tactics. The soldier crept as close as he could then sprinted into the open, within easy bowshot.

"I told you to run. You did not heed my warnings. Now pay the price!"

He got off three well-placed arrows before one of the terrified mob had the sense to grab a bow, then he retreated to the woods, laughing. He stopped in the shelter of a tree and listened.

The leader was haranguing his men, trying to get up a charge, but they were having none of it. The bandits gathered their belongings, looking apprehensively towards where Jhanes had stood. Then they headed down the road, straggling in small groups: the leader and his two horsemen in the middle, the women with the packs behind, glancing fearfully over their shoulders as they walked.

But their enemy was in front of them, looking for a good ambush point a candle or so down the road. He found a rocky outcropping, high enough to be hard to attack, but sloping at the back for easy escape. Jhanes doubted that any of the weary men below could outrun him, but he remembered his promise to Sarha and vowed not to stay too long.

He allowed half of the straggling mob to pass him, then started shooting at those in front, killing one and wounding another. *I'd like to get the leader, but he always stays in a group. Smart trick. Cowardly.* Then he aimed at those approaching, downing another before they spotted his perch and got up the nerve to attack. He waited until the charge reached an opening below him, took two more easy shots, then faded back down the ledge. By the time the bandits reached his former position, he was well out of sight around the corner of rock, jogging steadily towards the next town. He saw no evidence of the lads who had brought the warning and assumed they had circled to go back to the village safely or waited to return the following day.

He could do a better job if he went in front to prepare the locals. Now the marauders would find farmsteads barricaded and bare. With the lack of food and his harrying tactics, the remnants of the band would soon be running for the border.

In the end, events worked out as he had planned. He alerted the town guard at Cdeile, who picked up several bandits making a desperate try for food. The rest of the mob detoured widely around the town, allowing Jhanes a comfortable few hours' sleep in the guardhouse and a hot meal before he took their trail again. When seven exhausted and wounded thieves reached the border, a troop of guards, warned by a runner sent ahead by Lord Feister, swept them up with a simple ambush. By the time Jhanes arrived, they were in the blockhouse awaiting their fate. The women had faded away, probably to show up innocently somewhere else. *Well, I have no quarrel with them, poor souls. I hope they survive without committing any crimes serious enough to warrant chasing them down.*

While he had no authority here, Jhanes introduced himself and spoke to the sergeant on equal terms. "I see you have netted my quarry. By my count, there should be about thirteen left."

"Less than that. How many were there when they started?"

"I figured a bit over thirty before they attacked the village."

"And how many left the village?"

"Well over half that."

"So where are the rest?"

125

"The farmers will take care of the bodies. Or the wild animals will. Depends where they died."

The old soldier looked Jhanes up and down. "What did you do to them? They were so terrified by the time we picked them up they were practically begging to be arrested."

"Old tricks I learned as a kid. Kill from ambush, stalk at night, use their fear against them."

"All by yourself?"

"Easier that way. No chance of getting shot by a friend by mistake."

The sergeant grinned. "Sounds like you had an interesting childhood." He reached for paper and a pen. "I have to write up a report."

"Go ahead. I never saw this bunch before morning, day before yesterday, but I'll give you all I know. I'm thirsty, though. Road's drying out. Dusty, even."

There was a bark of laughter. "A whole lot dustier for them as you left with their faces in it."

A mug of cool ale appeared. The soldier guzzled half of it without pause, then started talking.

When they were finished, the sergeant put away his paper and pen. "Well, soldier, I'd like to save a whole lot of trouble and hang this bunch, but King Gerth has given his orders. No summary executions. Everything legal and fair. You'll be brought back to Cdeile to testify."

"They're a sorry lot. I don't imagine they'll all swing, just the leaders. What happened to the horses?"

"What horses?"

"There were three horses last time I saw them."

The grizzled head shook. "Not when we picked them up."

The soldier slapped his thigh in exasperation. "Then you didn't get the leader."

"No?"

"Why would he have gone on without horses? I'll bet if we look back along the road, we'll find some clever spot where he

126

cut into the brush, circled round and crossed the line on the smugglers' trails."

The sergeant nodded. "That's what I'd have done. Well, I'll send out the patrols, but I'll do better to warn my counterpart on the other side of the border in Velikii. I doubt if we'll see anything. If he had horses, he's long away from here."

"Not those horses. They were staggering two days ago, and I never gave them time to graze."

The sergeant was on his feet. "Good enough. I'll thank you for your help, Jhanes, and get some mounted patrols out right away. Will you stay the night?"

The soldier looked at the sun. "No, I can make it back to Cdeile before dark, and Lord Feister will want a report. Thanks for taking over my little problem. I want word to get around that nobody meddles with the people of the Free Counties."

"I think word will get around, soldier. Any use askin' if you'd like to join up?"

"Thanks, Sergeant, but I'm an innkeeper, now. Got myself a warm spot to retire in."

The man looked him up and down. Then he laughed. "Check yourself next time you see a mirror. Innkeeper? Hah!" Then he was gone, shouting orders.

The soldier strode happily toward home in the fading light. Now that he was looking for it, he found where the horses had left the road along a ridge of rock, their unshod hooves making no mark that an average tracker would notice. He kicked himself for missing it the first time, but he didn't bother to track them. *Let the army do its duty.* Still, he began to pay more attention to his surroundings. *No sense giving a straggler a chance of revenge this late in the campaign.*

He was received with great courtesy by Lord Feister, who was grateful that his people were saved from possible marauding.

When the soldier finished his report, the lord sat back in his gilded chair. "You know, I'd be happy to send you a couple of good men for a while, but King Gerth was very specific. None of us lords are to interfere in the Free Counties. Damned shame, I say. Leaves a big hole in this part of the country. His patrols are spread too thin. Times like this, he needs a permanent force in your area."

"I'll let him know, my Lord."

Lord Feister grinned. "You'll let him know, will you? And he'll listen to an innkeeper, will he? Even such a forceful-looking innkeeper as yourself? I doubt it."

"I don't talk to the king, my Lord. But Lady Zoysana does."

"Ah, Zoysana. The king listens to her. I would, too, and I was him. She's one smart lady, that Zoysana."

"I couldn't agree more."

"Well, you and I are in agreement on many things. I won't interfere, but if you need any help, just call. Can I put you up for the night?"

"I wouldn't mind a corner to curl up in, my Lord. I've been too busy for a full night's sleep, the past few days."

The lord laughed again. "I gather you have. I think we can do you better than a corner. Supper's on any moment now, and maybe you can entertain us afterwards with your story."

"I'd rather not, my Lord."

"I thought you said you wanted word to get out that your people weren't to be meddled with. You'll gain more credence telling your tale in my hall than down in the inns." The lord leaned forward. "You're new at this game. Soldiering was a simple and straightforward job. Now you have to learn all sorts of new talents. Time enough to start."

The soldier twisted out a smile. "I suppose you're right, my Lord. Time I started learning."

It wasn't such an ordeal as he had expected. There was no need to stand up in front of people and talk for hours. It was a small group at supper, and once he had outlined the bare details, the questions came thick and fast. All he had to do was answer. Finally they wound down, and Lord Feister leaned back in his chair, smiling.

"Now, if I do my arithmetic right, you killed or wounded ten men in the battle, seven at the first farm, and nine more at various times after that. Am I correct?"

"I suppose so, my Lord. I wasn't looking at it that way."

"No, I don't suppose you were, and it does you credit. Still, it's some accomplishment."

"I still don't want to look at it that way, if you don't mind. When I was a soldier, it was all straightforward battle. You defended yourself and killed anybody who attacked. Only fools kept a score. I didn't enjoy most of this, especially near the end when they were all just running. I stopped shooting them after they passed here. At the beginning I didn't mind, when it was necessary and there was so many of them. That was a real challenge. But later on, I couldn't bring myself to it."

The lord laughed quietly. "Well, I guess we won't make a killer out of you, then. Good thing. Killers aren't much good when peace time rolls around. I imagine King Gerth will prefer you as an innkeeper."

"Thank you, my Lord."

The lord didn't ask for what. "I suppose you are headed south again tomorrow?"

"Yes, Sir. People at home will want a report."

Feister beckoned him to lean closer for private conversation. "And you sent Lady Talia on through?"

"Yes. I would have preferred she stay, but she wanted to take the wounded man as soon as possible."

"Thoughtful of her. I don't know about that girl. Brave as all get out, but didn't know what she was getting into."

"She has a better idea now, my Lord."

"But that carriage!"

"I know. She'll get a smaller one in Tsalk."

"Any chance of catching up with her in a faster vehicle?"

"I wouldn't think so, my Lord. She has a three-day start."

"Fair enough. Now here's what I'd like you to do. You have a chance, you get a message to her that I'll have that behemoth of hers brought back here, fixed up and waiting for her return journey. Road to the border's good from here. Tell her I don't mind at all. Fact is, I'd be pleased to have her in my debt, however small. Her father's a powerful man back in the Duchies, as I suppose you know."

"She didn't let on, but I was beginning to suspect."

The lord smiled. "Oh, yes. You wouldn't be surprised to see her at the castle, and they'll be calling her 'princess.' She's not really a princess, or not quite, but close enough. I hear Gerth's looking for a bride?"

"Is that why she came?"

The man shook his head and grinned. "I'm only a local landowner. I don't pretend to know what goes on in the heads of the mighty."

The talk turned to other subjects, and soon the soldier was free to slip away to his room. There was a fire burning, cutting the evening chill, and he lay on the bed, relaxing in its softness but wishing his feet didn't hang over the end. It would be good to get back to the inn. The linen there wasn't so fine, but the bed fitted better.

In the morning, he breakfasted in the kitchen with soldiers of the lord's personal guard, swapping stories and correcting the rumours they had heard about him. His stomach full and his pack replenished, he was about to leave when a page stopped him.

"Lord Feister would talk with you. He's in the stable yard."

"Lead on."

When they reached the stable, the lord was standing beside a big bay mare: too small for a destrier, but longer in the leg than the average plow horse. Even the soldier, no great judge of animals, could see her qualities. "A fine steed, your lordship."

"She is at that. I hope you get along."

"Me?"

"Yes. I can't have you walking all the way back to your little village, with your friends waiting and all. You can ride Megrah, here."

"Thank you, my Lord. I'll have her returned as soon as possible."

"No, don't worry about that. She's not much use to us around here, just the wrong size. Too small for battle and too tame. Too big for most people to ride comfortably, too slow for hunting, and too long in the leg for plowing. Seems to me she'd fit a man your size. Let's consider her on loan for as long as you need her."

Jhanes remembered what the lord had said about having people in his debt, but didn't hesitate. "She would suit me, I'm sure, and I'd be pleased to ride her. Thank you, my Lord. Thank you many times."

The lord smiled. "I think I'll be seeing you again, Innkeeper, or Soldier, or King's Agent. Megrah is thanks for the lives of my people you saved this quarter-month. A good journey to you."

Jhanes bowed, then mounted. The mare snorted and danced, but soon settled.

"She's a fine animal, my Lord. Thanks again, and farewell."

The lord raised his hand, and the soldier lifted the reins and trotted off.

11. Homecoming

Later in the afternoon, Jhanes met a farmer on the road: a weary man trudging along, pushing a bloodstained handcart in front of him. Too tired to be careful, he allowed the armed soldier to get much too close, then looked around in terror when he found himself confronted with such danger.

"Good evening. A bit of blood, there."

The farmer recovered his wits enough to nod.

"Somebody hurt?"

"M...my son, sir."

"You'll be from the farm that was attacked, then."

"Aye. Had to take him to the village for help." He gathered his courage. "Wh...what do you know about the attack?"

When Jhanes explained who he was and asked after the people at the farm, the farmer looked around.

"You're the one what drove 'em off! Thought you looked familiar. Where are your men?"

"I didn't bring any men."

"You killed all of them yourself?"

He shrugged. He was getting tired of all this story-telling. "It was necessary. They were thinking of attacking your house. Probably would have in the morning."

The farmer nodded. "We knew. We just couldn't figure out what was goin' on when they didn't. Then when you stepped out and started shooting, we thought the soldiers had come to rescue us. Then everyone disappeared and nothin' happened. It wasn't till the next day that we come out and found the dead horse, and all those men with arrows in them."

The words seemed to tumble out of him, now. "We didn't know what to do with the bodies but we couldn't just leave them there, so I sent over to Frum's and they came and helped haul them away. They buried them, I guess.

132

"I was worried about leavin' the wimmenfolk, but my son wasn't mendin', and I had to take him into the village for some help. I wanted to bring them along, but we decided they was safer at home than out on the road."

"I agree. Was your son wounded badly?"

"Just an arrow in the thigh, but it wouldn't stop bleedin', and we were hopin' someone at the village could help."

"Well, there's the old woman who does the medicines; she's got potions for that. I have plenty of experience with wounds, and I'll check him over when I get there."

"They said he would be fine, and they'd send him home when he had healed a bit."

They parted cordially, the farmer promising to visit the inn soon and to bring all his friends there. Not a likely situation, since these people had very little cash for that level of luxury, but the thought was important.

Jhanes hurried on, more and more anxious as he got closer, his mind full of things that might have gone wrong at home after he left. The new mount was in far better condition than his faithful old plodder, but soon her breathing became laboured, and he slowed her to a walk again.

No sense using up a good horse when probably nothing's wrong. This is just new to me. Have to get used to it. He thought of Sarha's worry, going on for five days with no end. That started him off again, but he controlled himself and set the horse to her most economical trot. *Settle down, soldier. You can do better than this.*

It was dusk by the time he entered Lanil's Rock. Unfamiliar hoofbeats brought the village dogs swirling out to greet him, and the mare warned them off with dancing feet. Young Kletch was on guard at the north gate and greeted him with a loud whoop. This drew anxious faces to the doorways, but the smiles lit up when they saw who was swinging down from the big horse.

By the time he reached the inn door, he had quite a following, and they burst into the common room as he lifted

Sarha high in his arms and swung her around twice before setting her down. The crowd cheered, drowning her flustered speech, but her tears showed him what she had gone through these past five days of waiting. Then she regained her poise, her head flung back, and she grabbed his arm, spinning him around, checking him over.

"No cuts, no bumps, no sprains or strains?"

He laughed. "Not a one, my dear. I have come through with no more damage than an inflated opinion of myself."

They laughed at that, and several voices called out for a drink to celebrate.

"Only home a minute and I have to go to work. Can't you wait at least until I unsaddle my horse?"

Sarha snorted. "You'll not be takin' time to unsaddle any horse or pour any drinks tonight, my lad." She raised her voice. "Somebody take care of his horse, now, for there'll be no drinks for anyone till it's done."

Then she stopped. "What horse is that, now? Odred rode your horse south."

"Oh, I picked up another one: on loan, mind you, but for as long as I need her. Come out and see. She's a beauty."

The crowd poured out into the street again to admire the horse, who took all the attention as if it was her due. It had been a long day, and she was much more interested in water and grain than a crowd of noisy, gawking humans.

Soon she was led away, and the crowd returned to the inn. Jhanes was ensconced by the fire, a mug in one hand and a huge turkey leg in the other, and commanded to tell his story.

He laughed, took a bite of the juicy meat, a larger slug of hill-apple cider, and began. Having told the tale several times already, he found it easier. He still didn't feel right about too much bragging, but no longer tried to hide his accomplishment. It was important that the story should spread, and a poor tale went nowhere. Again, when he was finished the questions flew, and he answered good-naturedly. It was rather fun being a hero, although the situation had never become truly dangerous, a point he was careful to reassure Sarha about several times.

Once he had finished and the others had told him their tales of what had happened after he left the village, the crowd broke apart to their separate tables, rehashing the battle, discussing the new information.

Only then did Jhanes notice the stranger in the corner. A lanky man dressed in fine-stitched leather, an instrument case leaning against the wall beside him. When there was a lull in the action, the minstrel rose to a considerable height, strolling across the room to shake the soldier's hand.

"I am Solonstan. I have been impressed by your exploits."

Solonstan the songsmith. He of the barbed tongue, the acid wit. The king's favourite singer.

"I'm sorry, sir. I should not be holding the floor when an entertainer of your value is present."

The musician folded himself onto the nearest bench, waving his hand. "No, no, it was fine to hear your rendition, roughly stated as it was. It is only fair that the crowd's pennies go into the appropriate pocket tonight. People here owe you much."

"I don't like all this talk of debt. I was here, I was able, I did what I could. What good would I be as an agent of the king if I didn't protect his people when they needed it?"

"An admirable attitude, but not one that will gain you safety."

"Who is looking for safety? It would be enough for me if word got around that it was unprofitable to bother the people in this area. We have no lord to protect us, here in the Free Counties, and the king's patrols cannot be everywhere."

"The king is not unaware of the situation."

The soldier shot a glance at the singer's impassive face, remembering again to whom he was speaking. "Have you, by chance, seen Lady Zoysana?"

The man smiled. "Ah, fortunately I have, and not long ago." He reached into his cloak and pulled out a package. "She sends you this, along with her warmest greetings. She would have been here with me, but she turned back to give Lady Talia safe escort."

"I'm glad to hear of that. The lady's safety has been on my mind. So she made it through, then?"

The singer laughed. "She did at that, she and her big carriage. It now looms on the village green in Tsalk. I could have made a month's takings selling chances to sit in it. What a vehicle! It's a credit to her and her men that they managed to push it so far."

"More credit to her horses, I say."

"A good point. Fine animals they are, and very merry now, pulling that little two-horse carriage along. They will be at the castle by tomorrow night at the latest, and then Zoysana will turn straight back for here. She feels this area needs her attention, as you will know when you have read her messages."

He knows the contents of the messages he carries. Hmm. He filed this information away. If he ever needed a trusted messenger, this was one he could count on.

"Would you like to sing for us?"

Again the slender fingers waved a negative. "No, no, I meant what I said. I will not compete with your talents tonight. Besides, I have had a long walk today and would rather rest and chat."

The soldier pondered this information. So Zoysana had been headed in this direction. Forced to turn back because of Talia, she had sent Solonstan hurrying ahead to check things out.

"And will you have a similar walk when you return tomorrow?"

The long face lit up with a pleased smile, and a low chuckle rumbled for a moment. "You catch on fast, my friend. No, I see no need to hurry back. Zoysana will be here when she can, and there is no urgent need any more. I must say, I am glad to see that her trust was not misplaced. Tell me again about your visit with Lord Feister. He spoke of sending troops here?"

136

"He was very careful to offer help only if we ask for it. He is keenly aware of the king's feelings towards the Free Counties and made it clear that he was abiding by the king's wishes."

"An intelligent man, Feister, and a diplomat. He'll do well in Gerth's regime."

"Yes, I'm sure that beautiful horse I have loan of is not merely in appreciation of my heroic deed."

"Probably not, but I do not see any serious obligation incurred."

Jhanes nodded. "I wouldn't like anyone to think I was accepting a bribe."

"I doubt that Zoysana would take that opinion," Solonstan grinned, "especially when the gift is so obvious."

"I'm not known for my subtlety."

The balladeer nodded towards the heavy sword leaning in the corner. "Not exactly."

Jhanes looked for Sarha. She was standing in the kitchen doorway watching him. With a toss of his head, he motioned her to join them. "You should be listening. This is business." He handed her the package. "We'll check these over later. Solonstan says there's nothing pressing, now that we've solved our immediate problem."

"Now that you've solved it." Her hand caressed his cheek. "How did Lady Talia get on?"

"With a light new carriage and Zoysana to escort her, she'll be just fine. What happened to the farm boy who came in with the leg wound?"

"Old Ferdla took care of him. It wasn't pretty."

"Oh?"

"Yes. She said she was worried about infection, and the wound needed cauterizing."

He winced. "Hot iron?"

She nodded. "Good thing it wasn't too deep. Also a good thing Lady Talia left some of her sleeping powders. He'll need to rest for a couple of days, then he can go home."

Sarha did not need to go into more detail. A red-hot rod inserted the full depth of an arrow wound was a good way to solve any bleeding and infection problems, but it wasn't exactly fun for the patient. He had participated in a few such operations, and the smell would never leave his memory.

The fire eventually burned low and the crowd dispersed. An early morning awaited everyone as usual. Solonstan strolled up the stairs to his room, and soon the common room was empty.

"I suppose I have to start work tomorrow." Jhanes rose from his stool, stretching luxuriously.

Sarha grinned at him from her place in the kitchen. "There are many here who would allow you a well-deserved holiday."

"But not you." He leaned over the counter, watching her.

Then she was there in front of him, her arms around his neck. "Jhanes, you do anything you like. As long as you're here, I don't care."

He laughed, returning her embrace across the counter. "Such is the formula for laziness, my Hostess."

"I don't care. It's enough to have you here."

"It was hard on you, wasn't it?" He came around the end of the counter, held her closer.

She leaned against him. "I won't deny it."

"Now you know why most soldiers don't have wives."

"Now I know why most women won't marry soldiers."

"Well, I'm not a soldier any more."

"Not until the next time."

"How do you know there'll be a next time?" He knew how unconvincing it sounded, even as he spoke the words.

"Just listen to yourself, the way you talk. These have become your people, under your protection. The next time danger threatens, you will be in the front again, leading your people to defend themselves."

She leaned closer to him, her voice slow and thoughtful. "I don't like it. In fact, I was in tears every night worrying about you," she pulled away to look up into his face, "but I was so proud when you came back, and everyone was so impressed and relieved. So proud."

He laughed, pulled her close again. "I'm glad of that. I can't seem to get too proud of myself. Goes against everything I know. But there's no reason you can't do it for me."

"Well, I am. Very proud. When you came riding through the village on that big horse," she shook her head and smiled. "Oh, yes, I watched you, with everybody running alongside, trying to get close to you. I said to myself, 'That's my man out there. He's goin' to be someone important soon, and I'll be the wife of an important man. And I know I'll have to pay for that. But it don't matter right now. He's coming home to me. It's me he'll be in bed with tonight, when they've all gone away. It's me his arms will be around, and I'll feel safer than I've felt for a long time.' Oh, I was proud, right enough."

"Now that's a thought to consider. Bed."

She smiled, almost coquettishly. "Trust you to be thinkin' of that."

"That's true, my love. You can trust me for a lot of things, but that's one of the most reliable. Come, now. Bed time."

Laughing, they trooped up the stairs together, his hand on her waist.

They need me here. All of them. And this is where I want to be. Life doesn't get any better.

12. More Problems

They read Zoysana's message the next morning after Solonstand left, but little she said was important, since most of it contained suggestions of what to do in case their bandit problem wasn't over. It was interesting to see how the lady's mind worked and some of the creative solutions she offered.

One action he did take was to begin roughing out a message system, so that each farmer in the surrounding area could be informed of any new threat as soon as possible. Over the next two days, he made the rounds on the bay mare, his big sword slung on his back, aware of the increased status these trappings gave him. He was going to be the military leader of these people, and they needed to see him in that light.

He also invited them to the village for a meeting in two days time to discuss defence. By that time, he hoped Zoysana would be there to give them some ideas. Their traditional ad hoc militia was neither efficient nor trained enough. If the Free Counties were to remain independent, they would do well not to need constant help from ambitious surrounding landowners.

However, two days passed and the farmers arrived, but Zoysana did not. As the time for the meeting approached, Jhanes got more and more worried. *What am I going to say to these people? I don't know what to say, and I shouldn't be telling them what to do, even if I had a way to make them follow.*

"What's botherin' you, Jhanes? You're bustin' around here like a bear outa winter sleep early."

He stopped moving, turned to face his wife. "What will they say when they hear Zoysana couldn't make it?"

"They'll say nothing. Nobody promised she would."

"But what can I tell them? They aren't going to listen to me. I'm a stranger."

"You're the man who took out a bandit mob single-handed. They're worried. They'll listen."

"You know, I sometimes wonder if I'm way over my head, here."

"Huh! And this is the man who was wonderin' if bein' an innkeeper would be too boring for him!"

"Sarha, this isn't a time for jokes!"

"I wasn't jokin'. Look, Jhanes. You done your hero bit. That gets you the respect. Now you have to do the rest of the job. You don't have to be a hero any more. Just help them with what you know. You can do that."

"I guess."

"So do I. Just go in there and pull them all a mug of ale. That'll relax them." She grinned. "It'll also remind them who you really are."

He turned back to her in amazement. "You know, you can be very subtle."

"Comes from dealin' with you lot all the time. Some of it had to rub off." She slapped him on the shoulder and propelled him towards the common room.

A long time later Jhanes was back in the kitchen, wiping the last clean mug and lining it up on the shelf. He stood back to look at the long, even row with satisfaction and smiled over at Sarha. "They're a lot like Inari, you know."

"They are?"

"Oh, yes, in their own way. Independent. Touchy."

"I suppose."

"One way they're different."

"What's that?" She hung the rag on the mantel rail and turned to him.

"They're afraid, and they're not afraid to admit it."

"That helps?"

"Oh, yes. It makes them agree quicker to any idea. It's also a problem, of course."

"A problem? I thought you said it helps."

141

"Aye, but that's a problem for me. I didn't want to admit that I had no solution to their problem." He thought a moment, then grinned. "Of course, if I had come up with one, they all would have fought it, just on principle."

She answered his grin. "Just like Inari?"

"Right. After I figured that out, I started making progress. I treated them like Inari."

He didn't wait for her to ask. "You don't tell Inari what to do. You ask for ideas, listen to them, and if you're smart you find a piece of somebody's idea that matches yours. You support that. Then if you're real smart, you find another part of somebody else's idea that matches with yours, and work that point in. Then you can slip a bit of your own stuff in as well. If you do it right, you end up with most of your idea, and they all think they had a part in it."

"And you complain that I'm subtle!" She glanced up at him. "Then what happens if none of them have any ideas that are anything like yours?"

"Then you didn't have a chance, anyway."

She frowned and stared at him, her head to one side. "You know a lot about the Inari."

"Aye. Some day I'll tell you about it."

She shrugged. "Whatever suits you. I ain't pryin'. I took you as you are, and so far, I'm satisfied." She looked back to him. "Unless it's somethin' I need to know."

He rocked a hand back and forth, palm down. "There have been rumours coming up from the South all spring, and I don't like what I hear. I think the Inari will be more trouble this year than usual."

"For us?"

He put an arm around her shoulders and gave a quick squeeze. "Not a chance. That's the king's duty, and it's half the kingdom away from us. We have our own problems to deal with."

"I was only listenin' in part of the time. Once they decided to keep meetin' after supper, I had to get busy. What was the outcome?"

"Nothing definite, when I come to think about it. I didn't expect to end up with a full defence plan drafted out. Not on the first meeting. We mainly agreed on a few important things: what everybody really wanted, how important merchants and travellers were, who had jurisdiction over the road, under what circumstances they would allow others on their lands. That kind of thing."

He frowned. "Why is it such a problem, letting people cross their land to chase down bandits? I would have thought they'd be happy, but a lot of them baulked at the idea of regular patrols."

She nodded. "They will allow the militia access to their lands to follow bandits. If they didn't, it might look like they were helping the bandits. Regular patrols are different. It's how the law works. If you allow somebody the right to cross your land in a certain place on a regular basis, after a while everybody thinks it's a public path. Sooner or later, it becomes a public path, and you've lost control of that part of your land."

"Does the law really work like that?"

"Believe me, these farmers know a lot about the law. To hear them talk in the public room after a few strong ales, you'd think they know more than the advocators. In fact, I think some of them do. Several of them advocate for themselves, you know. The argumentative ones who end up in the assizes every year or so. They come back here, get drunk and re-run the whole trial over again. Whether they win or lose." She grinned. "And sometimes the winner and the loser show up at the same time and they start the problem all over again."

She pulled him into the public room and cocked her head at the ale barrel. When he nodded, she went to pull him a half-mug. "So how did your part of the meeting go?" She sat opposite him at the window table. "Pretty good, I guess?"

"Yes, it did. I shouldn't have worried about them not listening. They do bow to my expertise," he grinned wryly, "as long as my ideas don't stub into their toes."

"Told you they would."

"Guess I should have listened. I'm just not used to putting myself forward to a bunch of people."

"Well, learn to, my husband." She slapped him on the shoulder, left her hand there and kneaded the muscle. "I have a feeling it's going to happen a whole lot more."

He took a deep pull from his mug. "I don't know if I like that idea."

"New challenges, husband. Keep you from gettin' bored." She slapped his shoulder harder. "And keep you out from under my feet. Can't do better than that."

* * *

Zoysana and Tadeo arrived in late afternoon the next day: their faces drawn, their mounts stumbling with weariness. Hearing the fast-moving hooves, Jhanes was out to greet them.

"Lady Zoysana, we expected you yesterday."

Her answering smile was forced. "We got delayed but we made up by moving faster afterwards. That's one advantage to being light; the horses last longer. We used two sets to get here. Treat these boys well. They've done their duty."

Patu stood like the horses, head down, suffering from the heat in his shedding winter coat. They all laughed as he ducked his head up past the ears in the horse trough, then shook water all over the courtyard.

"I hope you left some in there for the horses!"

"No worry, my Lady. We'll have plenty out of the well soon enough." Jhanes handed the reins of her horse to little Frey. He had appeared the moment Zoysana rode in, anxious to do something to help his idol. There was no risk to the lad, with the horse too tired to do more than plod.

The soldier hauled several buckets up and refilled the trough, allowing the horses a short drink, but no more. "Road's getting dry."

She nodded. "Positively dusty in spots. Freight wagons will be moving."

"Several passed through. You'll have seen them."

"We talked briefly. The traders are happy with the new rules. None of the lords have asked for tolls, and the merchants have been very generous with their prices in response. These are smart men and they know how to make a good bargain in the long run."

"And any who aren't smart enough to give good deals will find they can't sell anything because the prices will be down."

"Jhanes, you're turning into a man of commerce."

"Among other things."

She turned to him, her face serious. "I hear tales of you, up and down the road. You have gained a reputation – well deserved, I gather."

"I'm not exactly happy with all this. I never wanted to be a hero." He shrugged. "I don't mind, I guess, if it keeps the bandits away."

She grinned and clapped him on the back as they headed for the inn doorway. "Don't worry. I have news on that front as well. Tell you about it later." Then they were inside greeting Sarha, and the bustle of unpacking gave way to the business of eating.

Jhanes couldn't help but notice that while Zoysana was mostly cheerful, lauding his deeds and laughing about Talia's adventures, there were moments when she was thoughtful, as if something serious nagged at the back of her mind.

When the table was cleared, Zoysana looked around. "Is it possible to close the inn early tonight? We need a private talk, and there isn't much time." Her glance included Sarha. "I'm glad to see the situation so organized here, because we have other things to worry about."

It didn't take long for the few local customers to drift out. They were flattered that the famous lady who was the king's agent had come to consult with their innkeeper.

When they were gone, Zoysana asked Sarha to fill up the mugs. They filed into her conference room and found seats around the table.

"First, here's to your people, Jhanes. They have acquitted themselves well and have proved once again that the Free Counties can take care of themselves."

"With a bit of help." Tadeo spoke seldom, but it was always to the point.

Zoysana grinned as she lowered her mug. "That was my second toast. Here's to our redoubtable Innkeeper, who turned the tide single-handedly."

They all raised their drinks, as did Jhanes, his face hot.

"Don't be shy, man. You did a marvellous job, both here and on the road. I can also see the improvements you have made to the defences of the town. Good thoughts."

"I had a great deal of help there, especially from anyone who held a weak spot in the fight." He grinned. "Like the smith. He is very enthused about anything that does a better job than a cart at blocking his alley."

They all laughed, but Zoysana spoke seriously. "The king is now aware of this situation and he is concerned, in spite of your success. New trade will attract new trouble. Better-organized and better-equipped bandits will show up as word gets around. It is not enough to have the villages safe. The roads must be safe as well.

"The coffers of the realm are not exactly overflowing at the moment, but Gerth is counting on better times to come and is willing to take a financial risk to ensure they come soon. So he is going to increase the patrols on this road. The Warlanders on either side of us will be expected to cover their portions, but it is too far from the castle for soldiers to march all the way here and back. Besides, they spend too much time marching through areas that are the responsibility of the landowners.

"The solution is to have a post somewhere in the Free Counties. Somewhere central. A place with local resources to provide food, with an existing organization so that everything can be set up quickly and with little disturbance."

She smiled around the table. "Somewhere like here."

There was a moment's silence as Jhanes and Sarha took this in.

"What will this mean, my Lady?"

"Please, Jhanes, none of this 'my Lady'. What it will mean is that a new barracks will be constructed here and small garrison set up."

"Under their own officers, though? They won't be answering to me."

Zoysana eyed him a brief, piercing moment. "Their officers will liaise with you, as representative of the local militias."

He frowned. "Why me?"

Her eyebrows shot up.

"Is it official? Am I the representative of the militias?"

"Look around." She held up her hands. "Do you see anyone else with your training and abilities?"

"I suppose."

She nodded. "That's what the king is expecting. I told him you would do it. I wasn't wrong, was I?"

Jhanes kept his sigh to himself. "No, no, I'm the one, I suppose." He forced his mind to the task at hand. "How many men? What kind of services do we have to provide for them?"

"Twenty soldiers, plus their officers and a few auxiliary personnel."

He calculated. "That means about thirty new people in the village."

"Unless some of them have women with them."

He shook his head. The economics of the whole thing astounded him. "We must tell the local farmers. There is still time to plant more food crops." He grinned. "I'll put in a larger supply of cheap liquor." Then he became serious. "I assume our smith, carpenter, and others will have more business. They'll want to prepare for it."

"I knew your input would be valuable. If the farmers want to sell any timber for the new building, they must have it drying right away."

"How soon will the troops arrive?"

"Next quarter."

They gaped at her. "Next quarter? That gives us almost no time for preparation."

"They can live under canvas for the summer. The officers will take over this room at the start, I suspect. How soon can you have your addition to the inn ready?"

"The plans are all made. Only this little dust-up with the bandits stopped me from beginning. Three quarters should see it done if we push. Maybe a month."

She nodded. "With these new circumstances, you may want to adjust your schedule. Unfortunately, I won't be here to help."

Now it comes. "Why not?"

Zoysana shook her head. "Things look very good on the northern front. Trade is increasing, everything is settling down quickly after the Troubles. In the South, it's not so good."

"The Inari. I was just telling Sarha the other day."

She nodded. "It was a poor winter on the high prairie. Much colder than here, with more snow."

The soldier suppressed a shudder. A cold winter up on the windswept steppes. Even a normal cold season was bad enough, with the cruel wind probing every corner of the tent, and if heavy snowfall hid the dung they used for fuel... He wrenched himself from his memories as Zoysana continued.

"Their herds did not winter well, and I have been doing some research in the archives. When the Inari have a tough winter, the raids always increase. So I sent out some feelers. They didn't all get back, but those that did say they couldn't get close to any of the tribes. That in itself is a warning. There is also word that they are grouped in a huge multiple-clan camp near the Barrier instead of spreading out over the land as they usually do in the spring. Nor are the new Fighters out on their usual spring raiding. Bad signs, all of them."

"So what does the king plan?" He listened, a sinking feeling in his gut, as Zoysana laid out her ideas.

"He hasn't made up his mind, what with the lack of information. That's one thing he learned from Barent." A shadow crossed her face, and she paused. "First you need information. Then you gather together a lot of different ideas. When the time for action comes, you can improvise."

"So he needs more information, and you're going to get it."

She smiled at him, but there was little joy in her face. "For a simple footsoldier, you certainly know your tactics. I'm not looking forward to the job, but it is best that I go. Our other guides don't cope very well up there on the steppes. Our men are good, but they are used to trees, forest and mountains. This restricts them to the foothills. When they hit the prairie, their skills do not help."

"And yours will?"

"No. I don't plan to stay hidden. I'm going to ride right into the camps as Gerth's emissary. We calculate that as the only way to get to these people. If we can deal with the leaders, perhaps we can offer aid, keep them alive without them coming to take what they need."

"Forget that."

She stared at him. "Pardon me?"

"They won't take aid. Especially from a stranger. Weakness is death to them. They take what they want. If you aren't strong enough to stop them, you deserve to die."

"We discussed that. I still have to try."

"How big a party?"

"Just Tadeo and myself."

He nodded. "That might work. They admire courage. They would never take advantage of you. If anyone wants to kill you, it will be in the open Circle in a one-on-one fight. Who is your interpreter?"

"That problem we haven't solved. We hope to find someone before we leave the castle. There are traders who speak Inari."

His heart sank. *What can I say? Why did it have to be now?*

"Well? What is it, man?" Zoysana frowned. "I can see you're not happy. Don't just sit there, tell us."

He looked around. All three of them were staring at him. "It won't work. Those traders only speak Chinotuk. Used to be called Tradespeak around here years ago, but nobody uses it anymore. The Inari won't talk serious politics in Chinotuk. It's a trading language, and they look down on traders. They trade among themselves: weapons, horses, breeding livestock. But that's more like a sport, though they take it very seriously. They disdain those who make a living at trading. They deal with them out of necessity, but they consider them a lower class.

"The Inari have a tricky oral tradition, and their diplomatic language is full of conventions and traps, highly dependent on a sense of irony. You dare not trust one of their people to interpret for you, because the word-for-word translation may mean something completely different from the intent. You need one of your own people who speaks Inarituk."

Zoysana took a moment to think, then turned her face full to Jhanes. "And that person is you? You speak this Inarituk language?"

He shot a glance, then a full look at his new wife. "I'm sorry, Sarha."

She was mute, unmoving, and he knew what was going through her mind. *Only three days respite from the last time of worry, and now...?*

Zoysana touched the other woman's hand. "I know it's a difficult sacrifice, Sarha, but if he can help in any way, he could save hundreds of lives. Thousands, perhaps. I do not exaggerate when I say that Gerth and Torey have considered the possibility of the tribes attacking en masse, with the

150

intention of overrunning the whole area. This is a crucial moment in our kingdom's affairs, and we must do our best to nudge the balance our way."

There was no argument from Sarha, only a lowering of her head to stare at her calloused hands on the table in front of her.

Jhanes felt walls closing in around him.

With a final glance in the woman's direction, Zoysana turned to Jhanes. "This all comes as a surprise to me. I think we need to backtrack into your personal history. I need to know the abilities of those I work with."

"Not much to tell." He took a deep breath. "My family was poor, took the risk of farming up in the foothills of the Barrier. My father trapped to make ends meet. The year I was eight, there was a poor winter over the mountains, and the Inari came south in larger numbers to see what they could pick up. What they picked up was me. I was taken over the Barrier, kept as a slave until I was big and tough enough to make my own way. It's a rough life up on the steppes and they don't care where you come from, slave or not, if you're a worthy addition to a hunt or a war party. It took extra work on my part, because I had no older family members to train me. But I managed, and once I grew, my size helped, at least in the fighting. Not so much in the woodcraft."

He grinned. "In fact, my adult name, translated from Inari, means something like 'Hidden Twig.' As I said, they have a great sense of irony."

"And are you willing to go with us?"

"I must, Lady Zoysana. Unless you can come up with a better interpreter, your mission has little chance of succeeding. The only other way you could succeed is by challenging every Fighter they have in one-to-one combat and working your way up to the leaders. Beat all of them and they might listen to you."

She nodded grimly. "We had considered that possibility."

He shook his head. "I have great respect for your abilities, but they are a ferocious people. It would only need one of them to be lucky, once."

"I know. It would make a great deal of difference if you could come. The fact that we didn't realize how much we need you shows how much we need you, if you follow my meaning." She smiled wanly. Then her eyes turned to Sarha again.

Sarha raised her head. "Don't all of you be lookin' at me like that. Sometimes we got choices and sometimes we don't. I can't see that any of us has a choice, here. None of us likes it, but none of us is backin' down." She had her own unhappy version of a smile. "After all, I'll be sitting back here in civilization protected by twenty new soldiers an' makin' a fortune off their drinkin' habits while you're up over the Barrier risking your lives every day. I'd be a poor person to complain."

Zoysana's eyes lit up. "I knew I chose the right people. Don't worry; we won't be risking our lives every day. Only once or twice when it counts the most."

The soldier laughed. "The Inari are going to like you."

"That's probably important."

"Oh, yes. If they like you a lot and fear you a little, you've got it fixed before you start."

"Well, we'll have to work on that."

"So when do we head south?"

"I have to go to Cdeile tomorrow to talk to Lord Feister, let him know he will soon have a regiment of soldiers on his doorstep. Not that he isn't expecting it, but it's good manners to reassure him that it's not on his account. I'll be back the next night. We can talk to your local people then. If that's all, I hope we can leave the rest of the business in Sarha's capable hands and start back immediately."

"Is there that much of a rush?"

"Gerth doesn't like a lack of information, and neither do I."

"Especially where the Inari are concerned."

"Exactly."

"You'll want to rest up tonight, then. Your rooms are ready."

"Then we'll make it an early night."

"And an early breakfast tomorrow?"

"Your very best, Sarha. We have a long ride, and our horses are tired."

The soldier had a thought. "Take mine. The bay mare's fresh, and Lord Feister will be pleased to see we're taking good care of her. The old gelding's a plodder, but he's in better shape than either of yours. Don't know what I'm doing with two horses, anyway."

"That would help. Thanks, Jhanes. I'm not thinking as straight as I should be."

"A night's sleep will fix that."

"I could use it." She stumbled as she rose but was moving again before Tadeo could help her. From the way he took the stairs, he wasn't in much better condition, and Jhanes hoped they would get a day or two of rest somewhere before they challenged the Barrier Range and the Inari on the steppes beyond.

He turned to Sarha, still sitting at the table, her shoulders slumped. Words tumbled through his head, but none of them would solve anything. He laid a hand on her shoulder, but when she didn't respond he patted her twice and stumbled up the stairs, leaving her staring at her hands in the dim common room.

13. PRELUDE TO BATTLE

Zoysana and Tadeo's horses were in fine fettle when the three riders pulled out of the village, having enjoyed five days of rest. Jhanes felt guiltier and lonelier each stride they took away from the inn. And Zoysana...worried him.

She had been on the road most of every day, but somehow she kept going. Just when it looked as if she really needed to rest, she would dig down into her hidden reserves of strength and move on, faster even, and sometimes with a smile. The only difference the soldier could see was that her face was thinner and the cords and muscles showed more starkly under her skin. Patu looked gaunt, too, his hide tight along his ribs, his belly curved inward. He ate more than ever and never flagged in his steady pace beside her horse.

Jhanes regarded Tadeo, but he could see no difference. The slim, dark man still showed his even temper and quiet strength, and a youthful grin sometimes softened his features. The Inari would say they were a pair to cross the mountains with. He hoped they considered him in the same light, because they were about to cross some very tough mountains.

They passed Lady Talia's carriage – standing forlorn and askew on the village green in Tsalk – and reminded the local people to leave it alone. A reminder from Zoysana was stronger than an order from one of the nobility, and they had little worry that it would be bothered. As for stealing it, who would try? It could hardly be transported, let alone hidden or used.

As the trip continued, Jhanes became torn between his feeling that Zoysana needed rest and his desire to prove himself to his new companions. For this latter reason, he could not hold them back, yet he didn't know quite how to handle the matter otherwise. Finally, she solved the problem for him.

They were just starting out from Tsalk when she motioned Tadeo to ride ahead and swung her pony in beside the soldier's big steed. "So what's bothering you?"

He looked down at her in surprise. "Bothering me, my Lady?"

"Don't go all formal on me, Jhanes. Are you still thinking too much about Sarha?"

"No, Lady Zoe. I think of her, but not enough to bother me."

"But something is bothering you."

He sighed. "It is. I don't know quite how to handle this because I don't know you well enough. If you were an officer in the mercenaries, I wouldn't feel bad about speaking up. But with you, it's different. I don't know how, but different…"

She frowned up at him. "Well, Jhanes, if you want to treat me like an officer and that makes you comfortable, then why don't you? I can't stand riding along with someone who has a thorn in his blanket."

He looked down at her and grinned. "This is not a time to be making any mistakes. You can't get up here to bite my head off, but you'll find something you can reach, I'm sure."

She sighed and passed a hand over her face. "I'm sorry, Jhanes. I think I've been on the road too long."

He nodded. "And that's what's bothering me."

Startled, she looked up at him. "What do you mean? You haven't been on the road three days yet."

"No, but you have. I don't know you that well, but if you were anyone else, I'd say you were strung pretty thin at the moment. When we get into the Barrier Range, I want you in top shape. In my opinion, Lady Zoysana, you need a rest." *There. I've said it.* A small part of his mind wondered how bad it was going to be.

She rode along for a while, looking straight between her pony's ears. "Is it that obvious?"

"Not to someone who didn't know you before, perhaps, but…well, hold out your arm."

With a puzzled frown, she did so.

"Look at the muscles."

She regarded her arm for a moment, turning it slightly. Then she nodded. "I'm in good shape."

"Too good."

Her face turned puzzled. "How can you be in too good shape?"

"I've seen it before. You're strung up tight, stretched out hard. It happens to soldiers in the middle of a long campaign. You may be in top fighting form but you have lower reserves, both in the flesh and the mind. About that time, you stop thinking and just fight, or march, or dig, or whatever needs to be done. It's not the condition you want to be in when you meet the Inari."

"No, that's true. I need to be rested, thinking straight." She rode along for a while. "I'll just have to make time, I guess. I know Gerth wants us to get up there as soon as possible, in case there's a real attack coming." She held up a hand before he could speak, and grinned up at him. "Don't say it. There's no use going up there in poor shape and making mistakes. That would be worse than not going. Thank you for your advice, Jhanes. It was good, as it always is. I will do my best to follow it."

"That would be a pleasant change." The voice floated back from where Tadeo rode ahead, close enough to hear their conversation.

"Tadeo, the soldier says I'm stretched pretty tight right now."

He turned in the saddle, regarded her seriously. "Is that a threat, my Lady?"

She smiled sweetly. "No, Tadeo, it's just a statement of fact. Information you might find useful in keeping your head on your shoulders."

Jhanes chuckled. "I think Lady Zoe needs to relax."

Tadeo pushed his horse farther ahead. "I always agree with the expert."

"What does she do to relax, Tadeo?"

The dark face flashed a white smile. "She fights."

"What?" He looked down at the round face beside him.

She shrugged. "He's right. I don't really do anything that relaxes me more than a serious training session."

"Oh."

"But it's a good idea."

"It is?"

"Oh, yes. I've been too tired to train lately, and that's not good for me. We'll have a sparring session when we stop for the night."

He shook his head. "That's not the kind of rest I had in mind."

"We'll just stop early, then, shall we? We've made good time today."

He sighed. "Lady Zoe, I don't have to remind you that you're the leader. We'll do whatever you say."

She grinned, straightened her back. "That's one advantage I have over the Inari. At least my troops do what they're told."

* * *

King Gerth laid his hands flat on the War Room table and gazed around at the select group sitting there. "Let me set this plan out. Zoe, with the help of Tadeo and Jhanes, will head straight into the Inari main camp. No hiding, no subterfuge. If she handles herself right, they will treat her as a visiting dignitary. She will then present our ideas to their leaders. If everything goes well, she will make initial deals with them to trade our meat and metal goods for their raw metal ores and furs. Once she has broken the ice, our traders will then be able to approach the tribes with their own deals. Have I stated it about right?"

Zoysana nodded. "If all goes well, that's what we hope."

157

Gerth looked around the table. Then his eyes swept back to the soldier, rested there a moment. "I don't see any enthusiasm, Jhanes. What have we missed?"

Getting no response, the young king grinned. "Feel free to speak up, man. At least you're big enough that I can't knock you down."

The soldier returned the king's smile, but he was gathering his thoughts. This was the point that so many intelligent people missed in their understanding of the Inari.

"It's their way of leading, your Majesty. Here in Petrella, you are the king. If you make an agreement, your people will honour that agreement. If you say a thing is to be done, it is done."

Gerth smiled wryly. "At least in theory. In practice, I have found I have to be careful what I ask for."

Jhanes nodded. "With the Inari, it is even more so. A man becomes a leader through his reputation: fighting skill, bravery, intelligence, and success. In any given situation, a different man may lead. Even in a war party, different leaders might take over at different times. So you can't set up a deal with any one person and expect it to hold for everyone else. All you can do is present them with an idea and let them make up their own minds."

Zoysana frowned. "Does it work that way within each clan as well? Isn't that very difficult?"

"In practice, it is simpler. Normally, no member of a clan would dare to question any specific decision by the Clan Leader, or Potentara. To do so, he would have to challenge the Potentara's – we don't have a word for it – Designated Fighter, I suppose. Since the Designated Fighter is the best in the clan, the challenger would end up dead."

Gerth's eyes narrowed. "That sounds like the Clan Leader can give an order, and everyone must obey."

"Yes, but not always. He can't order the whole clan to do something they don't want to do. They just won't do it. They won't follow him and all at once he won't be the leader. So he won't make a decision that goes too much against his people."

"But on a day-to-day basis, the Clan Leader makes the decisions and everyone toes the line?"

"With the help of the other elders."

Gerth nodded. "Then what causes the big problems?"

"It's only when someone wants to change his status in the clan that things get rough. Then they can get very rough."

"Someone dies?"

"Yes, and if someone makes a mistake of protocol, if the dead man's supporters feel slighted, it can get ugly."

"A feud."

"That's right, your Majesty. Which is why Clan Leaders are respected. If they have the wisdom to keep everything balanced, the clan prospers. If they give way to favouritism, greed, or stupidity, the clan suffers. Clans have been known to split up."

Lady Kenna had not spoken until now. However, the moment she opened her mouth, all eyes were on her, as if everyone had been waiting for her opinion. "So we cannot influence these people by normal political means. Power comes through personal reputation, so we must impress them."

"We must, my Lady."

"Which brings us full circle to Zoysana's plan. What do you think of it?"

"I think it has the best chance of succeeding, my Lady."

"Gerth?"

He shrugged, grinned. "I think she's impressive." His smile disappeared, and he turned back to Jhanes. "How do the Inari see a woman's status?"

"Not easy to pin down, your Majesty. Since women don't usually fight, they can't have a reputation in the Circle. This limits them. There is a Wise Woman who keeps the lore, but she is a historian, not a leader. An intelligent woman, though, can get a reputation for astute advice or good planning and she will be followed. As I said, they follow the person who has the best chance for success."

"Are there any female fighters?"

"They can all fight. Usually, the women are archers. That way they can protect the camp, fighting on foot. They also train with their own weapons: poles, knives, buckets."

Gerth laughed. "Now that I'd like to see! How do you fight with a bucket?"

Jhanes smiled. "It's very dark inside a tent, coming from bright sunlight outside. Many an invader has had a bucket over his head and a skinning knife working on his guts before he knew what hit him."

Gerth nodded soberly. "You don't have to tell us they are formidable fighters. We get plenty of evidence for that in the raids every year."

He raised his head, slammed his fist on the table. "God's seven curses, that's why we have to find a way to end this. We could probably beat them in a head-to-head battle, but I don't want the chance. We'd be much better off making trading partners of them. When our people came down off the steppes so long ago, we left behind wonderful sources of iron and copper."

There was a series of nods around the table.

"All right, then. Let's get going. Zoysana, Jhanes and Tadeo, there's a lot resting on you. We all have confidence in your ability to handle it."

The three glanced grimly at each other, looking for the same confidence in themselves.

14. THE INARI CAMP

The party of three sat their horses and surveyed the huge tent camp stretching along the banks of the river as far as the eye could discern through the haze of dust and campfire smoke. Jhanes breathed it all in, the memories crowding over him.

Then he broke from his reverie to regard his companions. "From this moment, I'm in charge. As we discussed, Lady Zoysana, you remain aloof. You don't talk to anyone; make no responses. If anyone presumes to even touch your robe, kill him, as quickly and openly as possible. I'm serious. If you are to act like a Clan Potentara, and they will deal with no one of lesser rank, you must act this way. Take your cues from me.

"Tadeo, I'm sorry, but from now on, you're a slave. You do what you're told; don't speak until spoken to. If you break any rules, I will hit you. I'm sure you'll have no problem rolling with the blow, but don't duck too successfully or I'll have to hit you again. No Potentara would ever travel without a slave. However, the Potentara's slave must be a ferocious fighter. If someone offends you, so much as steps in your path, look to me if you can for a signal. If you can't, kill him anyway. Better yet, put him on the ground without using a weapon. That will send a message, and incidentally a serious insult, to his clan."

"Is an insult wise at this point?" Zoysana was still regarding the camp, a frown marring her smooth features.

"By interfering with your slave, the offender has offered grave insult to you. The only response is a similar insult. The offender's clan will then decide what reply to make. Then the Clan Council will decide if the response is warranted. Our advantage is that this must all be done in the open, by the rule, and under the strict control of the Council of Potentaras. They will be careful in their choice of ways to test us. Since we are all confident in our abilities in this respect, we should pass the tests. Believe me, the tests will happen, and someone will die. Let's make sure it isn't us."

He took a moment to look each of his companions in the eye. "We have been trailed by their scouts for the last day, and we are under even closer scrutiny from here on in, by a people who train their whole lives in the Arts of War. They learn to note the slightest change in stance, the first tense muscle that shows fear. Remember, any show of weakness will be fatal."

He nodded towards two figures standing in front of them "It's about to start. They've known we were coming for two days now. It looks like they're going to let us do what we want, watch us and learn as much as they can from what we do.

"They will force us to work our own way up to the leaders. We are being tested at several levels. What we have here is an unofficial reception committee. A couple of young hotheads who wish to prove themselves before we get caught up in the formalities, when they'd never get a chance. I hope they're smart ones."

He dismounted and tossed his reins to Tadeo, not looking to see if he caught them. "Take care of the horses. You don't ride into camp. That's an insult, too."

He strode forward as if to ignore the two boys. When he got close enough to see the colours on their vests, he halted and gave a correct and formal greeting. *Aguilana and Espolo: an interesting combination.* He allowed the boys one degree more in age and rank than they probably deserved. *That should be enough to salve their pride.*

The two confronting him paused only a moment. The one on the right, the Aguilana with the plain vest and the worn moccasins, brought his hand out, palm up and empty, in a deliberate gesture of acceptance. But the other, the large one with the fancy Espolo beading and the fringed leggings, started to raise his hand, glanced at his companion, then dropped it. A sneer crossed his handsome face.

"The foreigner speaks with a strange accent."

Jhanes reached out and took the young man by the neck. He twisted, there was a snapping sound and the body dropped to the side in the dust. Regaining his stride, he spoke to the remaining lad. "My Potentara will be pleased with me, that I found courtesy in the Clan of the Aguilana. She would be honoured to speak with the Clan Leader whose following includes such a wise young Fighter."

The boy's eyes widened, but he contained himself as he walked alongside the larger man. Jhanes could see the thoughts whirling as he tried to find words for a question that could not be taken the wrong way. He took refuge in ceremony. "I am Mantinello, of the Aguilana Clan. I would be pleased to offer the *boal* and *aaruul* to your Potentara. Would your Leader be the woman, small in stature but subtle in movement, who walks with the Balagueratu?"

The soldier smiled inside. He had hoped someone would bring up the old tales of the Balagueratu, or Grandfather Wolf. "The young Fighter has exceeded his training in the eye-before-hand."

A pleased red suffused the boy's face. He was not more than sixteen winters, the down on his cheeks undarkened. "Please, sir, it is nothing to note that you, yourself move with the gait of one fully trained in the Circle. Perhaps elsewhere as well. One need only to know this, and your Leader's lack of tension shouts her training to the world."

His voice lowered. "I cannot help but notice that your servant moves..." He glanced up at the soldier's face and froze.

"I have overstepped, sir. If you wish your servant to meet me in the Circle to chastize me, I will oblige, although not willingly. I would not be seen as causing disharmony, merely to create opportunity for advancement."

The soldier paused, then walked on slowly, allowing the boy time to catch up. "I am going to enjoy meeting the Clan Leader of such a Fighter. Surely such wisdom must come from a Great Potentara." *Let's see how honest he is.*

The boy's face fell. "I am sorry, sir, to disagree. My family is a smaller clan. If your Leader wishes to meet with the Great Potentaras, I will lead you to the tents of their clans. The only reason I was here to greet her as well was because my unfortunate friend Rabos, of the Espolo Clan, chose to come."

Jhanes considered, then made an undiplomatic decision. "Then do you withdraw your offer of hospitality?"

"Oh, not at all, sir. I would not present your Leader with such disrespect. I feel that it is my duty to my esteemed guest to offer her all the options that she might choose. My father would be honoured to meet her and offer his hospitality, humble as it might be."

It would be a true pleasure to meet the man who sired this diplomat. "So we are greeted by the son of the Clan Potentara. My Leader would be pleased to join you for *boal* and *aaruul*."

Mantinello nodded soberly, but Jhanes noted the sparkle in his eye. *The lad is taking a risk, but a calculated one.* His impetuous and now dead friend had interpreted the situation in a different light. He had seen it as an opportunity to raise his personal status by killing a stranger. This boy had seen it as an opportunity to bring status to his clan, if these visitors turned out to be important. If they were unimportant or caused a problem, then his clan might lose out. *So the risk is taken, and now the boy has a full stake in seeing that all goes well. Ally number one.*

While they were talking, they had intruded between the first few tents of the great camp. Escorted as they were, no one came near them, although a crowd began to gather and follow at a prudent distance. Small children and big dogs swirled in a wide circle around them, though the dogs were not putting up their usual challenge. One smell of Patu was enough. He stalked along at his mistress's side: ugly, dignified, powerful.

There was a flash in his peripheral vision, and he heard the sound of Zoysana snapping her fingers. Glancing over, he caught Tadeo in the act of lifting a small boy by the nape of the neck.

"He tried to touch her robe. What do I do with him?"

"It's a game they play. Give him back to his mother."

Tadeo looked around, then strolled over to a distraught woman, placing the boy firmly in front of her. Then he flicked the child's nose with one finger, grinned, and resumed his place, picking up the reins of the horses and following.

"My cousin is too brave for his own good."

The soldier nodded. "My mistress is forgiving of children."

"He would be angry to hear that. He does not consider himself a child."

"I am sorry, Mantinello. He will learn, or he will die."

"I greatly fear the latter."

There was genuine regret in the lad's voice. The Inari loved the children who survived, and as long as they did not flagrantly break the rules of society, indulged them. The environment they lived in was harsh enough. Tadeo's actions had gained them more allies. The truly confident do not fight with children.

"Trouble coming." Jhanes spoke quietly in Petrellan, although the tone of his voice warned his escort as well. From his superior height, the soldier had seen a small knot of Fighters waiting in the middle of the path between the tents. Mantinello stiffened.

"Eye before hand, my new friend. Observation before action."

The boy, calmed by the words of the Training Circle, moved forward more easily. Six young men, all older than Mantinello, awaited the approaching party with wary but determined looks.

The youth who stepped forward was about twenty, taller than most, with finely embroidered leggings and shirt. His pose was superior and unbending. "Greetings, Fighter of the Aguilana Clan. What business brings you through the tents of the Pregotas?"

"Greetings, Pregota Fighters. I am escorting important guests to my Clan Leader's tent. The route, I believe, is open to all, though it does, in truth, pass through the tents of the honoured Pregota Clan."

Don't lay it on too thick, lad. The confidence of strength is the path, here.

The Pregota youth spoke with condescending and elaborate courtesy. "If these guests are so important, perhaps they should be directed to the tents of a Great Potentara, such as my father?"

Mantinello's back stiffened. Jhanes slid into the "full relax" pose of the Circle, hoping the boy would take the hint. Sure enough, the back relaxed, and the lad shot him a grateful glance.

"That would be a choice, which our visitor has been offered. However, she has exhibited a specific desire to meet with my father."

A sneer twisted the handsome young face. "She? You bring a woman and call her an important guest?"

"Tadeo, I need you."

Before Jhanes finished speaking, the slim man was at his side. He spoke Petrellan in even, conversational tones. "Kill this one. Kill him quick and obvious the moment I snap my fingers." He turned to the boy at his side and spoke in Inarituk, matching the tone of overdone courtesy.

"I apologize for interrupting our conversation, my host, but I must request your permission to have my servant deal with this intrusion."

Before the boy could finish his nod, Jhanes snapped his fingers. He had worked with the two Kyabrans in practice, but even so the speed of the attack shocked him. Tadeo was back at his side before the body hit the ground, blood pouring from an opened throat. The soldier spoke evenly to his Inari escort as Tadeo calmly turned his back and picked up the reins again.

"Perhaps your good friends of the Pregota Clan would escort us to your tents. These small misunderstandings become tedious."

"Yes, I'm sure they would love to oblige."

Stepping around the body in its pool of blood, the party moved on. Without a word, the five remaining Pregota youths fanned out ahead. There were no further incidents.

Their escort dropped back as they turned off on a smaller path where a stream trickled down into the river. The Aguilana Clan encampment was separate from the other tents, but in a pleasant spot upwind of the rest of the camp. Perhaps not a large or powerful clan, but well off, by the decoration on the tents.

Before their escort departed, Jhanes spoke to them directly. "Thank you for helping us avoid unnecessary disturbance in the Tribe. Please inform your Potentara that my Leader considers the insult sufficiently amended." The lads looked shocked at this, but their Leader, if he had any brains at all, should be happy to be let off with the loss of one hotheaded son. When the results of an insult could be so serious, only the stupidest people, or the wiliest, chose to break etiquette.

Mantinello led them into the Aguilana camp. "If you would enter my father's poor tent, your horses will be taken care of. You may wish refreshment after your morning's ride."

They passed into the cool interior of the felt-lined tent, to sit on embroidered rugs where servants were already pouring honey-sweetened *boal* into bone cups. The soldier was overwhelmed by a wave of aromas and memories, the conflicting emotions they aroused covered by the ceremony of their entry. He bore down mentally, forcing the feelings into the background, concentrating on the present situation.

Their coming was expected. Their host apologized for leaving them, saying he must report to his father. Doubtless they had things to talk about in private.

"What did he say, that last bit? It obviously had something to do with us."

Jhanes grinned and repeated the message. "He's a born diplomat, that one."

"Seems to be. So we've killed two already. How are we doing?"

Jhanes explained the situation as well as he could. "...the youngsters are in an aggressive mood. I suppose it's because they weren't allowed to go raiding this spring."

"So you chose to ally yourself with a smaller, less influential clan, and risked insulting a Great Potentara. An interesting course of action."

"I know, Lady Zoysana. I'm not sure myself why I did it. It just seemed right. I hope it was my Inari training taking over. They appreciate loyalty, don't like opportunists. Also, you notice that we have made contact directly with a Potentara. In a larger clan, that might not have happened."

"We'll have to see. The boy seems young but confident. Moves well when he's relaxed."

"He said the same about you."

They all laughed.

"By the way, it isn't safe to assume that no one here speaks our language. Some slaves do, for sure. So we had better not say anything we don't want passed on."

She nodded. "Standard trader's precautions."

They were interrupted by the return of their host, bringing with him an older man, his skin wrinkled and weather-scarred, but his back straight and his hands firm.

"My son speaks highly of the intelligence and ease with which his guests handle themselves. I am Terenno of the Aguilana Clan, and I am honoured and intrigued to entertain such folk."

The soldier rose. "I am Jhanes, of Petrella. My Leader is Zoysana of Petrella and Kyabra. Her servant, Tadeo, is of Kyabran heritage as well."

The Leader nodded. Solemnly lifting a plate upon which were spread four small balls of *aaruul*, he presented the ceremonial food to each, then sat on a cushion no more ornate than the others. "And how was the winter, north of the Barrier?" He used the Inari term for the mountains, which translated as something like "End of the World".

Jhanes crunched down on the cheese ball, savouring the sharp tang of mare's milk and the memories it brought. Once again he had to force his concentration back to the present question. This would be nothing the Inari didn't already know. "It has been a good winter, if any winter can be called good. Because of our recent Troubles, there was little seed grain left, but it is all planted now and in the hands of the Weather Gods. The herds were thin last fall, but most have survived the time of famine. Slim times, my Host, but better times ahead."

"You speak with confidence of better times. Has your king made a bargain with the Weather Gods? Such bargains often turn out like a sunny spring morning, with thunderclouds in the afternoon."

"Excuse me, sir, while I make your words known to my Leader. She does not have the advantage of the Inari tongue." At the man's nod, he translated.

"Why is this clan so well off, if they are small?"

"The Aguilana deal with traders, as I recall. See all the bronze around the tent? That comes over the mountains."

Zoysana thought a moment, then smiled at their host. "So their status suffers, but those who watch them prosper must give them their due. Fine. Tell him about the trading."

Jhanes mirrored her smile on the Potentara. "My Leader assures me that King Gerth has no more influence with the Gods of Rain and Wind than any other man. His hopes for future prosperity rest on trade."

The old horse-trader's glance flicked to Zoysana and back, but his face remained impassive. "You could explain this further, if it amused you."

Jhanes described the changes that were taking place north of the Barrier, including the influence of the Kyabrans. At the end of it, the Potentara nodded.

169

"So this woman, your Leader, is the perfect envoy. She represents both major powers that are moving the Northern World."

"That would be accurate, Leader."

"And my son says she must be a Fighter such as most have never seen, if her slave is so fearsome."

Jhanes translated, and Zoysana looked noncommittal. "I'm going to risk the truth here." He turned to the Inari.

"You understand, Terenno, that the Petrellans do not have slaves there in the North as we do south of the Barrier. However, Tadeo, a formidable warrior in his own right, is bound to her as Guard-of-Life, a term that does not translate well into Inari. Taken in literal translation, it might sound as if her life needed his protection." He smiled. "The Inari will appreciate the misleading quality of such a statement."

The older man chuckled. "I have heard of the demise of the Great Potentara Callar's most troublesome son. That Leader owes you a debt of gratitude which he will not admit aloud but which he must privately acknowledge. The lad was the son of his favourite wife, who took advantage of her status to indulge the boy. The father saw his mistake too late, and still loves the boy's mother, so what could he do? Something like this was bound to happen. It is good that the death was clean and in the popular view. There were many witnesses, and the insult was unforgivable. Your Leader is magnanimous to consider the matter closed so lightly."

"I thank you for the information, Clan Leader. As you know, we are new to this situation – all, that is, except myself – and are in need of guidance if we are to accomplish our mission." He translated this exchange to a pleased Zoysana before the Inari continued.

"We are not unaware, Hidden Twig, of your identity," the man smiled. "Your stature would be hard to conceal. While your departure years ago was understandable, yet there are some who felt betrayed. If you will accept more advice, you must make your peace with the Cerdana Clan. Otherwise, the disharmony there will cause the rest of the proceedings to move…less evenly."

Jhanes again thanked the man for his help, then translated for the others. "I agree with his analysis. I think I can handle it."

"You don't sound confident. What are your options?"

He thought a moment. "It all depends on who is influential in the clan, now. I had few enemies in my own group, and there are people I spent many enjoyable times with, now that I remember. I think I might still have allies." Memories sped unbidden across his mind. "Even friends, I suppose."

"Let's leave that, then." Zoysana sent an appraising glance at the other Potentara. "When do we broach our real mission?"

"Not here. We will only talk to the Council of Potentaras about that. They know why we have come. Let them make the moves. Sit back and enjoy the hospitality. We are among friends, here."

The conversation turned to other topics, such as the weather and the condition of the mountain trails and pastures. Jhanes was kept busy translating, sometimes wracking his brain for the appropriate expression to convey the intended meaning. He took an opportunity to pass along a compliment about the intelligent behaviour of the Leader's son. In spite of his trader's face, the man smiled, then became serious.

"You have done me a greater favour there than you know. I did not approve of my son's companionship." He raised a hand to still the boy's protest.

"Mantinello is known for his intelligence, and the Espolo lad used Mantinello's ideas to make himself look good, never giving credit. But he had leadership, and who can tell the young where to choose their friends? If my son comes out of these events with enough status to create his own following, it will be to his credit and to his greater good. I hope that Madana of the Espolo Clan is intelligent enough to understand, but he is one to think with his heart, not his head. There is where you will meet resistance in your negotiations, no matter what your intentions here."

It was as close to a request for information as they would ever hear, so Jhanes complied. "A man of your wide-ranging experience will recognize my Leader's objectives. Since they deal with trading, they should match with yours. Could you advise us on how to present them?"

"Straightforward is always best," the Potentara stood, "and I have monopolized your company long enough. The drama of your entry into our camps has achieved your aim. The other Leaders have had enough time to gather, but not enough time to reach any firm conclusions based on their lack of information. So it would be good to go to them now."

Needing no translation, they all rose. Outside the tent, Zoysana looked around. "We walk?"

Jhanes nodded. "It's considered poor manners to ride in camp unless necessary, and then only at a walk. Too much dust and too much chance of causing insult to someone on the ground. The Inari are very careful about seeming to place themselves higher than anyone else."

15. The Circle of Stones

So they walked. There was no need to change their clothes, as they had dressed in their best this morning before breaking camp. They penetrated to the centre of the huge encampment, on a wide, grassy area beside the river. In the middle of this field a circle was laid out with small white stones; a line of figures sat on embroidered cushions in a horseshoe shape, the opening towards the circle.

Their host led them to the mouth of the horseshoe with their backs to the circle and the river, then bowed and left them to take his place on a vacant cushion out near the end.

"Don't step into the circle."

"I can imagine why not." There was no disguising the rusty splotches that tinted the grass within the stones.

They marched into the horseshoe in their usual formation: the soldier in the lead to the right, Zoysana a bit left, and Tadeo in the centre rear. Patu walked where he chose. When Jhanes reached the focus of the assembly, he stopped.

"I am Jhanes, known to many of you as 'Hidden Twig'." It is many years since I have been among the tents of the Inari, and it gladdens my heart to see that your people have prospered since the time of my visit with you." He used forms of speech that accented his distance from them, to remind them that his stay had been involuntary. Hopefully, a lack of loyalty could be ruled out as a source of disharmony.

"I would like my friends among your people to know how successful I have been as a Fighter in the world Beyond the End of the World. The training I received from my Inari instructors has served me in good stead. You see me now as companion and thrall to one of the most respected Fighters in the whole Lower World: a trusted advisor and friend to King Gerth, the powerful monarch of Petrella, your trading partner over the

Barrier." Let every one of them that ever gave his wife a bronze comb think about that.

"My Leader, Zoysana, presents herself in friendship to the Potentaras of the Combined Clans of the Inari."

There was a moment of silence as the Leaders allowed his words a courteous moment for thought. Then a Potentara seated near the centre stood. *Only two removed from the Great Potentara himself. A good sign.*

"We welcome your Leader, Zoysana, who walks with the Grandfather of Wolves. It is interesting to see a legend come to life." The Grandfather of Wolves, who had been sitting, his ears pricked with interest, chose that moment to flop down on his belly and let out a great yawn. A chuckle arose from the horseshoe, although there were a few frowns in a well-dressed group close and to the left of the Great Potentara.

"I will speak briefly, so as not to bore you," the speaker grinned. "I am Nohedeya of the Verneta Clan. We do not often see your people south of the Barrier unless we invite them, as you are aware."

Jhanes was aware. He gritted his teeth and relaxed his body, knowing he was being tested.

"Especially not important ones such as yourself and your Leader, Zoysana. What honour brings you to us?"

He translated quickly to Zoysana.

"Get right to the point, don't they?"

He grinned. "Wait till you see the horse-trading part. Do you want to speak now?"

"Yes, I want them to hear my voice. You translate." She stepped forward, and he stood behind and to one side, speaking when she paused.

"Leaders of the Inari. I thank you for your warm welcome into your tents. I come in hope of mutual benefit and in peace." She held out her hand in the gesture Mantinello and Jhanes had exchanged. "I have been enjoined to speak clearly and truthfully, so I will go straight to the heart of the matter.

"It has not been a good winter. We understand that here above the Barrier, the Weather Gods have severely tested the People. In my country, the testing was at the hands of men, but it was a testing nonetheless. With less food grown and more fighting over the last year, my people are prepared for war and little else. It has been difficult, I admit, to prevent the strong from taking what the weak have been able to save. However, due to the strength of King Gerth and his allies, an uneasy peace lies over our realms. The tools of war are set aside. For the moment.

"We understand that your people have felt the effects of the Season of Snows and are hungry as well. I do not ask for information. I repeat what is in the minds of our Leaders, down in the Lower World.

"My problem is to strike the right note with your people. I come to investigate the possibility of our helping each other. There are some among you who will say I come in fear, offering bribes so you will not attack. There will be others who say I come as an opportunist, trying to take advantage of the need of your people, to make profits for myself.

"I hope that somewhere in the middle we can find a truth that is palatable to all. Somewhere, there is a way of looking at this where both peoples can agree to an understanding that will benefit everyone and take us through this time of trouble. When hard times come, it is known that all must pull together to support each other. I know this is true of your clans and of your tribes, as it is in our kingdoms. Could it not be true of our two peoples?"

When Jhanes had finished translating this last comment, she said no more, waiting for an answer. A bald man placed two to the left of the Great Potentara stood up. "Why should we bargain with traders? What can you give us that we need? What can you trade" – he spoke the word as if it soiled his mouth – "that we cannot simply take?"

There was a mutter of agreement among the seated men, and some shouts from the standing mob of younger Fighters behind them.

175

Jhanes translated for his party, adding, "Callar, Great Potentara of the Pregota. A well-respected leader, but ultra-traditional."

Zoysana stood forward, waited for silence. "It is simple, oh Leaders of the Inari. There is no doubt we have what you want. You have just said so. The question is whether you trade for it or take it by force. I am here to persuade you that you would do much better to trade for it."

The man had remained standing. "Why would we do better? We do not fear you!" The shouts of his supporters rose higher.

She smiled. An honest, friendly, smile. "You do not fear us. What is there to fear? Our farmers have no wish to come and break up your steppe-land to plant their crops. They would not survive here. Your land is too hard for them."

They yelled in agreement when he translated this, and again she waited them out.

"However, knowledge brings wisdom, and I would caution you not to act in haste. In the first place, we farmers may not wish to invade you, but we also have no desire to be invaded. Farmers protecting their homes have a great deal of courage, and many of you would die."

She held up her hand to stem the muttering this caused. "I know you are not afraid to die. Rather a waste of courage though, to die at the hands of a farmer with a shovel." They laughed at this.

"And that brings us to the main point. Assume you attack." She described in detail a plan of warfare very similar to the last Inari raids: what was successful, where they were repelled.

"And when it is all over, what have you? You have covered a small part of the poorest portion of our kingdoms. You have taken the goods and food from the harshest of our farming land, from the poorest of our people. The good farmland is beyond your reach, away down near the shores of the Inner Sea. Protected by the mounted Warlanders of Petrella, by the formidable Kyabran Masters, by the knights and mercenaries of the Inner Duchies.

176

"So you attack, and you take your meagre winnings and your wounded, and bring home what to your starving families? Pride? Glory? Good trophies for your young Fighters, but poor solace to your people.

"Instead, I am offering you food brought to you on wagons from the farms of the Inner Duchies. I am offering you beef from the plains of Kyabra, driven carefully so it remains fat and tender. That is the difference between trade and warfare, my friends."

Here, she raised her head and her voice to speak to the assembled Fighters. "I apologize to those who would prefer the honour. I would ask you to sacrifice your chance at glory that your brothers and sisters might eat. Some other time," Jhanes imitated Zoysana's shrug as he translated this, "some other time we might oblige your young Fighters with a chance to die. But not now. Perhaps you should wait a few years, time for our people to get fat and lazy and forget their warlike feelings of the moment. But not now."

Jhanes translated this last jibe with an inner qualm. She was picking up the ironic twists of Inari society with ease. He wasn't sure if this one was over the line.

There was a chuckle, though, when he finished, and then a rising buzz of conversation. Cutting through this came a new voice, not loud.

"Enough."

There was instant stillness in the field. The Great Potentara had spoken. Now he rose. Chuko wasn't a tall man, but the muscles corded from his shoulders to his head, concealing his neck completely, and as he stood the bulk of his chest pushed his hands out from the sides of his body.

"We thank Lady Zoysana for her lesson in tactics." There was a chuckle in the crowd. "We thank her also for her fine arguments on both sides of the question. It is doubtful if she has left anything to be said." Again, a good reaction from the crowd. *Yes, this bull-necked man is far more than a simple Fighter.* "However little is left, I am sure we will be saying it for some time to come. So let us put it aside for the moment. It is not often we greet important visitors from Below. Let us show them how we entertain ourselves."

There was a general hum of agreement, and Chuko signalled. More cushions were brought and placed within the horseshoe near the head. The Great Potentara left his spot and had his cushion set next to Zoysana's. Jhanes sat on a carpet between them to translate, but little was said.

The afternoon's 'entertainment' was semi-judicial. Those with grievances could come before the assembled Leaders to settle their disputes in the Circle. There were serious bouts that ended when blood was shed. Others, the more status-oriented, were weaponless, although broken bones were not uncommon. These ended with a fall. To the Inari, staying on your feet was everything. Jhanes and Zoysana chuckled about the smith's technique, and he was required to translate the joke for the company. As the roars of laughter subsided, he spoke to Zoysana. "The ability to laugh at yourself is highly prized here."

"As in most cultures. It is an important safety valve."

The matches were over when a lone man stepped forward. He was older and walked with a familiar limp. The soldier's heart fell. "Assembled Leaders, I have a request for honour to be satisfied which you may wish to deny me, and I will not complain."

This caught their attention.

"Speak up, Pagris of the Cerdana Clan. What is this claim which you find so important, yet so unimportant?"

"It involves one of the guests of the Aguilana."

"I see. Then you must deal with Terenno, Leader of the Aguilana."

Their host of the afternoon stepped forward. "What is your claim, Pagris of the Cerdana?"

"This man who is your guest was once my friend. He fought beside me, hunted with me, stood the lonely watches of the herds with me. I considered our friendship a rock, footing I

178

could count on, no matter how hard the battle. And then he left. He abandoned us, and my footing was no longer sure. I claim the right to meet him and throw his disloyalty in his face, to sweep his feet from under him as he did to me."

Terenno raised his eyebrows at Zoysana. Quick glances of understanding passed among her party. "This is what we expected, isn't it?"

"Yes, but I wish it wasn't him."

"Well, you know him and you know these people. Handle it the way you think best."

The soldier stepped forward and raised his voice. "My Leader and my Host give me permission to meet this challenge. I only ask one favour."

The man stared at him a long time, then answered. "I have no right to refuse you any favour you ask, Hidden Twig. You were my friend."

Jhanes nodded. "I was your friend, Pagris, and you were mine. When two men are friends, then size or age or tribe cannot come between them. But I was not Inari. I grieved to leave you, you above all my friends of the Cerdana Clan. But I had to go. I had to search for my people, my family. I hoped you would understand that."

The older man's head bobbed. "I suppose. So what is this favour?"

"Will you fight me weaponless?"

"Weaponless?" It came out in a shout of laughter. "Why, you big clod, I'll fight you with toothcleaners, if that's what you want. But weaponless? Your brain must have gone soft, down there in your so-called civilization."

Zoysana, puzzled, asked for a translation. "I can see why you wouldn't want to use weapons on an old friend. Why is he laughing?"

"Because he was the best weaponless fighter in our clan and many others. It didn't do him a lot of good, as any serious fighting is done with steel, but he got a lot of status inside the clan because of it."

179

"And you?"

He grinned. "I was always too big and clumsy. He made me look like a fool often enough, and I don't want to look like a fool now. I've picked up a few tricks since. They may be enough."

"Come on, Hidden Twig. Let's have the two old men in the Circle."

Stripping off his doublet, the soldier followed his old friend across the line of rocks.

"Need those big boots, now, to keep your balance?"

He thought a moment. The steel-toed, hobnailed boots were weapons in themselves, and he was comfortable in them. He stepped out of the ring and removed them. "I don't want any advantage over you."

Pagris snorted and began to circle.

It was very slow at the beginning as they tested each other out. Pagris was still his old, sly self, though his game leg slowed him, especially when turning left. However, Jhanes soon found that he was hard-pressed to stay facing his opponent, who attacked and moved and attacked from the next angle, or feinted and backed away just as the larger man thought he had a good swing. The one thing Jhanes had learned in his years of swordplay was never to commit his weight. As long as he stood balanced, he was impossible to move, as Pagris found out when he tried his first throw. There was a grunt as their chests collided, but Jhanes was unmoved, and the smaller man slipped out of his encircling arms.

"Huh. I see you learned something, all these years."

There was no other conversation as the two continued the testing. The crowd had started out yelling, but was calmer now, as nothing happened. They began to get restless, shouting for action.

"We have a problem, my old friend."

"What's that?"

"Unless one of us does something interesting soon, we will both get laughed out of the Circle."

His opponent's only answer gave him what he asked for. Driving off his good leg, Pagris kicked, the ball of his foot striking Jhanes in the lower ribs as he turned away to protect his stomach.

The soldier tried for the foot but missed it and backed away until the fire in his side subsided. "Sorry I mentioned it."

Pagris only smiled grimly and continued his circling. Jhanes decided he was done with caution. He moved more surely now, using his weight and reach to entrap his opponent, taking a few hits but scoring a few of his own, more damaging for their power. Both were breathing heavily by this time and the soldier thanked the rough trip up the passes for what endurance he had. His winter at the inn had slowed him.

So the fight continued, with Pagris chipping away, Jhanes hitting harder but less often, trying to just once get his hands on his slippery foe. Pagris was waiting for his old friend to get off balance, just the slightest bit, so he could slide in and finish the job. Finally, Jhanes realized the futility of it.

"How important is it for you to win this?"

Pagris stopped and backed away. "What do you mean?"

"Would it mean anything for you to win? You've been wanting to plaster my ugly face for years, and now you've done it, several times. I have no reason to want to beat you, except so I won't look silly in front of all these people. If I go easy and let you win, you would know it, and then you wouldn't be satisfied. So I don't know what to do."

That deep voice rolled through the crowd's murmur. "I think the two of you are wasting our time."

They both turned to the Great Potentara. "We think we're wasting our time, too."

"Then get out of the Circle. You're too old to be indulging in such silliness. If you want to kill each other, get swords and go ahead. But this is beginning to bore me."

The two grinned at each other. "Fair enough?"

"Fair enough."

The moment he stepped outside the Circle, Jhanes was engulfed in a pair of steel-band arms. "You old clod. It's good to have you back."

He could see tears in the other man's eyes. "You don't know how often I've missed you. Every time I was in a tight corner, I'd think to myself, 'If only Pagris was here, this would be so easy,' and then I'd have to get out of it myself and I'd be mad at you for not being there."

"You, mad at me?"

"Aye. Mad at you for being Inari, so I couldn't ask you to come with me."

"Why didn't you ask me?"

"I thought about it. But you'd have been honour-bound to stop me."

"I guess I would. Did you really think of asking me?"

"Almost did. I was young and stupid in those days."

"So was I. I might have gone. Too bad."

"Want to go now?"

"What?"

"Things have changed. I come and go as I please. You can come with me."

"I couldn't."

"Why not?"

"I'm too old. I don't know the language."

"Anybody here keeping you?"

His friend shook his head. "Remember Esperati?"

"Oh, yes! You married her?"

Pagris nodded. "Died two winters past. Coughing sickness. I just couldn't keep her warm enough."

"And children?"

The old face brightened. "Of course. Two boys and a girl. The girl's married, now, no kids yet. Boys are both strong Fighters. Good at weaponless, but they still can't handle the Old Man."

"I'm not surprised. Neither could I."

182

As they talked, younger folk were moving around with platters of meat and skins of wine to serve their elders. Zoysana had need of Jhanes for translation, so he had to leave his friend.

"I'll visit you tomorrow. Bring the boys over, let you meet them. I've told so many stories about you, they can't wait."

"Good enough."

Back with his party, the political conversation rolled on. "Well, Jhanes, I guess you solved your problem with him. How about the rest of his clan?"

"I think they'll follow his lead. He always was well respected."

"And the rest? Will we get an answer soon?"

"I don't think we'll get an answer."

"None at all?"

"No. Our best bet is to stay awhile, talk to people, ride with them, hunt with them, and then head back north."

"And what do we tell Gerth? Nothing? We had a good time and went hunting?"

He grinned. "Don't worry. We've made plenty of contacts already, and we'll make more. We also have to stay long enough to give the opposition a chance to take their try at us."

"We do?"

"It's only fair. They'll need a day or so to figure us out, and then they'll try something. Oh, don't worry; it won't be a sneak attack or anything like that. But they will try. And we have to let them. If not, they'll never come over to our side, and we'll have lost. The Tribes solve problems by consensus. Everyone has to agree, or nothing happens. So enjoy yourself and wait."

"Some advice."

"That's what you brought me here for, remember?"

16. A Different Hunt

It was supposed to be a friendly hunting trip. In Zoysana's usual fashion, she had made friends across clan lines, and Pagris had brought his sons and his son-in-law, while three of Mantinello's clan tagged along with him, hoping to learn some Petrellan. Among the other hangers-on were two Vernetas, probably sent to keep an eye on the situation, but young and enthusiastic nonetheless. They were out on the prairie to the north of the camp, where the mountains of the Barrier Range soared straight up out of the flatlands. Multiple streams ran down their flanks, and protected valleys held forests, meadows, and other habitat where game was plentiful.

As were the predators.

They took it for granted that they would be followed, either by prudent scouts keeping the foreigners under their watch or by enemies looking for an opportunity. It was a political necessity, but it didn't make for good hunting. After half a day's futile search turned up plenty of tracks but no game, Zoysana faced Jhanes. "I'm getting tired of this."

He shrugged. "It is difficult to hunt with ten or twenty outriders bothering the game."

"That many?"

"Difficult to say. These aren't kids out on a lark. They're the best of their clans."

"Time to play a different game." She turned her horse and started at a slow walk back towards the prairie. "Is there another hunting area nearby but not too close?"

"East about half a candle's ride."

"Anywhere we can duck into in a hurry?"

He turned to Mantinello for a quick conversation. "Yes, he says there's a hidden draw we can cut up if we're far enough ahead of any pursuit."

"I'll leave it to you. Most of them are farther up the mountain than we are, not hurrying because they think we're headed for camp. When we're at the right spot, we turn east at full gallop."

"I'll let you know." He signalled to Mantinello, and sent the boy and his friends to set up a screen behind. "If any try to get by, discourage them."

The lad regarded him a moment to be sure of what he meant. Then his face sobered and he nodded. "They will not pass."

"Report in at that last outcropping. If they are far enough behind, we will gallop east."

"I will be back." Mantinello signalled his friends and they turned their horses back along the trail.

Sure enough, as they passed the small cliff, Mantinello trotted alongside. The shoulder of his shirt was in tatters, and his horse was bleeding from a long scrape on its hip. The boy followed the soldier's glance and shrugged. "Got too close to the rock. The Espolo rider didn't realize there was no room outside us. It was a long way down."

"How far back are they?"

"We have three or four bowshots lead."

Jhanes nodded and caught Zoe's eye, pointing his finger ahead.

Without warning, she kicked her horse to a gallop, and their party thundered away along the prairie. Glancing back, the soldier was pleased to note that their pursuers did not appear before they had cut into the mountains again. Here they slowed, and Jhanes pushed to the front.

Once he was certain that the trees were thick enough to hide them completely, he began to disguise their trail, finding flat rock to ride across, changing directions at times, riding straight at others. Pagris and his two sons disappeared, going back to erase what tracks they could.

They zigzagged through the foothills for a candle, finally hitting a well-used path up into the mountains again. Here they turned north, and he sent out trackers to look for game. He slid alongside Zoe. "They'll figure it out sooner or later, but this will give us some time to hunt in peace."

She grinned. "Then let's get hunting."

Jhanes gestured her to lead, but stopped for a quick word with Pagris. "You don't mind missing out on the hunt?"

"With enemy fighters behind us, I believe I could be of better use. I'll take Greccio. He wants the practice."

Jhanes nodded, and the older Cerdana tossed his head towards his son and reined his horse to the north, the lad following.

Jhanes had just finished taking down a buck with a shot at a range none of the other bows could match and was feeling rather pleased with himself when a gesture from Tadeo brought his attention away from the hunt. A horse was approaching openly and at a good pace. Soon, Greccio was dismounting, to stand formally and bow to Zoysana

"My father sends information to Lady Zoysana."

She looked to Jhanes, and when he translated, she nodded. "Tell me what to say in response."

He repeated the phrase twice in Inarituk, and she turned and spoke it to the lad.

"You said that well."

"I'm starting to get the cadences. What did I just say?"

"You accepted his position as messenger and complimented the father on his choice."

"I did? Now, why did I do that?"

"It's a formal exchange that is rarely used, because..."

"...because the only time it would be useful would be when strangers are allied in something like a battle."

"Correct."

"Stop messing around. Get his message."

Greccio stood tall. "My father says all their watchers have pulled back."

Jhanes took this in. "But they know where we are?"

"Oh, yes. Father thought it was strange and wanted you to know. He's making one further sweep."

"He's right. Were there any Espolo in the watchers?"

The lad thought a moment. "I saw none."

Jhanes turned to Zoe and spoke in rapid Petrellan so no one else could follow. "Most of the clans watching us are those who oppose our trading, with a few from other clans. But the Espolo, the clan of Mantinello's friend that I killed, have not been watching. I cannot believe they had no interest in this. They have been holding back with a larger force. Now the others have backed off, taking the neutral watchers with them. This leaves free rein for the Espolo to do what they will unobserved."

"How does that action fit with their codes?"

"I have said over and over that these people are savages. They work under a very strict code of conduct to keep from destroying each other. This group has decided that you do not fall under their codes. Thus there are no restrictions. If you are captured, you will not be treated with honour."

She nodded, her countenance grim.

Jhanes faced the group, alternating between Inarituk and Petrellan and accenting his speech with gestures as he explained the situation. "My friends, this is not combat in the Circle of Stones. The Espolo are intent on revenge. There will be no honour here. We kill or we die. Because of their actions, they can allow none of us to leave this forest alive. Does everyone understand this?"

There were serious nods.

"See to your weapons." He gestured at the approaching rider. "Pagris will have more information."

Pagris swung off his horse, his face grim. In a few terse sentences, he outlined the situation.

Jhanes passed it quickly to Zoysana. "The rest of the watchers have gone, but we have about thirty Espolo fighters trailing us in two groups. The first ten are coming soon. The rest are a few bowshots behind."

"And we are under no rules, no conventions?"

"None."

Zoysana nodded. "Then we attack. We choose the ground and we keep the advantage as long as possible. We wipe out the leaders, then run if we can. If we cannot, we put our backs to the wall and let the bones fall as they may."

Jhanes nodded. "Pagris?"

"There is a spot just ahead, Hidden Twig. A narrow defile we can lure them into with a few fleeing riders. We can hide our horses above, then set on them as they pass below us."

"Let's take a look."

The small canyon looked good, and they slid into position on either side. Everyone had a bow drawn and three more arrows laid out. They planned to send four flights, then follow with a flank attack from both sides.

Soon a rider appeared. Sure enough, he had Espolo markings. They allowed him to pass and proceed up the trail, where two Aguilanas waited to take him down. After him came the rest of the advance group: ten men on horseback, well armed, each with a bow in his hand. When they spotted the decoys, turning away in seeming panic in the canyon, they surged ahead, heedless of their peril.

They stood little chance. By the second flight of arrows, the little canyon was a mass of screaming horses and dying men. Jhanes halted the barrage, and they charged down to clean up.

It took too long. Before they could regain their higher position, the rest of the enemy tore out of the forest below them, bows drawn. Jhanes and his allies responded with a flight of their own arrows, and then the Espolo were among them, flinging themselves off their horses to engage in the enclosed space of the gorge.

Jhanes and Pagris formed a wall at the bottom end, with Tadeo, Zoe and Patu backing them.

"Don't let them draw us out."

Pagris grunted and ran an enemy fighter through. "They're above us!"

Jhanes glanced over his shoulder. The Espolo Clansmen had divided and were descending on the gorge from either side. Zoysana's fighters now found themselves at the same disadvantage as their enemies at the beginning of the fight, struggling against superior numbers driving down on top of them.

A large group of the enemy forced its way down on the leaders, jamming a wedge between Jhanes and Zoe. Two huge Espolos with the look of brothers attacked the soldier, driving him back. Tadeo and Pagris were fighting back-to-back against five enemy. The bottom of the gorge was stuffed with bodies, wounded men, and dying horses.

"Zoysana!" At Tadeo's anguished cry, Jhanes turned to see the Kyabran woman go down under a welter of flailing arms and bodies.

He redoubled his efforts, but the swordsmen he fought were too tough to be intimidated. They worked in tandem, and he was hard pressed to keep them off balance enough to prevent a concerted attack. Circling to keep one in front of the other, he was forced to turn his back on the struggle on the ground, but soon his foes slackened their onslaught, their attention drawn to action beyond his sight.

And then the screams began. Inari fighters dragged themselves away from the tussle on the ground, blood streaming from their faces and necks, their stomachs, all the soft spots of the human body. Soon, the sounds of the other fighting faded as everyone watched the melee in the bottom of the gorge.

Then Zoysana's head worked its way into sight and she forced her way upward, bodies rolling away from her, two small and bloody knives flailing in all directions. Those unlucky enough to have no room to run were scored and stabbed as they scrambled to safety.

Finally she stood there, blood covering her robe, her breath rasping, her eyes wild. She pivoted raggedly, her left knee trying not to buckle, her right hand held lower than her left, the arm shaking with strain. There was silence in the clearing except for the moans of the wounded.

The Inari's arms fell to their sides, and they all stepped back, sneaking glances at their friends, then returning to stare at the woman who confronted them. Then one of the Espolos in front of Jhanes wiped his sword on his sleeve and sheathed it. He bowed deeply to Zoysana and Jhanes and took two steps backwards. Then, with a beckoning motion of his hand, he turned away. The others mirrored his move, their bows deeper. In a moment, the enemy had disappeared, their casualties carried with them.

Mantinello was moving, scouting out the fallen that remained, calling for help for one man, covering the face of another. Soon the other Inari stirred, likewise caring for their wounded. All skirted respectfully around Zoysana, their heads turned her way as they passed.

After a while, her breathing slowed and she sought Tadeo's glance. He went to her, his manner grave.

"Are you well?"

She wiped a hand down her cheek, smearing the blood that flowed from a cut on her brow. "As well as could be expected." She hobbled a step. "A bruise on my upper leg, I think. The knee's all right."

"Your arm?"

"Wrenched shoulder." She rotated it gingerly. "It'll be fine in a couple of days." Her head came up. "How's everyone else?"

It was Mantinello who answered. He held up two fingers. "Dead, Zoysana. Verneta, Aguilana." With a combination of hand gestures and his few Petrellan words, he did a creditable job of reporting the various injuries of the rest of the troop.

She nodded and responded in what Inari she knew. "Treat those who can walk. Three litters." She turned to Jhanes. "Will we have trouble going home?"

He shook his head. "They have learned respect."

"Good." She looked up at him. "You did say they would test us."

"Yes. I did not expect an all-out attack like this. There are higher stakes in this game than I thought, and I suspect it has little to do with us. Chuko has refused to throw his weight against you, making his opponents desperate."

"And they will be more desperate now?"

"Word will get around how this attack went. Nothing official will ever be said, but rumour and gossip affect the Inari like any other society. Your status has risen. Especially because of the way you ended the fight. How did they get you off your feet?"

She smiled. "I did what no Inari would do. For them to lose their footing is death. For me? When I am attacked from all directions, the safest place to put my back is to the ground. They can't use their swords because they get in each other's way. Then they come close enough that I can get at them." She pulled a cloth from her sleeve and cleaned her knives, returning them to somewhere inside her sash. Soon, except for the blood, she was tidy again.

"Do you want me to look at that cut?"

She wiped her forehead again. "Please do." She handed him the cloth. "Scalp wound. Bleeds a lot."

He cleaned her face, then folded the cloth and pressed it to her forehead. "Hold that." When she complied, he shucked out of his pack and dug for bandages, wrapping her head in a tight cocoon.

Even before he finished she had regained her composure, glancing around to see that her troop were being looked after, calling out instructions for the treatment of various wounds.

In a short time, the cavalcade meandered down out of the forest to the plains, wounded and dead on litters slung between two horses, bandages evident on all. Pagris rode supporting his son-in-law, who insisted on riding though his face was white. Late in the battle he had taken a blow to the head that left him reeling.

Jhanes and Tadeo were among the few uninjured. The soldier glanced over at the young Kyabran, who did not seem his usual stoic self.

"Something troubling you?"

Tadeo glanced at him. "It is difficult for the Guard-of-Life when his Master is injured and he is not."

"I feel the same way, but I don't think we could have prevented it. Their whole strategy was to separate her out and mob her. Those assigned to keep you and me busy had little need to push their attacks home." The soldier grinned. "I suppose I should be jealous. They only sent two after me. You got five."

"Nonetheless."

"You fought fiercely."

"But not enough."

"But we are in thrall to one who outdoes all." Jhanes shrugged. "In that respect, our plan is passing as it should."

"I hadn't thought of it that way."

He grinned. "That's because I've been at this business about twice as long as you have. Consider it part of your learning experience."

Tadeo bowed in the saddle. "I thank you for your wisdom. I will remember."

Jhanes reached out to clap the young Kyabran on the shoulder but Tadeo's mount slipped sideways and the hand hit empty air. The soldier grinned. The lad was getting back into form. "Let's keep our eyes open. There are no guarantees in this business."

"I will take the point." Tadeo lifted his horse to a trot and soon was far ahead. Jhanes noted Mantinello nodding to one of his friends, and the young Aguilana pulled out of line and faded behind them. As they reached the flatlands and the trees thinned down to brush and then grass, their scouts ranged farther afield.

Mantinello led them around the main camp, bringing them into the Aguilana tents without meeting too many people. Those they passed gave them their privacy, but Jhanes could see the curious looks. Gossip would rage through the clans tonight.

* * *

Three evenings later there was a feast, and all were invited. A mass of people gathered around a beef and four deer turning on barbecue spits near the centre of the camp. As the sun sank towards the mountain peaks and the smell of the sizzling meat arose, a mellow mood pervaded the gathering.

Zoysana and Jhanes had been regaling Chuko and some of the more progressive Potentaras with stories of the world below the rim, but partway through, the Great Potentara slapped Jhanes on the shoulder and turned him away from the gathering. "My people have a problem, Hidden Twig. It is a very delicate problem, and I feel it might offend your Potentara if it were to be placed before her."

"My Potentara has an open mind, and is wise far beyond her years."

"Still, could I mention it to you, on the understanding that it will not get to her if it might trouble her honour?"

"I don't think I could promise to keep anything from my Potentara. I assure you that she is not easily offended, and I will do my utmost to persuade her that no offence is intended on your part."

"Fair enough. The problem is this. My people have seen you fight, and frankly, it was a poor test of your abilities. A few saw your servant fight, and word has spread that he moves very, very quickly. And there was another testing, but that is only rumour and must remain so, happy though I may be that your Potentara comported herself so well.

"My people know enough about the world to understand that folk in different places abide by different rules. Were she

193

Inari, she would have no need to demonstrate her abilities. But even though a twelve-year-old with basic eye-before-hand can read the competence in her every move, many are blind to that which they would not see. They say she has done nothing to prove she has abilities deserving of her status. You understand, I see."

Jhanes thought it over. "Perhaps I should explain Lady Zoysana's position more clearly. In Petrella, she plays many roles. Compared to the Inari, I suspect her position would be closer to Designated Fighter than Potentara. A little of both, and a personal friend of King Gerth, as well."

The Great Potentara glanced sideways at Zoysana. "For a woman of her stature to attain such a rank is impressive. However, that does not help my people to understand."

The soldier considered. "I can reassure you that she will not be offended by this problem. I will discuss it with her."

Zoysana's response was swift. "What do you suggest? Do I go into the Circle? How many do I have to kill?"

Jhanes was about to respond when the Great Potentara stopped him. "Please translate what she just said."

Jhanes had no choice. "She is not offended. She asked how many it would be necessary to kill in order to solve your difficulty."

Chuko grinned, nodded thoughtfully. "A Fighter's solution."

"May I advise her?"

"Please do. I have no doubt this woman will have a Potentara's solution as well."

Jhanes turned to Zoysana. "It's not that easy. You are King Gerth's Designated Fighter. The correct person to challenge one of your status would be their Champion, the Great Potentara's Designated Fighter. He will be the very best. He could probably kill you, and you cannot fight the Champion to anything but death. If you were to beat him, that would open a different set of problems, because you would be expected to take his place. There is little chance of leaving that post without dying."

"So I have to persuade them I am who I say I am without fighting anyone. I have been expecting this." She glanced out over the fighting Circle, where the late afternoon shadows of a few straggling cottonwood trees cut across the ring of stones. "I am glad it did not happen while the sun was high. Tell them I will dance for them."

He was perplexed by more than this strange proposal. *What does she mean about the sun?* "My Lady, I..."

Then he found new reason to believe who she was. He had never heard such steel in her voice before. "Tell them, Jhanes, that I will dance. Now."

The Great Potentara watched this byplay with interest. "What did she say?"

One further glance at Zoysana choked his arguments. "She says she will dance for you."

A great laugh went up from those nearby, echoed as others heard the news. Jhanes looked at Zoysana, trying not to say 'I told you so.'

The Great Potentara regarded her as well. "Women dance. The only dancing a Fighter does is in the Circle."

Upon translation, Zoysana nodded. "Because I am a woman, I will dance. Because I am a Fighter, I will dance in the Circle. It suits me perfectly."

In the silence that followed, a young voice called out something, and the crowd snickered. Jhanes winced. "What he asked was if you needed a *morinkhour* to dance to. That's a stringed instrument like a violin, with a horse's head where the tuning pegs are. Because the horse's head is at the top, and the place you play it is...well...lower down, it also has a connotation I would prefer not to translate."

She waited until he had finished, then stepped forward to speak to everyone. "When I am finished, any man who still wishes to dance with me may have his opportunity." Her gesture made it clear what she meant with no translation. Silence descended.

"Tell them I will dance 'The Robe' for them."

This announcement was greeted by uncomprehending silence. She paced into the centre of the green Circle, her robe swirling around her to the swing of her steps. As she reached the place where the shadows fell, her concentration deepened, and a hush gripped the crowd. She held her position while she gathered her energies, then suddenly she was fighting: leaping, guarding, attacking, and all the while the swirl of her robe obscured and defended her body. Now she increased her speed as the swirling multi-hued cloak blended with the grass and the shadow in one smooth rhythm of movement.

She slid along a line of shadow, her fists flicking out to flash in the sunlight. She sprang out of the shadow towards the watchers, and they leaned back in a mesmerized wave. Up and down, along the grass and high in the air, she beat out the tempo of her battle. Then gradually she slowed, and there came a moment when she was still, motionless except for her lightly heaving breast and a trickle of sweat down her cheek. Her eyes held the Great Potentara's for a long moment, and then she made the inviting gesture again. There was silence, and no one moved.

She nodded, satisfied, and strode from the Circle. None who had witnessed this scene could ever look at her swirling robe or her small stature in the same way again.

The Great Potentara nodded. "A fine solution to our problem. Please thank the Potentara for me."

When he had done so, Zoysana nodded as well. "Tell me, Jhanes, is there some way Tadeo can demonstrate his skill without killing anyone? Don't they do anything for fun around here?"

"I can't think of anything they do for fun that doesn't involve hurting someone, but weaponless combat between friends can be relatively harmless."

"Good. Tadeo, would you like to put on a show? Don't hurt anyone much, but throw them as quick as you can."

He grinned and nodded as Jhanes translated Zoysana's request for the Potentaras.

"Will you find someone of appropriate rank to fight him? Perhaps someone of Pagris' clan with good weaponless training."

The Great Potentara called out, and soon Pagris was there. "Can you recommend a good opponent in weaponless combat for the servant, Tadeo? One of your best, but not too large. We want this to seem fair."

Jhanes held his tongue and stifled his grin, bringing an appraising glance from his friend.

Pagris nodded. At his gesture, a young man stepped forward, stripped to the waist. He was more heavily muscled than most of the Inari, on the lines of the Great Potentara, but with a slimmer frame.

The young man strode to the centre of the Circle and waited.

Tadeo stood beside Jhanes, reading his opponent. "What are the rules? I don't want to spoil it by cheating."

"No weapons. That's about all. Gouging eyes and punching the throat are desperation moves, so winning with one of those is not definitive. Otherwise, the man who puts a hand down or steps outside the circle loses."

Tadeo shucked his robe, since it was full of concealed weapons. He then removed his sash, again covered with equipment of various sorts. Then he moved into the Circle. His demeanour contrasted with that of his young opponent: darker, slimmer, moving slower and with more relaxed confidence. As he approached, the young man's manner changed as if he now realized what he was up against. Tadeo simply walked towards his opponent and kept on walking. When he got within range the boy reached for him, seemed to slip, and fell heavily to the ground. He lay there a moment, dazed, then got up, looked around, and slowly left the Circle, shaking his head. The crowd, too, was silent.

Tadeo looked back at Zoysana as if asking for instructions, and Jhanes stepped in. "Have you any better than that, Pagris?"

The Inari called out, and another man stepped forward, this one older, more sure in his stride. He stood on no ceremony, reaching for the Kyabran's arm. Tadeo grabbed the man's arm in a mirroring move. There was a sudden flurry of movement and a sharp slapping sound. The Inari flew backwards to the turf as if pushed by a huge hand. He lay a moment, gasping for breath, then arose and bowed to Tadeo before he crossed the stones, shaking his head as had the man before him.

He walked over to stand beside Pagris. "Don't bother sending any more, Great Potentara. He's stronger than I am, and faster; no, fast isn't the word. He's quick as a striking adder. And I don't mean to exaggerate. He is that fast, I wouldn't step in there with a sword, and him with empty hands."

"I would."

The young man who stepped forward was almost as tall as Jhanes himself, though slimmer. "Tell him it was my brother he killed, and he won't be so lucky with me."

Jhanes looked to the Great Potentara, who shook his head. "You know I cannot keep him out if he chooses to enter the Circle."

"Tadeo, this one's angry."

"I caught the family resemblance. Pregota?"

Jhanes turned to the Great Potentara. "He says he is sorry for the mother who raised the impolite child, and hopes this brother will not disappoint her so badly."

"He didn't really say all that."

"Tadeo fights better than he speaks. What he really said was not to bother sending someone with such a handicap."

The Great Potentara turned. "He's right, lad. You can't walk in there angry. He'll use it against you."

The boy's face was set. "I will treat this opponent with the utmost honour and respect. I will not disgrace my family or my clan. But I must have my hands on him."

There was no answer to that. The boy slung off his shirt and strode into the Circle.

198

Tadeo could hear the emotions, if he could not understand the words. "He will have his chance, then."

Zoysana nodded, and the Kyabran bowed deeply to his opponent.

The lad did not grapple with him at first, moving around him, feinting and ducking. Tadeo remained calm in the centre of the action, only responding when a move came close enough to require reaction. After a few of these semi-attacks, the lad gained more confidence, and the onlookers began to shout encouragement. He pushed a few strikes home, and while Tadeo avoided them easily, he leaned into his blocks enough for the boy to feel his strength.

After the third such attack, Tadeo stepped back and dropped his hands. "Have you stopped being angry?"

The boy couldn't understand the words, but again, no translation was necessary. He bowed as if the match was just starting, then crouched, a look of determination on his face. He knew the power of his opponent, and he had no room for a luxury like anger.

"Then let us fight."

Now Tadeo met block for block, strength with strength, his fists and feet punishing any slips. Still the boy bored in, absorbing the damage, scoring a few punches of his own, to the great delight of the crowd. Only a few could tell how desperate he was becoming. His moves were quicker, less smooth, but for a moment they carried him onwards through sheer bull strength.

The soldier could read the Kyabran's responses, sense the waiting. *Any moment now...*

And then it was over. The boy lunged forward, his arms grasping a quarry that wasn't there. Tadeo's hand moved like lightning, and there was the audible smack of flesh on flesh. The young man dropped where he stood and did not rise. Tadeo knelt by him, checked the pulse on his neck, then raised an eyelid.

"He'll be all right in a while."

"What was that strange ritual he performed over his fallen enemy?" the Great Potentara wanted to know.

"To make sure he hadn't killed him."

"Killed him? With a punch?"

Jhanes shrugged. "I don't know. You heard that punch hit. What do you think?"

The Great Potentara looked thoughtful. "It was charitable of him to let the boy have his chance. You and I know he could have won at any time."

When Zoysana had this translated, she agreed. "When you have no opponents at your level, it is often necessary to impose restrictions on yourself, in order to progress. Tadeo chose not to use any moves that would turn the lad's movements against himself."

"Your servants have great powers of discretion."

"In his homeland, Tadeo has high status in a powerful family."

"The servants of the very great must be great as well."

That was the end of the entertainment for that day, and there was notable warmth towards Tadeo as the young men gathered around the fallen lad, waiting for him to revive. Unable to understand Tadeo, they still joined him, demonstrating holds and moves. Soon the group was having the greatest time merrily comparing ways to kill people.

Then the food was served, along with strong drinks, and the mood became even more relaxed. It was late when Jhanes and Zoysana returned to their host's tent and sat awhile, reviewing the evening.

"What do we do now?"

"I think we have solved all the problems we can. We have gained credibility, we have conquered enemies and forced their respect, and we have shown respect in turn. That is all that can be accomplished, unless you want to wait around for a couple of quarters, listening to them rehash this over again every night."

"So you think it's time to leave."

"Yes, before we have time to make any mistakes."

"Fair enough. What's the protocol?"

"There is no formal reason to tell anyone except our host that we are leaving. However, it would be foolish not to give the Great Potentara and the council a chance to say their last word."

Sure enough, once their intention to leave had spread, they were invited to speak to the assembled Potentaras. This would be their last chance. They speculated as to what would happen, but even their host could give no hint as to what this might be all about.

They approached the horseshoe as they had on their first meeting, although Jhanes could see less hostility on the surrounding faces. As they waited, the Great Potentara stood; he was not letting anyone speak for him.

"Jhanes, who is Hidden Twig among the Inari. We have been pleased to have you with us again, even for such a short time. You have chosen a Leader who is worthy of your loyalty, and worthy of the friendship of the Inari, and you may tell her that."

Zoysana responded that she felt honoured to be accepted by such courageous people.

"Thank her and tell her that, whatever the outcome of our deliberations, whatever the future holds, the three of you – yes, even her 'servant' – will always be welcome in the tents of the Inari."

"I will let her know what a great honour has been bestowed upon her."

The Great Potentara smiled sardonically. "Not necessarily a great honour, for one from the centre of civilization to be invited to the smelly tents of a bunch of savages."

Upon hearing the translation, Zoysana did not even blink.

"Tell him that, depending on the definition, the word 'savage' can be a compliment."

"The concept of defining a word is foreign to them, but I will try."

He must have been successful, because the laughter roared out across the river. "Tell your Leader that she should leave now. If she waits until the shadows grow long, she might lose herself in them and never depart."

Jhanes turned to Zoysana and translated the last image. "I have rarely heard anything so poetic from these people. He's quite a man."

"You can tell him that, as my opinion as well."

The Great Potentara thanked them for their compliments and wished them a good journey home. The audience was over, and the lack of comment from the other Potentaras was notable.

As they mounted their horses outside the camp, Zoysana commented on this. "Does this mean he has them all under his thumb, or just that it wasn't the place or time to complain?"

"A bit of both. As I told you, they'll be talking about this for weeks. That's one thing sure. There won't be a concerted attack for a while. Don't be surprised if the usual raids start, though. There's nothing to stop them until a decision is made."

"We'll have to pass that analysis on to King Gerth."

17. Running the Gauntlet

The ride north started out pleasant, although later on the steep downhill grades were hard on the horses. At least the figures shadowing them this time wouldn't be so likely to put an arrow in their backs.

Mantinello escorted them to the treeline of the foothills, and as soon as he turned back, they all noticed the extra attention. Zoysana laughed out loud the first time a pair of feet hastily withdrew into a bush. "That one had better learn to think ahead. That was a thorn he dived into as we came around the corner. Or should we be laughing? I don't want to cause any trouble out here."

Jhanes shared the merriment. "I imagine all his friends are laughing, why shouldn't we?"

"I didn't think the Inari would be that inept."

"This close to camp, our shadows will be boys trying their skills. Any serious challenges will come later in the higher mountains or on the other side of the pass."

"Will they attack?"

"There are no guarantees with these people. I doubt it, though. And if they do come, it will be out in the open. An ambush against such as you would not provide enough honour to satisfy them."

"So what do they want?"

"To see who can get closest. Maybe steal something and get away."

"And we have to put up with this for the next two days?"

He shrugged.

"What should we do about Patu? If I send him, he'll clear them out. Or would they consider that cheating?"

203

"Better to handle this ourselves. Shows more confidence. Also, he's too vulnerable to an arrow. They probably won't shoot us, but they might shoot him."

She grimaced. "This could get very boring. Especially with only three of us to share guard duties."

"It's only a game. Keep that in mind if it helps."

Zoysana nodded. "A game to be played carefully by someone who knows the rules. Jhanes, I don't know what we would have done without you. I see now the problem of communication with these people. Their code of honour is not that much different from ours, but they adhere to it so strictly. I was astounded when you reached out and killed that first boy, but now I understand. They live in a harsh world, and one mistake could harm the whole clan. So no one is allowed to make a mistake."

"That's about it. I've tried to think of a way I could have kept either of those lads from getting themselves killed, but I haven't found one. Many of the Tribe were glad to see them gone. Overt pride is not a quality they cherish, though real pride is everything to them. It's a strange dichotomy."

She glanced up at him and shook her head. "Where does a soldier get a word like 'dichotomy'? Not in eight years as a slave to the Inari."

"He reads, Lady Zoe. He reads anything he can get his hands on. There's a lot of boredom in a soldier's life."

"Good answer. That's where I learn much of my knowledge as well. I wish there were more books."

"Are there not many books in Kyabra?"

"Yes, but they are hard to get and very expensive. Writing a copy takes even the best scribe many quarters."

"There needs to be a way to produce them without writing each one by hand. Couldn't you make several copies of each page at one time?"

"That might be more accurate, but we are still restricted by the speed of a hand writing."

"Perhaps a number of pens, all connected, all guided by the same hand."

She looked doubtful. "It sounds very complicated."

He shrugged and scanned the hills on either side of the path. "Ask a soldier about books and you'll get strange answers."

"Ask an innkeeper about the Inari and you might get a surprise."

They rode on, thinking their own thoughts.

That night, the game began in earnest. They let the fire burn low before full dark to develop their night vision to its strongest. Even so, it was long before time to sleep when Jhanes stood.

"I feel a pressing need, which I think I will satisfy. Right over by that tree."

He strolled over, untying his pants, and urinated beside an exposed leg, its owner having frozen as he approached. Then he ambled back to the fire. By the time he sat down again, the incompetent observer had disappeared.

"That'll make them more cautious."

They were not bothered the rest of the night, but they were careful all the same, leaving one on watch with Patu while the others slept. The next morning they climbed higher in the mountains. There was less cover for the watchers, who had to retreat farther and farther away. Zoysana commented on the mountaineering skill required.

"They are beside us and above us all the time, and yet we are on the only trail. I thought these were plains people."

"Some tribes spend more time in the mountains and forests. Our hosts, the Aguilana, control this area, which is why they are so involved in trading. I am pleased to see such skill. Some of these at least will be Aguilana, and they will be certain that the rules are followed."

It was Tadeo's turn to catch a prowler the second night. A light rain set in, and they had camped in a stand of trees, sheltered in a small valley. He was on watch near midnight when he nudged Jhanes with his toe. The soldier came awake without moving. Zoysana and Patu had their heads up, eyes piercing the darkness to the west. Tadeo leaned over him.

"I'm taking a walk. Someone's messing with the horses."

He was gone and back in a few minutes, slipping into invisibility against a rock, his Guide's cloak blending in the starlight. "I thought that was a bit much. Someone unable to get close enough was throwing stones at the horses to attract my attention, so I left camp in the other direction. Sure enough, one was sneaking in on that side. I left him tied to a tree. Then I went for the one who threw the rocks, but he must have heard me get his friend, and he was gone."

"How did you tie him so quickly?"

"Used his legs. It's a trick Zoysana taught me. You lift him up, cross his legs on the other side of the tree, and sit him down. If you fold his legs right, he can't get them out, and he can't pull himself up. This one will get away soon. There are no trees of the proper size."

"I think we're winning the game."

Zoysana checked the surrounding trees in the dim starlight. "Is that a good idea? Are we giving anything away?"

"I don't think so. These youngsters have little clout back in the tents but they do talk, and we achieve status by staying cool and playing along. Do you want me to go out and set a fire under a couple of them?"

"Could you?"

"I probably shouldn't. Remember the name they gave me, and I'm out of practice. Anybody who is still with us this far from the plains is one of their better mountain scouts."

"And they're going to keep this up all night?"

"No reason to believe anything different."

"I am tired of this. I am tired of watching, I am tired of waiting and I am just plain tired." He could see her squirming around in her bedroll. "Did you say rosemary had something to do with the burial ceremony?"

"Yes, they put rosemary on the body before they bury it."

"Good. There was a patch of rosemary over by that tree, I recall. Patu!"

The armigerent came to her as she rose from her bed, dressed in common Guide's wear instead of her Kyabran robe. She spoke to him a moment, and his head swivelled around, his ears questing, nose snuffling. Then she snapped her fingers and pointed at Jhanes.

"You stay there. Jhanes, don't let him follow me. I wouldn't want him to make a mistake and kill somebody."

Jhanes was about to comment that the beast was likely to do whatever was in his mind to do when he realized she had disappeared. He glanced at Tadeo, who only shrugged.

"Best get some more sleep. She'll be a while. I'll watch a bit longer."

"Nobody has to tell a soldier twice to get more sleep." Reassured by the Kyabran's calm, he set his worries aside and soon was asleep, the rough hair of the dog's mane under his hand. He woke some time later when the armigerent pulled out of his grasp. He thought he also heard a metallic clank, but when he looked, Zoysana was just getting back into bed.

"No problem. I'll put Patu on watch, in case. Sleep."

He woke again with the before-dawn birdsong. He raised his head to have Patu's calm eyes meet his. Then the armigerent sighed and flopped his chin on his paws, but his ears remained erect. Zoysana and Tadeo were two shapeless grey lumps. The soldier lay in his warm cocoon, listening in vain for any untoward sounds in the forest, waiting for enough light to start breakfast.

He was rolling sugar onto the first pancakes when Zoysana's voice came quietly. "Visitors."

The armigerent's head was up, looking back down the trail. The soldier's hand slipped nearer his sword, but he could see nothing. Then there was movement in the shadows, and soon a file of Inari, leading their horses, moved openly up the trail towards their camp.

"They're on foot. I take it that's a good sign?"

"It's how you approach a friendly camp."

"Great. You'd better cook a few more of those."

It wasn't quite an order, but the mystified soldier couldn't think of anything else to do, so he went back to his pans.

The Fighters arranged themselves in a line across the clearing, twelve of them: young and tough-looking, well muscled, with wide shoulders. They were bare to the waist except for the swirls of grey and brown paint that broke up the body's outline against rock or tree.

"Ask them to join us."

He passed on the invitation; they ground-tied their horses and stepped forward. The youth in the centre, a dark-haired lad of about twenty, held out a sprig of rosemary. "I am Guils of the Verneta Clan. Will you ask your leader if she will accept these from us? They are all we have."

Jhanes turned to Zoysana, but she did not wait for translation. "What does it mean when someone offers you his knife?"

"His knife? It means he wants to join your clan. What does that have to do with rosemary? He said it was all he had."

"Oh, what a pity." She flipped back her blanket to reveal a pile of knives.

"Wait a minute. Are you telling me that you went out last night and stole their knives? Were they all asleep?"

She looked piqued. "They were not. That one," she balanced a knife on her fingertips, pointing at the leader, "was behind that tree." She flicked her hand, and the knife spun across the clearing, heart-high.

"There were two more behind that log," a double 'thwack', "and one was actually up that tree." Her underhand spin sent a knife slicing up beneath a branch. She wagged a finger at a younger boy near the end of the line. "He was difficult. The others," she spread the knives out on the ground and covered them with her blanket until only the pommels showed, "were asleep." She tucked them in like a girl playing with dolls. "Invite our guests to sit, and watch the pan."

208

At his gesture, they retrieved their weaponry and sat in a semi-circle across the fire from her. He tossed a ball of dough onto the sizzling pan.

"How did you know where they were?"

"Patu knew where every one was."

"And I suppose he told you."

She looked at him, then shrugged. "You don't believe me. All right, watch. Patu." She did not raise her voice, but the armigerent was instantly on his feet. "Horse. Get my horse." She snapped her fingers in the direction of the picket line. The beast shambled off. A moment later there was a thud of hooves, and Zoysana's horse plodded towards the fire, the armigerent at her shoulder.

"But she was tied up."

Zoysana batted at the short piece of rope hanging under the horse's chin. "And this little demonstration will cost you the price of a new halter rope when we get back to the castle. Understand?" She gestured, and the armigerent shouldered the horse back to his place.

"The more I learn, the less I understand around here." He went back to sprinkling sugar into the cakes on the pan.

"So, does it mean anything if I feed them?"

"Means you accept their loyalty."

"Is that a problem? What about their original clan?"

"It's not so difficult, though it can get complicated. You can belong to two clans at once. For example, everyone has a family clan they're born into. That's permanent. But sometimes, for example if a clan member wants to learn a trade that the clan can't teach, he joins another clan."

"Temporarily."

"Unless he marries a girl there, which can happen. Most times, he moves home after he's finished with what he went for. Keeps it simple."

"So these boys want to apprentice themselves to me. What are they offering?"

"Loyalty. They'll fight for you, to the death."

"And I have to offer the same?"

"You have to lead them well, so that they only die if it's absolutely necessary."

"Oh."

"It's not much different from the relationship between an officer and a soldier, if you think about it."

"Easy in theory. You've been a soldier. Why do they want to join up with me?"

"Woodcraft, I guess. If you really went out in the dark and stole all their knives and left a sprig of rosemary in the sheath of every one of them, I think I'd like to take lessons, too. They might find a more respectful name for me. Where did you learn to move like that?"

She smiled, a slow, reminiscent smile. "I started young, and I learned from the best."

"So do I feed them?"

"If they're as hungry as I am, I guess they'd like that."

He grinned. "Yes, Lady. I hear and obey."

"Darned well better or we'll get another cook."

"I could handle that."

"It's not one of Tadeo's stronger skills. Keep up the good work, Soldier."

The Inari lads enjoyed the sugar-filled pancakes, and they drank Zoysana's special tea with a little less enthusiasm.

When they were finished, they sat expectantly across the fire, and Zoysana sat looking at them. "What do I do with them? Can I keep them?"

"Probably not. I can't see you wandering around the castle with a bunch like this following you. And they wouldn't be safe without you."

"I can't just send them back. I've accepted their allegiance, but I haven't given them anything in return."

"They aren't in any hurry. Just to be accepted is enough, for now. It also means they won't be taking part in any raids. At least not against Petrella."

"Well, invite them to continue the game, then. Except this time I'll be on their side."

"Who gets Patu?"

"You do." She grinned. "You'll need him."

Jhanes explained the situation to the young Inari. They grinned, elbowing each other. He turned to Zoysana, but she had disappeared. Tadeo, smiling as well, attached a new lead rope to her horse's hackamore. The soldier indicated to the Inari that their place was out in the surrounding hills, and they jumped to their horses, milled about briefly and stampeded back down the trail, leaving behind a cloud of dust.

Jhanes packed his cooking supplies.

As they proceeded, it seemed that their pursuers had disappeared. If it hadn't been for Patu's nose and ears, the soldier would have thought he and Tadeo were alone on the trail. It was a steep and tortuous path and his concentration was divided, but he spotted no one all morning.

They stopped for lunch just past the summit, and the Kyabran blew a long, quavering whistle between his fingers. A short blast answered him from behind a nearby rock, and Zoysana appeared, grinning. Jhanes called the Inari command, and Zoysana's Clan began slipping in from wherever they had been hiding. Some of them had been amazingly close.

"How did it go?"

She shrugged. "Not bad. How did you do, boys?" She held out her hand, showing three long hairs. They looked sheepish.

"Where did you get those?"

"From the tail of your horse."

"What?"

"I got the first two the easy way," she mimed what she was doing for the benefit of the Inari, "by lying in wait until you went past. The last one, I came up from behind."

"And Patu didn't see you?"

"Probably. He wouldn't have reacted to me. I hope you weren't counting on him?"

"No, I was watching pretty carefully myself. Tadeo?"

The Kyabran held up his empty hands in innocent denial. "I was in front."

Jhanes grinned. *A political answer.*

At that moment, the last Inari showed up leading the horses of the rest, and they pooled the lunches they had gleaned in the sparse forest. When they had finished, Jhanes stood up. "I think it's time the lesson ended."

"Do we have to send them back? I was just starting to have fun."

He shook his head. "They're well out of their own territory now, and there could be soldiers or Guides around anywhere. People who shoot first and don't bother to talk if they see an Inari."

"I suppose. Well, explain it to them. Tell them to look me up when the war's over, and we can go play together again."

He translated this, and they grinned in unison. They lined up, and each one shook his hand, then Tadeo's. The first in line knelt briefly to Zoysana, then rose and stood before her.

"What do I do now?"

"Whatever you can think of. There's no set ceremony. Just don't kiss them. It wouldn't go over too well. Or it might go over too well. You never know."

"Thanks for the valuable advice." She reached out both hands and clapped the lad soundly on the outside of his shoulders. Then she made a lighting kick at his head, pulling her foot just before contact. He stood the test beautifully, not so much as blinking. She laughed and the lads behind him whistled in appreciation. As each Inari stood before her, she made a different attack, and each held his poise while his friends cheered. When they were all on their horses, she motioned them away and they wheeled as one and sped off up the trail for home. Feeling lonely, the three headed down the pass in the opposite direction.

Soon another escort appeared, in the form of two Guides who dropped out of the woods on either side of them, their horses lathered.

"In a hurry, gentlemen?"

"We were just checking to be sure that your friends headed in the right direction."

She grinned. "Thanks. They didn't start out as friends. Friendly opponents in a little game that could have turned serious at any moment."

"Well, unless they are playing a very devious gambit, they've headed back over the pass."

"Don't worry about that bunch. It's the ones you can't see that you have to look out for. Tonight we sleep, and you can stand guard. I'm beginning to doze off in the saddle."

"Whatever you say, Lady Zoe. King Gerth will be very happy to know you're back. The messengers headed for the castle as soon as we knew it was you. Take your time." He shot her a worried glance. "Unless there is reason to hurry."

She laughed. "No hurry. We've bought a little time, at least." She turned to Jhanes. "Do you have any advice for the Border Patrols?"

"Be on the lookout for small parties as usual. They'll slip down out of the mountains in ones and twos, some with horses, some on foot. They'll group up where the trails are easier, then start hassling people. Keep your eyes open, as you always do, I'm sure."

The Guide smiled. "You can count on us to do that, sir. Take it easy. You're in friendly hands, now."

Jhanes tried not to react, and Zoysana shot him a knowing smile. "Get used to it, soldier. You're an officer now, whether someone gave you a badge or not."

It didn't seem as if they had much of an escort, but while they were in the steeper foothills and among the hill farms, many people stopped on the trail to chat and receive Zoysana's reassurances, then stepped aside to watch the small party down the path. There were a lot of smiles, and Jhanes could see that the people held Zoysana in a high regard bordering on awe. Several Guides dropped in during the day, made their reports to her and faded back into the forest. The three ambassadors slept well that night, guarded by four more Guides who appeared at their campsite near dark.

18. A New Troop

They reached the castle at mid-afternoon of the fourth day. Summer was approaching in the South, and the day was warm and still, with most of the inhabitants driven indoors by the heat. They gratefully reined into the shadow of the wall, turning their horses over to the stable boys who came running. One boy was especially friendly with Zoysana's horse, rubbing her muzzle while she nuzzled him.

"So, Ardu, did I take good enough care of Luby?"

"Of course you did, Lady Zoe!"

"And how's my favourite kid?"

"Growing like a weed, Lady Zoe. He butted me the other day when I wasn't looking. Knocked me clean over."

She grinned. "That'll teach you to keep your eyes open. He starts knocking people over in the stables, it's out with the herds he goes."

"Oh, he's very polite, Lady Zoe. He was playing with me."

"He's a goat, Ardu. It is the nature of goats to butt things. Manners don't enter into it."

"I know."

"Where's the king?"

"Hunting with Lord Torey and Lady Talia since early this morning. They must have had a good chase, to stay out in the heat."

She dismissed the boy with a friendly shove in the direction of the horses. "Take good care of them, as you always do." She turned to her travel companions. "I guess we have time to clean up and rest a bit. I'll let you know when Gerth wants us."

Jhanes returned to the room where he had slept on the way south to find all the equipment and clothing he had left behind cleaned, polished, and laid out on the bed. Marvelling at the luxuries of castle life, he pulled off his sweat-damp clothes and

215

poured a basin of water to clean himself up. Then he lay naked, luxuriating in the coolness of the water drying on his skin. He half-dozed until a soft knock roused him, a polite voice inviting him to the main hall to meet with the king.

He was dressed, pulling on his boots, slicking back damp hair and out the door before the page had time to get bored.

He entered the main hall to see King Gerth standing near the throne with another large figure beside him: Lady Talia, venting her huge laugh at something the king was saying. Zoysana and Tadeo were there, as well as Lady Kenna, Varli, and Loreline. Everyone turned to look as he hurried up to bow before the king.

"I'm sorry to be the last, your Majesty."

"Don't think about it. I wanted to have a chat with Zoysana first. So you had a good visit with your old friends, I gather?"

"It was rather tense for a holiday, your Majesty, but thinking back on it, I did meet some I was pleased to see."

"Zoysana tells me you were invaluable. Keep up your reputation and explain, please, what you have accomplished." The king led the way to a table in a corner of the huge room and motioned them to sit. "We're meeting here because it's cooler on this side of the castle, and my mother has taken it into her head that the small meeting room needs to be cleaned out." He grinned at Lady Kenna, who pointedly ignored his jibe, except for a wink she shared with Zoysana. "So, Jhanes, what have you to say?"

Thankful that the king had chosen this interruption to give him time to collect his thoughts, Jhanes took a moment longer.

"When so many clans get together, it takes a long time for them to make a decision. From what I picked up listening around the camp, they were in the process of deciding whether to make a serious attack, either here or all along the Barrier, wherever they could get through. My guess is that sooner or later they would have invaded. Now it's not so certain, though some of the hotheads will be disappointed, and some of the

216

traditionalists will disagree with any compromise, even if it means cutting off all trading.

"But the main thing is that there will be no invasion until everyone agrees, and that will take a long time. A couple of quarters, at least."

"But the onslaught will come."

"I don't think it will. The Great Leader is an exceptional man. He thinks before he moves. I hope he will see the benefit for his people in trading."

"What about the others?"

"As I said, there will be many who do not agree. So if there is no major attack, there will be some who wish to act on their own and no one will stop them."

"So at best we will still suffer raids."

"I'm sorry, your Majesty, but I don't think there ever was a chance of stopping those. The Inari are a very independent people."

"I understand. I am not disappointed. If you've put off a major attack for even a few quarters, it will be a great advantage. If you have staved off the invasion, you have achieved more than I had hoped. How do you think we will find out their answer?"

Jhanes shrugged. "When you see the Tribes pouring through the passes, your Majesty. They don't sign treaties, because they don't write. If they decide to attack, they will attack. Your scouts had better be on their guard. They will be the first targets."

"So do you suggest we mass our forces at the two major passes?"

Jhanes hid his astonishment that the king was asking a mere soldier for his opinion on the deployment of troops. "If you wish to abandon your hill farmers, I suppose you might. The problem is that the small raids are a sure thing. The large-scale invasion is not. Less than an even chance, I would say."

"You've hit the target. Do we protect our people from certain attack, which will do little harm to anyone except those scattered farmers, or do we sacrifice them and keep all our forces here to protect ourselves from a major attack which may not come, but if it did would be devastating?"

"Except..." Then he realized he had interrupted the king.

"Please, Jhanes, don't hesitate to give any thoughts you may have."

"I was just thinking, your Majesty, that it would not be good for the small raiding parties to meet with no resistance."

"How so?"

Zoysana answered. "The Inari don't know if we are bargaining from strength. We did our best to persuade them, but many want to believe otherwise. If they push a few raids down the minor passes and no soldiers resist them, they will report back that we are weak. That is an argument even the moderates will listen to."

Gerth nodded and grinned. "Thank you. It is always nice to have someone come up with good reasons for something I was going to do anyway, no matter how stupid it sounded. We'll garrison the small villages near the passes. I couldn't have left them undefended. Tell me, Jhanes, what approach will work best against the Inari?"

"Depends on the pass. If horses can get through, you'll need cavalry: light and fast, because that's how they move. If the Fighters are on foot, you could use our Light Horse against them, but you'll need light infantry as well. That's if you want to take the fight to them. To fortify your villages, your heavier troops will do. But don't send out any skirmishers who can't move fast and respond quickly to changes in the situation. The Inari move well and act independently. They are brave and tough. Never count them out of the battle unless you've seen all the bodies, and even then, watch them carefully."

The king nodded grimly. "That jibes with everything I have learned over the years. I have fought them myself. I know to leave most of my fighting gear at home and carry a short sword. An armoured Warlander just gets in his own way trying to follow them through the woods."

He stood. "I need a conference with Lord Torey and the southern Warlanders. You'll have to be there, because they'll want your impressions, numbers, things like that. You don't mind hanging around the castle for a few days, do you?"

Jhanes knew an order when he heard one, no matter how politely it was put. "Of course not, your Majesty."

"In fact, you're going to be invaluable to us this summer. Have you any plans?"

His heart sank. *Here we go again. How do you say, "No," to a king?* "Well...your Majesty, I hadn't thought of taking up soldiering again. Lady Zoysana and I have been making plans for the Free Counties, and..."

"And I gather you have a new wife out there. According to Zoe, your Sarha is a pretty good organizer herself and will keep information rolling in from the Free Counties while you're gone. In return, we'll make sure they don't have any trouble, fair enough? And I don't want you out fighting. You'll be with me, where I can talk to you when I need to."

My family is safe, and the king needs me. And that's supposed to make me feel better? A memory flashed through his mind. His mother, on her knees, blood running down the side of her face, pleading as the Inari Fighters dragged him away. It was the last time he saw her. She had died of overwork and, for all he knew, sorrow, years before he grew strong enough to escape his captors.

Jhanes looked at the king, but his moment was gone. Gerth was pacing, the ideas flowing to match his long strides. "What we need to do is get you together with all the experienced men, the ones who have dealt with the Inari: traders, trappers, officers, some of the soldiers and Guides, maybe even a few hill farmers who have survived the raids. Then we can thrash out some techniques that might work.

"Let me see. If we send out the Guides now, we can have everyone here in two days. Give you a day or two to meet, put something together...Zoe, you've got nothing to do. Will you take care of this? You're the best one to deal with a disparate bunch like that, pull them all together. I'll give you five days, then bring me a report. I'll get going with Lukin and the Lords, start deploying the footsoldiers and Light Horse right away. Torey will have to handle his own passes. Loreline, you heard what he said about the scouts. Pass it along. Mother? Any suggestions? Or are you too busy making the castle uninhabitable to worry about a little thing like an invasion?"

Lady Kenna smiled regally. "I'll try to take some time off from my important duties to have a chat with a few people. There are some who will need persuading that this scattered approach is the safest."

"Thank you, Mother. I knew I could count on you. Well, everybody, let's get cracking!"

He brought his hand down on the table in a resounding slap, and his subjects jumped to their feet.

Zoysana laughed. "Are you sure you don't want to just go up there and take them all on by yourself? You look ready for action."

He grinned sheepishly. "It's been hard with nothing to do but wait, not knowing what was going on up there. Nice to have a chance to do something for a change."

Varli leaned over with a mock frown and whispered in the king's ear. Gerth spun on his heel, pointing an accusing finger at Zoysana. "That's right. I'm the king. You can't make fun of me like that!"

"Of course, your Majesty. I deeply apologize. I forget myself sometimes."

"Hah! You forget nothing. Now let's get to work!" He strode out of the hall muttering something about 'insubordination and insolence' as he went. Varli flashed a grin backwards as he followed.

Jhanes shook his head. As a common soldier, he had no picture of a policy meeting at this level. He had never expected it would be exactly like any family gathering, with jokes and gibes as well as serious talk. He turned to see Zoysana and Lady Kenna exchanging proud glances.

"He's doing all right, isn't he?"

"If we say it, as shouldn't."

The two chuckled at that – it must be a private joke – then Zoysana turned to Jhanes. "I'll be a while getting this all organized. You could spend your time well by having a chat with Loreline." She nudged the other woman. "That's an experience our dear innkeeper has yet to enjoy. Try not to wring him too dry."

Zoysana and Tadeo left with Lady Kenna, their heads already together as they walked, deep in their plans. He turned to Loreline. He had barely met her, and even after their months of correspondence he did not know her well.

"What did she mean by that?"

The tall, spare woman did her best to look innocent. "Wringing you dry? Oh nothing. She thinks I put a little too much pressure on when I'm trying to get information. I hope you have a good memory. Come on down to my workroom, and we'll get started."

He took advantage of the walk to ask a few questions of his own. "What does Lady Kenna do that's so important? She isn't the type to meddle in her son's business. Hardly spoke a word."

"Lady Kenna is subtle. She's a kind person: chats with everyone, well liked. People tell her things. She knows what's going on, keeps it all organized in her head. Then, when it's important, she nudges things along. Nothing obvious. She happens to run into certain people, has an informal word, and suddenly everything falls into place. Quite the opposite of King Gerth, who likes to be out there in the centre of the action. Preferably swinging his sword."

"Sounds like a great combination. And you provide them with the knowledge they need."

"That and more. Sometimes I send information out as well as bringing it in. The right facts for the right people, the wrong facts for our enemies." Entering her office, she kicked a chair towards him and gathered writing implements at a big, battered table, clearing a space between the piles of papers.

"And speaking of our enemies, what do you have to tell me?"

By the time supper was called, he knew what Zoysana meant. He had thought, with his soldier's training, that he was good at observing details like numbers of men and types of weapons. He was amazed at how well the two of them were able to estimate the number of Fighters in the huge Inari camp, given the number of tents, the average family size, even such small facts as the age at which the mature men stopped raiding. She wrote it all down as he talked, but she never referred to her notes and he had the distinct impression she remembered everything he said.

He sat with her at the meal as well, Gerth being sensitive to those conservative lords who might resent having an innkeeper at the High Table. Zoysana sat where she chose, and no one would think to make note of it.

Loreline relaxed more over the food, spending part of her time making pleasant conversation, the other part bringing him up to date on the various lords at the High Table. Soon, Jhanes felt comfortable enough to ask her a few more questions, especially about the semi-mythical Sivan.

She turned and stared at him for longer than seemed necessary. "Why do you ask about him?"

"I just wondered if you knew him. I have heard a lot, but it's very hard to separate the truth out of it all."

The answer seemed to satisfy her, and she smiled. "That's as he would have liked it."

"So you did know him."

"Oh, yes. He trained me, and I'm now performing his duties. Not as well as he did, but I'm doing my best and getting results. Sometimes I think he's still looking over my shoulder."

"But where did he go? I never heard that he died."

"He's not dead. That would be much too simple. He got himself out of a situation where his loyalties were divided."

"How divided?"

"That takes a bit of explanation. You knew King Barent, Lady Kenna's brother?"

"By reputation. I never figured it out. He was supposed to be the best general in a thousand years, but then just about the time he became king, everything went wrong – nobody could say why – and the kingdom almost fell apart. I never knew whether it was his fault like some said."

She nodded. "Near enough. Some would say it was mostly his fault. He made the wrong moves for the right reasons, and that's not good enough. Then he had to make a bunch of more wrong moves, and he lost track of the reasons. That was the Sivan's problem. He wanted to be loyal to Barent, but Barent was way out of line, and the Sivan felt it was wrong to continue helping him. So he ducked out. I know that doesn't sound like a very honourable thing to do, but that's what he did. The other options were less honourable. But I don't think he went too far. I think he's still nearby, still meddling."

"You do? Why?"

"Oh, I worked with him enough to know his style. Every once in a while, I get a sniff of something that only someone of his devious mindset could concoct."

"Can you give me an example? One that I'm allowed to know, I mean."

She grinned. "What do you think of Lady Talia showing up here?"

"I don't know what to think. It seemed a hare-brained scheme, but except for the carriage, it turned out she was really well prepared."

"Exactly. And her father won't let anything stupid happen to his only daughter, whose sons will be next in line to his dukedom."

"So why did he let her go?"

"And where did she find such a talented escort? Her man Gavess is very resourceful, but not in that area. And why was she allowed to come with that incredible carriage?"

He shrugged. "I gather from the coachman that it's not that unusual, back in the Inner Duchies, where the land is flat and the roads are smooth."

"True, but any trader could have told them it was too big for two horses in this country. But they tried and didn't get through, so they came on without it. Sounds very convenient, but for what, I haven't figured out."

"Are you sure you're not just over-sensitive?"

"You have to be over-sensitive in my line of work. You have to catch every small nuance of every circumstance. Collecting information is the easiest part. The trick is to decide which details are the important ones."

He nodded in sympathy. "I know what you mean. When I send you all that information, like the list of people who stay at the inn, I sometimes wonder what you'll do with it, so disconnected and random."

"I look for patterns. Incidents that are similar but in different areas of the realm, or spaced out in time. Ideas that repeat. People who do something you wouldn't expect. Or do what you do expect too often."

"How can I make the information I send more useful?"

"It already is more useful, now I've met you, talked with you. The better I know you, know your prejudices and inclinations, the easier it is to analyze your material. What you can do to help is send parallel messages. The first is the usual information. The second is your opinion and interpretation of the information, and the reliability of the source. If I have the two together, it helps."

He nodded. "That seems a good idea."

"It ought to be. It's another of the Sivan's." She laughed with him a moment, but then her face went sad, and she stared across the hall, unspeaking. He wondered if that meant something. *It might be interesting to look out for this Sivan, see if I could find him. After the Inari problem is solved, of course.*

Then she snapped out of it. "You say Lord Feister offered to fix her carriage and take care of it? Has he already got it?"

"He did offer, but he's waiting for permission."

"Good. I think someone should look over that carriage before it gets into his hands."

"Looking for what?"

She shrugged, grinned. "I don't know. But if the Sivan had a hand in it, nothing is done without a reason. Check it on your way back, if you ever do get back."

"Certainly." He changed the subject. "I was surprised to see so little action in the castle. If King Gerth is worried about a war with the Inari, you'd expect him to be building up his armaments heavily. But I only see average work in the shops."

"Barent was all prepared for an invasion last fall and it never came. We have an incredible amount of materiel put away: supplies, spears, arrows, other weapons. The soldiers are working in the fields, helping with the early hay harvest. They can be here quickly if they're needed. We are depending on enough warning of a major attack."

"I hope you will get it."

"Oh, I think we will. The Inari may be subtle, but you can't move any size of army over even Broken Boulder Gap in a short amount of time. It's just too slow a trip."

"As long as you have enough of your Guides out to make sure one gets back here with the warning."

"We have that covered as well. They have a regular schedule for checking in. If they don't show up – well, no news is all the news we need."

"And they are reliable enough that this system works?"

"Always has in the past. You haven't worked with our Guides yet. They're not up to the standard that Barent and the Sivan had them to, but we're working on it. A lot of the old hands drifted back in over the winter, and the group is coming together well, now."

Trust is all very well, but I wonder if any of them ever decide to throw it all away, to forget the duty and the glory and just go home. He shook his head. *I know better. I'm here for the summer, and there's nothing I can do about it.* He put these distracting thoughts aside and returned his focus to the matter at hand.

225

Jhanes stood beside Zoysana at the big table of the War Room, sizing up the group. There were several Guides and soldiers, mostly older men, wiry and active looking. Two ragged men in sheepskin vests must be hill farmers. *Did my father look that poor and hard-bitten?* From his childhood memories, his father had been a huge, solid man who laughed seldom and worked long and hard.

A well-dressed trader was sitting beside a Light Horse officer, sharing something from a jewelled case. *Candied ginger from Costabonne, if I read the trader's robe pattern correctly.*

Zoysana shifted her weight forward, and every eye in the room turned to her in anticipation. Everyone had some idea of why they were here, and every man had good reason to want results from this meeting.

"Gentlemen, welcome. It is good of you to come when you would rather be defending your own interests. The only thing I can assure you is that you will not be wasting your time here.

"The Inari will be raiding soon. Some of them will be through the passes already. King Gerth has sent forces to all the villages, and we hope that, for the moment, it will be enough." She held up her hand as several mouths opened to speak. "But in the long run, that is not enough. Too long has our response to these raids been simply a reaction. We wait until they attack, then we send our forces. By the time our men arrive, the Inari have moved on. We don't have enough soldiers to defend every small farm, every traveller, every day of the year.

"And so we turn to you. Every man here has fought the Inari, fought and won, or he wouldn't be here."

There was a grim chuckle around the table.

"I, myself, have had only one visit with them. Jhanes was brought up by them. He has had their training, knows their tactics, how they think, how they feel. Our task here is to figure out a campaign that will allow us to counter their threat without filling the Southern Frontier with soldiers. What do you think we should do?"

There was a wary silence around the table. Most were strangers to each other, only introduced this morning, and no one wanted to make the first move. Jhanes was to say nothing. Zoysana had made that clear this morning before the meeting. "If we want their ideas, we have to listen to them. You do the reacting this time. Look at the discussion from an Inari point of view. Get into the feeling of being Inari. What would an Inari think of this meeting? I'm counting on you for that."

Zoysana's gaze swept slowly around the room, and she waited.

"Take it to them."

Everyone turned to the last member of the meeting. The trapper, Ferlen, sat straighter, as if uncertain that all this attention was what he wanted.

"Explain, please."

"They don't often come far enough north to bother me, and I'm not on my trapline much in the summer, but if they do show, I don't just hole up, waiting for them to come and find me. The moment I see a sign they're around, I go looking for them. I find them and walk into their camp. That gets me respect. I know a few words in Chinotuk, the trading language, and some of them do, too. So we have a chat and exchange information, like where they saw any fur animals, or what snowfields are likely to slide. Then they go away."

One of the farmers let out a snort that was half a laugh. "They just go away?"

Ferlen's back straightened further. "That's right. They go away."

Jhanes glanced at Zoysana, and she nodded.

"That's what I would expect." He waited while the attention of the table turned towards him. "They are hunters themselves, and that's how they treat other hunters. If he sat in his cabin and waited for them to sniff him out, they would see him as fair game. If he takes the initiative and shows them he has similar

227

skills to theirs, they will treat him like another hunter. You don't keep information from another hunter, especially information about animals or the safety of trails."

He grinned. "And you're way too far north for them to just happen on you by mistake."

"You figure they come looking for me?"

"I suspect somebody in one of the clans brings his favourite bright boys for a special challenge. Any of them ever find you?"

"Once. I came back to one of my line cabins and found a couple of tracks on top of mine. So I went after them, as usual. Come to think of it, when I met that bunch they seemed real cheerful."

Jhanes nodded. "You made somebody's day."

The Light Horse officer crossed one high boot over his thigh. "So what I'm hearing is that if you fort up and wait for the Inari to attack, he will. If you go out in the woods and play tag with him, he'll give up and go home?"

Jhanes grinned. "You're more right than you know. For them, this is a game. Unless it has been a bad winter, they rarely take anything of any great value back across the passes. The Inari who raid here in normal years are young fighters, looking for adventure, for ways to prove their skills and valour. If we go out in the woods and play tag with them, there may be deaths, but not many. In their forays against other tribes, there are very few casualties. The game is more important."

One of the Guides leaned both hands on the table, staring at Jhanes. "So we should go out after them, show them we're on their trail, that we can out-think them, out-track them."

Jhanes could see that this idea appealed to the Guide. He shrugged his shoulders and remained silent. It was time for others to speak.

"That don't help *us* much."

Zoysana regarded the farmer who had spoken, a gaunt man with a shock of blonde hair. "What do you usually do when they're around?"

"We hole up. We got a place up in the woods, a cave. Got it hidden real good, and we drive the stock up there and rub out all the tracks. We take enough food for a week or so, and they don't hang around that long."

It was the trapper's turn to snort. "And what do you do while they're around? Hole up with the stock?"

The farmer regarded him, deciding whether to take offense. A quick glance at Zoysana helped him make up his mind. "Naw, I can't stand bein' cooped up like that. I go out and look around, keep movin'. If I find them, I watch them till they move on. If I can't find them, I watch my back and keep layin' tracks to confuse them, keep them from findin' my stock and my family."

Ferlen smiled, then raised his eyebrows to Jhanes.

The soldier nodded. "They know where your stock is."

"What?"

Jhanes glanced at the Guides, trying to keep the conversation widespread. The older man nodded judiciously.

"He's right. I doubt if you could move even a few head of stock around up there and hide the trail so's I couldn't find it. And I'm no genius at trackin'. The Sivan always said you could track anythin' but a man. Even a single horse trail can't be hid from a good tracker." He glanced defensively at Zoysana, who nodded in her turn.

"I remember him saying that."

"Then why don't they attack?"

Zoysana waited, and it was the trapper who answered. "They don't need your stock. They only need enough to live on while they're down here, and they aren't wasteful. If they come across one of your animals on their way home, they'll kill it to take back a leg, but generally they don't care. If your stock and your family are well hidden in an easily defended spot, they'd much rather chase you around."

"Chase me?"

"Sure. You said you went out hunting for them, but you left them alone when you found them. That's your game, and they play the same."

229

"But last year they overran Brenner's farm completely. Killed everyone, ran off all the stock."

The Ferlen's shrug tossed the onus back to Jhanes.

"Contempt. Nobody ever said they were civilized. They have nothing but contempt for a coward who won't come out and play with them. If you sit in your cabin and shoot arrows at them, they'll wipe you out because you don't deserve to live. Not in their minds. You can be hunter or prey. There's nothing in between."

The farmer shook his head. "Could be, I suppose. I allus thought I was pretty good at trackin' and trailin', but nothin' real special. I never could figure how those Inari, who was supposed to be so good, never found my hideout. So you think they knew all along?"

"They don't know before they come. They find out when they get here. It's a different bunch comes down every year, pretty well. All the new young lads, with a few older ones to keep an eye on them. Nobody tells them too much; they're supposed to figure it out themselves. I imagine they're told that you're fun to play with, and that's all. They come, try their skills against you, and move on."

Zoysana's voice dropped into a moment's silence. "Do we have agreement on this? In your experience, and I know you are all experienced, is this analysis close to the truth?"

After a moment's thought, there was a series of nods around the table.

"Do you realize what this means in terms of our present strategy?"

The Horse officer nodded again. "It means it will be as successful as it always has been."

"Which isn't great."

"And with the larger threat being posed this year, because of the restlessness above the Passes?"

"We could have a lot of people getting killed."

The second farmer had sat silently through all this. He was an older man, short and stocky, and he seemed to move slowly

230

and think slowly. "So you mean that we got only two choices. We bunch up in groups too big to be attacked, or we go out in the bush and play games with them. Anybody in between is in the most danger."

Again a wave of nods swept around the table.

"So what do we do?"

"Take it to them."

"I think I heard that idea before somewhere." Zoysana grinned at Ferlen, and the group chuckled. "How do we take it to them?"

Another Guide leaned forward. "We watch the passes, and when they come through, we go after them. We don't have to kill them. We just chase them around, keep on them." He looked to Jhanes for confirmation. "A lot of them will not try to kill us, they'll just see if they can turn the tables on us and get behind us."

Jhanes nodded. "But don't be fooled. Some of them are not nice people at all. Some of them would be happy to slit your throat if they caught you sleeping, just for the joke of hearing your friends when they woke up the next morning and found you."

Zoysana nodded as well. "A good solution, and one I would have expected from a Guide. You do what you do best. Anyone else?"

Ferlen and the first farmer both started to speak at once, and it was the trapper who deferred to the older man.

"We hide our stock, well-defended, and go out and play games with them? I can't see that working too well. Most of us are farmers, not trackers. We do well enough, but not up to your standard. Besides, we can't take the time. We have work to do. How long is this all going to last?"

Zoysana looked grim. "This isn't a normal year. Between the weather and the politics up there, I think they'll be raiding most of the summer, if nothing breaks our way. So our problem at the moment is to give the farmers some time to do their farming. Any other ideas?"

231

The Light Horse officer raised a hand. "What about horses? Sometimes they're mounted, sometimes not."

"Depends on the pass. Some they can get horses through, some they can't."

"That's right." The first farmer's hand smacked on the table. "We never see 'em on horses, but the pass above Fermsted is real narrow, 'ith one chibney a horse'd never get down."

The discussion flowed, and Zoysana started to write, noting the various passes and what was likely to be the threat from each one. After a while, the conversation wound down, and it was during a pause that the slow drawl of the second farmer slipped in.

"Sounds like we need our own Inari."

All eyes turned towards him. He shrugged as if it all seemed obvious. "They come and want to play. The Guides'r' too busy watchin' the passes for serious trouble. The farmers want to farm. The traders want to move their stuff. The soldiers..." he glanced apologetically around, "...well, no offence, sirs, but you ain't trained up in this stuff. It ain't really fightin', if you get my drift."

It was Zoysana's turn to slap the table. "So we need someone whose only interest is going out and beating them at their own game."

A general hum of agreement around the table.

"So where are we going to find them?"

There was a moment's pause, and then the trapper laughed. "You're going to train them, Lady Zoysana. You and my brother-in-law, the Hidden Twig!"

There were several uncomprehending looks passed, but enough of the party had heard the story of the Inari camp to understand.

"I think he's right, my Lady." The Horse officer was grinning. "From what I hear, you're the one to do it. You and your big friend there. Maybe you can bring some of your tribe down to help."

There was general laughter at this, but Jhanes noticed that Zoysana's heart wasn't in it. In fact, her mind was elsewhere as the meeting broke up. As they walked across the courtyard, she stopped and turned to him.

"Jhanes, how would I say 'Zoysana needs her tribe' in Inari?"

"You're not going back up there!"

She smiled. "How do you say it?"

"All right. I suppose it's the best way, but you don't need to learn how to speak Inari. I'm going with you."

"No, you aren't. You're staying here to screen the recruits, gather them together and get them up to the camp at Broken Boulder Gap by the end of this quarter." Her tone changed. "Now, how do you say it?"

About to protest, he glanced at her face and re-assessed the situation. He told her the proper phrase, and she practised it until he was satisfied that it was perfect.

The next day she was gone up the trail, and he was getting ready to screen the new troops. *And take them up to Broken Boulder and train them. And after that, what can I do but take them into the field? So much for staying safe back here in the castle. Oh, well, I'd probably be bored here.*

19. TEAMWORK

It was a strange confrontation. Or meeting. Whatever you wanted to call the group that assembled on the field in front of the officers' tents of the force guarding the foot of Broken Boulder Gap.

On one side, the most uniform group: the twelve Inari Fighters of Zoysana's original Tribe with another dozen of their friends. Mantinello stood in front grinning, and Pagris nodded to Jhanes from a more solitary position at the rear. On the other side ranged Jhanes and his motley bunch of recruits: twice the number, double the age.

Word had spread, and the soldier's only difficulty had been to select a small enough force from the mob that responded. The Guides were well represented, along with Ferlen and a few of his fellow trappers. Only three hill farmers had passed the quick but rigorous elimination session Jhanes had improvised. Woodcraft and stamina had been his first measures, fighting skills second. There were no other criteria. Anyone who showed up had the requisite motivation.

In the small band of mercenaries standing together at the side, there were even two girls. Correction; 'girl' was a poor word to describe either. Maura was a woman of about thirty, lean and tough-looking, who had broken the nose of a young soldier who made a disparaging remark at the wrong time and got himself weeded out as a result. The other, Anine, was a hulking peasant girl of about eighteen, round-faced and stolid, but with a strength that had Jhanes shaking his head.

He knew Zoysana would be pleased to see them, and he had no difficulty with their presence. Women who made it through the tough training of the mercenaries had a good reputation in general: fierce, motivated, and more level-headed than their male counterparts, they were prized for the versatility they afforded their company, especially in the wide variety of duties the mercenaries hired out for in times of relative peace.

The only recruits that concerned him were three squires who had badgered Varli into sponsoring them. There was no doubting their enthusiasm, their valour or their fighting skills, but Jhanes wondered if they could fit into the social hodgepodge of this strange bunch.

So far they had been fine, and Varli himself was rapidly demonstrating his worth, talking to everyone, learning all their names, creating private jokes. He already had tried out his limited Inarituk on Mantinello, and received a certain amount of laughter for his mispronunciations. Jhanes was beginning to see why Zoysana and King Gerth gave the lad so much of their trust. He was going to be a portion of the glue that held this disparate bunch together. There was a talent that some men had – laughing when the conditions were the worst, turning difficulties into triumphs – which did wonders for the morale of the troop. It was not one of his skills, and Zoysana, for all her ability to attract loyalty, was too serious to create that level of camaraderie.

In all, this was little different from any other troop of recruits he had faced in his long career. A lot of hard work, danger, and dependence on each other, combined with a small but public weeding of the unfit, and soon the group would be welded together into a decent fighting force. This would only be different because of the experience of the men and the independent nature of the task they had ahead of them.

Out of the corner of his eye he saw Zoysana step forward with that sense of purpose that always brought the group's attention. She surveyed the assembly, then gestured them to gather around her.

"Sit down, friends. Too many of you are too tall to see me properly." Her face remained serious, and as he translated for the Inari, he wondered if she was even aware of the joke.

When they were seated, she looked them over once again. "As you can see, we are a very diverse group. You still sit with your friends, avoiding the others. This is a small troop, and we must get to know each other quickly. Let's see if we can get a quick start. Form a line."

She swung a hand, and despite a few puzzled frowns, they jumped to obey.

"Now, what we are going to do is introduce ourselves to everybody. At the end, the person who can recite the most names wins." She turned away, then raised a finger, turning back in time to catch Varli's grin half-formed. "Except for Varli, of course, because he already knows everybody."

The squire froze, his face a mask of dismay. Then he advanced on her, sputtering, his finger shaking at her. "You can't do that. That's not fair. Look at me. I'm smaller and younger than most of this lot," his hand swept out to include the group, "and you're going to take away my one chance to be the best!"

As his arm swung towards her, she flicked out a hand to grasp his wrist. With a quick tug she had him off balance and spinning around to fall flat on his back at her feet, his arm twisted up. She casually placed a foot on his chest and regarded him with benign interest, then looked around at the men.

"Is there anyone else who doesn't understand the rules? Good. If the first man in line will just turn around and introduce himself to the next man, then move down the line, followed by everyone else, by the time we finish, everyone will know everyone. All you have to do is remember them. Got it?"

There was no further response. She took her foot off Varli's chest and helped him to his feet. He grinned and winked at the first man in line, speaking in a stage whisper. "I told you she was mean. Next time you'll listen to me."

Jhanes could see the pattern forming. Varli would be the jester, the complainer, and also the conduit. Problems that men were reluctant to voice would come into the open through his exaggerated grievances. There was a complainer in every group. In this case, it would be the most loyal of them. To the men, the message was clear. They were well aware that, had Varli's belligerence been serious, he could have ended in the same position with a broken arm.

In the end, one of the squires won the competition. Mantinello came a manful second and would have won, but he mispronounced several of the Petrellan names so atrociously that everyone agreed, with a great deal of laughter, that they did not count. Anine, the big mercenary woman, came third, and Jhanes decided to keep an eye on her.

While it was an unorthodox beginning, Jhanes could see how useful it was, for the names were repeated over and over as each contestant tried to speak them. Zoysana was watching them all, forming her first impression of their personalities, as he was.

After the "Naming Ceremony," Zoysana started them off with some training exercises, moving quickly into those requiring two to work together, and changing the pairings frequently. Although she seemed completely serious, she put them through several gyrations that were almost impossible to perform, resulting in many undignified postures that elicited gales of laughter. Again, Varli was the leader in spectacular failures. Finally, when almost everyone had stopped their own work to watch him, Zoysana stepped in.

"Are you having a problem, Varli?"

"Just a bit, Lady Zoysana, ma'am. This exercise is only completely impossible for a normal human body."

"Come on, Varli. Try a little harder."

"Aw, come on, Zoysana. It's impossible!"

She regarded him. "Are you going to try again, or do you want me to help you?"

"I'm trying, I'm trying." He dove into the beginning position so quickly that he stumbled, caught himself, glanced at her in mock horror, then skinned through the exercise without a slip. He stood and looked down at her, panting.

"Zoysana, you are such a good motivator!"

She said nothing, but cuffed him, none too gently, on the back of the head as she turned to see what the others were doing. They all became very busy, but Jhanes could see the hidden grins. He allowed himself a smile. *Yes, things are progressing. Time to push.* He walked over to where Anine and Maura were working together. "Looks good. Come with me."

He brought them over to where Pagris was working with Mantinello. "Here, you split up and work with these two. Your ages match, if nothing else."

He turned the Inari towards their new partners, one hand on a shoulder of each, and spoke clearly. "They understand some Petrellan. Speak slowly." He shoved the men forward, then frowned at a nearby Inari lad who had started to smile. "The Inari aren't used to women fighters. They have to get used to you. Don't worry; Zoysana has them prepared."

The older woman shrugged and stepped towards Pagris. "Let's go, tough guy."

The Inari looked at Jhanes. "What is 'tough guy'?"

Jhanes gave him the proper phrase, and he laughed. "Tell her I'm too old to be flattered by such talk."

"Tell her yourself."

"How do I say 'flattered' in Petrellan?"

Jhanes told him and turned away, confident that this pair, at least, would have the maturity to cope with the situation. Zoysana was nearby, watching.

"A good move, that. If they lead the way, the younger ones will follow."

"I agree. But no fighting yet."

She nodded. "Someone might go overboard trying to prove himself. We'll leave it now for supper. Then we'll give them a chance to show off. Create mutual respect."

The evening was a great success, with everyone demonstrating feats of strength, agility and good old trickery while the rest tried to copy. Jhanes could hear nicknames tossed around; when soldiers didn't know your name, they soon found one that stuck in their heads.

They turned in early, and Zoysana had them out of their tents and on horseback just as the first rays of the sun were reaching through the trees to the ground.

"I have a spot of work for you today." Her pony was laden with ropes and metal rings. "Climbing sounds like a useful idea."

Their practice area was a good hour's ride south toward the pass, but at an angle to the west. They dismounted in front of a huge rock face about the height of the castle wall, but fissured in places with wide and narrow cracks.

"All right, troop. Up you go. We'll meet at the top." She threw the ropes down and stepped back.

They looked at the rock, then at her. Realizing she was serious, they studied the face again. A few stepped forward, testing the rock with their fingers. Others stepped back, scanning the wall from top to bottom. Soon there was a swarm of men on the face, some moving slowly upwards, some frozen in place, others retreating. Most were able to get about three head-heights up but then ran out of handholds. Mantinello and his Aguilana kinsmen fared better than their plains counterparts, but all found the climb impossible. After a few slips and one forced jump, the trials slowed down, sore fingers and tired arms combining to create a general lack of enthusiasm.

Varli had not tried the climb yet, but was standing far back, his neck craned upwards, staring at the wall.

"What do you think, hotshot?"

Varli turned to Zoysana, his face serious for once. "It's a tough one. Shouldn't be too hard to get up the first half, but over there," he pointed to an area on the right, "it looks pretty smooth. The left-hand route starts good, but peters out in that overhang."

"So, which one are you going to try?"

He smiled down at her. "Whichever you aren't. Is this a race?"

She frowned. "Never. Not for fun. Some day you may have to do this in a hurry, but not in training. Mountaineering is difficult enough. Racing makes it suicidal."

"Point taken." Varli seemed unquenched. "I'll take the right side. You try the left. If you run into trouble, call, and I'll come over and give you a hand."

"Fine. But don't go to the top. Leave a double-supported ring about halfway up, then come down. Once we've got them working on that, you and I can go up the centre, where it's interesting."

All eyes turned to the centre of the wall, where the cracks were slimmest and no one had even tried to climb.

As they approached the wall, each with a coil of rope slung over a shoulder, the rest of the troop stood back to watch. There were mutters of amazement at the speed with which the two moved over the rock, slowly but steadily inching upward where none of the others had been able to climb. About every two head-heights, they took a twisted metal ring from pouches they carried. Flexing it into a convenient crevice, they ran the rope through it and carried on. Each reached the halfway point at about the same time, and they stayed there for a long while, fiddling with the lines.

Then Zoysana looked across at Varli. "You ready?"

He yanked once more at the rope. "Any time."

"Let's go!"

At once, both let go, falling down the cliff in a bounding leap. Then the rope caught them, and their feet braced against the rock. They sprang out again, dropped and swung in against the face again. The fourth jump brought them to the ground, laughing and shouting at each other. The ropes remained, hanging down the cliff face.

"There you have it, folks. Easy as pie to go up, lots of fun coming down. Any takers?"

Several enthusiastic volunteers stepped forward.

The troop worked on the lower face until everyone had made it up to the halfway point. Anine had the most difficulty, as her superior strength was not in proportion to the weight of her body. However, through a good deal of sweat and gritting of teeth she made it, and used the doubled rope to come down, just in case. When she reached the ground, Jhanes clapped her on the shoulder, grinning.

"Well done. I know what it's like to get yourself off the ground. Uses a set of muscles you didn't know you had."

She nodded, then glanced up at him. "So, you don't climb?"

He laughed. "Oh, yes. I've been doing it since I was a kid. I won't go up until they need me."

"Need you?"

"Yes. The best path to the top is up the centre. It's harder down here, but easier once you get going. Zoysana will need somebody tall to boost her past that smooth spot; you see the one over there?" Her gaze followed his pointing finger up the cliff.

"So she can't make it up herself?"

"She probably could, but that's not the point. If it's easier to do it by teamwork, that's how we do it. We're not in this to prove anything to anybody. Just to get the whole lot of us up that cliff before supper time tonight."

She scanned the height of the wall. "Everyone?"

"Everyone who is a part of this troop. And that includes you."

She looked at the wall again, shrugged, and smiled. "Well, I made it halfway. I guess I can make it the rest."

"Good attitude." He cuffed her shoulder again. It was like slapping a side of beef, hard and heavy. He kept the unflattering opinion to himself and grinned at her. "You'll make it."

Several of the men had gathered to hear the end of this conversation.

"Did you say we all have to make it to the top before supper?"

Zoysana's cheerful voice came from behind them. "That's right. So you'd better have a large lunch now, because it might be a while before we eat again."

They sat munching on the bread and cheese they had carried with them and passed a skin of watered wine around. Just as everyone was settling down to digest it, Zoysana stood. "All right, Jhanes. You've had a nice rest all morning. Ready to go?"

He shrugged. "Any time. You going to drag me up, or shall I lift you?"

She looked up at him. "I'm not dragging you anywhere. Get up there and show us you're not dead weight."

He wrapped the rope around his chest, tugged twice at the knot to test it, and headed up the wall. It was nice rock, firm and rough to the touch. He jammed his fist into a vertical crack and started up. There was no foothold, so it would be a hand-over-hand job. He moved up quickly; it was hardly comfortable, holding most of his weight on one hand stuffed into the rough rock of the crack.

As the crevice narrowed, he found he could only get two knuckles in, and then it began to get painful. When the crack got even narrower, he slid his fingers in, elbows wide, and created enough friction by pulling as if he wanted to widen the gap. There was a ledge about four head-heights up, and he made it, gasping quietly to himself. He planted a ring and motioned Zoysana to follow him.

She found it easier because of her strength and light weight, and soon Varli joined them. They stared upward.

"I can't see anything for the next two head-heights."

Jhanes leaned out against the rope. "Nothing until that nub up there. Think you can reach it if I lift you?"

"It will be a stretch for both of us. Let's have a go."

He held his hands together in a stirrup and boosted her up onto his shoulders. Then, taking her heels on his palms, he lifted her up to the length of his arms. She stood there, and he began to wonder how long he could hold this pose. Then the weight was gone and a triumphant shout from the men below told him she was on the next ledge.

"No one can do that bit alone. I'll double-rope here, put in an extra ring for safety, and you two can come up."

After she had finished, they mounted the rope, walking their feet up the rock face. From the next ledge there were ample handholds. Jhanes looked up to see Patu's shaggy head peering down at them over the edge. There were other routes. Varli scrambled to the top to place the safety ropes, and Zoysana started back down.

"You stay here to belay everyone past the difficult part as they hand-over-hand up the ropes."

He nodded and sat on the ledge, his feet dangling over empty space, and looked out at the valley below him. Over to his right, he could see smoke columns from the fires of the main military camp. In front of him, the road to the castle showed because of the fresh slashing to make room for the supply wagons. Over to the left, some of the lower foothills were cleared, and he could see two of the low log cabins of the hill farmers. A burst of smoke from below the treeline caught his attention.

"Varli, look out there. What can you see?"

There was a moment's pause. "Looks like a barn in flames."

"Anybody around?"

"I don't see anyone at all. Strange."

"Not if it was set by Inari and the farmers had the field of fire covered with their bows. I think you'd better come down."

"Right."

Jhanes looked down. Zoysana had just reached the ground. "There's somebody in trouble out there, Zoysana. Barn on fire. Looks like the attack is still going on. It's that farm that gave us the berries the other day."

She craned her head upwards. "Any sign of troops going to help?"

By this time Varli was beside him, and the boy shook his head. He shouted down again. "We're the closest help they've got."

Zoysana looked at the men gathered eagerly around her. "Well, friends, it looks like we've got our first assignment. Leave the equipment. Weapons only. Mount up." She looked up the cliff, where Jhanes was descending. "Varli, you'll be the last down. Ride to the camp and have Lord Tour send us a troop of Light Horse, just in case there are more of them than we can handle."

The youth nodded and started down the rope.

By the time Jhanes reached the ground, the clearing at the foot of the rock held only dust and piles of discarded rope. He ran to his horse, slipped the bit into its mouth and mounted even as he was turning the animal down the trail to the east. Varli was right behind him, spinning his horse towards the west.

20. First Battle

In the half hour he rode, Jhanes didn't catch up to anyone, but there was no missing the shredded forest floor and the dust hanging in the air. Then he rounded a bend and found the whole troop dismounting around Zoysana. He swung down and shouldered his way to her.

"All right, we have two choices. We can go in there like the cavalry, scare them off with noise. Or we can try some of our own tricks. Sneak up behind them and take a few of them out before they even know we're there. Are you up to it?"

She shushed the rising murmur of their voices. "Good. Then it's quiet from here. Pair up. One man to come in front on foot, the other to stay back with the two horses. If we run into trouble up front, the horsemen come in at a gallop. Make up your minds as we ride. No arguments. I want the best woodsmen on the ground, and you know who you are."

Jhanes translated this to the Inari and made sure they were paired as she had instructed. He added a further warning to them. "Anyone who doesn't follow Zoysana's orders to the last detail goes back up over the mountain tonight. Do you follow?"

They all nodded. He knew there would be no trouble with the division of the pairs; they were used to making this sort of decision in raiding situations.

The troop mounted up, two by two, and walked their horses quietly down the trail. Soon they stopped again, and Zoysana signalled the attackers to dismount. Jhanes stayed on his horse, and she caught his eye.

"You'll know if we need you." She turned and slipped off through the forest.

He was sure he would. Leading Zoysana's mountain pony, he pushed to the front of the horsemen and moved even more slowly along the path. Then he stopped. There, in the clearing in front of them, was a line of Inari horses tied to trees. Two still figures lay stretched on the ground beside them: sentries who had paid the price for inattention.

The last of Zoe's attackers was just disappearing down the trail. As he dismounted to tie up the unconscious Inari, Jhanes looked upwards to see the black smoke ahead. They were very near now, and he wondered at the silence.

"If they catch on to us, some of them will be back for their horses."

Jhanes nodded to the Guide who slid up beside him. "We should post a guard."

"Is that what Zoysana said?"

"No, but that's what she will expect. You do a lot of improvising in times like this. As long as we're ready to bring the horses in quickly when she needs them, we can do what we need to."

He positioned his men in a guarding circle around the Inari horses, keeping the Petrellan soldiers and squires closer in, sending the Guides and Inari out farther. "Remember, lads, this bunch must be some of the best. The Guides won't have let them come over this pass, so they've brought their horses from farther away and they haven't been caught yet. Keep your eyes skinned for any movement and don't be afraid to shout for help if you see anything. Again, no hero stuff. We do this together. That's how we'll beat them. Try to stay within sight of me so I can signal you. And watch the ground near you. They can sneak up amazingly close."

He loosened the thong on his sword but left it sheathed, and readied his bow.

"Anine." The big mercenary was still mounted nearby. "How are you with horses?"

She grinned. "All my life on a farm."

"Some of them will get through our lines. They'll try to stampede their stock so they can pick them up in the forest. Get down among their horses and be ready. Watch the horses, not the forest. They'll tell you if anyone is near. If they cut any loose, keep as many as you can under control. But don't leave your back uncovered. One hand to your sword at all times."

She nodded and slipped off her horse. He had given her a dangerous job, but he was too short of men to send two. He would try to watch out for her, although other things could interfere.

He scanned as many of his command as he could see. Everyone was keyed up, alert. He responded to several glances, signalling some to better positions. They waited.

A high, wavering cry rang out over the forest. His men reacted, listening and looking. He raised his voice just enough that most would hear. "Zoysana. She'll be starting the attack now." Still there was silence.

Then a flicker of motion attracted his attention. One of his outposts had slipped to the ground. Not knowing whether the man had been attacked or had ducked because he saw something, Jhanes chose to be pessimistic and reined his horse nearer. Sure enough, the sentry lay unmoving, and there was no other sign of life.

"There's one inside, Anine." He looked back. One of the enemy sentries was gone. The other looked still unconscious.

"Two inside. Everybody move in and watch your backs." As he spoke, Jhanes was swinging the bow around.

A head broke from the grass at the feet of the horses, but his arrow was on its way before the man could rise, and he sprawled, arms outflung, back to the ground. "Anine, look out for the other one!"

The girl had her back to several horses, one hand on their halters, looking up at them. "He's over there!" She pointed to a clump of willows at the edge of the clearing. Jhanes had another arrow nocked, but the Inari burst low from the other side of the clump and slashed at halter ropes with his knife before disappearing behind the horses. Several mounts stampeded out into the forest.

"Stay where you are and don't shoot inward!" He glanced around as he pushed his horse closer, crowding some of the freed horses into the centre of the clearing. He had to keep moving; someone in the forest could target him for an arrow. He circled the stock; the Inari had disappeared, probably on one of the horses, but he couldn't depend on it.

Gradually the mounts settled, and stillness returned. Everyone waited, heads up, but there was no repeat attack. The second sentry had not moved. Jhanes rode over to the fallen Inari; his chest was pierced. Dead. The mercenary who had fallen was finished as well, his throat a bloody mess.

Then Zoysana's whistle lifted through the trees. He whistled back, and she responded. "The fight's over, but there are still lots around. Zoysana is sending help, and we'll move the horses to the farm. Don't let down your guard for an instant."

They held their position until Zoysana and Patu reappeared with four of her Inari. "We snuck up on them, had to kill a few. Five or ten slipped out when the fight started. Have to keep a sharp eye. How'd it go here?"

He reported briefly. She walked over to the dead mercenary and stood, looking sorrowfully down on him. Then she shook her head as if waking from a dream. "I'll take over the watch. Bring them all to the farm." She strode off, spreading her Inari and Guides through the woods ahead of them.

Jhanes and Anine gathered the horses while two others put the bodies and the still-unconscious Inari sentry across saddles. They reached the farm without incident and rode into the open field where they could relax their vigilance. The rest of their troop was scattered, either on sentry duty or hauling buckets from the stream to throw on what was left of the barn. A scorch mark up the side of the cabin showed how close the attackers had come to succeeding.

They laid the bodies next to three dead Inari and one lad, scarcely more than a boy, who wore peasant's homespun. A woman sat holding his head and moaning. The arrow transfixing his chest left no doubt he was dead. Jhanes turned away to check the situation. The creek was out in the open, more than a bowshot from the forest edge, so the firefighters were safe.

"Maura and Anine, take these three and scout the property." He indicated two Guides and an Inari standing nearby. "One of them could be hiding anywhere." He translated for the Inari. "Don't overlook anything. Stay in a group."

They passed the bodies and the weeping woman as they started out, and he knew they would be careful.

Just as Zoysana's scouting party slipped in from the woods, there was a thunder of hooves and twenty Light Horse swept into the clearing, Varli in the lead. He pulled his lathered mount to a sliding stop, surveying the scene.

"Well, Jhanes, it looks as if you have everything in hand here. How did we fare?"

"We only lost Madhuran."

Varli swore. "He was a great bowman."

"But he never looked down." They both turned to see Maura, her lean face grim. "He had the bowman's problem. Always scanning for a target. He ignored what was close to him. I always told him, but he wouldn't listen. He wouldn't listen..." She turned away with a potent curse of her own and went back to scouring the immediate vicinity for Inari stragglers.

"They were friends." Anine spoke softly, then followed the other woman.

"I gathered." Jhanes turned to where Zoysana and the Horse captain were talking.

She gestured to a disconsolate row of Inari. "What do we do with the prisoners?"

He considered only a moment. "Let them go, if they want."

The cavalryman stared at him. "Let them go?"

He shrugged. "Take them to the bottom of the pass and send them home. They won't be back."

"How can you be sure?"

"Rules. They belong to Zoysana, now. Slaves. Her clan took them prisoner in battle. She can keep them or set them loose, but they'll still belong to her. She can collect them at any time, and they can't do anything against her or her clan, which means all of us. If she tells them not to come back, they won't."

"Are you sure?"

"I'll talk to them, if you like. They may want to stay here, though."

"Why?"

"They've been defeated. They've lost the game. They won't want to go back empty-handed and enslaved. But there's no shame in serving someone who is so good at the game as to beat them. Especially since it's Zoysana, who has a powerful reputation and will gain an even bigger one, now. Most will want to join us."

Zoysana nodded. "Do we want to keep them?"

"Might be embarrassing at times. You've never owned slaves, have you?"

"I should hope not, and I don't plan to start!"

He grinned. "You may think that. They have another point of view. Maybe we should talk to them."

They strode over to the dejected group of five Inari sitting on the ground, the sentry conscious now, but still holding his head.

"The Leader Zoysana would like to speak to you."

They were on their feet immediately, even the injured one.

"The Leader Zoysana has accepted your surrender."

Their heads drooped.

"What should the Leader do with her new slaves?"

The youths glanced at each other, then one stepped forward. "The Leader Zoysana has proved her superiority. We are impressed at her craft and that of her clan. We also bow to the Grandfather of Wolves." He actually bowed to Patu and rubbed a forearm that was fang-scored, top and bottom. "We would serve our new master in any way she wishes us."

"And if she told you to return to your clan and never come back?"

Anxiety passed over his face. "The Potentara Zoysana would not be so cruel. If we return defeated, we go to a poor life. We would not get good brides. We would be sent to the farthest edges of fire and tent. Far better to be a slave to the great Leader Zoysana than to live such a life."

"And what if the Leader sends you to fight against your kin?"

The lad thought. "That would be difficult."

"Would you do it?"

He shrugged. "If our master ordered, we would have to." He regarded Jhanes, then Zoysana, and raised his chin. "But it would be best for our master to know that against our own clan we could not fight as honorably in her cause."

Jhanes translated. "A good answer. This lad just took a calculated risk, based on your reputation. He hopes you will appreciate his honesty rather than empty promises."

"Well, he's right."

"Shall I tell him that?"

"He already knows." She allowed a small smile to quirk her lip. Then she sighed. "Tell my new 'slaves' that there is work to do. There is wood to gather and graves to dig. Not the one with the sore head. Tell him to rest."

They were late to supper that night. By the time the Inari funeral pyres had burned down and Zoysana had spoken the words of the Lady over the graves of the mercenary and the farm lad, it was approaching dusk. Leaving three Inari ponies and all the captured weapons with the farmer and his family, they jogged their horses back to the main camp.

Once the meal was finished and the wineskins had passed around, the mood changed. Each part of the battle had to be retold for those who had been elsewhere, or who had not noticed the stunning feats of their mates. As the wineskins emptied, the battle seemed to get larger and the feats greater. Toasts and tears remembered Madhuran, their first casualty, and his past exploits and feats of daring were recounted by his mercenary friends. Finally, Maura got to her feet, a half-empty wineskin dangling from an unsteady hand.

"It is time to put Madhuran to rest. He was a good friend and a good soldier. He saved my life a few times, and I returned the favour. But one thing he left us might save our lives again. The lesson he didn't learn. Watch your feet! When you fight the Inari, watch your feet."

The response was instant. "Watch your feet!"

They chanted the mantra several times before the sound died away. Maura took a long pull at the wineskin, then looked around, puzzled, as if she couldn't remember why she was standing there. Then she plopped down and said no more for the rest of the evening.

Soon, the troop staggered off to their tents, slapping the shoulders of anyone within reach. Jhanes and Zoysana watched them go.

"It went well."

He yawned. "Yes, it did. They are beginning to gel."

She yawned too, then fell silent, her hand at the medallion she wore under her shirt. "And Madhuran was a part of that."

"A necessary part. It had to be someone. It was him. Lady be kind to him."

She nodded, swallowed, gripped the medallion tighter. "Lady be kind to him."

"It isn't easy, I know."

"I've lost men before."

"It still isn't easy. It shouldn't be. And you didn't lose him. I did."

She turned to face him. "No arguments. We lost him. It's hard. But we did well otherwise. You did what I expected of you."

"It's the only thing I can do – what you expect. I'm not brilliant, but I'll never surprise you."

"I don't need surprises from my second-in-command."

"Is that what I am?"

She paused, then shrugged. "We never discussed it, but that's what happened. In fact, it's been obvious from the beginning. Now it's official."

"Will that cause any problems?"

"Can you think of any? The men – and women – won't have any trouble with it. Most of them are commoners. Those three squires are so in awe of you, just from Varli's stories, that they would do anything you told them. The officers of the other troops here are used to dealing with mercenaries. They don't care who the leader is, as long as his men do their job. And we are going to do just fine."

"I think so, too. Good night, Zoysana."

"Good night. And Jhanes?"

"Yes?"

"Watch your feet."

He grinned as she strode away, aware of the significance of the words. Madhuran, their first loss, would live on in Zoysana's troop.

21. Visitors

Jhanes stumbled as he rounded the corner of his tent. It wasn't so much that he was tired, although he was: bone-weary. But he wasn't paying attention. Too much else on his mind.

It had been a frustrating day. He had taken a mixed squad out, and the sharp eyes of the Inari had picked up a group of invaders coming down off the mountain. However, by the time Jhanes and his troop reached the area, the intruders were gone. It was disheartening work, trying to move quickly while remaining unseen and unheard. This bunch of Inari was good, and their trail was very difficult to follow, finally disappearing completely over a slab of solid rock. The men came home in a ragged mood, and Jhanes felt it keenly. He was sitting slouched over the small table in his tent when Zoysana's voice broke his reverie.

"Anyone home?"

"Come in."

"My, such enthusiasm." She swung a camp stool around and sat, eyeing him. "Is there a problem?"

"I suppose not. Well, we didn't have much success today. Saw a bigger bunch than usual across the valley, coming down along the shoulder of the Lavenhorn. But by the time we got over there they were gone, and we lost their trail on the rocks above Ansler's Creek. It was a tough, hot day with nothing to show for it, and the men came back pretty discouraged."

"It's happened before. We'll just have to keep a close eye on that section. Did you put it on the chart?" There was a large map of the area in the command tent where everyone marked the progress of bands of enemy they had spotted.

"Yes. But that's not the problem. It's the men's morale. I should have found a way to turn it around. It's poor leadership to leave them down like that at the end of a day."

Zoysana grinned, slapped him on the shoulder. "Jhanes, you're worrying over nothing. You can't have complete success every day. Let them stew. Good for their strength of character."

He returned her smile sheepishly. "Well, speaking for myself, my character doesn't need any more strengthening."

"Perhaps. But the group needs adversity. It will do them good."

"I suppose. Better this than losing a battle."

Her smile dropped. "That has to come, too."

"I know. I hope I'm up to that, when it comes."

"What do you mean? You've been through it a score of times."

"Not me. Them. I'm the leader. I have to get them through it. You know how it happens. When things get tough and morale is low, that's when you find out the real problems. That's when you find out if the men really think you're the leader."

"Jhanes, do you think the men have any doubt you're their leader? The king himself appointed you. I support you in every way. How could they doubt?"

He sighed and leaned both forearms on the table. "I don't know. It's different for me, I guess. I've been a soldier too long, watching the leaders, figuring out what mistakes they made. Now I'm the one that has to cope. And then there's the Inari way."

"Their leadership style?"

"That's right. With the Inari, being appointed by somebody doesn't mean pig slop. You earn it every time you take the troop out."

"And do they expect success every time?"

"No, I suppose not. Nobody wins every battle."

Her smile returned. "So what are you worried about?"

He shrugged. "It sounds so logical when you say it. But I'm not dealing with Inari here. I'm trying to lead squires from noble families, veteran soldiers with superior rank to mine..."

"Nobody has superior rank to yours in this outfit."

"You know what I mean."

"Ah. But this has nothing to do with the men. They all have the greatest respect for you. You need to have more respect for yourself."

"In other words, kick myself in the butt and get over it."

"If that's what it takes, yes. The one thing that will cause you real trouble with the men is if you lose confidence in yourself."

He nodded. "I've seen it happen."

"Right. So, when you were a soldier, you watched the officers' problems. Now you've got them. Can you deal with them?"

"Because if I can't...?"

She didn't answer. They both knew the answer.

"I guess I'll deal with them."

"I think you will." She clapped him on the shoulder as she rose. "And now I have a more pleasant task. I'm riding out to meet Gerth."

"Is he coming in now?"

"About a candle's ride out, according to the scouts. I'm getting dressed in my best and going to escort him. Varli and I and a couple of my Inari, just for fun."

"Well, don't waste your time coddling me. Away you go."

She turned back with a level stare. "I have my priorities straight." Then she grinned and disappeared through the tent flap, leaving him deep in thought.

He knew what she meant. He'd seen officers go through this. If an officer got to worrying about his own competence his men would know, and he would start to feel their knowledge. That would make it worse, and the problems would start. Orders would be questioned or obeyed half-heartedly. The officer would react by being more demanding. The men would get sullen; the officer would get picky.

Some officers reached a rough balance and managed to stay there, uncomfortable as it was. They considered that the "price of command" or some such excuse. For the Inari, and especially for Jhanes, there could be no such situation. *I have to buck myself up, right now. No more snivelling. Get down to business, as my commanding officer has reminded me.*

Then he remembered. *Gerth is coming.* He'd been so immersed in his own problems he had missed that. *Are the men ready? Do they know? I'd better go and see.* Relieved to have something to do, he jumped to his feet and strode out of his tent.

With the activity and the enthusiastic response of the camp, Jhanes felt a whole lot better as he stood in front of the ragged line of his troop as the king rode in. Gerth looked impressive as usual on his big bay horse, a handful of Warlanders of his personal guard following. Zoysana, riding beside him on her pony, looked even smaller than usual, and Varli…

He regarded the young squire again.

…Varli was not his usual cheerful self. A frown clouded his face, and anger twisted every line of his body. His horse was skittish, responding to its master's mood. With uncommon lack of ceremony, the boy swung aside as the cavalcade swept into camp. The men cheered as Gerth, smiling and waving, swung down from his destrier then turned to the tall Warlander riding beside him…

…and helped her dismount. Long blonde locks flowed from under the helmet and a rounded hip instead of the usual metal tasset lifted as she swung her leg over the cantle of the saddle.

"Why did he bring her here?"

Jhanes looked down to see Varli, his eyes flashing with rage, standing next to him. "What's the problem?"

"He shouldn't have brought her out here. There's a war going on! It's too dangerous. Oh, she looks big and strong with all that armour on, but you know what she's like with a sword. He never should have brought her."

Jhanes glanced down at the boy, then turned back to watch Gerth and Talia. They were both enjoying themselves hugely with everyone's surprise and delight at having the lady in camp. He decided to be noncommittal. "Good for the men's morale."

"Not so good as it will be bad if she gets hurt or killed. I thought he liked her."

"Oh, he likes her, sure enough."

Varli shook his head. "I mean really likes her. You know…"

"Enough to marry her?"

Varli nodded. "It would be a good match. He has to form strong alliances, and Uncle Cheyne is one of the more astute diplomats in the Inner Duchies. But it won't do anybody a lot of good if she comes out here and gets killed."

"Maybe that's the point."

"What?"

"I've heard the strategy sessions as well as the gossip. Gerth needs a queen who can cope with our life. If she can't handle it, now's the best time to find out. That's harsh, but it's true. I doubt if he would have brought her if he didn't think she could handle herself. Give the king credit for a touch of intelligence. And if you don't, at least credit his mother."

Varli relaxed, but he was still frowning. "Yes, Kenna must have approved. Still, I'm worried."

"So am I. So is every man in camp. I think she'll be well protected."

Varli glanced up at him. "You're probably right." Then his face became grim. "But I'm still going to give them a piece of my mind." He started forward, but the soldier laid a big hand on his shoulder.

"I'm sure they're expecting it, but not just now. Let them have their fun." He felt the boy relax, and the two of them stood, watching Gerth and Talia accept the greetings of the men. *The morale problem is solved for the moment, anyway.*

Then Zoysana stepped forward with her two mercenaries. "You didn't bring attendants, Lady Talia?"

The lady gave an unladylike snort. "Lateda was the only one who would come."

Zoysana grinned. "Well, Maura and Anine here will help keep the men away while you bathe."

Jhanes was pleased to note that both his soldiers kept their dignity, bowing appropriately, although he could see by Anine's flush that she was nervous.

As Talia laughed and followed them off, he heard Maura's voice lowered in conspiracy. "My Lady, there really is a tub, and if you wouldn't mind waiting, we could get some water heated…"

* * *

The next day during practice session the morale rose even more. Jhanes was enjoying the men's new enthusiasm in their sparring when a voice came from behind him.

"Ah! The innkeeper. I've been looking for you."

He swung round, and there she was, with Gerth a step behind her, grinning. She was outfitted in a helmet, short-sleeved chain-mail shirt and a set of forearm bracers that looked more like jewelry than armour. She offered him the largest practice sword in the rack.

"Come and work with me. The others are afraid to, and Gerth doesn't want to hurt me, so he holds back."

"And you don't think I will?"

She looked at him candidly. "If I ask you to, you'll push me as far as I can go. If I get hurt, that's the way it has to be."

He nodded. "I'll do my best." Then he grinned. "Not ashamed to be seen fighting the innkeeper?"

She gripped her weapon with fake grimness. "I doubt if anyone else thinks of you that way."

He hefted the sword, clapped on his helmet liner with the other hand. "If that's designed to lull me into inattention, you're succeeding, my Lady."

A grin broke through. "Then 'ware thyself!"

With a helpless look at the king, who was enjoying this immensely, he backed onto the practise ground, Talia following, sizing him up. As she stepped forward, he watched her with a professional eye. She moved without hurry, planting each foot firmly, her weight centred. *Not bad. Maybe she has learned something.* He began to circle around her, his sword swinging, but she refused to be drawn. She waited, composed.

He tried a simple overhand attack, which she parried with a careful swing: not too quick, not too far. He continued with a regular three-pattern over-under, and she was able to cope. A varied tempo almost threw her, but she stayed with him. Purposely, he allowed some openings, waiting to see what she would do. Sure enough, she countered with a quick backswing that made him dance away. She grinned and moved in at her own speed, slowly but surely, her sword meeting his with strength.

He parried hard, twisting his sword to make her ripostes difficult, but she hung on, her grip sure. He tried to shake her with several sudden jabs, which she avoided with difficulty but kept her poise. A bead of sweat appeared on her upper lip, but there was no sign of weakening.

Now he had her measure and was impressed at her level. The awkwardness she had complained about was absent. Her movements had a long way to go to achieve the fluidity of the professional and she was using too much strength. Still, he was pleased. He paused a moment, his sword on guard.

"Time for work, my Lady."

She nodded, adjusting her grip.

"Not too tight. Keep the wrist supple."

She nodded again and swung her sword back and forth, ready.

"Now we fight." He started a short backswing, but she was before him with an unconventional jab straight to the heart, which he slipped sideways to avoid, bringing his sword around in a short arc towards her helmet. She ducked in turn, twisting her sword in a quick move around her wrist to make a chop at his thigh. By this time he was back in balance and she missed, but she recovered as well with a backswing that forced him into a more conventional exchange. He began to vary his timing and level of attack, and she followed, her face grimmer now, the sweat staining her cheek.

With a quick twist, he forced her sword into a bind and pushed against her, testing the strength of her wrists. She slid away in a standard escape that he could have beaten, but he let her go, continuing his attack instead. His sword whistled closer to her, nipping here and there, not hard. She held on, trying her best to keep up, but her breath was coming heavily and the tip of her sword was lower. He worked against her wrist and she brought her left hand into play, working the weapon two-handed, a move that restricted her mobility but saved her strength.

He worked to the outside with a touch to her shoulder, then sudden low cut that bounced off her greave. When she swung a low backhand to counter, he reversed and rattled two fast ones off her helmet before she could straighten.

He was prepared to stop at any time, but she recovered in desperation, several wild slashes driving him away while she regained her balance. It was the proper time, and he pushed her far enough back, then grounded his sword. Panting, she did the same. He smiled and nodded.

"Very good, my Lady. What happened to all that clumsiness you used to complain about? Was that a ruse to put me off my guard?"

She shook her head, fighting for breath. "Nobody gave me a big enough sword."

"Pardon?"

She swallowed, breathed deeply, then smiled. "A big enough sword. The little ones don't work for me. I can't move in rooms full of small furniture and small people. I need space and a big sword that keeps its own path, so I just push it along."

They turned to walk to where the king and the others were waiting. "Well, my Lady, you certainly surprised me. Who's been teaching you?"

She dimpled. "Just about everyone. It turns out I'm a good pupil, and they all want to take credit for my success."

He raised his voice as they approached the king. "Credit where credit is due, my Lady. That was a good workout you gave me."

Gerth laughed. "She's good, isn't she?"

Jhanes sobered. "With due respect, your Majesty, she isn't."

There was silence, and he felt obliged to continue. "It would be doing her a disservice to tell her she was good. She has improved a great deal and she should be very proud of herself, but we are in a dangerous situation, and it would be perilous for her to have an inflated opinion of her abilities." He bowed his head. "I'm sorry if that displeases your Majesty."

Then he looked the king in the eye.

Gerth nodded, then reached out to clap him on the shoulder. "I believe you are right. We were playing a little game back at the castle that was a lot of fun. We came here to be serious, and you have reminded us of that. I know you will be honest. Where would you rank Lady Talia's abilities?"

Jhanes paused to think while relief coursed through him. "If she were a new recruit, I would be pleased to have her in my unit. A month of training and strengthening and she would be fit to hold her place in the line."

The king nodded. "I'm glad to hear that, Jhanes. I would have been more charitable than that, but perhaps I am too close, being one of her trainers."

...and more than that. The soldier noticed the look that passed between the two. "Are you rested, my Lady? Would you like to try against someone else?"

She hefted her sword. "Everyone is always telling me I'm supposed to keep going, no matter how tired I am. Who's my next victim?"

A mischievous thought flashed into his head. "Varli, perhaps?"

Her eyes lit up. "Oh, yes, where is my little cousin?"

Varli was at her elbow. "Right here, Cousin."

Jhanes handed him the sword. "Would it bother you to work with the lady?"

Varli snorted, and his eye slid to Zoysana. "I was trained by a lady. But take this big club away. I'll use one my own size." He took a smaller sword off the rack and moved into the practice field, working the swing of it, loosening his shoulders. Jhanes strolled beside him.

"Work her hard, Varli. She came for the reality. But don't hurt her too bad."

Varli grinned. "The king might be displeased at bruised merchandise."

Jhanes walked back to the side of the field to watch, wondering how Varli would express his displeasure. Perhaps he would feel differently about it when he felt the power in her swing. He suspected that this bout would not be so levelheaded as the last.

Sure enough, Varli seemed determined to show his cousin the reality of the situation. He attacked quickly, a rapid pattern that suited his lighter sword. He scored twice before she recovered and returned a huge, looping swing towards his head that brought him up short. For a moment she controlled the tempo, but soon he had her measure and took advantage of her longer, slower swing to get inside her guard. The "thwack" of wood on padding resounded several times.

Still she fought on, her moves more ragged, but stronger in her desperation. She scored once, a glancing blow to the top of his helmet, which brought cheers from the assembled watchers. Varli shook it off and bored in with determination.

She saw his bind coming and pushed it off. He tried to twist her sword away, but her wrist was too strong. He jabbed a few times, scoring at her stomach and thigh then dancing away before the big sword could come around. Still, she refused to be shaken, stalking after him at her own pace.

The pattern continued for a while, with Varli scoring more often and Talia's swings increasingly wild. Then, just as Jhanes was starting to wonder if he should step in, Varli stood back.

"Well fought, Cousin. Shall we rest?"

Her breath was coming too fast to answer, but she grounded her sword wearily.

"Don't ever lean on it." His voice was sharp.

She started upright. "Why not?"

"Because you might need it. If you're leaning on it, you can't get it into play fast enough. Zoysana taught me that. The habits you develop on the practice field come out when you're weariest, when it's the most dangerous."

She leaned the sword against her thigh and used her left hand to mop sweat from her cheek. "Good point, Varli, I'll remember that."

He grinned. "Good enough. I see his Majesty has improved your skill a bit, though."

"Do you think so?"

"Oh, yes. You almost got me once, there."

"Almost! I made your head ring, admit it."

"A glancing blow. But a good effort, I grant you that." They started off the field, and the other soldiers, who had paused to watch, returned to their sparring. "She's come a long way, your Majesty."

"In more ways than one, Squire." Gerth seemed pleased, in spite of the drubbing she had taken. "How do you feel, Lady Talia?"

She tipped back her helmet and smudged a dirty hand across her brow. "Like I need a bath. Not a hot one in a little tub."

Varli winked at Jhanes. "Well, we made a small lake by damming the creek."

264

She looked at him a moment, wondering. "Is it cold?" She thought a moment more. "Is it private?"

He swept her a bow. "Both can be arranged, my Lady."

She nodded regally. "Then arrange it, please." She lifted her arm in that simple gesture of hers and Gerth managed to be there to take it.

Jhanes chuckled to himself. *The king is getting trained as well.*

22. THE TRAP

"Not a chance. You're not taking her on patrol. Please, Gerth!"

Jhanes turned to see Varli facing up to his king.

Gerth raised his hand. "I know, Varli. It's a risk. But don't you think it's worth it?"

Varli wasn't about to be put off. "Your Majesty, as the representative of the Medure family here, I have to look out for the best interests of my cousin. I admit she is much more adept than I had expected, but still..." He seemed for once at a loss for words. "She said it herself. We are in a war here."

The king smiled. "Varli, could anyone persuade your cousin not to come to Petrella?" He paused, but there was no answer. He turned and, putting his arm across his squire's shoulders, led him away from the crowded area, motioning Jhanes to follow. "Exactly. And it was the same this time. So either she's right or she's wrong. If she's right and she can handle it, then she has proven herself. If she's wrong, it's best she finds out now, before it's too late."

Varli's head twisted back towards Jhanes. "That's what he said."

The king glanced back to the soldier, then continued walking. "It is good for my officers to keep a picture of the whole campaign in mind, not just their own part in it. Zoysana and I both feel that way. Jhanes has been given enough information to make the observation on his own. Do you see how much easier it is, now that I don't have to waste time persuading him?"

Varli shook his head. "I suppose you're right. But I don't want to be the one to tell my uncle if anything happens to her." His shoulders drooped more. "And I will be, won't I?"

Gerth clapped him between the shoulder blades, hard enough that the lad stumbled. "We'll have to make sure nothing happens, then, won't we?"

They had slowed while this conversation took place, and Jhanes paced up beside the king. "One thing we must be aware of, your Majesty, is that she is a disruption in our battle plans. If everyone thinks only of her safety, they will not hold their proper positions."

"A good point. I suppose you have a solution?"

Jhanes thought furiously. He had done a certain amount of bodyguarding, winters when there was no soldiering. "She needs an assigned guard, responsible for her safety. Then the rest of us can concentrate on our own duties."

"And who have you in mind?"

"She brought her own three mercs for camp duty, but they're flatlanders. I wouldn't take them into the forest or up on the rocks without training."

"You would take Talia out in the forest, but not a trained mercenary?"

He shrugged. "I wouldn't take any of them. You're the one who wants her to have the experience. One person like that is enough in a scouting party. Three or four, and it becomes exactly what our enemy loves. A big, clumsy mob."

The king nodded.

"Our two women are the obvious attendants. In fact, if we were to dress Anine in similar costume, from a distance they could be taken for each other, which might confuse anyone who knew who they were after. Maura is better than average with all weapons, and Anine has the strength and brains to make up for her lack of experience. I think they would be excellent choices. She should never be out without a full squad, Inari and other Clan. I think Lateda, skilled though she is, should stay in camp, at least at first. She won't like it, but she'll understand that this is a different style of fighting than she's used to."

The king nodded. "It's up to you to arrange it." He grinned. "Which, I just realize, you already have. Well done, Innkeeper." He turned to Varli. "Satisfied?"

The squire nodded. "As long as I go along when she's out of camp."

Gerth grinned. "She might not appreciate a nursemaid, but I'll leave that problem to you. She's your cousin."

Varli nodded wryly. "That she is."

So for the succeeding days, Lady Talia and Gerth joined Varli and Jhanes on their patrol. As time passed, the lady's pace quickened, and the constant training firmed her wrist and smoothed her fighting. Jhanes watched her with increasing respect. *She doesn't quit. Gerth is lucky to have found her.*

One day they were on a routine sweep on foot through a rocky section farther out from the mountain than usual, and it should have been safe. Jhanes fanned three Inari out on point and the rest of the squad moved in a loose group through the rugged terrain with Gerth and Jhanes to the front, Talia and her bodyguards in the centre, Pagris on rear guard. The sun was just getting hot enough to have them thinking about a break and a drink when a bird whistle cut the air.

Everyone froze, and Jhanes answered. Then another came from the left, repeated twice. Gerth turned a questioning face to the soldier. He whistled twice, sharply, and turned to the king.

"We've got a problem. For some reason, there are three groups of Inari in the area. We weren't expecting any, but that's the Inari for you. I've called the scouts in to get a verbal report. If they are here in force, we'll retreat to camp and get reinforcements. If you wish, your Majesty."

Gerth shook his head. "You call the game here, Soldier. I'm just a visitor. Let's wait till the scouts report." Jhanes nodded, but he could see the king's right hand slip up to touch the hilt of the big sword slung across his shoulders.

Pagris grinned. "Good Inari style."

The king raised an eyebrow, so Jhanes explained.

268

"The Inari don't follow the same leader for everything. A good hunter is the hunt leader. A good tactician handles the larger battles. An especially brave or strong fighter might lead a frontal attack. Different leaders for different jobs."

Just then, the first Inari appeared and spoke a few words. The second man's report was just as brief. The centre man had seen nothing.

Jhanes turned to the king. "It looks like this. There are two big groups, maybe ten men each, one on either side of us, and a smaller group headed at an angle about to cross behind us. That means they'll cut our trail, and also that there's no retreat for reinforcements. At the moment they don't know we're here, and the only way out is to keep going."

The king nodded. "What do you suggest?"

"Added to this, these are Pregota Clan, the group most opposed to trading. They are the traditionalists, the ones who are pushing the raiding the most. I'm worried at the number of fighters. If this is the whole attack, that's not a problem, except for us."

Gerth nodded. "But it might be a larger push."

"Exactly. Which is why I would like your Majesty to forget his visitor role. There are larger policy matters to be considered."

"True. I think we need to get word through to camp, no matter what. But if these are the best men of the worst troublemakers, it's too bad we can't give them a lesson."

Jhanes nodded. "Perhaps we can, your Majesty."

The king's face brightened. "How?"

"What I suggest, first, is that we take care of the other details. Two Guides should start now, off to our flanks and back to camp. One will pass behind the small party and the other will pass in front. The one in front will take great care not to leave a trail. When they are clear, they should make their best speed to camp and tell Lord Tour to double the patrols in this area."

"And the other detail?"

Jhanes nodded towards Lady Talia. "Her safety is next. I think Varli and her two guards should move her somewhere safe and hold out until we finish off the rest."

Varli agreed. "But if you attack them, won't they break up and fade away? That will split them up and make it even more dangerous for us, if we're trying to stay out of sight."

Jhanes grinned. "We give them a reason to attack us."

The king looked intrigued. "And what reason do you have in mind?"

"You, your Majesty."

"Me?"

"They can't resist a challenge. You need only to make a stand and they will all come running to try their might against you. It's the only way to get them to stay in one place."

One of the Inari touched his arm, asking for an explanation. Jhanes gave a brief rundown of his plan, and the scout spoke enthusiastically. Jhanes turned to the others.

"There's a perfect spot just ahead and to the left, a narrowing canyon that seems a perfect trap. A small squad of men could hold off a larger group for a while, just long enough for the rest of us to get behind them and crush them between us. The trappers trapped. They only outnumber us two to one. Shall we try it?"

Gerth considered. "Are there any other options?"

"I had thought of starting back in the same formation as before, but with double flankers. We encircle the small group coming up on our trail, wipe them out and fight a running battle home to camp with the rest, who will follow us for a while and then disappear, knowing we're aware of their presence. It's a less risky plan, but it would work."

Gerth shook his head. "I like the first one better. As long as Talia is protected."

The lady's chin rose. "I didn't come out here to be a hindrance. You do what you think is best. We can take care of ourselves."

A look of pride came into Anine's face, and Maura's body straightened. Varli merely rubbed his sword hilt.

"Fine, then. Jhanes, give the orders, and let's get moving."

The two Guides were soon on their way to camp, and half of the troop was hidden on a ledge overlooking the faint trail they had been following. Gerth and the rest, led by the Inari scout, made a clear track up the valley towards where they would make their stand.

It wasn't a long wait. Jhanes had been watching their back trail, and soon a head appeared, right where he had expected one. Seeing the path clear, the scout signalled, and a group of young Inari fighters, well spread out, slipped by. There were only seven of them, all Pregota, and the Guide had reported nine. Jhanes worried about those numbers, but considered that if he had been leading he would have sent messengers to bring the two other parties onto the trail.

Soon the second party appeared, eleven in number. They, too, glided past and faded up the canyon.

He waited a while after they had gone, then motioned everyone out of hiding. "Varli, you and Talia are best staying here. You're well hidden, and the less movement, the better. It's a good spot to fend off an attack."

Varli was about to speak when a faint shout startled them. "The first group has found Gerth."

Jhanes nodded. "Let's move. We don't want him to have to handle all of them for too long. We'll want point, flank, and rear scouts, in case the small group comes up behind us." He translated his orders for the Inari, assigned the scouting positions, and with one last reassuring look at Varli and Talia, moved out towards the faint sounds of battle ahead. As they crept along, he listened to the noise. It was good because it covered their approach, and also because it indicated Gerth and his group were still fighting. As they got closer, they could pick out Gerth's voice above the rest, directing the battle.

"Watch your back, Catis; keep them in front of you. Baroten, you take the little one, I'll handle the other two. Come on, you sneaking thieves. Are you afraid of me? That's better. Come on, I can handle two at once. I can handle three at once. No, Catis, let them try. Only help if they get on my back and start bouncing up and down." This diatribe was interspersed with Inarituk insults, which Gerth was learning rapidly.

Jhanes swept his group to a halt. A sentry, left to guard the backtrail but too interested in the battle to do a good job, was standing half-hidden beside a small pine. Pagris slipped up, and Jhanes motioned him forward. The man grinned and mouthed "Just like old times," as he turned away. Very soon, the sentry stiffened and slumped to the ground.

A quiet voice came from back in the troop. "Didn't watch his feet."

Pagris motioned them forward, and they crept up to his vantage point and saw the battle. Gerth stood with his back against a boulder, his men covering him on either side. Dead Inari were strewn around him like straw after a storm. There was blood on his left shoulder and his right thigh, and he looked grim as he hacked through the guard of the young giant facing him and kicked another attacker, who slammed against the rocks and fell like a rag. A ring of Inari, not bothering to hide themselves, watched with interest.

Jhanes signalled his men, and they spread out. There was a brief lull in the battle. Gerth threw up his sword and Jhanes lifted an arm in return. When the soldier dropped his hand Gerth attacked, his men behind him. The startled Inari had little time to raise their weapons when the second group fell on their rear, killing half of them in the first moments. The tide of battle turned so rapidly that Jhanes barely got out the call for encirclement before it was over. As far as he could tell, not one invader left the area. As the last one fell, the soldiers started to cheer, but Gerth held up a hand for silence.

From far back down the draw, an urgent whistle sounded.

"Varli!"

Their fatigue forgotten, they raced down the canyon. As they approached their former hiding place, they slowed to listen.

Nothing. They burst forward to emerge on a scene of stillness. Maura lay on the rock, her head cushioned in Anine's lap. Talia knelt beside her, holding a limp hand covered in blood. Varli stood nearby with drawn sword, watching outward. The rest were Inari, six of them, all down and out. One was completely decapitated.

Jhanes motioned four men to sweep as Gerth strode forward, dropping to his knee beside Talia. "What happened?"

She raised a face stained with sweat and tears. "They found us."

Varli spoke, his voice low, strained. "Some of them were smarter than we thought. They must have been scouting around and heard the battle, but they were moving slow enough to read the signs. They knew we were up here and attacked. Four from the front, two from above. I don't know how they got up there or how they got down without killing themselves, but when they came in behind us, we had to fight out in the open."

Jhanes gently moved Talia aside, looking down at Maura's pale face. "What happened to her?"

"I don't know. I was on the other side." Varli indicated Anine. "Ask her."

Anine looked up, her face tear-stained. "She saved me."

Gerth kept his patience. "How?"

"They were all over us. Three went for the lady and Varli, and Maura and I cut the other three out. I...I couldn't keep two of them away, and they were going to separate and go around me to Lady Talia, I could tell. So I just jumped on them."

"Both of them?"

She nodded. "I took them to the ground. Surprised them, I guess. Banged their heads together. But then I was down and the third was on me, but Maura took him herself. He caught her hand with his knife and she went over, hit her head, I guess, because she didn't get up. When he went for her, I got him with my sword. By the time I turned around, it was all over."

Gerth smiled. "Well done, Anine. And Maura too. That counts three of them. Varli?"

The boy shrugged. "Like she said, three came for us. I took two of them, left one for Talia. She was doing all right, but the other two had me cornered, and I could see one was about to get behind her. I dove for his legs, a real desperation move, and the other jumped me. Talia turned around and swung, took his head right off. Then she stood over me. I didn't even get off my knees. I remembered what you and Zoe do, you know, the high-low trick. That shook them, and we finished them off real quick."

Gerth turned to Talia. "You took his head off?"

She nodded slowly. "It was so easy. I was holding my man off with my big sword. He only had a short knife. I could see Varli was in trouble, so I tried something different. Instead of parrying with my sword, I took his knife on my armband." She held up the arm; some of the blood was her own. "Damn piece of jewelry was too soft, and he got to me. But his knife caught in the metal, and I twisted it away. Then I swung at the one that was after Varli. I swung, and I was so scared that I was too late, and I swung really fast, and his head...just...just came off!" She buried her head in her hands and began to sob. "I thought I wanted to go to war, but I don't. I'm not cut out for this. I'm sorry, Gerth, I can't do this kind of thing."

Gerth just stared helplessly, so Jhanes gave him a nudge. The king gathered his wits and took the crying lady in his arms, comforting her. "Don't worry, Talia. You did fine. Nobody ever expected you to have to fight like this. Varli says you were wonderful."

Varli spoke up on cue. "For certain, Talia. I'd have you at my back any day. With that big sword of yours swinging over my head, I felt safe as a castle."

She frowned at him. "You did? But you all got hurt protecting me."

Varli frowned. "Of course. That was our job. But you protected yourself, too. You took a knife in your arm and turned it to an advantage. You changed tactics in the middle of the fight. That shows creativity, doesn't it, Jhanes?"

The soldier grinned. "The soft metal armlet is a good trick, my Lady. Maybe you can get another one made with a bit stronger underlay."

She looked down at her bloody arm as he snapped the bracelet off. "Damned piece of jewelry." She winced as his fingers prodded the cut.

"Not too deep, nothing important severed. We'll get Zoysana to sew that together later. She does neater work than the surgeon. You'll have a nice scar to remember this by, but not too obvious." He smiled at her and turned to the still body of Maura. "Now, what have we here?"

Anine looked up, her brow furrowing. "There's a big bump on her head. She must have hit a rock."

He explored the swelling, thankful that she couldn't feel his prodding fingers. No softness or dent. "Only knocked out. No sign of bones broken. What about that hand?"

He turned the hand over and winced. A deep gash ran across the inside of the palm, and the fingers moved too easily. "Tendons cut. We'll wrap it up for the moment. Make a litter. There's a stand of saplings back down the canyon."

The men jumped to obey, and he wrapped the injured hand in a clean cloth from his battle pack, tucking the edges of the wound together as well as he could, although he knew it would do little good.

They placed the unconscious woman on a stretcher made with their coats and two poles, and made their way back towards camp, every eye alert. The scouts found no new intruders, although the funeral party he sent back to the site of Gerth's stand reported that two of the Inari were gone.

"Good."

Gerth looked at him, puzzled.

"There's no use smashing them like that if no one knows what happened. We want someone to take the story back over the mountain. They need to know what it's like to face King

Gerth and his big sword. I hope they aren't too badly wounded. I suspect the ones Anine took down will recover, too. That's why I broke their swords."

"I wondered about that. I thought it was just so others couldn't use them."

"That, and it's a sign of disdain. Like we don't think their weapons are good enough to keep."

Gerth nodded thoughtfully, and they continued their careful pace. When they reached camp, Gerth strode to the command tent, but Lord Tour met them at the door.

"Any reports?"

"A few, your Majesty. There's definite activity. Zoysana's Inari say they are all from the Pregota tribe. They must have come down the pass in force. I sent riders to every camp with a warning."

"Any fighting?"

"Only two skirmishes, Sire."

"Any killed or captured?" Jhanes broke in.

The Warlander turned to him. "None that I know of. Why?"

Gerth also looked at him. "Is that important?"

"Yes. Did you notice that all of ours were young? Only a few were out of their teen years. That's good. When they start sending their best over the pass, we'll know it's war."

Lord Tour nodded. "I'll keep that in mind when I'm taking reports, and I'll let you know. What happened with your group?"

Gerth stepped back, indicating that Jhanes should report, which he did, in detail. The old Warlander nodded when he finished. "So we have a big rush of them from the one clan. What does that tell you?"

Jhanes considered. "The big test. Remember, I told you they couldn't make up their minds if we were bargaining from strength or bluffing. Now they've called our bluff, found out how strong we are. If we can find a few more, it would help."

"Zoysana's troop hasn't reported in yet. I imagine they'll have some success."

Gerth grinned. "I hope so. I wouldn't want to keep all the fun to myself." Then his face sobered. "Would you like to see to your wounded? I'm going to check on Talia."

They left the general poring over his maps and went to the injuries tent. There, a surgeon was wrapping the bandage on Talia's arm while Anine held a cold cloth against the lady's head. Maura lay propped up on pillows on a cot, cradling her left arm, her face grim.

Gerth immediately went to Talia, and Jhanes approached his injured soldier. "Glad to see you awake. How does it feel?"

"I don't know, sir. You tell me. They say you tied it up."

"I did check it over before I wrapped it."

"Give it to me straight. It don't feel right, somehow. How bad is it?"

He knelt beside her. "I'll give it to you straight. The thumb and forefinger are all right, but you have some tendons cut for two or three outside fingers. Good thing it's not your sword hand."

She flexed her good hand, staring at it. "I knew it might happen. Knew I might invalid out. But I hoped it would be later." She turned to him. "Done with soldiering, ain't I?"

He rocked his head, side to side. "Maybe, maybe not. There's lots of service done off the battlefield."

"And you aren't done with my service, either." Gerth's voice boosted across the tent. "I won't forget how you got your wound." He smiled. "There's plenty of places in the castle for people with loyalty and bravery."

She looked to Jhanes for confirmation, and he couldn't help but feel a rush of pride. He nodded, grinned. "He's the king, and he said it. There's a place for you."

A tear ran down her cheek. "I...I...Thank you, your Majesty. Wasn't expectin' nothin' of the sort." Her back straightened. "I'm a mercenary. I take my pay and I take my chances. But it's good to know I won't be turned out."

Her gaze turned to Jhanes. "Thanks to you, too."

Jhanes felt his cheeks warm. "I didn't do anything."

She grinned, white teeth bared in a pale face. "Sure you didn't, sir. You took me on, gave me a chance. If I can, I'll stay with the Clan. Do you think she'll still have me?"

For a moment he wasn't sure what she meant, then it all came together. "Zoysana? Of course she will. Mind you, if she's really mean, she'll put you to training the recruits."

The woman ignored his joke, nodding. "I could do that, couldn't I?"

"Let's not worry about the worst. Maybe your hand will heal."

She gave him that flat stare. "Don't let's fool around. We both know that hand will never be the same. Don't worry about me. I always made a place for myself before, and I'll find one again. A good one, now you give me the chance."

Jhanes smiled, slapped her good shoulder. "That's the spirit, soldier. When Zoysana gets back, I'll send her in to look at you. She knows a lot about wounds. She and the army surgeon will do the best they can. How's the head?"

Her face relaxed, a real smile this time. "A whole lot better than it was before you come in, sir."

Jhanes turned away, his heart light. It was hard to have one of his own wounded, but support from the king made being an officer easy.

23. KIDNAP

With the excitement over, life settled back to its usual level. Gerth made wider sweeps to check on the camps that guarded the various other passes. He often left Talia behind, because they were fast, hard-riding forays into rough and dangerous territory. While she was in camp without him, Talia went out on the closer patrols, her usual troop with her, now including Arderton and his men. Even Lateda began to ride out, more for the exercise and the relief of boredom than any desire to become a horsewoman.

Late one afternoon Talia went on a short excursion, and disaster struck. Jhanes was settling down to get some paperwork done when Varli galloped back into camp just before dark, his troop behind him on lathered horses. He was shouting as he entered the clearing, and he rode straight to the king's tent without dismounting. "Gerth, Gerth, she's gone! They took her!"

Gerth had just returned from his own patrol, and strode out of his tent, still in his fighting rig. "What? Who took her? How?"

Varli shook his head. "We didn't have a chance, Gerth. It was too well-planned an operation."

Zoysana rushed up. "What happened?"

Varli's shoulders sagged. "It was Fedus, that Inari we captured in the fight at the farm. He's been trying so hard to fit in, we all thought he was doing the right thing, so we trusted him. But they had it all laid out. Fedus must have handled it at our end.

"It was the last patrol. Lady Talia said she'd been lying around camp all day waiting for Gerth to come in, and she wanted to work up an appetite for supper.

"It all went well at the beginning. Then, when we were almost at the far end of the route, Fedus came in from point duty. He reported a large invading group, off to the right. We

279

used the same technique as last time, splitting our main force off to attack, and Talia going to safety with her guard. It was her usual guard this time: five of us plus Lateda. Fedus said he had a perfect place to defend.

"But he led us into a trap, a narrow gully between the rocks. They dropped a log down behind Anine and me, and we couldn't get back to Lady Talia. A bunch of horsemen came out of a side gully and went for Arderton and his men, held them off just long enough to make the grab. They dropped a rope over Talia and lifted her off her horse as neat as you please. She tried to get her sword out to cut the rope, but her arms were pinned. By the time we got up the rocks on foot, they were gone. There was a trail there, but we couldn't get the horses through to it."

There was blood seeping through a rough bandage on Arderton's upper arm. "Fighting on a horse in a gulch like that is useless. There were four of them, and they had no interest in attacking, just keeping us away from Lady Talia. Soon as they had her, they were gone. Rolled a pile of rocks back down into the side gully behind them and plugged it."

Zoysana was pacing. "It sounds like they had this well planned. How could they be sure you'd fall into it?"

Arderton's lip curled. "Your tame Inari. He led us into it like a herd of sheep."

Jhanes shook his head. "Poor fool."

Gerth scowled. "How can you have any sympathy for a traitor?"

"Zoysana was his only hope. He could have gone back to his clan, but to a lower position because of being captured. Now he will get an even worse position because he has lost more honour by spying. Not only that, but his whole clan will lose prestige when word gets around that they have used such low tactics. I can't see why they did it, unless they are really desperate."

Zoysana stopped pacing. "Where's Lateda? She was with you, wasn't she?"

Jhanes looked around. He had forgotten the wiry servant girl.

Anine shook her head. "I never seen nothin' like it. After they grabbed the lady, they took off like lightnin'. But somehow Lateda got up on the rocks, and she was waitin' when they scrambled up the gully. As they rode by her, she jumped down behind the last Inari and slit his throat before he knew what was goin' on. She dumped his body off the horse and went after them. I got no idea what happened to her, but she never come back."

Varli nodded. "By this time, the rest of the patrol had returned after discovering that there were no other invaders. We sent Serus and Drak to keep track of them and hot-footed it back to camp."

Anine looked around. "Yes. I wanted to take off after 'em, but Varli said there wasn't that much rush."

Jhanes nodded. "He was right. They won't do her any harm."

Gerth frowned "Can you be sure of that?"

"It depends on why they took her. But I'd guess it's to make a point."

Zoysana tossed up her hands. "I can't see what the point is. What do you think, Jhanes?"

"It could be just a stunt. Some young fighters, just to prove they could do it. But it seems too well organized for that. If they wanted a slave...no, same reason. They don't use hostages, so that's not it. The only thing I can think of is a challenge. They took her, you have to come and get her."

Gerth reached up and drew his big sword. "That suits me fine. Let's go."

"But your Majesty..." Jhanes looked helplessly at the king's back, then to Zoysana.

"I think you'd better listen, Gerth." There was that note in her voice again.

The king spun. "I'm not waiting around all night!"

Zoysana shook her head. "I imagine Jhanes wanted to tell you that there's no point stumbling around up there in the dark. It's too dangerous, and even our Inari couldn't follow."

Jhanes nodded. "That's about it, your Majesty. Our two scouts will leave us a trail, and we can make good time in the morning as soon as it's light enough to see."

Gerth slammed his hand against his leg. "Dammit, Zoysana, why do you always have to be right?"

She smiled, walked over and took his arm, leading him towards his tent. "Come on, I'll keep you company. Jhanes will join us and we can make plans, check our equipment. We'll be on the trail a while, and we want to be as prepared as possible."

Despite an almost-sleepless night, Jhanes led a file of riders from the camp as the first greyness touched the eastern horizon. Gerth was easily persuaded that only a small party was required. Varli and Talia's mercenaries could not be left behind. Zoysana and Tadeo, on their small, shaggy ponies, with Patu ranging at the side. Five Clan Inari, the only ones in camp at the moment, took up scouting, pulling in from the flanks as the path got too narrow.

As the light grew, the tracking became easy. The kidnappers had made no effort to hide their trail, and the two scouts had left ample sign to follow. During the day several more Inari dropped into line; some on horseback, some afoot. They spoke little but changed places often, flanking when the terrain made it possible. Suspicious as always, Jhanes sent scouts to sweep their backtrail, but they rode all day undisturbed.

Nearing dusk, Zoysana, who was in the lead, pulled up with a quiet exclamation, staring at something on the ground. Jhanes signalled more scouts out before he joined her.

There, deep in the dust by the side of the trail, was a pool of blood, dried dark brown by the heat of the rocks. There were scuff marks in the dirt, but no other sign of a fight. They scanned the boulders that closed in their skyline, but only received "all-clear" signals from the scouts.

282

Zoysana dismounted and scanned the ground. "Lots of footprints."

Jhanes stayed on his horse. "Yes, they stopped here to rest." He pointed. "See the marks on the rocks at the side? Unshod."

Gerth stared down at the blood, his face working. "So what happened here?"

Zoysana and the soldier exchanged looks. "Somebody died. There's too much blood for anything else."

Zoysana pointed, standing well back. "See the impression. I think he fell there and was dragged that way. There's too many walked over the site to tell more, but the horses wouldn't walk in the blood, so..."

The young king's face twisted at the possibilities running through his mind. "So no reason to hang around. Let's go." Pelex, unfazed by mere blood, put a huge foot in the middle of the dried pool as the king spurred onward. Exchanging another glance, his followers urged their mounts after him.

Jhanes had a sinking feeling. *Gerth has discovered that this is not a game. I hope it doesn't get worse. Because if it does, I don't know how I'll fix it. And I'm the one that has to try. No matter the consequences to me and to my family. This is why soldiers don't marry.*

It was full dark, and they had stumbled around looking for the trail several times before Gerth would agree to camp for the night.

"Any sign they stopped?"

Jhanes considered. "No. I imagine they went all night the first night. Tonight, they'll stop. They know we're not close behind them. They can easily check their backtrail for a large group like this."

"Will they have a squad trailing behind them?"

"I would. But we won't see them. If they survive Serus and Drak, that is."

Gerth nodded, silhouetted against the stars. "We'll have to stop, then. I hate to think of them almost two days ahead."

From out of the darkness, Zoysana's saddle creaked as if she were dismounting. "We've been moving fast. They aren't that far ahead." She gave directions in simple but correct Inarituk, and soon a small fire gave them enough light to arrange themselves. They lay on their bedrolls, chewing dried meat and passing a skin of watered wine.

"She'll be all right."

Jhanes heard the undertones in the young king's voice. "She's trained up for a ride like this after all she's done this summer."

"What about Lateda?"

Jhanes took the straight route. "We haven't seen her body. We haven't seen any walking footprints. She's with them and she's on a horse."

Zoysana was farther from the fire, leaning her head on Patu's side. "She's too valuable to harm."

Jhanes had his own opinion about that, but he kept it to himself. The Inari despised weakness, and he hoped the lady could keep her wits about her and her spirits up. She would be tested to the extreme, physically and mentally, and everyone here knew it.

"She'll do fine."

"She will."

In the long silence that followed, some slept, some tossed on the hard ground, but there was nothing more to be said. Just past midnight a bright moon rose, and when the shadows had shortened enough, Zoysana stirred.

"I can see fine."

Jhanes shrugged the blanket from around his shoulders. "You can only see in the moonlight, and the shadows are twice as dark because of it. If we were tracking it wouldn't go."

"But we aren't. We're following our guides' markers."

"That's right."

There was no need for more. Gerth had risen as they spoke and was already strapping his blanket behind his saddle. They gave the horses a quick drink and stepped into the stirrups. With one Inari leading on foot, followed by Patu and Jhanes, they made their way up the mountain.

They reached the end of the pass just after dawn, and the grey-brown expanse of the steppe stretched before them. There was no sign of any large party on the trail, but as they descended the first pitch, Drak was sitting his horse beside the path, waiting.

"What news?"

The Inari shook his head. "Nothing, Sha-nes. They are headed straight for the multi-clan meeting ground." The lad smiled down at Zoysana. "We had to discourage three of their scouts who thought they would ride sweep. It was not hard. Our Lady has taught us well."

"Any sign of the lady?"

"Tell your king we could not get close enough to see clearly. But everyone is riding well, so the lady is keeping up."

"Thank you." That came from the king himself, in accented but correct Inarituk. The guide grinned and gave the king a fists-together salute.

"Let's move then. I'm sure she's all right, but she'll want us to get there as soon as possible."

They stepped up the pace as the trail dropped, careful on the steep grades, the flankers spreading more as the terrain smoothed. When the trail widened, Zoysana pulled up beside Gerth. Jhanes followed to listen.

"See how quickly the mountains fall away to flatland here. No foothills at all."

The king grunted in reply, his mind elsewhere.

She reached up and touched his knee. "She'll be fine, Gerth. They have no reason to harm her."

His attention came around to her. "Oh, she'll be fine. I'm just thinking about what I'm going to do to them if she's not. I may do it anyway."

Zoysana glanced up at his face, then looked again. "You know enough about the Inari to handle this, Gerth, but take Jhanes's advice. That's what got us through last time."

The king looked back, caught the soldier's eye. "I think perhaps our Jhanes is a touch too cautious. I don't feel quite the same constraints. But I will listen."

Zoysana, too, glanced back and grinned. "Good enough."

Jhanes caught the message. He would give his advice as usual. The king would take it if he chose. If he didn't choose, well, he was the king. He could get them all massacred if he chose. *I have to give my advice in a way that he will listen. I hardly know the man. He's in love. How will I make him listen?* Jhanes had a fleeting vision of Sarha and little Frey waiting back at the inn, but pushed it out of his mind. *Thoughts of home get in the way. At least I'll die in good company.*

It was late in the evening of the second day when the trail led them straight to the big multi-clan camp. Serus was waiting at the outskirts, a few other Inari sitting their horses in a loose group around him. They made no hostile moves as Gerth's party approached, wheeling their mounts away to make room, then turning in behind as the Lowlanders passed.

Jhanes noted the colours braided in their hair. "Serus, these fighters are from your clan."

"They are, Sha-nes." He tossed a grim smile over his shoulder. "Go straight through. Our quarry came in last night and went to the Pregota Clan camp. I have waited here since morning."

"Well done; you left us a good trail." He translated for the others. "I suggest we go straight to the centre where the Circle is. They know we are coming. They will be there."

The king nodded. Then he looked at Jhanes. "All of them?"

"All. Most are not involved in the deed, but all the Potentaras will be there to discuss its outcome."

Gerth turned his horse and rode into the Inari camp.

The king was aware of the etiquette. He knew what he was doing.

286

Here we go. Jhanes glanced over at Anine, riding beside him, a scowl on her face. Talia's guards all blamed themselves for the disaster, and glum looks abounded. He gestured her to take position to Gerth's right. *At least I know how she will react. Like an experienced mercenary. The rest of them…?*

The camp was smaller than in the spring, although the results of over-grazing showed on the barren prairie around. Many trails ran empty between bare camp spots, showing that whole clans had returned to their traditional lands. However, there were enough people around to form a substantial crowd that stood silent as the king and his party rode through. As the Petrellans approached the central green, the horseshoe of Potentaras was already assembled, almost as large as before.

Jhanes pushed his horse up beside the king's charger. "This would be about the right distance, your Majesty."

Gerth's lip twisted. "Then we'll go a few paces farther." He suited actions to his words, then swung down, dropping the reins and pacing forward, not looking back. When he reached a point halfway between the Circle and the Great Potentara's seat, he stopped. He did not ask for translation, he merely stood, waiting.

The Great Potentara rose and strode towards the king, stopping a few paces away. He was a head shorter than Gerth, but his shoulders bulked broader. For a moment they faced each other, the old leader and the young. Then Chuko spoke, slowly and calmly, but his eyes never left the king's face.

"Sha-nes, tell your impetuous young king I sympathize with him, but there is nothing I can do to solve his problem. Warn him that the relationship between our peoples is at a balance here, and how he acts in the next ten breaths may mean thousands of lives."

"He's on our side, your Majesty."

Gerth exhaled slowly, his eyes riveted on his opposite. "Explain."

Jhanes translated the Potentara's words as precisely as he could.

Gerth's hand left his sword-hilt, and he nodded. "Fair enough. Can't or won't help?"

"He holds a delicate balance of power. If he were to make the wrong move in this case, he could lose control. Then the opposing clans would gain strength and we'd be in worse shape than before."

"So if he's on our side, what can he do for us?"

"Nothing. But he can stand aside and let us handle it ourselves."

A small, unpleasant grin twitched Gerth's lip. "Now that's the kind of help I can use. Who do I need to deal with?"

The Great Potentara returned to his seat, a satisfied set to his face. The King of Petrella stepped back, and his eyes swept the arc of Inari leaders, meeting each gaze with a level stare. Then he stopped.

"Him." He pointed at the Pregota Potentara. "He's the one."

He turned and strode to the centre of the Circle, drew his big sword. "I know enough about their ways to deal with this."

Jhanes felt no need to translate. He glanced at Chuko and caught a feral gleam in the Great Potentara's eye. A lot of people were about to get a serious adjustment to their outlook, and all to the advantage of his allies. As long as Gerth handled it right.

Gerth waited, staring at the Pregotas. "Jhanes, what's the word for 'afraid'?"

Jhanes told him, and the king repeated it with relish.

There was a roar of anger from the Pregota ranks, not all of it directed at Gerth. The Pregota leader shifted on his cushion, his eyes flashing to the Potentaras on either side. Receiving no assurance, he had no choice. With a curt gesture, he sent his Designated Fighter forward.

The Designated Fighter of the Pregotas was a big man, his bare back and arms corded with muscle. He swaggered forward drawing a short stabbing sword, a steel-rimmed buckler strapped to his left arm. Approaching the stones, he slowed as he realized the size of the man confronting him.

Gerth scowled. "Do I have to fight this character? When does the real culprit pay for his deeds?"

"Don't worry, your Majesty. If you beat the Designated Fighter, the Potentara falls. The worse you humiliate the fighter, the worse the disgrace."

Gerth shifted his grip, flexing his fingers along the sword hilt. "Now that appeals to me."

Zoysana slid forward to the edge of the stones. "Gerth, don't be too confident. He's their best."

"Don't worry, teacher. I'll make you proud."

Jhanes watched, tension rising in him as it always did before a battle. *I've never seen Gerth fight. If he loses, I'll have to step in, and I doubt I can beat this one, either.* "He's an excellent swordsman." He rolled his shoulders and checked that his sword was loose in its sheath.

Zoysana shook her head as she stood back, folding her arms. "I'm sure he is. But he thinks he's fighting another swordsman."

"What do you mean?"

"He sees Gerth's big weapon and he's thinking 'sword' right now, and how to deal with it. That'll be his mistake. He's fighting someone trained in Weaponless by a Kyabran Master." She tossed a tense grin over her shoulder. "That's me."

He tried to answer her smile, and they turned to watch the fight.

The Fighter moved into the Circle and slid gracefully forward. Gerth stood watching him. The Inari was uncertain of how to deal with the length of Gerth's sword, and the king wasn't giving him any hints, refusing to take a defensive position.

The Pregota Fighter decided to attack. He raised his sword, ducked behind his shield, stepped forward and swung.

Instead of using his sword, Gerth stepped forward. His left hand met the Fighter's arm at the pivot point and his foot hooked behind the man's ankle, pulling forward before the foot reached the ground. As his foe spilled to the grass, Gerth swung his knee against the sword arm, and the weapon fell to the

289

grass. With the tip of his own weapon, the king flipped the sword into the air. It hung a moment at the top of its arc, and he struck it. Two halves of metal fell to the grass.

As the Fighter jumped to his feet, Gerth moved in, his left fist striking the temple with a meaty thud. The man dropped and lay still. The whole fight had lasted about two breaths. Gerth regarded his fallen opponent a moment, then turned to face the Pregota Clan. He strode closer, then pointed his sword at the deposed Potentara.

"Bring her."

There was no mistaking his meaning. After a brief pause, there was a stir in the ranks, and a path blew open. A harsh voice cut the air, rolling out in the accents of the Inner Duchies.

"Watch it, you slime. I don't know where you're taking us, but if you touch my Lady, I'll hand you your fingers in a sack."

The gap widened, and Lateda strode forward, her eyes flashing, a dagger in either fist and curses spewing from her mouth. She was so busy threatening the Inari around her that she almost reached Gerth before she realized who it was. Then she stopped. Without missing a breath, she reversed the daggers in her hands and dropped in a perfect curtsey.

"Good afternoon, your Majesty. My Lady will be so glad to see you."

Jhanes could hardly suppress a laugh, but there was a tremor in the girl's hand as she slipped her weapons away. No one else noticed, as their eyes were on Talia.

She strode forward through the crowd, her head high, a light, formal smile on her lips. When she reached Gerth, she dipped a curtsey, holding out her hand. "Your Majesty, so good of you to come."

Gerth's grin widened as he inclined his head. "My Lady, wild horses couldn't have kept me away. Have you been treated well?"

She pretended to consider. "Well enough, my Lord. They are a people who learn quickly. After Lateda found it necessary to chastise two of them, they became very polite."

Gerth turned to look at the young woman, standing demurely to the side. If anyone had told him of her true nature, he hadn't believed it until now. He smiled, then turned back to Talia. "Is there any action you would have me take?"

For a moment her poise slipped. Her eyes shot toward the discredited Potentara of the Pregota Clan, who quailed at her glance. "Fortunately for some here, there are diplomatic considerations which preclude personal desires."

Gerth strode over to tower above the seated Potentara, and again Jhanes felt no need to translate. The king stared into the man's eyes until they dropped. Still Gerth waited. Finally the Pregota Leader rose, slipped off the cushion and disappeared into the crowd, which parted before him, closing quietly behind. Then Gerth turned and offered his arm. The lady took it, and they faced the Great Potentara. Jhanes stepped forward as well.

Chuko smiled slowly. "Sha-nes, I'm sure King Gerth has had a long ride. Ask him if he would accept our hospitality for the night. We have much to speak of."

Gerth nodded at the translation. "So that's how it's going to be? He really did want me to win?"

Jhanes nodded. "Most definitely, your Majesty. The Pregota Clan made a serious mistake by using treachery to kidnap Lady Talia. This is good for Chuko's power and discredits the whole reactionary movement. For you, personally destroying one of the best fighters in the tribe gives you a certain status as well."

Zoysana came up on Gerth's other side. "Yes, you've caused a problem there. You defeated the Designated Fighter and faced down the Potentara. That means you're now the Potentara of the Pregota Clan."

Gerth's eyes widened. "I could take over the whole clan?"

Chuko roared with laughter when he heard this. "I don't know, Gerth, Leader of Petrella. If you wanted to try."

Gerth smiled and shook his head. "I have enough trouble ruling a kingdom of people I grew up with. Let Zoysana be the only Potentara from below the Edge of the World. I'm sure someone in the Pregota Clan would do a better job than I could."

Jhanes translated this loudly, and he could see a certain amount of relaxing in the clansmen to Chuko's left.

The Great Potentara tilted his head in an Inari bow of respect. "I am sure Lady Talia will welcome you to her tent. When you are refreshed, we will eat and have entertainment. Perhaps your Lady Zoysana will dance for us!" Laughing in high good humour at his own joke, Chuko swept off amid his advisors, leaving the Petrellans shaking their heads.

Gerth turned to Talia. "You have a tent of your own? I thought you were kidnapped."

She smiled over at Lateda. "At first they were quite rough. But Lateda corrected their manners, and they became more polite. When the rest of the clans discovered who their guest was, there was pressure on the Pregotas to treat me with proper respect."

Gerth grinned. "You mean, while we were spending two days on the trail in constant worry, you were relaxing in a comfortable tent?"

"You could say that. I'd rather have been with you."

Zoysana regarded Lateda. "Just what was this 'chastising' she is talking about?"

"One of them laid a hand on her, so I cut his throat."

"About halfway up the trail?"

Talia nodded. "And the first night here a man tried to get into my tent. I remembered what you said, Jhanes, and I put a pot over his head. Lateda finished him off. They had to change all the carpets along that side."

Gerth laughed, then stopped abruptly. "Are you really all right, Talia?"

She sighed, a great gust. "No, I'm having a great deal of trouble keeping my knees from collapsing. I've never been so glad to see anyone in my life. But don't worry. I won't let you down. I'll never show weakness in front of these savages."

Gerth gave a whoop of laughter and caught her against his side with one arm. "What do you think about that, Zoe? Didn't I tell you she'd cope?"

Zoysana smiled. "Many times in the last two days, as I recall. Not that anyone was arguing with you. Well done, Talia." She turned to Lateda. "It sounds like you acquitted yourself with honour as well."

To everyone's surprise, the woman blushed. "I did my best, my Lady."

Jhanes slapped her companionably on the shoulder. "I'm pleased you listened to my stories."

Talia laid a hand on his arm. "They saved us, Jhanes. If we hadn't known how to act, I don't know what would have happened."

Jhanes looked down at the smaller woman. "I have a feeling Lateda would have done the right thing anyway. She's that sort of person."

Zoysana grabbed each of them by a shoulder and steered them to where two high-ranking Potentaras were waiting in escort. "If you are comparing her to the Inari, you may or may not have insulted her terribly, and I'm going to distract her before she makes up her mind."

* * *

The next night, as they sat around their campfire halfway down the pass, Talia put down her mug of tea. "Oh, in all the excitement, I didn't get a chance to tell you. I met someone else important in the Inari camp. A woman."

Gerth's forehead wrinkled. "An important Inari woman?"

"That's right. They have a Wise Woman. She must be the female equivalent of the Potentara."

"So what did she say to you? Assuming that you could understand anything."

293

Talia grinned. "That's what was so strange. She can speak Petrellan!"

Zoysana sat up straighter. "She spoke Petrellan?"

"In a strange way. She spoke very correctly and slowly, and she had the strangest accent. It was like she was pronouncing every letter. You know. If she said 'knife,' it came out 'kaneefey'."

"So you spoke to her. What did she say?"

"She mostly asked me questions. She was very interested in who I was and where I came from. Had an idea about the Inner Sea, and was interested in how far it was. Oh...and she was impressed that I could read. When I told her that Gerth could read as well, she was very surprised. Shocked, even."

Zoysana frowned. "Inari is only a spoken language. What would she know about reading?"

Jhanes chuckled. "You have only to ask."

Zoysana turned on him. "What have you been keeping from us?"

He shrugged. "I have not had time to tell you all I know about the Inari culture. Of course, I know very little about the Wise Woman and what goes on in her Tent, and no Inari male knows any more than I do."

"Do you know anything about reading?"

"No, except some of the women can definitely read."

"But what do they read? Is there an Inari written language?"

"Not that I know of."

"Um, Zoysana?" They turned at the new voice. Anine stood hesitantly at the edge of the firelight.

"Yes, Anine?"

"I couldn't help listenin', Lady Talia. How the Wise Woman talked?"

"Yes. Using all the letters."

"That's how I sounded at first when I was tryin' ta read aloud. I'm...uh..." She grinned. "I'm gettin' better, now."

Talia nodded. "So what you're saying is that if it seemed like she was sounding out the words as she spoke, it means that she reads Petrellan but she doesn't know how to pronounce it."

The big girl shrugged. "Seems like."

"The Inari Wise Woman can read Petrellan, but doesn't speak it." Zoysana turned to the soldier. "Jhanes, how does that sound to you?"

He shook his head. "Sounds like women's business that men don't mess with if they know what's good for them. The Inari call Petrellan 'Seaspeak,' if that helps any."

Zoysana frowned in thought. "The Kyabrans say the Petrellans came off the Great Southern Ocean some time in the recent past. They say our language is far too full of references to water to have developed on the Prairies."

"So the Inari women learned to read from the Petrellans when they passed through?"

"Sounds like it."

"And kept the knowledge alive for generations?"

"Doesn't sound too likely, but who knows?"

Talia nodded. "I have to visit the Inari again."

Gerth planted his elbows on his knees and leaned forward. "Not very soon, I don't think!"

She laughed. "I'll wait until you boys have finished your fighting. Then I'll drop in on the Wise Woman and we'll sit down for tea and a chat."

Zoysana joined in. "I'll go with you. What do you say, Anine? Want to learn to read Inari?"

It sounded like a joke, but the big mercenary nodded. "Tell you, I'd like that. Just gimme a chance to learn Petrellan proper first."

Zoysana looked around and grinned. "There we have it. Journey postponed until everyone gets more civilized."

"Oh, I ain't thinkin' about gettin' more civilized, Zoe. I'm just learnin' to read."

24. TREATY

The following morning, their trail home spread out through a series of high mountain meadows, and Jhanes finally got up his nerve. He pulled his horse alongside Zoysana's pony.

"Lady Zoe, can we have a talk?"

"I suppose it's time."

He glanced down at her. "You already know?"

"In essence. Gerth asked you to stay as an advisor, and you have done your duty admirably. The Clan Fighters are trained to the point where they no longer need you. You want leave to go home."

"Umm...that wasn't exactly it, but close enough. I...it's hard to put into words. I don't need to go home, but I think I should."

She frowned up at him. "That's about the strangest request for leave I've ever heard. You don't want to go home?"

"It's not like that. I have spent the summer up here training and fighting. In the past half month, I have not thought of home. It's as if they didn't exist. No, that's wrong. I thought about Sarha and Frey once, just before going into the Inari camp. But I put them aside, because they were a distraction that would reduce my effectiveness.

"And I don't want them to be a distraction. As I told you when I hired on, I know how it works. Once you've started, the duties pile up. I've had a lot of success this summer."

"You certainly have. You're a full-fledged officer now, and good at it. I knew you would be."

"That's the problem. I'm having success at my old life, just when I want to concentrate on my new one. That could be dangerous, for several reasons."

"It could, but so far you've handled it admirably. But this is only one battle we've won. Chuko still doesn't have control over his people. I doubt he ever will. We've still got three clans

296

attacking, and you're our best defence. Oh, I know we are capable of handling them. We shouldn't need you. But what if we do?" She rode in silence for a while, and he felt it best to let her think.

"I can talk it over with Gerth. I was expecting him to take you back to the castle with him in any case, as he promised. I can handle things here for the moment. At the castle, you can play it as it happens."

"I guess that's the best I could hope for."

"Success breeds success, doesn't it?"

"Aye. That it does. But what kind of success?"

"That's for you to decide."

I wish it really was for me to decide, but I can hardly say that. They rode along in silence.

* * *

Zoysana and her Clan peeled off to the east where the trail forked above Broken Boulder Camp, and the group escorting Gerth and Talia back to Arlyn Castle cut west down the mountain. It was a cheerful bunch, buoyed by their success. They took their time, camping in a pleasant mountain meadow that night, feasting on a young mountain sheep that Gerth had brought down just beside the trail.

As the senior officer, Jhanes commanded the escort and sat beside Gerth when they ate, with Talia and Varli on the other side. It was only natural he should share the conversation with the king and his lady and match them in drinking the wine that passed around.

So it was a cheerful evening, and he went to his tent around midnight with his mind spinning, partly from the wine and partly from the heady experience of being treated almost as an equal by the nobility. When he called up the image of the old inn and its tattered thatch, his enthusiasm for going home paled, and when he thought of Sarha, he wasn't sure he remembered her face very well.

Back at Arlyn Castle, Gerth swung into his role as king, handling all the duties that had piled up in his absence, and Jhanes had little to do but wait around in his "advisory capacity" for his knowledge to be needed. When it wasn't, he relaxed with the other Clan, the castle soldiers and the King's Guard. They all treated him with friendly respect and often asked for retelling of the king's summer exploits in the mountains. Since mugs of ale always accompanied such requests, he found himself on a schedule of late nights and later mornings.

I should be heading home. I haven't even asked the king.

But it was good to be off duty for a while. His gear needed attention, and he enjoyed dropping down to the Mercenary's Rest after supper for a drink and having someone else pour the ale. Which made him feel even more that he should be at home if he wasn't needed here. He missed Sarha and Frey, but he didn't really miss the inn and the constant round of chores. Which Sarha was probably doing on her own, making him feel even guiltier about enjoying his leisure so much.

That was one thing about soldiering. There were moments of hard work and fear, but also times of leisure and well-earned relaxation. He thought about that for a while, comparing the two lives, but that made him feel guiltier still. He drained his mug and went back up to the castle.

The following morning, he was in his room dutifully mending his sword belt when a page pounded down the passageway.

"Sir, you're needed!"

Jhanes swung around, laying belt, needle, and thread on the table. He heard the tension in the page's voice. "What's going on? Another attack?"

"No, Sir, it's one of the Guides. He's just come in, all beat up. Says he was a prisoner."

"Where to?" Already, the soldier's long strides made the little page run.

"The War Room. King Gerth is already there."

When the two entered the War Room, the injured Guide was stripped to the waist and Loreline was wrapping his ribs with a long bandage. His face was bruised and his left arm hung in a sling, but otherwise he seemed chipper enough, drinking a great slug of ale from a mug that Varli held out to him.

"So, Jhanes, I finally got to meet your friends, face to face."

"What friends are those, Lavorsil?"

The man grinned. "The bull-necked one with the big hands."

"Chuko?"

"That sounds like the name. The man who translated didn't speak Petrellan much, but I got the gist. They want to talk."

Jhanes looked at the king, who was staring at him in glee. "Does this mean what I think it means?"

He considered. "I hope so, your Majesty. They don't talk if they're going to fight. May I hear the whole story?"

"We've just heard the main parts. Let's make ourselves comfortable, and Lavorsil can tell us the details. Are you up to it, man?"

The Guide grinned and took another slug of ale. "Your Majesty, I'm so glad to be sittin' here talkin' to you, I could jaw all day."

"Good." The king looked around. "Loreline, you'll want to take notes. Everyone else, let's see what's happening."

The Guide settled himself, adjusting his injured arm. Then he shuddered. "I thought I was dead, or worse. 'Course, they was out to capture me from the first. I'm stationed at Broken Boulder Gap, auxiliary to Lord Tour. I was way up on the shoulder of Old Grandad, you know, where it overlooks the main pass? We was watchin' real careful, 'cause there haven't been any parties sneakin' through there all quarter.

Then I seen a troop of 'em comin' along where they shouldn't have been, 'cause the path goes nowhere, dead-ends up a canyon. But I thought maybe they'd found another way down, so I followed them.

Next thing I know, they're all over me. I put up a fight, but there was too many, and they'd ambushed me...well, I don't know where they came from, just up out of the ground."

Jhanes nodded. "They're good at that. They can hide on flat prairie where you'd swear there was nothing but grass."

"I'd have to agree with you. So they grabbed me and tied me up, put me on my horse, and back over the mountains we go, full gallop, not waitin' for nothin', or tryin' to hide. Just up over the pass. Rode all day, half the night. They got a camp at the top, a big one. No families or nothin', just all their fighters. And I thought, 'This is it. This is the invasion force, and they'll never let me out alive to take news north.'

"So they took me to this big tent, and out in front there's this guy sittin' on a cushion. He's about as wide as the castle gate, and his arms don't even hang down beside his body, there's so much muscle on him. There's a bunch of others sittin' around, but I know the boss when I see him. He's got this older guy to translate for him. They don't waste any words, that bunch. Sound's like the translator's got it memorized.

"The message was, 'Tell Hiding Branch we will talk.' I couldn't figure it out, but he said it again. 'Hiding Branch will know. Tell him we come.' Then they put me on my horse, and back we come, full speed again.

"By this time, I'm almost fallin' outa the saddle, what with the bad arm and gettin' hit on the head and ridin' all night, but they don't stop 'till we're down off the mountain. I'm ridin' along, and then I realize they're not there any more. Neatest disappearin' trick I've ever seen. Next thing I know, Coresu and Nalle are pickin' me up, and here I am."

"And that's all they said? 'Tell Hiding Branch we will talk'?"

"Yep. They said they was comin', didn't say when."

Jhanes turned to the king. "Your Majesty, I've got to get out there right now. If the Great Potentara says he's coming to talk, then he's coming, and he won't come alone. If Lord Tour thinks they're coming to fight, he'll attack. Then this will all be for nothing. There's two Castle Clan here now, and maybe a handful of Guides."

The king nodded to Varli, and he rushed out. "So you don't think he's come to attack? What about that army at the top of the pass?"

"I'm not too worried about the army. The Great Potentara wouldn't be there without a lot of his people. He may need a show of force to keep the other clans in line. But I do have to go, and quickly. If he's here to talk, we have to have someone to talk with him."

Gerth headed for the door and everyone else scrambled to keep up, leaving Lavorsil sitting, his weary head drooping over his mug.

"Zoysana can be my representative. Do you know where she is?"

Jhanes shook his head. "Last word,she was at Gisbon Valley. They've had trouble with invaders coming down that pass and heading to the Arvan border. There are no Clan at Broken Boulder right now, because they went along to help out. Tour will send for her, I'm sure. We have to hope she gets there in time."

"It's more important you get there in time. If she isn't there, you're in charge. Do what you think is best. If you can get him to come here to the castle, that would be great."

"Do you want him to see inside here?"

"Maybe not. But I'd love him to look up at it from the outside. Maybe we can set him up on the parade ground."

"He'd rather stay in the open. I doubt if he's ever slept inside stone walls in his life."

By this time they were in the stables, and servants were saddling horses and filling saddlebags. Soon, he and the two Clan were mounted. With no further speech, the king slapped Jhanes's horse on the rump to send her snorting and skittering towards the main gate.

But Jhanes had a thought. He reined back.

"Your Majesty! A few pack horses of grain, half a dozen prime steers. Can you start them after us as soon as possible?"

The king raised his hand in acknowledgement, and then he was lost in their dust. As Jhanes settled down to ride, he couldn't help but notice. *Here I go again. Back to battle. Is this what I want?*

It was a tough ride, because they had to save the horses as much as they could, which meant getting off and walking up the steeper hills. Still, one of his escort was from the Light Horse, the other was a trapper and they were all in fighting shape. The half-dozen Guides that Gerth sent behind had no chance of catching up.

When they reached the camp at the bottom of the pass, they could see trouble brewing. The infantry were formed up in their squares, and the Light Horse were milling about on the field beside the palisade. Six Warlanders in full armour sat their chargers quietly to one side, disdaining a show, but menacingly ready.

Jhanes kicked his horse to a final spurt and slid off in front of Lord Tour. "What's happening, my Lord?"

"Hello, Jhanes. Wanted to get here in time to fight, did you? We have report of a fair body of them headed down the pass. No slinking and sneaking this time, just riding straight down the trail. I guess this is the attack we were hoping wouldn't come."

"I hope not, my Lord. We've had a messenger come through. One of the Guides. He didn't stop here?"

"No, he didn't. What was the message?"

"The Great Potentara of the Inari is coming down. To talk."

"Talk? Are you sure?"

"Looks like it. They captured a Guide, picked him up on purpose. Sent him with the message they were coming to talk. It might have saved a lot of trouble if he'd stopped here first, but they dropped him off farther down the trail. He was injured and in a hurry to get to the castle to report to King Gerth."

Lord Tour stroked his beard. "I sent word to Lady Zoysana. She should be here any time if she was over at Gisbon where she was supposed to be. I bow to the king's orders and the king's expert. But if you don't mind, I'll have my men at the ready, just in case."

Jhanes grinned. "Oh, that would be a very good idea. The Great Potentara might be insulted if we didn't put on a show to greet him."

There was a brief whistle, and one of the Clan caught his eye. Alerted, he heard the sound of hoofbeats. Soon, Zoysana piled onto the parade ground, breathing heavily but looking as unperturbed as if she'd been out for a quiet stroll.

"So, Jhanes. What's going on?"

He sketched out the situation.

She nodded. "If it's Chuko, he will talk. He's an honourable man. I'm supposed to make the deals?"

"If necessary. His Majesty wants them to come to the castle, if possible. That's all we had time to talk about. I doubt Chuko will want to stay away from the clans that long. We hurried up here before there could be any misunderstandings."

"That's fine. We'll play the currents as they run." She glanced around. "Everyone looks good. Great welcoming committee." Then she frowned at Lord Tour. "Just make sure that everyone knows what's going on. The first man who makes a wrong move, I'll kill him myself. No mistakes."

Lord Tour nodded, almost a bow, and Jhanes kept himself from raising his eyebrows. Zoysana rarely changed the even tone of her voice, but on occasion she would speak like that to anyone, as if rank and position meant nothing, and people obeyed her without question.

Still, it won't hurt to explain. "Lord Tour, if you don't mind, it would be good for me to speak to your people about protocol. Our visitors have a very strict code of honour, and it wouldn't be good for anyone to be insulted by mistake."

"A capital idea, Jhanes. I'll have my officers brought here, the Warlanders, too."

303

It was an informal meeting, since the Warlanders preferred not to dismount, only taking their helmets off to hear better. The other officers stood in the front, while Jhanes tried to encapsulate eight years of life experience into one brief speech.

"Treat these people like you would a half-trained horse. Very firm but very careful. They admire bravery, but they are quick to take insult. They are proud, but hate to have pride turned against them. If they are on the ground, don't come anywhere near them on a horse. The Inari meet a mounted man mounted, and a walking man walking. And don't touch anyone, for any reason. I don't have time to explain all the rules, and you're sure to break one. If you touch one of them, be prepared to fight him.

"Remember, if these talks go well, the fighting here will be over. There will be pack-trains of goods going over this pass, not soldiers."

They all nodded at this, and he was thankful. No young hotbloods to deal with here. These were all serious fighting men in the middle of a tough campaign, happy to see the end. *Now, if the Great Potentara has only made the same choices...*

The Inari horses paced out of the forest and spread across the field. Jhanes grinned at Zoysana and Lord Tour in relief. "It's not the right people for a war band. This is for talk. Zoe, we'll form up like last time. Follow my lead as usual. Lord Tour, I'll signal for you at the correct time."

He nudged his horse ahead, and Zoysana and Tadeo followed, Patu choosing the downwind side. The Great Potentara moved out as well with his Champion beside him. Terenno came next. Jhanes could see the Inari's eyes taking in the troops in formation. In turn, he sized up the Inari fighters.

He spoke for Zoysana's ears alone, not turning his head. "Four major clans here, three important ones missing."

"No consensus."

"No attack." He bit down on a grin.

"So talk."

When their horses were within easy talking distance, they stopped. As host, Jhanes spoke first. "When I left the camp of the Inari, I had no idea I would be repaying your hospitality so soon."

The Great Potentara inclined his head. "Hidden Twig. Or I suppose you are Sha-nes, here in your country. It is agreeable to greet you and your Potentara, Zoysana of Kyabra. Please inform her how good it is to see her again."

The first sentence finished, Jhanes dismounted right away to show his confidence, the Great Potentara following by a half-breath. When both parties had followed their example, Jhanes turned to translate.

Zoysana smiled briefly. "Tell him the usual stuff, Jhanes. No sense two of us making it up twice."

"My Potentara greets you, and welcomes you in the name of Gerth, her king and mine."

The Great Potentara smiled openly. "Both you and I know, Hidden Twig, that was not what she said. But the thought is there. I note also that you address me personally, not as a simple translator and servant to Potentara Zoysana. Is this because of different customs, here below the End of the World, or because of a change in your fortunes since we last met?"

Jhanes translated this to Zoysana.

"This all sounds very informal. Is that a good sign?"

"I don't know him well enough. What do you want to do next?"

"So far, I'm leaving it up to you."

He turned back to the Inari. "As you have noted, my Potentara is leaving the content of the speeches to me. This is a sign of her growing trust in me and it gives me the latitude to make a more personal approach. In truth, your other guess is also correct. My people are less formal, and personal comments are not out of place in a situation such as this. In time, we hope you will meet again with his Majesty, King Gerth. In more ordered circumstances, you will see me speak in the formal manner, with due respect to the gravity of the occasion."

The Inari Chief nodded. "Quite right, Hidden Twig. I hope that your visit with us was agreeable enough to remind you of the pleasures and benefits of the Inari life you enjoyed in your youth. Enough perhaps to override the less pleasant memories of your original position."

Jhanes paused. "An important point, Great Potentara. My visit was a great cleansing for me. I had harboured memories that gave me an unbalanced view of your world. My visit has done much to restore harmony in my soul in that respect. Please excuse me while I inform my Potentara what we speak of."

He turned to Zoysana. "He is conscious that I am your translator, not his, and I have reassured him I no longer hold any grudges about being a slave. Isn't it interesting that I don't? I did before I went south of the Barrier. So, shall we start the dance?"

"As soon as we can. I'm all aquiver with suspense."

Jhanes could not stop his smile quickly enough as he turned, but he was pleased to note the Potentara's face relax in response. "Potentara Zoysana, in her usual straightforward manner, would like to get to the heart of the matter."

Chuko chuckled. "Will she not, in one quick speech, lay out both sides of the problem plus the solution so neatly as she did last time?"

"She is hoping for equal diplomatic skill on your part, Great Potentara."

"Good, good. I am ready, as I told your clumsy young Fighter, to talk."

The Great Leader passed a signal to his waiting men, and except for three sentries, they relaxed, dropping the reins of their horses and gathering in groups to chat. There was little anxiety in these clans. Jhanes wondered if they had been taking part in the raids at all. These were mostly older men, Clan Potentaras with their advisors and their Champions.

Jhanes stood and stared around the crowd, waiting for silence.

"Great Potentara. On behalf of King Gerth, his representative Zoysana, and his War Leader, Lord Tour, welcome. What would you say to us?"

The Great Potentara smiled at the general. "Tell the War Leader he has good men. I would fight them at no more than two-for-one any day."

Jhanes relayed the first half of the message.

Zoysana halted him. "What was that about two and one?"

He smiled wryly. "He said our soldiers are half as good as his. A great compliment, as you might guess."

She laughed out loud. "I have to learn Inari faster. I want to talk to this fellow one-to-one." She turned to the Great Potentara and repeated the phrase in decently accented Inari. "One-to-one!"

There was a shout of laughter from the Inari, and the soldier's explanation that she meant talking, not fighting, made them laugh harder.

Chuko grinned. "Talking and fighting are fine. Anything else, I'm not so sure."

Lord Tour smiled hesitantly at the laughter. "I'm glad this is all so relaxed. It didn't sound so funny to me."

"You have to get used to their sense of humour, my Lord. The Great Potentara doesn't make jokes with anyone of low rank. Zoysana has gained in status since they last spoke, either because of her actions in the fighting or because she is in control of what he wants. Hopefully both."

He turned to the Inari. "Lord Tour accepts your compliment to his Fighters and defers to Lady Zoysana when it comes to negotiating on a personal level." He used the Inari verb that could mean a contest of either words or arms, with sexual connotation as well.

When the Inari again burst into laughter, he grinned sheepishly at Zoysana. "You don't want to know what that meant."

She tossed her head. "Don't make any bargains for me that you're not willing to keep yourself."

He couldn't resist translating that, too.

When the laughter had died, the Great Potentara raised both hands, palms down, in a calming gesture. "Enough merriment. We are here for serious business. When you came to us in our encampment, you offered certain…items in exchange for ores, wool, furs. Are your intentions still the same, in spite of the actions of some of my over-eager kinsmen?"

Jhanes nodded. "We are not unaware, Great Potentara, that only members of certain clans have chosen to test the mettle of our Warlanders and Guides this spring. King Gerth is little dismayed by these small testings. They have their value. They keep his men fit.

"We have grain and beef available. They move slower than Lady Zoysana, but they move in our direction, nonetheless." He turned to his Clan Leader. "No idea how long it will take the supplies to get here. Another day?"

She nodded. "But we have plenty of stores here, don't we, Lord Tour? What about a small sampling?"

Jhanes grinned. "Perfect hospitality. Put your cooks to work, my Lord. Tell them to keep it rare and juicy. If the ovens are hot, fresh bread would impress them. We can talk while it roasts." He turned. "If Lady Zoysana approves?"

"Of course I do. A sit-down dinner for forty, if you please, Lord Tour. Preferably before dark. Jhanes, what's the word for 'hospitality'?"

He told her, and she turned to the Inari Potentara and spoke in his language. "King Gerth shows you hospitality. You will accept?"

He bowed. "I would be delighted."

She opened her mouth, but no words came, and she turned to Jhanes. "I don't have the vocabulary to say what I want to. Very frustrating. Tell him we'll have a quarter of juicy beef on the coals before he has had time to water his horse, or whatever you do before a party up there. Tell him we can chat about trading while we wait."

The Inari picketed their horses at the edge of the parade ground where they stood, and soon soldiers were bringing buckets of water and grain. The Petrellan Warlanders, careful to dismount at a distance, left their own steeds and helmets to their squires and joined the crowd. Jhanes stood and chuckled to himself as he watched Zoysana at her finest. At her order, the camp was stripped of carpets, pillows and stools. Saddles were pressed into service. A large oval formed, with the Great Potentara and Lord Tour seated across from each other in the centre of the opposite long sides.

The officers of the regiment sat in their usual positions next to Tour. The Inari ranged themselves in their proper spots on either side of their leader.

Jhanes leaned his head close to Zoysana's. "The Aguilana clan is on his immediate left. Partly a change in status, partly as the designated traders. I doubt if Terenno has learned enough Petrellan to be too useful as a translator."

"I'll make sure I speak slow and clear enough to be understood."

Jhanes refused the seat that was reserved for him, preferring instead to stand between Zoysana and the general so he was free to move. At times he would have to take the Inari Potentara's position and speak for him.

Now the bargaining went slower. The objective was to get the intent of the agreement established. Prices and details could be discussed at a later meeting, and it soon became clear that this would not take place at the castle.

Jhanes explained this to his people. "The Inari Potentara has no problem negotiating peace. That is a major function of his position, since wars are never negotiated. But even as progressive as he is, he will not stoop to trading. He will leave that up to the Aguilana Clan. As you can see, they have moved up in his trust, replacing the Espolo Clan, who are not present.

They are up in the mountains, still raiding, and it is they who will cause the most grief to this accord.

"Likewise, I doubt that the Great Potentara will come to the castle, or expect King Gerth to come here. Since there has been no war between them, there is no reason to meet."

Zoysana nodded. "Sounds reasonable. Ask him what he offers."

The Great Potentara had a simple response. "You send us cattle and grain. We send you whatever you wish in return, at a rate our agents can agree on. We guarantee the safety of your traders through this pass only, and no farther than the Sign of the Eagle. All other parts of the Barrier Range, including all the other passes, remain as they have always been: available to anyone brave enough to try them."

"And what does he expect of us in exchange?"

"Very little. Most of his people have no wish to come down here. He does not want us to come up there. There will be a trading village where he is now camped, just below the rim of the pass where the stream drops into the valley under the Sign of the Eagle. Anywhere south of that point is off-limits, and any lowlander who breaks this prohibition without the Great Potentara's personal permission is fair game for any Inari who can find him. In other words, just as it has always been."

"What is this Sign of the Eagle? Is it easy to find?"

"At the top of the pass, just before the prairie starts, there is a canyon. A huge rock has fallen away from the canyon wall, and it lies flat, like a bed. Or a coffin. That's why we call this Broken Boulder Pass. Above it, scribed beautifully into the stone, is an eagle in flight. It is a great mystery. Perhaps it is the Resting of a great warrior. No one knows."

He was about to go on when the Great Potentara stopped him with a quick word.

Jhanes grinned and translated. "He places no restrictions on Lady Zoysana. He suggests that he's already given you permission, and there's no point taking it away, since he probably couldn't stop you anyway."

He paused. "That last part, he was only half joking. You've impressed him. He made a comment to Terenno a moment ago, when he thought I wasn't listening. He told him to get Mantinello married to you quick or he'd put his own son in the running."

To Jhanes' surprise, Zoysana turned as red as her dark skin would reveal, but she ducked her head and said nothing. *So there is something that will get through that composed countenance.* He looked at his patroness in a new light. It was hard to remember she was only a girl. "Shall I tell him you're not interested?"

Her head snapped up. "No, you will not. Not until he opens the subject. Then…" she faltered, but her chin rose again. "Then we'll see. A lady likes to keep her options open."

"But Mantinello's just a boy, Zoysana. He can't be more than seventeen."

Her head swung towards him, and her eyes travelled his frame as if she were choosing the place to carve the juiciest hunk from a side of beef. Then her voice came low and even. "Maybe I'll go for the great man himself."

Since he couldn't tell whether she was joking, and he didn't really want to know, he decided to shut up.

25. The Carriage

A month later, Jhanes and Zoysana jogged their horses along the familiar road north from the castle towards the centre of Petrella. He had been thinking a great deal on the latter part of this trip, and finally he spoke his fear aloud. "I'm about to make a mistake."

Zoysana looked up at her second-in-command, where he rode beside her on his big bay mare. "Now where did a thought like that sneak in from?"

"I was thinking. I've been too successful. Things don't usually go this well for me. I've seen it happen to others. They get successful, then they start to expect it. The next thing you know, they're dead."

"Aren't you lucky you're not soldiering."

"I guess I'm lucky, then. I'm still worried. Certain, I'm making progress, but the more progress I make, the worse it will be when I mess it up. What do you think?"

She threw up her hands in mock dismay. "Jhanes, you're easily ten years older than me. I brought you along this summer to give me the benefit of your wisdom. So why are you asking me about this? I'm twenty-one and I don't know anything about life."

He was about to apologize when he noticed her grin. "I don't know, Lady Zoe. It's just something that happens to people like you. You're sympathetic, or something."

"Flattery will get you everywhere. All right. So you want my opinion?"

"We're still a day out of Lanil's Rock. Nothing better to do."

"True." She thought a moment. "All right, here it is. I don't think you've ever been aware of your own abilities. You certainly haven't been working up to them."

"I haven't?"

"Why was someone with your capability still a soldier in the ranks? I know, you said you didn't like to stay around and play the politics, but I also think you didn't want to stand out. You liked the anonymity of the ranks. Maybe it's something to do with your upbringing as a slave to the Inari, but you never put yourself forward. Not until this summer."

"I suppose."

"But now you have to push yourself. You have people to protect. The battle fell out so you had to win it because no one else could. So you tried, and you succeeded. It wasn't luck. It was ability. Your lack of confidence in yourself kept you from doing that sort of thing before."

"I've always been confident."

"In a way, yes. But it was the confidence of someone who was doing something easy. Something he was sure of succeeding at. Oh, I know you could have been killed any time. A soldier's life is like that. But given the same chance any other soldier has, you knew your superior ability, your size and your intelligence would get you through.

"Your test came on the road last summer when you faced me. You ran into something bigger than yourself, and it beat you. That shook you up. The first thing you did was retreat. You decided to quit soldiering, didn't you?"

"Yes, but wasn't that natural? I mean, my age..."

"Of course it was natural. It was as good a reason to quit as any. But you couldn't quit, could you? Circumstances made you keep on, push yourself, and you couldn't resist the challenge."

"So what has that to do with making a mistake?"

"Before now, you've never taken a risk. I don't mean your life. I mean a risk of failing. Now, coming with me to the Inari, you were taking a big chance."

"That's for sure. We could have been killed."

"Of course, but that's not the risk I'm talking about. I'm talking about the risk of failure."

"Failure?"

313

"That's what you're worried about, isn't it? Not death or injury: failure. I'll make a guess that for you, the worst thing that could have happened south of the Barrier would have been for me to get killed, and you to survive."

He thought about it. "Could be."

"See? That would have been failure. But you were up to the task. You succeeded beyond your hopes. Same with the Inari raids. Your knowledge was invaluable to Gerth, and you saved a lot of lives. By the way, will your Inari friends be upset about that?"

"Not at all. They would be upset if I did any less than my best. It's a game, remember."

"Good. So again you push yourself, and again you succeed."

"Which is exactly my problem. If I get too confident, I get complacent, and that's how a soldier gets himself killed."

"True. So what are you going to do? Sit back and do nothing because you're afraid to fail? Stop now and be careful because you're afraid of getting complacent? Or keep pushing yourself, to see what you're really capable of?"

"Which makes my real problem even worse."

"Because all this success in soldiering comes when you are trying to get out."

"Exactly."

She glanced up at him. "Welcome to the nobility."

"What?"

"The Warlander's constant problem. He wants to stay home, run his manor and live with his loved ones, but he's always being called away to protect them."

He thought about that for a while, the horses' hoofbeats stretching out behind them. Then he chuckled. "Well, at least we have the answer to your question."

"My question? Are you changing the subject?"

"Your question about why I'm asking you, when you're so young. You're a leader. I'm not. Oh, I can lead in a small way. I can make plans. But I don't look as far ahead or as deep as you do. I only do it when it's necessary, like planning for a battle. You do it all the time. You must. Don't tell me you thought this up just now?"

"Not completely. I haven't written a report on you, but I do think about people around me and consider how they would react if I had to put them into certain situations."

"That's it. Most people don't think about the possibility of putting anyone into any situation. You think like a leader. And I wasn't changing the subject. I have to agree with you. It's hard to admit that I've been taking it easy all my life."

"I wouldn't exactly say taking it easy!"

"You know what I mean. I haven't ever pushed myself. And now I have to. I have responsibilities, and I never had those before. I have a woman and a child to think about. Not that they wouldn't get on just fine without me, but I like to believe they will be better with me around."

She laughed out loud. "I think that's safe to say."

"So in answer to your question, I will continue to push myself. I am aware I might overreach, but I will not let that stop me from acting. In both sides of my life, and let the bones fall where they may."

"Good. I thought you'd feel that way."

Her face was impassive and innocent to his glance.

"Did you set me up for this conversation?"

She looked across, eyebrows up. "You were the one who brought up the subject."

"I suppose I did. But somehow it ended like you had it planned all along. All those nice things you say about me make me think I can do my duty to the Clan and to my family as well. And I'm not sure that's a good idea to try. I seem to remember Sarasha the Lame saying something about showing her a man doing two jobs, and she'd show you a man doing neither of them properly."

"So perhaps I'm trying to persuade you without you noticing?"

"As I get to know you better, I get more suspicious about how 'forward-thinking' you are. Sometimes I find you downright sneaky."

She laughed. "I can't help it. I spent too much time with the Sivan."

"Did you? What was he like?"

She mused a moment. "What was he like? Like an onion, I'd say."

He knew he didn't have to react, and after a moment she went on.

"Layers. Just when you thought you had him figured out, you would learn something different about him that changed everything. Oh, I could just wring his neck!"

"I thought he was your friend."

"Of course he was – is. That's why I want to wring his neck. He doesn't have to stay away and play his devious games from a distance. There's always a place for him in Petrella. We understand what he did, why he left. Why doesn't he come back? Loreline isn't going to wait forever."

"Loreline? You mean Loreline and he...? Oh. Well, there's my first mistake."

"What was that?"

"I had no idea. I was asking Loreline all about him. Some of her answers seemed a bit strange. She must think I'm an unfeeling clod."

"Nonsense. She loves him. She loves it when anyone wants to talk about him. Talks my ear off sometimes. No, your only mistake was in thinking you made a mistake. Don't make that mistake again."

Their peals of laughter startled their horses out of their plodding walk, and they cantered ahead to where Tadeo and Patu were waiting, wondering what the fuss was about.

The rest of the conversation took place in his own head as they travelled. He thought about what he had accomplished recently, and the complicated situation it put him in.

Success. I've never had success of this sort before. Now that Zoysana said it out loud, I see how it was always too easy. Now I'm challenging myself and succeeding. And it feels good. Being a soldier feels different.

But here I am, on the road to being an innkeeper again. With a wife and family to look after.

I wonder how I feel about that.

* * *

When they reached Tsalk, there was Talia's carriage sitting on the village green looking forlorn, like a huge old luxury barge stranded on shore. No one had polished the brass, and it looked as if someone had stolen the big lamps. Considering the difficulty of hiding such booty, perhaps they were just put away for safety.

Zoysana sat her horse a moment, staring at the monstrosity. "I still can't figure out why."

"Stupidity."

"Who, in that whole bunch, is stupid?"

"Not one I can think of."

"So, who is hiding the real reason? Who isn't telling all he knows?"

They dismounted and walked around the coach. Tadeo inspected the suspension, rocking the body. Jhanes stooped to check how his axle repair had fared. It seemed to be holding, although wear spots showed that it was no longer tight.

A thought occurred to him. "When they left it here, who was the most worried?"

"I see what you mean. We don't know because we weren't here. When I met them on the road, nobody seemed concerned. Talia did ask what I thought she should do about it."

"So what should we do about it?"

"How is the axle holding out?"

"Well enough to take it back to Lanil's Rock if we want, especially empty. Easier than taking it on to the castle."

"So did he count on that, as well?"

"Who? You aren't still thinking about your friend."

Zoe grinned at him. "I can't help considering the possibility. Now let's think. The Sivan would have known this monstrosity couldn't get to the castle. If he didn't send it, this is all a mistake, and it means nothing. But what if he did send it? He must want it here, part way."

"Or he wants someone to discover how bad the road is and fix it, so it can get to the castle. Along with the larger wagons of the Kyabran merchants."

"Surely there are more certain ways to do that."

Jhanes shrugged. "It's your game."

"No, I appreciate your ideas. Keep it up." He nodded, and she continued thinking aloud. "Let's assume he wanted the carriage to get about this far. Why? What does he want us to do with it?"

"This game is getting pretty far-fetched. How could he expect you to do anything? From what I've heard, he wasn't – or isn't, if you wish – the kind of man to take a wild chance like that."

"He doesn't expect us to do anything specific, like take it to some certain place at a certain time. He often sets things in motion so that he has a lot of different things in different places, waiting for him in case he needs them. Most of them will never get used."

Jhanes thought. There was something he half-remembered… "Wait a minute. Lady Talia. That first night, she talked about taking poor advice. She said she was told by someone she trusted to take bigger horses, but she took the matched blacks through vanity."

Zoysana grinned. "We can only guess who the trusted one was. Just shows that even the Sivan's plans don't always go according to his wishes." She scanned the carriage again. "That will be only one of his plans. Whatever is in this huge boat, it will be useful for many reasons." She looked around the green

318

to see if there were any listeners nearby. "If there's anything in it at all. I may be completely off the track. We might discover that it folds out into a travelling theatre, for all I know."

"So do you want a more detailed search?"

"Yes, but not with everyone watching. How much trouble would it be to get it back to Lanil's Rock?"

"Not a lot, if you aren't in a hurry. Is it worth it?"

"I think so. Did you have anything else in mind?"

He grinned. "Only getting home as soon as possible."

"Why? From all the reports, Sarha's getting along wonderf…oh."

He was gratified to see her blush. It wasn't often Zoe missed something like that. He decided to be gracious. "Another day won't matter. We'll need another horse."

"You can use yours?"

"This carriage is meant for big horses. She'll fit, but we can hardly use your ponies. We'll need harness, though, and it might have to be adapted to fit her."

"Well, that's why we carry the king's coin with us. Let's head for the smithy. They always know where to find things."

26. Home Again

So the innkeeper rolled home to his village on a hot day in late summer, driving the big, black carriage with Zoysana and Tadeo sitting comfortably inside, their horses trotting on leads behind and Patu's ugly visage panting from a window on the shaded side of the carriage. He looked funny leaning out, but he loved to ride that way, and the heat was hard on him, in his wiry coat.

As they cleared the edge of the forest, Jhanes eagerly searched for signs of change. Sure enough, a row of wood-walled tents backed against the outermost houses, a dusty parade ground stamped out in front of them. Something in the village looked strange: his inn. Its roof now stood out from the other buildings, and there was a lighter section of new thatch stretching it at each end. He could see two figures working on scaffolding at the east gable.

There was no official sentry at the edge of town, but an officer strolled over as they approached and nodded to them as they drove by. Jhanes grinned back, touching his helmet liner with his whip handle in salute.

There was the usual swirl of dogs and children, a cheerful sign. Remembering the rules of the Inari camp, he restrained the horses to a walk down the dusty street and pulled up in front of the inn. The workers turned from their job and looked down at him, grinning.

"Nice carriage there, Jhanes. Seems I seen it before, somewheres."

The other spat a stream of tobacco juice into the dirt. "Aye, but the owner had a prettier face last time."

He couldn't help but laugh when he turned to see Patu's bearded visage staring up at him. The two carpenters almost fell off the scaffolding at their own humour.

"I gather our arrival is no surprise."

"Naw, the boy came runnin' in a while ago, shoutin'. Then we seen you comin'. Get a great view from up here, ya do. Sarha says we can stay overnight once in the big guestroom an' we do a good enough job." His thumb indicated a large dormer window facing south, farther down the roof.

Jhanes swung down from the high driver's seat, chuckling at the landlady's methods of motivating her workers. He opened the carriage door, but Zoysana motioned him towards the inn.

"Don't play coachman now, you silly man. Get in there."

"Oh." He turned and started for the inn.

He didn't make it. The door smashed open and Sarha appeared, striding briskly – not quite running – towards him. He found himself rushing to her, picking her up, crushing her against him, swinging her around. Her arms were choking him and her face was buried against his collar. He stopped, and she leaned back to look into his face, a huge smile widening her mouth like the one that was stretching his own. Then she pulled him forward again, holding him tightly, murmuring nonsense in his ear.

"Young love. Ain't it somethin'?"

He turned to see Zoysana laughing up at him. He released one arm and spun Sarha, setting her down so that the two of them towered over the Kyabran woman. "Are you laughing at us?"

"Sure enough. Aren't you two a little old for that sort of display?"

He glanced down at Sarha, smiling up at him from the circle of his arm. "Nope. Never too old for this." To prove it, he bent down and slipped his arm behind Sarha's legs, gathering her into his arms, and spun her around again. She leaned against the spin, whooping like a child. When he set her down again, she was out of breath and red in the face. Again they confronted Zoysana.

"Well, Sarha, I brought him back safe. It was difficult at times, but I steered him through."

Sarha glanced from one to the other, then to Tadeo for confirmation. "And who kept who safe?"

Zoysana rocked her hand back and forth. "A team effort, I suppose."

"Well, bring the team in where it's cool and you can tell me all about it." She raised her voice to the roofers. "You two take care of the horses, please. It'll give you a break from the hot sun."

The men clambered down, grinning.

The travellers turned towards the inn and paused. "It seems you haven't been exactly idle yourself while we were gone."

She waved a hand airily, although the other arm remained clamped around his waist. "Oh, you know us women. Always wanting to make a little change here, a slight adjustment there. A new room here, a bit of extra roof there. Nothing major."

They walked into the cool of the room to see Frey struggling to lift a full mug of cider up beside the three already waiting on a table. Jhanes reached out and caught the boy up in his free arm. "New waiter, I see. She workin' you hard?"

The child smiled and ducked his head but didn't pull away. Jhanes squeezed gently, then put the lad back on his feet. "Won't keep you from your work. Carry on." He turned to Zoysana and Tadeo, grinning in the doorway. "Please enter my humble inn. I believe I detect the distinctive aroma of hill-apple cider," he imitated a sweeping courtly bow, "and I suspect this table is prepared for us. Please seat yourselves."

He followed them and sat, managing not to release Sarha in the process. They raised their mugs and clashed them together, top, bottom, then top again, and drank in appreciative silence. There was a long pause while they looked at each other. Then Zoysana shook her head in disbelief.

"We did it!"

They looked at each other again. Jhanes squeezed Sarha until she squirmed in discomfort and batted at his arm. "We sure enough did!"

Even Tadeo broke his usual reserve. "I can't really believe it, even now. We did it!"

They clashed mugs again, and the mellow cider ran down their throats and dripped from their chins.

Sarha looked around at them over the rim of her mug. "The three of you? All by yourselves? A pedlar went through here a coupla quarters ago, all full of the tale. You went up there over the Barrier and took on the whole Inari nation. Brought them to their knees, he said."

Jhanes looked at the other two appraisingly. "To their knees?"

They nodded together. "To their knees."

"To be honest." Tadeo lowered his mug. "We did have a little help."

"Did we? Oh, yes, later."

"Much later."

"With the raiding parties."

"After we brought them to their knees."

They nodded somberly. "Long after that."

"And," Jhanes held up a finger for attention. They waited. "I only drew my sword three times."

Sarha stared at him. "You're joking."

He played affronted dignity. "I am not. My sword stayed in its sheath unless it was desperately needed. I must admit, I used my hands once or twice. Fought weaponless once."

"And almost got dumped on your duff."

He ignored this jibe. "I used my hands. My bow a little. But I was very thrifty with my sword." His chin rose. "I am an officer now. I fight with my mind."

Zoysana nodded. "That's right. And I only drew mine once."

Sarha stared at them. "You didn't fight?"

"She danced."

"Danced?"

"True. She danced. Impressed the hell out of them."

Tadeo nodded. "Set them back on their heels, that did."

Sarha grinned. "Well, as long as you didn't sing."

"We wanted to trade with them, not scare them away."

"Please, let me get this straight. You went into the war camp of the Inari, just the three of you. You wrestled and you...you danced? And you scared them so much they decided not to attack?"

Zoysana sat back a moment, gazing at the three of them. "You know, I like her story."

Jhanes nodded. "So do I."

Tadeo added his solemn, "And I."

"Thank you, Sarha. You have made a beautiful story. We couldn't have said it better ourselves."

"Am I ever going to get a straight story about this?"

"You have it. You can tell it any time you like. We couldn't do better."

She jumped to her feet. "If it wasn't a battle, it must be the sun that addled your brains. I need another drink."

Jhanes was in front of her, serious, now. "No, Sarha, please allow me." He pushed her gently back down and gathered the mugs.

"I have been looking forward to this for a long time." *Now that I think about it, I have been.* He walked to the barrel, set the mugs down beside it and took the handle in his palm, feeling the silky smoothness of its polish. He drew four more mugs of cider: exactly to the rim, not a drop spilled. He carried them back to the table and set them down with a flourish. "Drink up, my friends. Your innkeeper serves you."

I wonder how I feel about that? I think I like it.

They laughed, but there was more than one meaningful glance passed around the circle.

"And why have you brought that big, ugly carriage back here?"

"Now, my dear, I'll not have you cast aspersions on Lady Zoysana's chosen means of travel. It may be large, but it is roomy and comfortable."

"Which neatly ducks my question."

"Well, we're not sure what's going on with that carriage, but Loreline and Zoysana both suspect it's not here by accident. In the morning I'll pull it into the yard where it's private and have a good look at it."

* * *

Under the pretense of checking the repairs, Jhanes parked the carriage in a corner of the inn yard where it was as far out of the way as something that big could get. Then he propped up the rear end and removed the broken axle. Scouting out his biggest hammer, he knocked off all the metal parts. He was left with the wooden axle, a deep crack running halfway along from one end.

Shrugging, he put it all back together and tightened it up. It would make it to the castle as soon as Talia wanted it.

He stood back and surveyed the carriage, checking the overall dimensions. Then he moved closer to examine the interior to see whether there was room for a secret compartment in the walls, ceiling, or floor. As far as he could tell, everything was the proper thickness. He checked all the joins to see if he could find a panel that would move. The carriage was frustratingly well crafted; there was no room to slip a paper into any joint.

He was just backing out the door after this inspection when he saw Zoysana watching him from the stable doorway.

"I can't find a thing. This boat's as tight as a drum. Boat! I bet it would float, it's so well made. You want to take a look?"

She shook her head. "No, I imagine you'd have found anything there was to find. I'm doing my looking from over here."

He must have looked skeptical, because she continued. "I'm not looking into the carriage. I'm looking into the Sivan's head. Why such a big carriage? Why so big a show?"

Jhanes stood beside her. "One thing for sure. No one who saw that thing would ever forget it."

"That might be part of it. If Lady Talia had to leave it behind, there's no way it could get lost."

"Which means that it must be of some value."

Zoysana moved closer in a slow curve as if approaching an unknown adversary. "But what kind of value? Value as an object, or value as in money?"

"The gilding alone would be worth a bit, if you took the time to scrape it off."

Zoysana froze. "The gilding?"

"Aye. See this trim that runs along the outside?" A band as wide and thick as his hand ran all the way around the carriage, top and bottom. "I bet that gold stripe is pure gilt paint. Notice how it shines, in spite of all the weathering?"

With an agile leap, the small woman was in the driver's box, a dagger appearing in her hand. She examined the strip, poking once or twice. She looked down at him with a strange smile. "I think you have it backwards, Innkeeper."

"Backwards?"

"That's right. You are not looking at a black moulding strip with a bit of pure gold paint on it. You're looking at…"

"…a pure gold moulding strip with a bit of black paint on it!" He glanced around to see if anyone was in earshot. "You have to be joking!'"

"Come and look."

His head was just the right level. Wherever she poked the black paint on the railing, a gleam of gold showed through. He peered closer, noting the structure of the moulding. "Not completely gold. There's a strip of wood on either side."

"Right. To protect it from bumps. Couldn't have the gold showing through every time the paint got chipped."

"It would be quite distracting, trying to travel with people running alongside, digging hunks off your carriage trim."

They stopped giggling and stared at each other. "I think we better look this carriage over more carefully."

From that point on, it was like a children's candy hunt. They discovered that much of the fancy trim on the carriage was cast in gold. The higher off the ground, the safer from chance knocks or scrapes, the more likely it was to be gold.

Finally, they gave up. "I know there's more, but why bother? We know it's there."

Jhanes shook his head. "Why would he send all that gold? There must be a king's ransom in there."

Zoysana smiled wryly. "Or a queen's dowry."

"Do you think so?"

"Why not? If all of Gerth and Janitra's plans come to be, then Petrella will soon become richer than any kingdom we know of. Combine that with the strength of our armies, especially our Warlanders in full armour. A small but influential ruler in the Inner Duchies would do well to be connected here."

"So Talia came, all ready to marry Gerth, with everything she needed, including her dowry."

Zoysana shook her head. "We're exaggerating the worth of this gold. I doubt if this is anywhere near enough. Besides, Gerth will be looking for trading concessions and political support, not money. This," she tossed a hand towards the carriage, "is small change compared to the riches to be made with the proper trade deals. This is just enough to set her up nicely, allow her to maintain herself for as long as it takes."

"Why didn't he do it the usual way? You know: ambassadors, letters of intent, all that political stuff."

"I suppose that's the way her father would have done it."

"Well, if her father didn't send her...you think the Sivan did?"

"That's been my theory all along." Zoysana shrugged. "I'm not even sure the lady herself knows she's been set up for this. Bet her father doesn't."

"It didn't seem like she knew about the carriage, did it?"

"She would have been much more concerned about it."

"And her people?"

"Only Gavess would have known, and he's showed no interest either. No, I think we're looking at the Sivan's shifty mind at its best."

"So what do we do with it now?"

"Besides a little touch-up painting? Nothing. It's safer here than it has been for the past month. We'll just have to get word to Lady Talia that the carriage is worth something to her and await instructions. From what I could see, she's doing fine. It doesn't cost much to visit our court if you live in the castle. But she won't be able to stay there too long. It wouldn't look right. If she moves to a more permanent residence somewhere in the town, she'll need some cash."

"And here it is." He slapped the gold, then checked to see he hadn't marred the finish.

"That's right. I'll send word to Loreline by the next messenger. You can expect orders back, some time this summer, to bring the carriage to the castle. With those big horses of yours, you shouldn't have any trouble."

"If I don't carry quite as much equipment as the lady did."

They both grinned. "Those poor horses! No wonder they were worn out. That gold must weigh more than Talia's luggage."

* * *

Orders came soon, and by unlikely messengers. Two quarters had gone by, and Jhanes was just getting comfortable in his routines again, adapting to the new demands of the larger inn with more customers.

One afternoon, just as the sun was slanting low enough to give scant relief from the heat of the day, Frey came trotting self-importantly down the road from his hiding place in the woods. The boy had grown, both in stature and confidence, and had been known to speak full sentences, sometimes even one after the other. He paused dramatically in front of the inn, where Jhanes and Sarha were sitting for a moment in the shade.

"Better rest while you can, Ma."

Sarha smiled. He had been calling her 'Ma' for some time now, but Jhanes could see it still gave her a lift.

"Why's that, Son?"

"Customers comin'. Important ones." He paused for a moment, then decided to try for one more sentence. "Friends o' yours, Pa."

Jhanes grinned down at the boy. "Friends of mine, Son? Now who would that be?"

The boy grinned triumphantly. "The girl with knifes."

Sarha stood. "Lateda. Who's with her?"

"All of them."

Jhanes stood too. "All of them? Lady Talia?"

The boy nodded and smiled at this reaction and held up his fingers.

"Six of them? You sure?"

He stared at his fingers. "Six."

Jhanes glanced at Sarha. "We can handle six if Lateda sleeps in with Lady Talia again. That merchant in the old room over the kitchen will have to move his servants in with himself or put them down in the barn."

"He won't mind when he hears who is putting him out."

They turned as a cloud of dust emerged from the forest, resolving itself into six riders and a packhorse, their mounts plodding, heads low.

"Where's her carriage?"

"No carriage, Ma. All ridin'."

"Even the lady?"

Jhanes laughed. "She's had an interesting time this spring. Between Gerth's usual court entertainment and fighting the Inari raids, she's been on horseback every day and loving it. I guess she came to get her carriage herself."

When the riders got close enough, he could see that several of them were astride horses much too big for normal riding. Tall and rangy, but with a good weight of muscle on them, the four matched blacks looked vaguely familiar. Then he had it. He strode forward to help her down, but she vaulted from the tall horse before he could reach her.

"Welcome, Lady Talia. I didn't expect a personal response to my letter."

She grinned and slapped her glove on the thigh of her riding habit, raising a cloud of dust. "It seemed the most direct way of taking care of things."

He held the horse, stroking its nose. "I see you've made friends outside the castle as well."

She laughed out loud. "Yes, Lord Oando was happy to lend me his team."

"Begging the lady's pardon, but I doubt somehow that the Duke let his prize team out of his sight without some serious persuasion."

She batted her eyes at him. "Why, Jhanes, don't you believe a pretty girl could make friends with an older gentleman? Would you impugn my virtue?"

Sarha stepped up, chuckling. "I don't know what 'impugn' means, Jhanes, but it sounds like you'd better think before you answer that one."

"Sarha!" The lady strode forward, clasping Sarha's outstretched hand in both of hers. "I gather you made the mistake of hitching yourself to this rude character. I hope he treats you better than he treats me."

"About the same, my Lady, but I get even less respect."

"Well, we'll have to get our heads together and see if we can reform him." She turned as the rest of her people dismounted. "What do you think of my horses?"

Sarha smiled. "They'll probably get you up to the castle. Especially since your luggage went with the teamsters months ago."

The lady waved her hand. "Oh, all that stuff. I have no idea why Gavess packed most of it. I haven't used half. Although some came in handy when we started out on this little foray. Didn't it, Gavess?"

The butler, slimmer and more cheerful than Jhanes remembered, appeared, the lead rope from the packhorse in his hand. "Most certainly, my Lady."

She looked at him. "You didn't even hear what I said, did you?"

His poise was unruffled. "Well, my Lady, in such a situation I find it expedient to agree from the start. I will have to sooner or later."

She turned back to Jhanes, shaking her head. "Insubordinate. I don't know how you train servants out here on the frontier, but it does something to their heads. You take a civilized man like Gavess here, send him out chasing Inari for a week and you can't talk to him afterwards."

"Chasing Inari? You sent Gavess out with the patrols?"

"I didn't send him out. I took him out."

Sarha looked again at Talia's clothing and demeanour, noted the sword slung at her belt. "Perhaps once we get you into the shade with a nice, cool drink in your hand, you'll have a tale for us."

Talia slapped her on the back. "Hostess, the only thing that kept me going the past hour was the thought of a mug of hill-apple cider, cool from the cellar." She raised her voice only a touch. "Lads, the quicker you get the gear off these horses, the quicker you get to join the ladies in the taproom."

With a wink to the silent Lateda, she strode into the inn, admiring the renovations as she went. Jhanes glanced at Sarha and raised his eyebrows. She smiled and shook her head slowly. There was a ruler in the Inner Duchies who would get a shock when his daughter came home.

Jhanes set up the mugs of cider while Sarha sat with Talia. "So, my Lady, you like it here in Petrella."

Talia took a long pull at her mug. It was difficult to tell if she was considering his question or enjoying the cool liquid sliding down her throat. After a moment, she spoke in slow, considered tones. "Yes, I do. I like everything about it. Oh, I don't like the dust and dirt on the road, but I doubt that anyone actually likes dust. You learn to put up with it. No, I like it here because...because..." she swung her arms out, "because it's so big. I mean everything is big. Even the furniture. I haven't knocked a table over for weeks. They're all too heavy, and they're far enough apart that I can move around them. You must understand, Jhanes."

He pretended to think. "Well, my Lady, I can't say as I've spent too much time in the dainty drawing rooms of the Inner Duchies, but I can imagine. Some of us take up more room than others."

Her laugh rang out again. "Couldn't have put it better myself." She took another drink, then looked around. "Speaking of big, I don't see the Grandfather of Wolves around. I was hoping Zoysana would be here."

"She's out and about. Not the type to sit around and relax, even if the war is over. She and Tadeo went over to Alderly yesterday. They'll be back later tonight or tomorrow. They'll lie over in some shady spot during the hottest part of the day and ride in the evening."

"Like we didn't. I know. But we're from farther north, where it gets really hot. This was merely uncomfortable. And we had hill-apple cider to think about." She drank again, draining the mug, and sighed. "I enjoyed that."

"Don't get too attached to it, my Lady. The king's soldiers are getting paid too much, and they've taken a liking to the good stuff. I've had to order another couple of barrels."

332

By the look on Talia's face, she had something she was dying to tell them. She glanced around at the reconditioned inn and turned to Sarha.

"You've done such a good job here, I should hire you. I'm building a house."

"A house." Sarha glanced at Jhanes.

"Yes. Don't just sit there like a couple of sheep. I'm going to build myself a house. A summer house. You don't know what it's like in the Inner Duchies in the summer. It's so hot and damp, and you can't get to sleep at night. Up here in the mountains, it's hot but it's dry, and it doesn't feel so bad. Then it cools down at night, and you can forget how hot it was during the day. I love it here!"

"So you're going to build yourself a summer place here."

"That's right. And I'll come here every summer when it gets unbearable at home. I'll bring my friends with me. We can ride, and hunt, and climb mountains, and slide down snowfields in the middle of the summer. I can't wait!"

"I didn't think there were too many people in the Duchies who liked that sort of thing."

Talia's laugh boomed out. "You haven't met my friends. Wait till next summer when I invite them here."

Jhanes set his mug on the table. "Do you think there's enough gold in that carriage to build a house?"

She shrugged. "We won't know until we get it to the castle and take the trim off. Which brings me to the next question. I have a favour to ask."

"Anything I can do."

"Well, we don't know what the value of the carriage is, but we know it's valuable."

"And you need an escort."

"Exactly. And if you were free…" She glanced at Sarha.

The landlady tossed up her hands. "Oh, take him. He's just under my feet right now."

Jhanes laughed. "Yes, take me away before I find myself brained by a frying pan. She's too used to being her own boss."

"And he's too used to being his. He won't listen!"

Talia's hands hit the table. "You know, I have the same problem with Gerth. We must put our heads together and compare techniques."

Jhanes dropped his smile. "So we have to take the coach to the castle? When are we leaving?"

"As soon as Zoysana is ready. Gerth wants her there because of some project or other, and this sounds like his excuse to get her to come home without actually sending an order."

Sarha frowned and smiled at the same time. "He's the king. Why doesn't he just order her back?"

Talia shook her head. "Have you ever seen anyone give Zoysana an order?"

Jhanes thought for a moment, then grinned. "It isn't something you do."

"True. Besides which, she's so cooperative, all you have to do is ask her."

"Right. And if she doesn't want to do it, she'll have such good arguments that you'll end up agreeing with her in any case."

27. A Pleasant Assignment

"Jhanes, I have a small duty for you."

He looked up from the garden where he had been hoeing weeds. "If it doesn't involve bending over in the hot sun, Zoe, I'm your man."

"I think I can arrange a holiday. Talia wants to visit Lord Feister. Thank him for his offer to take care of her carriage. It wouldn't hurt to have you come along to show you're taking good care of his horse."

"And incidentally reassure him that the Free Counties are thriving."

"That's it. Take four or five days. Is that all right?"

He started for the stable. "Better than what I was doing. When do we leave?"

"Oh, there's no hurry. Tomorrow will be fine."

"Oh. Then I have time to finish the hoeing?"

"Sorry."

"Ah, the trials of the landed folk."

"If you were in the army, you'd be digging fortifications."

"Not if I was an officer."

She paused to regard him. "Still worrying about that, are you?"

He shrugged. "Only now and then." He hefted the hoe.

"I'll leave you to your thoughts. I often find a repetitive chore frees the mind."

"Thank you for your consideration, my Lady. I will take your advice."

She slapped him on the shoulder and left.

* * *

Once again, the innkeeper was swept into the realm of the upper classes. He didn't expect to be seated at the head table, but he enjoyed sitting with Talia's mercenaries, reliving his army days with the usual tales and jokes. He was included in all the less formal meetings and events. His opinion was sought, and he felt he acquitted himself well. Talia's friendly treatment did him no harm, and he wasn't sure he was happy or not when it came time to leave.

Jhanes was in his quarters packing for the next day's return trip when a page arrived, panting. "My lord Feister wishes your attendance immediately, Sir."

He dropped his pack and strode after the boy. "Is something wrong?"

"Messenger came in, Sir. I don't know what he said, but the whole castle's abuzz. Shouldn't say anything, but the word is there's an invasion."

Jhanes frowned. *Who could possibly be invading? It doesn't match up.*

As he entered the lord's reception room, Feister looked up from his conversation with Talia and some of his advisors. "Ah, there you are, Jhanes. Need your advice here."

"What's this about an invasion, my Lord?"

"Don't quite know what to think. Just got a message from the border post. There's been an invasion. Farms burned, merchants waylaid, that kind of incursion."

"Any reason to suspect more than bandits?"

"There's something about uniforms running through all the stories."

"But nothing more than that?"

"The messenger is here. Do you have any specific questions for him?"

Jhanes turned to the young soldier, who was standing there, looking rather unhappy.

"How much is firm fact? Do we have numbers, armament, colours?"

The messenger ducked his head and looked sideways at the lord. Feister shook his head. "I already went down that road with him. Nothing of the sort, I'm afraid. Rumour and hearsay. Oh, there's someone out there, all right. Three farmers murdered, one small wagon train attacked and looted. There are too many reports of a uniform to discount them."

"What uniform?"

The messenger was eager to redeem himself. "Red with gold buttons, Sir. Three different people said that."

"If you substitute brass on the buttons, that describes seven armies I know of within a ten-day ride, including Light Horse."

Feister nodded. "Anyway, I've written up a report and sent it to Arlyn Castle. The messenger has orders to show it along the way, including to your commander at Lanil's Rock. So everyone will be prepared."

"Thank you, my Lord." Jhanes turned to Talia. "You'd be safe here. The trouble seems to be farther north. What would you like to do? Head for the castle?"

"The castle would be best, since we have no idea of the size of army facing us."

"You're well horsed. You'll move faster than any army."

"Shall we leave today?"

Jhanes shook his head. "We wouldn't get far, and I don't want to stay in a little hamlet with an army around somewhere. Their outriders might overtake us."

The lord nodded. "So you'll stay with us tonight, hoping for more news, then travel in daylight tomorrow?"

"I think that's safest, my Lord. If we ride hard, we'll make it to Lanil's Rock by dark. Lady Talia?"

She smiled. "I'm not likely to question your decision, Jhanes. Your advice has always been good."

"Do you want an escort?"

Talia glanced at Jhanes. "I hate to pull your soldiers away when you might need them. My troop is very competent. I'll be fine."

Lord Feister glanced up at Jhanes. "I can't argue with that. An early night tonight, then, and off at dawn?"

Jhanes nodded. "Suits me, my Lord."

Talia quirked a rueful smile. "Up at dawn for an all-day ride. And I came out here for a little adventure."

"Just making sure your every wish is satisfied, my Lady."

Her face lost its humour. "My wish for tomorrow is a sharp sword and a good horse."

"I'll take care of that, too, my Lady."

* * *

The next morning, the five of them trotted off to the south, bristling with arms, every sense alert. They were too small a group to afford outriders, so Jhanes led, with Talia in the centre beside Arderton, and the two other lads following close behind. He had only one order for them. "Arderton, you and your lads keep your eyes up and out. You had good training this summer."

The bowman gave a grim smile. "And you'll watch our feet for us?"

"I'll be watching for tracks. Talia, you look where everyone else isn't."

"What do you mean?"

"If we all look left, you look right. We're guarding you, so you don't have to worry about the first threat. You're watching backs in case trouble comes from two different directions."

"Right. I can do that."

They rode in silence, all business. Jhanes thanked their luck for Talia's experience in the mountains this summer. She knew to conserve her horse and her energy, and her sword was as sharp as anyone's.

By mid-afternoon they had put in a good distance from the troubled area. He was starting to relax when he heard the noises ahead. He pulled his horse to a halt, and his party did the same, quieting their tired mounts with little trouble.

Meeting Arderton's eyes, he pointed forward. Soon, everyone could hear it. Jingling of equipment, tramping feet. He signalled to the left, and they wheeled their horses into a stand of trees. Jhanes dismounted and scooted back with a branch. He couldn't cover their tracks, but the road was hard and dry, and at least he could mess them up enough that most regular soldiers wouldn't notice anything.

The riders were close, so he dove into the bushes to see Talia smiling at him.

"Wasted work, I'm afraid."

He glanced over his shoulder to where the travellers were rounding the corner. Two short, dark riders on mountain ponies. One mounted officer. Behind them, a small troop of soldiers with travel packs and a supply wagon pulled by mules. He swung up on his horse and followed Talia out on the road.

Zoysana pulled up. "What is this, an ambush?"

Talia grinned. "No, my Lady. Practising in case of need."

Zoe looked down at the muddled road. "That mess would have just piqued my curiosity."

Jhanes tilted his head. "A wise person taught me that any attempt to hide a trail serves to attract the attention of the one who can follow it."

Lady Talia nodded. "We have heard that quote many times this summer."

Zoe shrugged. "Having my lessons repeated to me shows how well my students are learning. Now to business. I'm happy to see you in one piece. What's going on?"

Jhanes shook his head. "It's the same as last year, Zoe. Rumour, gossip and fear. The facts well hidden in the hysteria."

"I read the message." She glanced up at him. "Last time there was a rumoured invasion, it was only me. This time, who can tell how large this group is?"

"We won't know until we find them. What are your plans?"

"I'm taking our soldiers as far as the border with Lord Feister's land. They'll set up camp and patrol the area. Then Tadeo and I will go on to Cdeile and talk to Feister, coordinate our defences and collect any more information that comes in. I'm of the opinion it's a big fuss over nothing. Well, more than nothing. There are bandits out there. But after Lupent's nastiness last year, the mere hint of a rogue uniform sets the whole countryside on its ear."

"Right. Any further orders for me?"

"Get Lady Talia back to Lanil's Rock and do your duty. Keep everyone there safe like you always do." She turned to Talia. "You're in good hands, and you should already be out of the danger zone. Don't worry."

Talia's left hand rubbed her sword pommel. "I'm not worried. Just being damned careful."

Zoe raised her eyebrows at the language but did not comment, turning back to Jhanes. "We all know what to do. I'll send a messenger direct to you when I have more information."

"I wish you good hunting, Clan Leader."

"I'm wishing you no hunting at all, Clan Second."

"Couldn't have said it better myself." He nodded to the officer and led his party down the road. The soldiers were standing and hefting their packs as he passed them.

Jhanes rode for a while, his mind churning. Then he let his horse slow, signalling Talia and Arderton alongside. "There's something not right, here."

"What?"

"We've been fooled by this 'invading army' rumour before. The people in this area are so traumatized by Lupent's atrocities last year, they're likely to be jumping at shadows."

"What does that mean, as far as what's actually happening?"

"I can't be sure, but the easy solution is that it's a smaller group than anyone thinks."

"That would be good news."

"It could be. But if they're small, they could be moving far faster than a full army. Zoysana is leading troops. She's thinking larger. We should think small."

Talia nodded. "You're doing the same duty you gave me today. Zoysana is facing the main source of attack. You're looking for threat from another direction."

"I didn't think of it like that, but you're right."

"So, what can we do?"

"We don't relax our guard. Let's keep our eyes open."

It was late in the afternoon when he spied it. He pulled up, staring at the road. "Arderton, what do you see?"

The bowman glanced down at the tracks, then to the left. "Bunch of men came out of the bush over there. Headed off down the road in front of us." As he was speaking, he was stringing his bow. The other two had their heads up, each scanning his side of the road.

After a glance to see that everyone was alert, Jhanes slipped off his horse for a closer look. The dirt was soft under the trees, and it did not take him long. He returned and mounted, stringing his own bow. "Seven men, all in boots. Three of them army style. Hobnails."

"Only seven?"

"'About that. Can't be certain. They're out on the road, headed for Lanil's Rock." He kneed his mount ahead. "Let's not rush into anything. Quick trot only, full alert."

Talia and the other two slipped the thongs off their sword hilts, Jhanes and Arderton arranged their quivers for access, and the party moved forward.

Confident in the abilities of his companions, Jhanes kept his eyes to the ground, but he saw no evidence that their quarry had left the road. As they neared the village, he became more anxious. "I don't like this at all. Let's pick up the pace. We'll be home before the horses wear out."

They came out of the trees at a gallop, to see the town buzzing with men, the barricades up. He pulled up at the north end and clambered over the logs. "What's going on?"

"We've been attacked, Sir. Seven of them. They marched into town, bold as brass. Went into the inn before anyone knew what was happening…"

Jhanes needed to hear no more. He sprinted to his home, fear burning in his throat. There was a crowd around the door, and he shouldered through them.

Sarha was sitting on the bench, a basin of water on the table in front of her, a cloth pressed to her eye. He glanced down. No blood. "Are you all right? What happened?"

She lowered the cloth. Her eye was red and the area around it was swollen. "I'm fine. Bastard took a swing at me when I said there wasn't any money. Didn't believe me, but there wasn't any, so what could I say? They raided the kitchen for food and wine. But I don't care about that…"

"How long ago?"

"About mid-afternoon. But that's…"

"Sarha, this is really important. The story is that there's an invasion of some sort going on. Is there any chance that this was a band of outriders from an army?"

"One of them might have been an officer, once. Red coat, black boots, filthy white shirt. The rest of them were dressed like a bunch of seasonal farm workers. With swords. Didn't act like farmers, though. Frey…"

He tried to look at her eye, but she pushed him off. "Leave that alone, Jhanes. That's not the problem. It's Frey!"

"What happened to him? Where is he?"

She clutched his arm, her fingers digging in. "He's gone!"

"What do you mean, gone?" A chill of fear ran through his veins. "They didn't take him. Why would they want a little kid like that?" He grasped her shoulders. "Tell me they didn't take him!"

"No, no. When they showed up, he disappeared. You know how he is with uniforms. He came back after they left. No crying, or anything like that. He was just standing there, his face deathly pale. Then he said, 'It's all right, Ma,' and turned and ran off up the road."

"Which way?"

"The same way the robbers went."

A pang of relief shot through his chest, followed by a jolt of concern. "By the Lady, he's gone after them!"

"What do you mean, gone after them?"

"They came and hurt you. The last time anyone attacked, I went after them and took vengeance. I wasn't here, so he thinks he has to."

"What? A little boy like that? What can he do?"

"He can survive in the wild better than most bandits, and I'm sure that includes stealing. I don't know what he has planned, but he's gone after them, and I'd better find him, quick."

He dashed to his room and grabbed his fighting pack, switching a few weapons into it from his travel equipment.

When he reached the common room, he stopped. Talia was there with Arderton.

"Talia...my Lady! I..." He looked to Sarha, then back to the lady.

"I know. Frey's gone after them. They told me."

"He's in danger..."

"That's right. And I'm not. Off you go."

"But my Lady, Zoysana told me to take care of you."

"She couldn't know this would happen."

"Still..."

"Jhanes. Your son is in danger. I'm in the middle of a town in a secure inn with all my men. Your people are using your admirable system to send word out and the local militia will be forming up immediately. I'm quite capable of taking care of myself. Why are we talking? Go!"

"Yes, my Lady."

A quick kiss to Sarha's tearstained cheek and he was off up the road in a ground-covering lope. A great weight lifted from him the moment he left the village. All other concerns faded, and he focused on his first problem. *How am I going to find the boy?*

28. A New Clan Member

He needn't have worried. Just where the road left the fields and entered the forest there was a path off to the left: Frey's trail up to the Rock. It was the first spot the robbers could have turned aside, but there in the road were three stones. One on top of the other, one on the side pointing south.

With a grin to himself and a glow of pride, Jhanes followed his son's sign. After that he made better time. He wasn't worried about following the robbers. If Frey missed their trail, that was fine. All he had to do was find the boy. The robbers had about a two-hour start, but Frey would be slower, reading sign, careful of a lookout.

But Frey didn't miss the trail. A few miles farther on, the robbers cut through the bushes off to the right. A clear boot track in a muddy spot confirmed it. *Sloppy. No experienced woodsmen.* Just in case Jhanes missed it, Frey had broken the top of a sapling down, pointing in the proper direction.

Jhanes quickened his pace and followed. He knew he was catching up when he began to see blades of grass and displaced bushes easing back into position.

Then he smelled wood smoke. If he could become any more alert, he accomplished it. He came to a junction and saw an arrow scratched in the trail. As he watched, a bit of soil fell into the gouge. The smell of smoke was stronger, and he crept forward with all the silence his years of training could muster.

Through the trees ahead he could make out a clearing, smoke drifting up from a fire in the centre, where a large pot bubbled forth a tasty aroma. As he neared, he could see the scattered belongings of a messy camp. Packs were strewn about, contents jumbled haphazardly beside them. He spotted an empty wine bottle near his feet in the undergrowth. *They drank their booty, and now they're taking a well-deserved rest while the stew cooks. Sleep well, my friends.* Creeping closer, he could see a man sprawled on his bedroll with a bottle in his hand, his head back, snoring. The others were in similar positions, none with a weapon close to hand. One man reclined against a tree, sipping now and then from a bottle, his eyes glazed. Two slouched on their bedrolls, their eyes glued drunkenly on a deck of cards. *Seven. No one on guard.* He slipped his bow off his shoulder and edged forward again.

Frey had been here, and for some time. The boy's prints cut off to the left, came back from the right. *He circled the camp, then continued...this way...*Jhanes followed the more recent trail, which spiralled in towards the edge of the trees, taking advantage of every bit of cover.

And then he saw Frey. The boy was halfway across the clearing, just sliding behind a bush, his eyes intent on the men in front of him.

Jhanes made an involuntary step forward and flinched at the rasp of his pant leg against a thorny bush. Frey's head snapped around, but then he grinned and flicked a wave. Jhanes tried to think of how to signal him back, but the boy made a definite "stay there" gesture, turned to the front again and rose to a crouch, his body tight and small. One more check of his quarry, and he eeled several steps to the next bush.

Accepting the situation, Jhanes moved into a backup role. He nocked an arrow and scanned the clearing, noting the positions of the sleeping men, looking for vantage points and escape routes. The next time the boy glanced back, he raised his bow, pointed to a large tree across the clearing and made a "go there" gesture. Frey nodded and returned to whatever mission his devious brain had concocted. Jhanes felt better. When he started shooting, he knew how his ally would move.

The boy's target was the fire, backed against a pile of rock in the dead centre of the camp. Jhanes watched, his heart pounding, as his son covered the rest of the distance, sliding in behind the rocks. One of the sleepers snorted and rolled over, and Frey froze, waited, then melted to the ground and slid forward, reaching around the rocks on the opposite side of the fire from the card players. It seemed to take an age, but finally he stretched his hand out to the simmering pot. He dropped something into the stew, glanced around at the robbers and then turned and started towards Jhanes, his back to the enemy.

Now that Frey could see him, Jhanes took control. One of the card players snarled at his opponent, and the man with the bottle laughed and called out a comment. The boy went rigid, his eyes on his father's face. Jhanes held him with an upraised finger, scanning the camp. When the game continued, he motioned Frey onward.

Soon Frey reached his position, and he sent the lad past. The two of them crept, ghosts in the forest, until they were a good distance from the camp. Then he strode forward and clapped a hand on Frey's shoulder. "What did you put in that pot?"

The boy reached down and pulled a plant from the side of the trail. "Roots." He pulled a small kitchen knife from his belt. "Shaved small."

"What does it do?"

"Sick. Very sick." He looked up. "Bad men, Dad."

"Yes, they are bad men. It won't kill them, will it?"

The boy shrugged. "Eat too much, maybe." He frowned. "Hurt Ma." Then he looked up. "Is Ma all right?"

Jhanes replaced his hand on the boy's shoulder. "Your Ma is fine, but she's worried out of her mind about where you are and what you're doing."

Frey glanced up with a small grin. "She's good at that."

"What do you mean?"

"Worries about you."

"Great. Now she's got two of us to fret about."

The boy shrugged. "We're fine. Send soldiers to get sick bad men."

He pulled his son in for a quick one-armed hug, then scooted him ahead on the trail. "Then let's get home and do that. The quicker we move, the less time Ma has to worry."

"So let's go." The boy broke into a trot, skimming over the ground at a pace that made his father step out to keep up.

346

When they reached Lanil's Rock, Jhanes sent Frey to the inn while he detoured to the officer's tent to describe the site of the robbers' camp. The sergeant only had five soldiers, but after a brief discussion, they decided the troop was up to the job.

"You should make a careful approach, but they might not be paying too much attention." He described what Frey had done.

"You mean the little imp snuck right into their camp, laced their supper and snuck out again?"

"They stole a bunch of wine from the inn and they didn't save much for later."

The officer frowned. "I hope he made them good and sick. We won't be giving them any breaks on the march back. We can't have people robbing and beating our citizens."

"I couldn't agree more. Now, if you'll take care of that matter, I'd like to see how my wife is."

"I'm sure you would." The officer clapped him on his shoulder. "You've done the hardest part of the job. Now we'll just go and clean up." A strange look crossed his face. "I hope we don't have to clean up too much."

They both laughed, and Jhanes headed for home.

As he approached the inn, there was loud talk and laughter from inside. He opened the door of the common room to find it full of Talia's party and villagers. As he entered, everyone turned and gave him a cheer.

He shrugged and held up open hands. "I didn't do anything. Frey had it all under control when I got there."

Everyone looked at the boy. He tried to slip behind Sarha, but she pulled him out. "What do you mean, under control?"

"I got there too late. He was already in the middle of their camp, slipping the poison into their stewpot. All I did was stand by with my bow."

"He never said that. 'We found the robbers and Pa is sending the soldiers.' That's all he said."

Jhanes grinned. "Oh, no, no, no. It wasn't like that at all." He swooped up the lad and set him on his knee. "Frey trailed them all the way to their camp. He left signs in the dirt like Zoysana talks about. I could have followed the trail he left in pitch dark." He continued to tell the story, making it as exciting as he could, while Frey alternately glowed with pride and squirmed with embarrassment.

When he finished, everyone cheered except Sarha. She frowned at her husband. "But once you got there, why didn't you call him back?"

He shook his head. "The middle of the enemy camp is no place for a family argument. He had the plan, and all I could do was back him up. Don't worry. I had my bow ready. If they had awakened, I would have shot three of them where they lay, and had my sword at the throats of the others before they could find their weapons."

"Aye, and I had a tree to hide behind, so's he didn't need to worry about hittin' me."

"But I thought..."

"Sarha, it was a simple situation, and a few hand gestures made it clear what each of us would do." He cuffed the boy's head gently. "Frey doesn't talk much, but he watches very well."

The group conversation broke up into several other topics.

A few hours later, the sergeant returned with his retching prisoners.

Jhanes went out to meet them. "What do they say?"

The old soldier grinned. "They got no stomach for argument, sir. There's only the seven of them, and they done all the raiding."

"That ties it up neatly, then. Shall I send out the message?"

"Could you do that, Sir? My men hadta half-carry a couple of 'em."

Jhanes went about finding a couple of local lads who were good riders and sent them off with the news.

* * *

348

The next day near noon, Zoe and Tadeo trotted up to the inn, dismounting with grins.

"There's a story up and down the road." As she handed her reins to Frey, she laid a hand on his head and looked into his eyes. "What have you been up to?"

"My duty, Clan Leader."

She looked up at Jhanes. "It's Clan Leader, is it?"

He shrugged. "You're my Clan Leader. He's my son."

She gave the boy a quick one-armed hug. "So you're the first of my Clan in the second generation, are you? It seems my status progresses."

Frey covered his embarrassment by tugging the reins of the horses, and away they went to the stable.

Zoysana glanced at Jhanes. "That ended well, didn't it?" Then she looked up at him again. "Is something wrong?"

He stared at his feet. "I must apologize, Clan Leader. It was impossible for me to do anything else."

"Anything else than what?"

"I know you were depending on me to guard Lady Talia. But..." He shrugged. "I couldn't. Frey was in danger, and Sarha was out of her mind with worry. I had to go. I'm sorry."

She nodded. "I've been thinking about that. If I have the story straight, those bandits raided your inn and injured your wife. Your son went after them. As soon as you got home, you went after him, leaving Talia safe in the middle of an armed village with her usual retainers on guard."

"That's right. Counter to your orders to stay with Talia and keep her safe."

"I know. And I wish you hadn't been forced to do that. There might have been other enemy around, and things could have gone very wrong. But the more I think about it, the more I see it differently, and you, of all people, should, too."

"Why me?"

"Because it deals with basic Inari beliefs, and you're supposed to be the expert." She smiled at his puzzled look. "Jhanes, you're not a mercenary with a contract. You're a member of Zoysana's Clan, right?"

"Yes, but that doesn't mean I'm not loyal. You can't have a clan member running off home in the middle of a campaign to wipe his kid's nose."

She stopped him with a raised hand. "I would prefer my clan members to do their duties without question like good mercenaries do, but I am well aware that the Inari don't work like that. Come to think of it, the Warlanders don't work like that, and neither do their levies. Do you think Gerth can give them orders and have them obey without question?"

"I suppose not."

"And you suppose right. Ask him some time. All the members of Zoysana's Clan are also members of their own clans and families first. You know better than I do how that works. I'd be a fool to expect you to drop your urgent family duties to do a task for me where you weren't needed.

"And there's something else we have to consider. Your primary duty now is to the Free Counties. Your people have to handle things like this bunch of thieves, and without help. That's how you maintain your independence. King Gerth wants it that way, so by doing your duty to your clan here, you're supporting the king and the realm. I have no complaint."

He grinned down at her. "So my clan is the people of Lanil's Rock?"

"If that helps you understand, I guess it is."

"And Zoysana's Clan is my secondary, just like it is for all your clan members."

"That's right. I'm the only real member of the clan." Her smile was replaced by a thoughtful look. "And I don't have a family."

He shook his head. "As far as I can see, your family is the Arlyns, your loyalty is to the Great Potentara Gerth, and your clan is the whole realm. You've got more duties than everyone else, not less."

She looked up at him. "So we both should be happy, then. We have our places and we have more responsibilities than we know how to handle."

"A problem we solve by depending on other people to help us out."

"And speaking of those other people, I believe we have a party to attend."

"That's a duty too, I gather."

After supper, they all sat around the fire, retelling their stories of the day. When there was a pause in the conversation, Jhanes reached over and slipped a hand behind Frey's head.

The boy looked at him.

"I have a present for you." He untied his smallest dagger from his belt. "You take care of that."

Frey stuck the sheath in his waistband. "Don't worry, Dad. I won't lop a finger off." He drew the dagger and dropped into a fighting crouch, scowling fiercely. "Least, not one of mine."

Everyone else laughed.

The innkeeper nodded. "We'll be working on that, too, son."

THE END

Here is the first chapter of "Mercenary's Dream," which wraps up the second trilogy in the Petrellan Saga.

THE MARCH HOME

She thought like a man. That was Anine's problem, and she had known it for a long time. How could she avoid it? Brought up on a hill farm with five older brothers, her mother dead of overwork before the only daughter reached her teens, she had fitted in as well as she could. When she left the farm to seek her fortune in the mercenary troops, her huge size and plain features made it easy for the men around her to treat her as an equal.

Well, she was fine with that. *At least, I ain't complainin'.* Sure, she knew she was missing something when the tavern girls moved in on their table as they always did. For a while she had toyed with the idea that she was really a man in a woman's body, but she felt nothing towards the girls in the bars, willing though some of them might have been.

No, she wasn't complaining. At least, not out loud, where anyone might notice. *I'll never be a beauty like men want, so that's that.* Oh, there had been chances. No real offers, mind you, but she had friends in the troop, men who had stood by her through the battles of the past three years, those she had stood by in turn. They liked and admired her. Last winter, in the loneliness and boredom of guard duty on the frontier, she knew that several of her friends would have accommodated her, but her natural reserve, combined, frankly, with her homeliness, had kept anyone from mentioning it.

Well, she had seen other girls and what love did to them, mooning and sighing and falling all over themselves. All very well if you were a milkmaid. A spilled pail of milk was soon forgotten. *In my profession a moment's inattention is likely to result in spilled guts, and that's a little harder to get over.*

She marched down the mountain path with the rest of the Clan, striding easily in spite of her bulk. Chasing Inari around the mountains was developing more than her fighting skills. She grinned over at the young soldier slogging beside her.

"Whaddaya think, Varli? You gonna get through this?"

The lad grinned. "Oh, Zoysana never really puts us in any danger of dying on the road. She'd sooner save us to get killed in a fight."

She smiled back, her trained eye going over his face for signs of real fatigue. "You look a bit hot, my friend."

He shrugged as much as the heavy pack would allow. "I didn't say I was happy. Just that I figure I'll survive." His glance became calculating. "If I was just a bit more tired, would you take the tent for a while?"

She laughed out loud. "I don't think so. Nice try, though."

They strode in companionable silence, the troop strung out evenly along the road, heads up, eyes moving, as proud and alert as any fighters in the kingdom. A warm glow suffused her: nothing to do with the late fall sunshine. It had been a good campaign for the final part of the summer, harrying the few Inari that snuck down over the passes, putting the pressure on so they had no chance to do more than minor damage to the hill farms of the area. With the coming of fall, the tribes had pulled back into the fastness of the Upper Plains, and Zoysana's Clan was headed back to the castle for a well-deserved rest.

"Whaddaya think's on the order slate for this winter? Didn't sound like she was gonna be payin' anyone off."

Varli shook his head. "Not a chance. You lot are too well trained to let go. Most of the rest of us will be going back to our usual positions. I have to go home to the Inner Duchies for a while," he grinned again, "to prove to my father that I'm not completely gone native out here on the frontier."

She nodded. It was easy to forget that the next soldier in this strange bunch could be a squire, a well-trained mercenary or a rough hill farmer. "Well, I got nowheres to go, so I guess it's the castle for me for the winter. I'm not really lookin' forward to it.

I mean, it's nice to be gettin' paid and all, but winter sentry duty ain't exactly fun."

The boy grinned up at her. "Oh, it'll be worse than that, count on it."

"What?" She looked across at him. "I ain't heard nothin' about any dangerous jobs comin' up."

He shook his head. "Not dangerous. Worse. Do you know how to read?"

Only the years of mercenary training kept her from missing a step "Read?"

"Yeah. You know, words on a page."

"I know what readin' is, Shrimp. I just don't follow what yer talkin' about."

He sighed mightily, as much as one can sigh who is breathing heavily from the exertion of striding at a ground-eating pace with a heavy pack. "I mean that if you're in the castle for the winter, and you have any brain for it, you'll be learning to read."

"Read? Me? You gotta be kiddin'!"

"Nope. Every one of the regular Guides learns to read. Useful, you know."

"But I'm not a Guide. I'm just a regular soldier. In case you didn't remember, I come off of a farm. I can't read. Well, not much, anyhow. I know all the letters 'n' how to write my name 'n' that."

"After this summer, you're not a common soldier any more. You're one of Zoysana's Clan. You don't stay where you are."

She paced along, wiping the sweat from her forehead. "That's for sure."

A quick, scoffing laugh. "You know very well that's not what I meant. I meant you have to make progress, get better at everything." He regarded at her a moment, seemed to come to a decision. "You're not as dumb as you act."

"Thanks a lot, Shrimp. You lookin' to get around me, all this flattery?"

He didn't laugh. "You know what I mean. Sure, you come from a farm, and my father's a noble in the Inner Duchies. But that doesn't mean you have to pretend to be stupid. You pick up things as quick as the rest. Quicker, most times."

She walked a moment, then made up her mind. "You put that in your report?"

"What report?"

She grinned over at him. "If I'm smarter than I act, then mebby I notice things you don't think I notice. You and Zoysana bin together a while, right?"

"She trained me for years."

She nodded. "So all that complainin' you do, and she knocks you around for it, I figger that's a warnin' to the rest. They know what she could do to any man in the troop if she wanted to. So you're the company sleeper."

"The what?"

She grinned over at him. "Mercenary slang you never heard. The sleeper is the man in the ranks that reports to the Commander what's goin' on with the rankers."

"Like a spy?"

She shrugged. "In some of the rag-tag companies, I guess. In a good company everyone knows who it is. There's always some guy who has a personal relationship with the brass. Can't be helped, can be useful. In Zoysana's Clan it's gotta be you."

Now he looked concerned. "Do all the others think the same?"

She shrugged her bulky shoulders. "The mercs probably. Most of the others have some idea. You don't exactly hide it."

"Oh."

She reached over and clapped him on the arm, staggering him out of line, although he recovered his balance quickly. "Don't look so disappointed. Like I said, nobody minds. In fact, if they trust you, most of them like it. If they got a legit complaint, they make sure you hear it. They know you'll pass it along, without nobody bein' singled out as a whiner."

"And do they trust me?"

She laughed again, more loudly. "I'm gonna let you figger that out yerself, lad. I said most of them like havin' you around. I don't mind it myself. At least with the company snitch, you know where you stand!"

"Thanks. I thought you said it was called the company sleeper."

"That's only if they like you."

"Great."

She laughed again at his glum expression, and slapped him on the shoulder again.

"Hey, Anine. You makin' up to Lord Varlinden, there?"

She turned briefly to glance at the grinning face behind her. "That's right, Beken. "I'm pushin' for a soft job in the Duchies this winter. While you're standin' sentry in a snowstorm I'll think of you fondly."

"Don't let her turn your inexperienced head, lad. She's slyer'n she looks!"

Varli laughed. "That's funny, Beken. I just said the same thing."

"Well, there ya go. If me and you said it, it must be true, us bein' the smartest heads in this bunch. Savin' Herself, there, o' course. So you watch it, youngster. She'll be tryin' her wiles on your innocence, and who knows what could happen."

The boy grinned over his shoulder. "She keeps shaping up like she has this summer, and that might not be too bad an idea." He glanced up at her and his face paled. "I mean...I'm sorry, Anine, I didn't mean anything by that, really!"

She strode ahead until the heat died from her face. Varli scrambled to catch up, putting distance between them and the pair behind.

"I'm really sorry, Anine. I didn't mean to talk about you like that. Zoysana says I'm always opening my mouth when I shouldn't. I didn't really mean it."

Seeing his obvious distress, she felt a bit better. "You didn't? That's too bad."

"What?"

She could smile, now. "I don't know. I sort of hoped you meant it. It sounded like a compliment."

"Oh, it was, it was."

There was a snicker behind her and she spun, walking backwards and raising her fist. The soldier held up his open hands. "Anine, I ain't laughin' at you. I'm laughin' at the youngster there, tryin' desperately to drag hisself out of the hole he dug, and slippin' in deeper at every word."

She stared at Beken, then nodded and turned back into the column. After a while, she looked over at Varli, who was walking just a bit farther away from her than the proper order of march. "So what did you mean?"

He glanced up suspiciously. "What?"

"Well, every girl likes a compliment, but she just wants to be sure. What did you mean, 'shaping up'?" She half-turned as hurried footsteps approached from behind.

"Oh, we gotta hear his answer to this, Anine. Please don't get mad and spoil it."

She turned to glower at the young squire. "Well, Varli, the troops need to be entertained on the march. Looks like you have to explain. With all of us listenin'."

"Yeah, Varli, this better be good. Ya know, Anine's a friend of ours. We wouldn't want to hear her gettin' upset."

The boy glanced back with a frown. The soldier looked half serious. "What I meant, Anine, was that...well, you're pretty big. You don't mind if I say that, do you?"

She considered a moment. "Whaddaya think, Beken? Another compliment."

The soldier laughed. "He's doin' great so far."

Varli smiled. "Well, when you started out this summer, you were just big. Like one of the other big guys. But you didn't have much...well..." He fumbled for the words, looking

357

sideways at her, then over his shoulder at the soldiers behind. They only looked on with interest. Finally he screwed up his courage, and the words came out in a rush.

"Well, I don't mean to offend, Anine, but you didn't have much shape."

There was a burst of laughter, which showed how many of the marching troops were listening. Anine joined in. Varli looked so worried she could almost forget he was talking about her. She stared at him with mock ferocity. "You're not gettin' too far out of the hole with comments like that. In fact, you're slidin' back pretty deep. Wanta quit now?"

He grinned. "No, no, now we get to the good part."

"Ya mean the punch line." Beken chuckled from behind.

"I sincerely hope not. What I meant was, we've all had a tough summer, climbing and training and fighting and chasing the Inari all over. Most of us have lost weight. And I think Anine has lost quite a bit. And if you don't mind my saying..." He glanced up at her, and she nodded. "In the right places."

There was a burst of laughter from the troops around, and she blushed again. She knew the only thing to do was keep going. "Why, thank you, sir. I'm sure you practise that sort of thing in lordling school, do you?"

He was immediately indignant. "I do not. I meant it, and it's true. Ask Beken!"

Beken raised his hands again. "No you don't, kid. You got yourself into this. I ain't stupid enough to jump in with you. Please, Anine, don't ask me!"

"Don't worry, Beken. I'll just have to let it remain a mystery. I've already got young Varlinden, here, in my debt; I'll take my winnings and quit the game."

She strode ahead, ignoring them, but she couldn't stop the warm glow that filled her. She had always loved being included in the rough joshing and insults, but this was different. She realized that Varli had meant what he had said.

Probably.

For a moment she was suspicious that he had another reason for the jest, but it was unlikely. He had spoken too thoughtlessly and been instantly sorry. He could have no reason to play games like that with her. There wasn't a mean bone in the young lord's body, and whatever role he played: jester, complainer, company sleeper, or mascot, he was loved by the whole troop.

They strode along in companionable silence, the faint jingling of their gear a pleasant counterpoint to their steady march. Even in full kit, Zoysana's Clan moved with little fuss. The fall sun slanted lower in the west, and soon they came into a small dell with a spring running across it. The cook tent was already pitched, and they set their own tents with a will, to the smell of fresh venison roasting over the fire. Two of Zoysana's Inari scouts were tending it, accepting the troop's jesting thanks with quiet pride.

"We quit early."

Varli grunted as he hauled on a guy rope, fastening it securely with a practiced twist of the wrist. "No sense rushing. The war's over for this year, and we've got the supplies. Might as well use them before they spoil."

Maura hauled the next rope to him one-handed, her scarred fingers covered only by a heavy leather glove.

"How's the wound healing, Maura?"

The older mercenary looked down at her left hand. "Feels fine. No more pain. Just two fingers with no grab. Tendons were cut, for sure. The third finger gave me some trouble, 'n' Zoe said that tendon was probably nicked as well, but it's loosened up now."

Varli grinned. "That's good. I'll be real glad to have you training us, now, instead of her."

"Who says I'll be trainin' you?"

He shrugged. "Word gets around."

She was instantly in front of him, her good hand lifting him by his shirtfront easily. "You know somethin' I don't, Shrimp?"

He laughed and twisted free; he'd had lots of practice with that move, too. "Nothing that you'll get upset about, that's for sure, and I'm not allowed to say."

She made towards him again, but he held up his open hands, a serious look on his face. "I mean it, Maura. I don't know much, and I'm not allowed to tell anything I heard. I just figured it out. We're short one Arms Master at the castle, and Gerth said there would always be a place for you."

The woman looked stunned. "Arms Master?"

Varli shrugged. "You see why I can't say anything. If I did, and then you didn't get the post, you'd be real upset."

Anine reached out and cuffed his shoulder with the back of her hand, "But now you have said somethin', you dummy. How are you gonna get out of this one?"

He flinched away, but she knew he wasn't hurt. "I'll just have to talk to Zoe, I guess."

"Did I hear my name mentioned?" The Clan Leader had an unerring ear for any disturbance in camp and could read stirred emotions over the usual hubub. She and Patu strode up, the soldiers all standing to greet her. Anine read the mistress's mood in the leisurely sweep of the armigerent's shaggy tail. Varli was less impressed.

"Yeah, Zoe, I was talking about you. Maura's been left hanging long enough, don't you think?"

The small, dark, woman reached up and ruffled his hair, then grabbed a handful, pulling his head down while she stared into his eyes. "And you have taken it upon yourself to decide when the announcement should be made."

"He was just makin' guesses, Lady Zoe. He didn't speak out of turn."

Zoysana released the boy and turned to Maura. "He always speaks out of turn. Don't stand up for him. How am I ever going to get him to discipline himself?"

The older woman smiled as well. "Oh, I think he's doin' all right. Sometimes he's even useful."

Anine took her courage in her hands. "Aye, Lady Zoe. Now that he's brought the subject up, do you have some plans for Maura?"

Faced by three serious faces, the Clan Leader relented. "Of course, and I'm sorry I didn't tell you sooner. I knew you would be concerned. Gerth needs another Arms Master at the castle," Anine caught a triumphant glance from Varli, "and he thinks you should apprentice."

"Apprentice? Me? I'm thirty-four years! Way too old to apprentice. Besides, where would I get the fee?"

Zoysana shrugged. "I don't see what age has to do with it. You can't fight anymore, so you'd have to take a new trade anyway. You might as well get your Master's papers. Your apprentice fee is your compensation for a wound received in battle. We'll start your four years from the day you signed on with us last fall. " The small woman's face crinkled in a grin. "I'd say you've learned a few things in the past year."

They all laughed ruefully. The summer had been a learning experience from the first day.

"So you report to the Armoury when we hit the castle. They'll find you a room there, and we'll talk to the Armourer about your training."

Anine was surprised to see a glisten in her friend's eye. "Thank you, and thank His Majesty, Lady Zoysana. It's more than I expected. Way more."

"What about the rest of them Zoe? Are they just going on Guard for the winter? I heard Gerth say you're not letting anyone go."

Zoysana shook her head. "Again, the Mouth o the Troop reminds the Leader of her duties. I suppose everyone is worrying about that." She looked up to see an expanding circle of mercenaries around her.

"All right. The plans are pretty well set, and you deserve to know. After supper tonight we'll have a talk. You," she pinned Varli with her glare, "I will talk to now!"

She spun on her heel and strode off, the huge armigerent glued to her side as usual. Anine clapped Varli on the back, reassuring him but shoving him in the right direction at the same time. He glanced appealingly over his shoulder at her and trudged off dejectedly, to the laughter of the watching troops. Anine was pretty sure he was in no trouble; it was just his usual act. The kid certainly did have his uses.

She thought it strange that she always considered him to be young; she only had two years on him. He had grown over the summer. Now the lad looked down on her, and the constant sword work had broadened his shoulders. However, her time had been spent with a mercenary troop, and it aged you. She thought of her blush at his jests, back on the road, and wondered if she really was that mature after all. *Life certainly does hand out the twists and turns.*

"Guess your little boyfriend's in trouble, now!"

She turned to face Beken's wide grin. "Beken, if you had a brain in your head, you'd be grateful to him. Now we're gonna find out what's happenin', and all because he opened his mouth. So don't make a complete ass of yourself, hey?"

There was an appreciative chuckle from the audience. The two women returned to setting up their bivouac, and the rest strolled back to their own tasks. *Beken is all right to have around, but sometimes his constant stupid jokes bother me.*

"Is it just me, or is he gettin' worse?"

Maura straightened up from her bedroll. "It's just you."

"You mean it?"

The older woman shrugged. "I haven't noticed him any worse or any better. He's just Beken, and you put up with him, just like you put up with the rest of us. He ain't smart and he ain't pretty, but he's a good man to have at your back in a brawl."

She sighed. "I guess you're right. He just bothers me today, that's all."

"Because of what Varli said on the road."

She sighed again. "That's right. How did you know?"

Maura grinned. "Because everybody in the troop knows, of course. It was a borin' day of marchin', and anythin' that spices it up is fair game. This time it's you. Take your turn, Anine, and put up with it."

"I suppose so. But it won't end tomorrow."

"You're right, there. These men have to have some shelf to put you on, some excuse to deal with a woman. You either have to be an old witch, like me, or young, innocent, and plain, like you were. Now, that's changed. Varli told 'em you're a woman. Their little male brains can't forget that. Now they gotta find another title for you."

"Another title"

Maura stretched out on her bedroll, her sore hand cradled. "Sure. They useta treat you sorta like a little sister, protect you, that sorta thing. Now they realize you're a woman, they gotta find another name. The kinda women they usually have, you don't want to be. Do you?"

"Not a chance! So what do I do?"

The woman shrugged. "I dunno. Be tough, is all I can say. This is a hard bunch. Oh, sure, they're the right kind to have with you in a scrap. But you hang out with a tough troop, you gotta pay the price in camp. They don't fight all day then turn into bunny rabbits at night, you know."

Anine grinned. "Bunny rabbits I don't need, either, right now."

Maura had a wicked grin. "Din't mean it that way. But th' fact remains..."

The big girl sighed again. "I know. It means they're all gonna be testin' me, just like they did when I first joined up. Dammit, is it always this way for a woman?"

"Till you get old and ugly, it is."

"You're not ugly!"

"Mixed blessing, believe me. I'd rather not be pretty, thank you very much." A pleased smile crossed the weathered face. "And now I'm gonna be a Arms Master! Thinka that! With

363

papers and everythin'. With Arms Master papers from Petrella, I could work anywheres."

"You wouldn't leave!"

Maura's smile became thoughtful. "No, guess I wouldn't at that. Arms Master at a king's castle is top o' the heap. But it's nice to know I could. Gives you a feeling of freedom, ya know?"

Anine sighed. "I guess. It'll be a while before I get that kind of freedom."

Maura sat up straighter. "Look, girl, you bin sighin' like you was in love or got the chest heaves or somethin'. It ain't that bad. You just gotta get out there. Chin up, stare 'em in the face, and give it to them straight if they crosses you. You're a Fighter of Zoysana's Clan, and they can't forget that."

"Give it to them straight, hey? I tell you, Beken mouths off one more time, I'm gonna paste him one."

Maura grinned. "That's the attitude, girl. If that's what it takes!"

Hiding another sigh, Anine stretched out on her bedroll to await the dinner gong.

More from Gordon A. Long

Available at Smashwords, Amazon and other outlets

"Zoysana's Choice" The Petrellan Saga Begins
Coming in early 2018
"Mercenary's Dream" Final book in the first trilogy of the
Petrellan Saga

"Out of Mischief" World of Change Book 1
"Into Trouble" World of Change Book 2
"Mountains of Mischief" World of Change Book 3
"The Trouble with Tents" World of Change Book 4
Coming Fall 2017
"Queen of Mischief" World of Change Book 5

"A Sword Called...Kitten?" Romantic Comedy with an Edge
"The Cat with Many Claws" Sword Called Kitten Book 2

"Why Are People So Stupid?" Social Humour with a Point

Look for Gordon's books, selected reviews, poetry and short
stories at <airbornpress.ca>

Gordon's opinions on humanity are at the
"Are People Really That Stupid?" blog
<airbornpress.ca/arepeoplestupid/>
Find his weekly reviews and his ideas on writing at
"Renaissance Writer" blog
<airbornpress.ca/newdir>

www.ingramcontent.com/pod-product-compliance
Lightning Source LLC
Chambersburg PA
CBHW060154260626
47160CB00001B/262